Deceptions

Deceptions

BY LAUREN MADDISON

alyson books
los angeles | new york

MANUFACTURED IN THE UNITED STATES OF AMERICA.

THIS TRADE PAPERBACK ORIGINAL IS PUBLISHED BY ALYSON PUBLICATIONS INC.,
P.O. BOX 4371, LOS ANGELES, CALIFORNIA 90078-4371.
DISTRIBUTION IN THE UNITED KINGDOM BY TURNAROUND PUBLISHER SERVICES LTD.,
UNIT 3 OLYMPIA TRADING ESTATE, COBURG ROAD, WOOD GREEN,
LONDON N22 6TZ ENGLAND.

FIRST EDITION: MAY 1999

99 00 01 02 03 **a** 10 9 8 7 6 5 4 3 2

ISBN 1-55583-490-6

LIBRARY OF CONGRESS CATALOGING-IN-PUBLICATION DATA
   MADDISON, LAUREN.
      DECEPTIONS / BY LAUREN MADDISON.—1ST ED.
      ISBN 1-55583-490-6
      1. NAVAJO INDIANS—FICTION. I. TITLE.
   PS3563.A33942D43 1999
   813'.54—DC21   98-49284 CIP

ACKNOWLEDGMENTS

With deepest gratitude to three very special women who never lost faith in my ability to write a book that might actually get published: Ali Maxfield, Dianne Deloren, and my agent, Sandra Satterwhite.

PROLOGUE

For she was beautiful—her beauty made
The bright world dim, and everything beside
Seemed like the fleeting image of a shade.
—Percy Bysshe Shelley

The way she drove a car was heartstopping. So, indeed, was the way she looked. But it was not simply a set of flawless features that distinguished the handsome woman behind the wheel of the sleek Mercedes convertible. Everything about her was alive! She projected the sort of boundless energy and enthusiasm that inspires the dreamer and annoys the plodder. Most men thought of her as spirited and enchanting. A number of women, on the other hand, tended to be less charitable, either out of envy or, perhaps, because they saw in her the wild, spontaneous, and slightly dangerous woman their mothers had cautioned them against. Whether from admirers or detractors, however, she always attracted attention, and a second look.

Today, though, given the breathtaking speed with which she maneuvered the agile car around the curves of Canal Road, even the most observant person would have gotten no more than a brief glimpse. She was driving substantially faster than the posted limits, but she was in a hurry, and it was part of her nature to assume traffic laws were more in the nature of suggestions.

Just past Glen Echo Park, where the abandoned roller coaster

stood as one of the last remnants of better days, she hit the brakes
hard and pulled off into a steep and narrow dirt road, the car sliding in the mud. She switched off the engine and sat listening to
the water in the canal and the ticking of the motor as it cooled.
An occasional car passed on the road above, but the small, dark-
metallic-green car was well-screened by the lush late-summer
foliage common to a city built basically on top of a swamp.

Rain was imminent; it had been drizzling off and on all day.
She pressed the switch to raise the top, and stepped out of the
car. She suddenly didn't feel like carrying the umbrella she had
taken from the back seat. Tossing it back inside, she shrugged
into her Burberry trench coat, carefully pulling her long hair
from beneath the collar and letting it fan out over her back. The
glistening chestnut mass was her pride and joy. She'd always
thought of it as her best feature, which perhaps demonstrated
that even those blessed with physical beauty are perfectly capable of insecurity.

The whole idea of this meeting, which had been arranged
with only a few hours' notice, greatly annoyed her, but it would
give her the chance to set things straight once and for all. The
situation had gone beyond her control, she thought, with a
scowl that pinched her aristocratic face, with its aquiline nose,
firm chin, high, chiseled cheekbones and finely shaped mouth. A
spasm of petulance swept over her, prompting her to slam the
door of the Mercedes. She hated people telling her what to do!
Admittedly, her temper had cost her dearly of late, but, on the
other hand, it was at least partly responsible for the sparks that
flickered in those astonishingly green eyes—eyes that made even
the most jaded human beings regard her with a certain amount
of wonder.

She reflected that her mood, far more pessimistic than usual, could be put down to the flowering of an emotion she disliked intensely—guilt. She wanted to place the blame elsewhere, to act as if her lover of so many years had set all of these events in motion with her sheer stubbornness. But, though slightly vain, extraordinarily impetuous, and even a bit selfish, she was basically honest, and generally a very loyal and faithful friend. Like most people, she initially resisted taking responsibility for her choices, but she usually ended up doing it anyway. This meeting was partly motivated by her desire to extricate herself from the situation into which her impulsiveness and quick temper had led her. She was beginning to see she might have miscalculated.

The delicate Cartier watch on her wrist read 4:10 p.m. It was already getting dark. The clouds and the overhanging trees screened the sun effectively. As she started along the towpath, the wide, packed strip of earth where harnessed mules once staggered along pulling heavy barges up the canal, she congratulated herself on having worn hiking boots and jeans, although she was aware of being uncomfortably warm. After all, it was only September 15 in Washington, D.C., where the temperature and humidity were usually within single digits of each other (often both in the 90s) until well into the fall. But, stylish flats or elegant heels would have been disastrous in this mud. And even in boots she walked with the lithe, upright posture of a dancer, a career she had considered and eventually discarded because all that rehearsal was so much like work.

As she strolled up the towpath toward the city, she once more reviewed what she would say—nothing too indignant, nothing threatening, something more along the lines of "let's put our cards on the table," or maybe, "let's put this all behind us." Yes, she thought, that's the tone I want to adopt. She was given to rehearsing her life in advance, a habit some people found annoying, but the technique had served her well all of her life to offset those dangerously impulsive moments; she was loath to abandon the habit now. Besides, a script was just a guide; one had to improvise, too.

When 20 minutes had passed, her calm certainty gave way to an odd mixture of anxiety and anger. How dare she be kept waiting! What if something had changed, something had happened that made this meeting unnecessary? Surely she would have gotten word on her cellular phone. Just as she decided to go back to the car and check her voice mail, a figure emerged on the path just ahead. She allowed herself a brief sigh of relief and stepped forward, her smile fading as she realized something was very wrong.

A couple of hours later, a D.C. Park Police officer, charged with protecting the public in designated federal park areas, including Canal Road, noticed the muddy tire tracks leading down into the pull-off. He left his unit with the flashers on and walked to the edge. Spotting the expensive car below, he made his way along the edge of the muddy track and examined the Mercedes. The doors were locked, as they should be, he thought, though he noted with disgust the leather briefcase and cellular phone left lying right in plain sight on the front seat.

"Serves 'em right if they get ripped off," he said to himself. "Probably some rich jerk pretending to be a jogger."

He noted footprints leading away from the car toward the towpath, but there was no sound near him other than the passing of rush hour traffic. He considered looking in the vicinity for the driver, and rejected the notion. This wasn't a restricted area, after all, and he wasn't a damned baby-sitter, just a cop with eight straight days on duty behind him, and a hot meal and a warm wife waiting at home. He pulled out his notebook and duly recorded the license plate number. Tomorrow he'd have someone check to see if the car was still here.

Then, in the true spirit of zealous police officers everywhere, he opened his citation book and wrote a ticket for illegal parking, placing it on the damp windshield. Satisfied, he labored back up the incline, tossed his ticket book onto the seat, and headed home.

CHAPTER ONE

———❦———

A solitary sorrow best befits
Thy lips, and antheming a lonely grief.
—John Keats

———❦———

Monday, September 18
Washington, D.C.

With a quick glance at the calendar on her desk, Connor Hawthorne confirmed her suspicion that this was indeed the 17th straight day of rain. The brick sidewalks and narrow streets of Georgetown were awash with leaves and debris. Though she couldn't see the Potomac from her window, she knew it was flooding in the usual spots. Rock Creek had upgraded its status to small river. She had decided to forgo her morning walk; an unexpected cold spell had settled on the city overnight, and the unrelenting dampness was even more miserable.

In the brick fireplace, the first blaze of the season crackled a little too merrily to be in keeping with her mood. The drumming of the steady rain was soporific, and her mind wandered far afield, so far in fact that she was startled by the burr of the telephone. The answering machine clicked on immediately. She ignored the low murmur of the outgoing message and the ensuing beep. Today, all she wanted was privacy. But her attention was snared once more by the familiar, deep voice of the caller.

"Connor, this is Malcolm. If you're there, please pick up...it's...it's important, no...it's urgent...come on, Connor, please." Despite her need for solitude, Connor could hardly ignore his tone. He was one of her closest friends. She half jogged to her desk and picked up, flicking off the recorder.

"Malcolm, I'm here, what's so urgent?" There was a long, long pause, so lengthy, in fact, she thought perhaps he had hung up. But then she heard his breathing, harsh and almost panting, in her ear.

"Connor, thank God you're there. When you didn't answer the first time, I called Valerie. She thought maybe you'd left for that seminar in Santa Fe."

"That's not until November. I'm sorry, I didn't check messages." Connor felt momentarily guilty for being so hard to reach, but she instantly regretted the feeling. After all, she was beholden to no one, at least not anymore. Irritation crept into her voice as she quickly added, "But what's so important you have to start calling my friends?" Again, the pause was too long. "Mal, for Christ's sake, answer me!" There was a twisting knot in her stomach, a knot of anxiety, because Malcolm Jefferson was not just her friend, he was also a cop, and cops sometimes brought bad news.

"It's Ariana." He stopped. She could hear his voice tremble. One more pause and she thought she would leap through the phone and shake it out of him. Instead, she waited, her knuckles white on the receiver. "She's...we found..."And then, as if all his police training came back to him at once, his tone became clipped, emotionless. "We found Ariana near the canal, washed up by the flooding. She's dead, Connor. I'm sorry, but she was stabbed to death, and...I'm so sorry." Malcolm's terrifying words washed over and through her as if a penetratingly cold rain had begun falling right there in the living room.

*Dead…Dead…Dead…*the word was a buzzing in her skull, growing louder and louder, squeezing her brain, crowding out every other thought. Her voice wouldn't work…she felt a horrible choking sensation as her heart pounded harder and harder in her chest. Her entire body prickled and burned as cold fingers of fear plucked and scraped at her skin. She dropped the receiver back in its cradle. She stood motionless, as if her body had turned to stone.

She couldn't take it in. It wasn't real, couldn't be real. *This could not be happening.* Air forced its way past her constricted throat muscles and emerged as a sobbing gasp. "Wake up, Connor," her mind shouted, as she fought against what must be, had to be, a nightmare, a horrible, horrible nightmare. But Malcolm's voice, the plain, cruel words he had spoken, they were as real as the pounding in her rib cage. She wasn't going to wake up from this.

Hot ice clawed at her guts, and her head was filled with noise. Connor's legs buckled, and she fell to her knees on the thick pile of the Oriental rug, clutching herself with both arms. She thought her heart would collapse under the weight crushing at her chest, or that she would simply cease to breathe. From her came the cries of a mortally wounded animal. They echoed through the rooms of the elegant townhouse, torn from a place inside her where such primal emotions had neither name nor remedy. The world darkened and swirled away from her, leaving her cruelly and irrevocably alone.

She had no idea how many hours had passed. A loud pounding began to seep through the haze of pain and anguish. She was lying on the floor; she could feel the carpet rough against her cheek. Her body was stiff, cramped, and that insistent noise kept on and kept on. "What was the noise?" she wondered. "Who was it?" Connor expected to be alone in the house. BeLisia, her housekeeper, had the weekend off. Then there were louder sounds, glass breaking, and some part of her felt a twinge of fear. Most of her, though, didn't particularly care. "Besides," her well-trained mind thought, "imagine the irony. Ariana's dead and now someone will break into my house and kill me. It all fits, it's all so...funny."

Hysterical laughter bubbled in her throat, and she pulled herself up against the back of the sofa, until she could look out into the hall. "Come and get me, you bastard," she shouted. "I don't give a damn! Just come and get me."

A huge figure loomed in the doorway, backlit by the lamps in the hall. "Jesus Christ, Connor," came the deep, rumbling tones. "What the hell are you talking about?"

An hour later, while Malcolm tried to put something secure over the window he had broken, Connor sat wrapped in a down comforter on the sofa in the library and stared dully at the fire her friend had quickly stirred up and to which he had added too many logs. Still, she couldn't feel the warmth of the blaze. Instead, she sat trembling inside, as if she would never stop. She could hear Malcolm's footsteps clomping back and forth in the hall. At 6'6" and 265 pounds, he was a big man. But he was incredibly gentle in his manner when he chose to step out of his "cop" persona. And even as cop, he never played the bully. During her years as an assistant district attorney, she heard more than once that Malcolm was a man who could do his job well without being cruel or overbearing, a man who never abused his authority. For 14 years she'd watched him rise through the ranks, had built a friendship with him that had deepened into a valuable relationship. He had to be a good friend, she thought, to be here now, at the worst of times.

She heard him pounding on something with a hammer, and a moment later he was back with her. The two friends sat in silence, one mute with pain, the other helpless to ease the suffering. Only one lamp was on, leaving much of the room in shadow. The fire's flames danced over the deep mahogany of Malcolm's somber countenance and were reflected in his soft, brown eyes. She knew he wanted to say something, but there were no adequate words. Once again, despite the fire and the down quilt, tremors passed through her body. The strong sedative he'd found in the medicine cabinet and the hot tea he'd prepared hadn't helped either. Malcolm moved to sit on the leather couch, the frame creaking softly with his added weight. Ever so gently he took her face between his hands and looked into eyes so devoid of any spark of life it frightened him.

"Connor, listen to me, please...listen." He dropped his hands to her shoulders. "I know what this is like. I know what you're feeling. You know I do. When Marie Louise was killed, I thought everything was over for me. The world just broke into a million pieces, and I couldn't put it back together. I didn't want to. Why go on without her, without my wife? But you made me see it differently, you kept me from eating my gun." He shook her gently. "Connor, you kept me walking and moving and taking care of the kids, and living my life. You told me everyone has a time when they have to go, and I had to stop blaming myself for not being there, not protecting her, not keeping her alive. You told me all that, and I believed you. Now you've got to believe it, too, Connor, you've *got* to. Sometimes people die."

Her eyes focused on him. His words sank in slowly. She remembered Marie Louise. Thinking about her brought a fresh bout of weeping, but at least they were different tears, shed for someone else. Malcolm's partner, Leon Petrusky, had called her the day it happened. She had not heard about the incident because she no longer watched the evening news as a matter of principle. Leon told Connor that Marie Louise had been at a Riggs Bank, getting traveler's checks for the family vacation in Ocean City. Armed gunmen had shot five people, killing three instantly, while escaping with only a few thousand dollars. Marie Louise had used her body to shield an elderly man from the spray of automatic-weapons fire. The old man survived, but Marie Louise died on the operating table. No one had seen Malcolm after he'd left the hospital.

Connor had immediately called Malcolm's sister, who was with the children, but Eve had no news of him and was frightened of what he might do to himself. When Connor did find her friend, she knew his despair had taken him to the verge of suicide. His face was gray with pain and shock as he sat on the bench by the tidal basin, clutching his service revolver. She'd only found him there because she knew it was a place he sometimes went to think late at night. Without a moment's hesitation, she had unflinchingly taken the gun from his hands and spent the next three hours reminding him of why he *had* to live. Now, in the depths of her agony, she was trying to recall why it had seemed like such a convincingly good argument.

"I do remember, Malcolm. How could I forget that night?"

"I listened to you because the things you said came from your heart. You have to let me do the same for you." He put his big hand on his chest. "What I'm saying now is from *my* heart."

She looked at his kind, handsome face, searching for answers he didn't have, answers no one had. Then her expression changed as a newfound source of anguish presented itself. "It's my fault, isn't it? Because we fought and she moved out. That was six weeks ago, and we've only spoken twice. I didn't even know..."

"Connor...no! Don't start beating yourself up over what you couldn't have prevented."

"But I could have done something...somehow..." Her voice trailed off.

"You couldn't have prevented this any more than I could have saved my wife."

Connor looked at him again, her eyes pleading. "Why, Malcolm...why did...? What happened to her? Are you sure it's Ariana? How could she be...?" The word stuck in her throat.

Softly he finished the question, "Dead?" Then took a deep breath. "I'm sorry, but she is, Connor. And I've seen her to make sure. You won't have to go down there to identify the b...to identify her." He held her close for a moment.

Suddenly she sat upright, pushing away from his protective embrace. "Oh, yes, I *do*." She started to rise, but he easily pulled her back down onto the couch.

"No, you *don't*! There's no reason to put yourself through that. And besides," he hesitated, and she turned to him, "I've pulled some strings to rush the autopsy."

Connor shuddered at the thought. She had been to more than one autopsy, both in the line of duty as a D.A. and to aid in her work as a novelist during the past several years. She clearly remembered the procedure—the incisions, the sawing, the peeling back of the scalp, the removal of the organs—the complete and final violation of the human body, but not just *any* body. Ariana's body. With this thought, her insides heaved violently. She leaped from the couch and ran to the small powder room under the winding staircase.

Later, she only vaguely recalled Malcolm holding her head and wiping her face with a warm, damp cloth. She remembered being carried, gathered in his powerful arms as he climbed the stairs to her room and placed gently under the covers of the king size bed she had once shared with her lover. The sedatives he had given her finally took effect, and her last memory was of Malcolm settling himself in one of the wing chairs by the window. In the next instant, she was unconscious. She finally found, in sleep, the only escape there could be from the horrors of death.

CHAPTER TWO

———◦◦◦———

No blessed time for love or hope,
But only time for grief.
—Thomas Hood

———◦◦◦———

Tuesday, September 19
Washington, D.C.

Sometime, long before dawn, Connor almost believed she was awake. Yet she also felt as if she might possibly be dreaming. Someone was speaking gently to her, someone she knew well. It was her grandmother, Gwendolyn Broadhurst, that wonderful, dignified old lady whose cottage in the English countryside had always been a blissful haven for Connor over the years. Of course, it wasn't unusual to dream about her grandmother, and yet this felt more like an actual conversation. And the odd thing was that Gwendolyn knew...she knew about Ariana, which she couldn't possibly know yet. But the elderly woman's voice was strong and clear in her mind. "To lose the one you love is horribly painful, and this will be a terrible time of grief for you, my child. But we are all with you. Those who guide and protect and comfort you are always near. Do not despair even in the darkness. There is always light when you are ready to look for it." Connor felt herself, or some part of herself, being gently embraced. Warmth flowed through her and around her. The pain subsided a little, and the stultifying darkness receded a bit.

She heard her dream-self saying, "I need you, Grand-mama. Please, don't leave me." And the voice replied, "I am always with you, my dear. Someday, when you are ready, you will understand how...and you will understand why. For now, child, go to sleep and let go of the pain."

Connor awoke in a dense haze, the echo of her grandmother's voice still reverberating in her mind. As she lay there, trying to make sense of it all, she made a slow and labored inventory of her body which revealed that her head hurt, her stomach ached, and several muscles in her chest and arms were sore. Unable to explain this state of affairs, she closed her eyes and tried to ignore the pounding in her skull. Out of long habit, she reached out to the place next to her to stroke the warm, sleepy softness of her lover. The sheets were cold as ice. Too quickly, she remembered why, and the brief reprieve of forgetfulness was over. She put her hand to her mouth to stifle the sound and buried her face in the pillow.

The phone rang, but before she could decide what to do about it, the bell stopped, and she heard what could only be Malcolm's resonant voice somewhere downstairs. A few minutes later, he appeared in the doorway, carrying a tray. If there was anything more incongruous than a 6'6" cop wearing a frilly apron, Connor couldn't think of it. Any other time, she might have laughed. As it was, only a ghost of a smile crossed her face. His expression was compassionate, but there was no pity there, something for which she was grateful. With the firm efficiency of a head nurse, he told her to sit up so he could put the tray stand over her lap.

"Really, Mal, I can't," she mumbled, looking at the toast, fruit, and steaming pot of coffee.

"Just try it…you've got to get on your feet, girl." She looked
at him quizzically, wondering if this were some sort of weird pep
talk about getting right back on the horse? She shook her head,
reached for the coffee pot and poured out a cup as he moved
closer and looked her in the eye. "Look, Connor, I need you. If
anyone's going to solve this crime, it's going to be you and me
working together."

She almost choked on the first sip of coffee.

"You can't be serious, Mal. Good God, how can you even
think I would…now? I just lost…." She fought back a fresh bout
of tears.

He sat down on the edge of the bed. "You lost Ariana, and I
lost one of my best friends. I loved her, too, Connor. But the
only thing I can do for her now is to make sure the scumbag
who killed her pays for it. And if you ever want to make your
own life right again, you have to be involved, you can't just sit
around here grieving for her. You're a woman who *does* things.
You don't let life run you, you run your life. Who was it that
figured out the pattern of those perps who killed Marie Louise?
Who did all the legwork and then practically got killed following them? You did."

He paused for a moment, looking away from her. "And who
made me arrest them, instead of killing them where they stood?"
He looked back at her again. "You knew my fellow officers
would have covered for me because they wouldn't blame me for
offing those bastards, but you also knew that I would always
blame myself, that I would always have to live with the fact that
I had killed someone in cold blood. I didn't want to be that kind
of man, or that kind of cop. You were there for me every step
of the way."

He stood up. "Now it's my turn. The only thing that will ease the hurting inside you is to find out who did it, and why. I know *you*. So drink that coffee, take a shower, and get dressed. We're going to the scene to look at it in the daylight."

"I can't do it." Connor's face was ashen, her misery written large upon her features, but she hadn't reckoned with Malcolm's stubbornness.

"Yes, you *can*. What happened to that stiff upper lip you inherited from your old Gran? What would Gwendolyn be thinking now if she were here?"

Thinking of the British side of the family and their unerringly courageous and brisk attitude toward life and death actually did make Connor smile for a moment. She could almost hear Gran, "Now, my girl, let's have none of that. Feeling sorry for yourself never made a bad situation better. Remember, the Broadhursts have backbone." Or was that the dream? Had she only just heard that? No, that was some other time. Conjuring up an image of that indomitable and outspoken woman, still striding through her Sussex village at 83 years of age, gave Connor something solid and even soothing to hang on to. Though the Broadhurst women had a reputation for being descended from Celtic priestesses who had once practiced magic, Connor had never known anyone more down to earth than her Grandmother. She kept the image firmly fixed in her mind as she sat up, pulled the breakfast tray closer to her, and poured out more coffee.

"I'll be ready in half an hour, Captain."

Malcolm smiled briefly at her and started out. He stopped at the door.

"Your father called from Lucerne. I told him what happened and that you were in shock, and almost unconscious by the time I put you to bed. He said he was glad I was here since he couldn't get a flight out of Switzerland for another 24 hours. He said he was sorry, and, well, I think he really meant it." Malcolm started to close the door and then hesitated again. "And there was an odd message from your grandmother. Must have come through while I was talking to Benjamin on the other line."

"Why odd?" Connor felt her chest tighten. She could still hear that dream voice.

He frowned slightly. "Well, I left it on the machine so you could hear it later. Something about…if you hadn't already gotten her message directly, she wanted you to know how sorry she was about Ariana, and that she was there if you needed her. Thing is, I can't figure out how she found out so quick. It hasn't been in the news."

Connor shook her head. "Don't ask." Malcolm shrugged and closed the door behind him. She sat back against the pillows, trying to get a handle on what was happening in her life. Unable to explain her grandmother's omniscience, she let her mind drift to her father, the enigmatic and sometimes harsh Benjamin J. Hawthorne. She knew he *was* sorry. He was fond of Ariana, unlike Connor's mother, who would maintain to her dying day the fiction that the gorgeous Italian woman with whom Connor had lived for over 11 years was nothing more than a glorified *au pair* looking after Connor's daughter, Katy. Amanda conveniently ignored the fact that Katy had been living in England with her great-aunt and great-grandmother for over two years, and had gone up to Oxford University this year, while Ariana had remained ensconced in the Georgetown house.

Despite Connor's increasing celebrity as a writer, invitations to the Hawthorne's sprawling estate in Potomac were few and far between. That suited Connor just fine. Frankly, she missed her horses and her Labradors more than she missed her mother's thinly disguised and remarkably vicious comments about her lifestyle. But then Mrs. Hawthorne had never found much to like about her only child. She believed that at almost 5'10" Connor was too tall to be graceful or marriageable. The girl insisted on pursuing sports; her shoulders became too broad, her muscles too well-defined for a "lady." She would rather read a book than attend social functions, preferred horseback riding over dating, and trimmed her hair to a short, easily maintained style before it was the least bit fashionable to do so.

Nor did this pillar of Washington society approve of her daughter's choice of law school over a graduate degree in fine arts, her eventual career as an ADA, the substitution of her middle name (Connor) for her actual given name (Lydia), or her decision to become a novelist, using her training to create popular, yet literate fiction centered around the criminal justice system. To her mother, Connor's novels were no better than Mickey Spillane's, books she referred to as sensationalist trash. Fortunately, she wasn't a literary critic, just a bitterly disappointed mother.

The only thing Amanda had ever approved of where her daughter was concerned was Connor's marriage to Alex Vandervere. It was a social and financial triumph to join the names and fortunes of the Hawthorne and Vandervere families.

For Connor, it was a nightmare, a sinkhole of lies and self-denial; mercifully, it was also a brief one. The only good to have come of that mismatch was Connor's daughter, whom she loved almost too much for the child's own good. But she'd had wise advice from both Grandmother Gwendolyn and Aunt Jessica, from whom Katy got her middle name. With three loving women and her doting grandfather, Benjamin, seeing to her growth, Katy had turned out to be a level-headed, intelligent, and lively young woman of whom her mother was justifiably proud. Connor wished for a moment that Katy were here now, but rejected the notion immediately. She wouldn't want her daughter to see her like this.

Connor sighed heavily, put aside the tray and her despair, and threw back the covers. She went into the dressing room that lay between the bedroom and the opulent bathroom, with its Jacuzzi and enormous multispray shower, in which Ariana had always reveled. "The plumbing in Europe is dreadful," she would exclaim. "There's nothing like a really great bathroom." Connor shook herself; she didn't need to think of that right now. She grabbed a towel and padded into the bathroom. The walls were mirrored on two sides and she was startled by her image. Her eyes were bloodshot; most of her jet black hair, shot through with strands of slightly premature gray, was matted to her head, while a few pieces stuck up here and there at absurd angles. There was very little color in a face that appeared to have aged years in just one night. She decided she looked a lot older than 41.

"I look like bloody hell," she said out loud. Fighting off the urge to run back to the bed and crawl beneath the covers and cry, she took a deep breath, stepped into the shower, and let the hot needled spray pound some semblance of life back into her.

———◦◦◦———

Thirty minutes later, clad in navy wool slacks, a creamy silk blouse, and a fawn-colored, light-weight leather jacket, she descended the stairs. Malcolm turned to look at her as she came in and was reminded once more of what a strikingly handsome woman was Connor Hawthorne. The thick mane of hair was cut to frame her face in soft, natural waves, though she had chosen the style more for the sake of convenience than out of an attempt to conform to fashion trends. Her chin was firm, though not overly prominent, as were the finely sculptured cheekbones. Crystal blue eyes were set beneath dark, expressive eyebrows that contrasted sharply with a pale, creamy complexion. Her nose was subtle, well-proportioned. The sum total of Connor's features was harmonious and compelling, bordering on the androgynous.

Still, Malcolm could see the sorrow etched into her face and that her normally rosy skin was now deadly pale. He finished talking to Leon, now his detective sergeant, and put the receiver back on the cradle.

"Leon's got the area cordoned off. The forensic team is still down there. You ready?"

For just a moment he thought she would crumble again, refuse to leave the house, but years of fighting for whom she was and whom she wanted to be, had toughened to sinew the spirit of the little girl who always knew she would turn out "different" and whose mother never stopped trying to browbeat her into conformity. There was a lot of Benjamin Hawthorne's backbone in his daughter.

"Yes. I'm ready. Let's take my car."

Malcolm understood her need to feel in control of something right now; driving her own car seemed like a good start. He nodded his agreement. "I'll get my portable radio and meet you by the garage door."

As with many of this neighborhood's elegant and historic townhouses, the garage was on the street level, the other three stories rising above it, tall and narrow. At one time, the imposing brick home, with its white trim and black shutters, had been the Hawthornes' city home. After Connor's divorce, Benjamin knew she would never marry again, nor was she likely to feel welcome in her childhood home. On her 30th birthday, he had deeded the house to her, complete with furnishings and artwork, over the strenuous objections of his wife. Connor and Ariana had called it home ever since. Malcolm remembered his first visit there, with Marie Louise on his arm. They were good memories.

He retrieved his portable radio and waited on the curb in the weak but persistent sunshine. The garage door slid up silently. From the dark recesses, the silver Lexus sedan emerged. She stopped to let Malcolm in, and even though the passenger seat was in its rearmost position, it was still a bit tight for him. He really was a Cadillac man, although he had flatly refused to let Connor buy him one for his last birthday. She pulled out of the driveway and headed down toward M Street. Just past Key Bridge, she made an illegal turn onto Canal Road where it intersected M.

"Hey, watch it, I'm a cop," he said, trying to elicit a small smile. His efforts were rewarded.

"So give me a ticket already."

He noticed, however, that her usually smooth and confident driving style was absent. She sped up; she slowed down. She jerked the wheel slightly. It was if she wanted to get there, and then again, she didn't. He was immensely grateful that Ariana's body was not there for Connor to see. He was sorry that he'd seen it, in the fading light, lying there on the bank. It was a sight he would never be able to forget, and it was the first crime scene he had ever walked away from. It was also a memory he would never share with anyone, least of all the woman who sat beside him, hands clenched on the leather-padded steering wheel.

Later that night, it had taken every ounce of objectivity and strength he could muster when the morgue attendant lifted the sheet covering Ariana Gennaro's body. He wanted to walk away. No, he wanted to run away. But he had to do it for Connor, make the formal identification. He didn't want her to live with that kind of image seared into her mind. Malcolm had seen a lot of bodies in his career, but this was still a horrible sight. Ariana had been in the water for two or three days; the corpse was bloated and pale, with little hint of the beauty that had been. Her long hair was twisted and wrapped around her face. The eyes were open—staring, lifeless, and no longer green. The pale sweater she wore had dried just enough to show the dark patches surrounding jagged rips in the fabric. He saw evidence of at least five stab wounds. She wore fashionable, but now sodden, leather hiking boots and tight jeans, which he also suspected had been soaked with her blood. Looking closely, he noted with his detective's eye, the defensive wounds on her hands, the deep scratches on her face. Ariana had not gone meekly to her death.

As if reading his mind, a habit they had both developed over the years, Connor suddenly said, "Tell me how you found her." He didn't know at first if she meant who had discovered the body, or in what condition the body was in. He decided to go with the easier answer.

"A guy was jogging down along the towpath. No one had been down there in a few days, what with all the rain. He saw her and called it in on his cell phone. Leon caught the report and found her wallet in her coat pocket. He called me." Malcolm didn't mention that the guy had thrown up in the canal twice before he could manage to dial the phone.

"What was she doing there, Malcolm?" He saw her grip on the wheel tighten even more. This was the crux of the matter, he knew. This was what truly tormented Connor. She didn't know why Ariana was there, because she didn't have any idea where Ariana had been for the past two months, at least not specifically. After the last big blowup they'd had, Ariana had moved to an apartment at the Watergate, refusing to admit Connor, or return her phone calls. She'd show up in the society pages on the arms of various officials and diplomats, and Connor had told him about reports from friends that Ariana had made a spectacle of herself more than once at a private club near Adams Morgan frequented by moneyed lesbians and a few "straight" women looking for some forbidden pleasure. Connor's pride, and her own integrity, kept her from spying on Ariana, though she had the resources and connections to do it. They had quarreled before, but Ariana had always come home, until now.

"We don't have a clear idea of what happened. We're not even sure exactly where she was killed. Someone may have brought her here after she was dead." He tried to keep his voice matter of fact, keep the tremor out of it. But Connor heard it, and steeled herself to ask more questions.

"Had she been...um...had she been assaulted?" Malcolm saw how hard it was for her to ask that particular question.

"Not that we could tell. The autopsy will give us more information." As they rounded a curve, they could see three Metro patrol cars and two Park Police cars on the shoulder. Connor pulled in behind them. An officer immediately started to wave her on with an annoyed scowl until he saw Malcolm, a recognizable figure in D.C. law enforcement. They got out and walked through the dense vegetation along the short path to the canal, where an area had already been cordoned off with bright yellow police tape. The air was damp and heavy with the smell of rotting leaves, brackish water, and death.

Over a dozen officers and technicians were at work on the

crime scene. Malcolm had given this every priority, a decision he was aware might be questioned, despite his captain's rank. But if it were, he was sure the Hawthorne name would convince the higher-ups of the wisdom of a full and rapid response.

He saw Leon a few yards away talking to a member of the forensic team. In the technician's latex-gloved hand dangled what looked like a belt. Leon took the object from her and walked over to his superior. He obviously didn't know where to look, what to say, or whether to say anything at all. Malcolm rescued him from the dilemma.

"Leon, Connor's here to help. She's going to be on this investigation with us until we find the perp, okay?" He was well aware that Leon did not favor civilian involvement, especially not when the civilian was more or less related. Fortunately, the sergeant had the good sense to save his protest for later.

"Sure...and I'm really sorry about Ariana." Leon was a man of few words. Condolences constituted a supreme effort for him.

Connor looked him in the eye and simply said, "Thanks...I know."

"What have you got?" Malcolm reached out and took the piece of fabric. Connor started to touch it, pulled her hand back.

"That could be the belt of Ariana's raincoat. It's the right color and it's from a Burberry...look at the buckle."

Neither Leon nor Malcolm would necessarily know a Burberry from a London Fog, but they took Connor's word for it. Leon motioned to the young technician who came over with an evidence bag, looking curiously and, perhaps, a bit appreciatively at Connor. Being a consummate professional, however, she did not linger, but took the belt, bagged it, and went back to combing the undergrowth. As they stood looking at the dark, redolent canal, Malcolm's radio crackled.

"Lieutenant, we've found a car up here, less than a quarter mile from your location, near Glen Echo."

"Make and model?" Malcolm was terse.

"Some kinda Mercedes...a convertible. Tan over green."

Out of the corner of his eye, he saw Connor's face harden, jaw clenched. She had given Ariana a Mercedes convertible just last year for her birthday—tan top and a dark green body. He turned to her.

"We'll drive up there." He spoke into the radio. "Tape off the area, don't trample all over the place." Then he motioned to Leon. "Get forensics sweeping the towpath from here to where the car is, on both sides...there's a footbridge between us and Glen Echo. It could have happened on the other embankment, between here and the river."

Leon's eyebrows did a skeptical dance. "But that's a lot of territory, it could take all...." He stopped, looking embarrassed. "Sure, boss. We'll get right on it."

Leon turned quickly and walked away, issuing instructions to the team as Connor and Malcolm made their way back up the embankment to the car. A couple of minutes later they parked behind yet another police vehicle and, for the first time that morning, Connor looked as if she might not be able to do this. But she opened the door, got out, and started down. Without a word, Malcolm took her arm. The car stood there in the shaded gloom. Given the angle at which it had been parked, even from several feet away they could see the three pink parking violation slips on the windshield, an amusing fact under other circumstances.

The wheels of law enforcement had ground on, but no one

had bothered to look for the owner, have the car towed to impound, or wonder why a $60,000 automobile had sat unat-
tended for at least three days. That it hadn't been stripped, or
at least burglarized, was probably due only to the fact that it
was fairly well-hidden by foliage from cars passing on the road
above. At least the citations might help narrow the time-of-
death estimate. Malcolm made a mental note to find the officer
who had issued them. He felt his chest tighten when he realized how close by help might have been when Ariana died.

Once the officer on the scene assured him the ground
around the car had already been carefully examined, they approached the car from the rear. There were no footprints at all
on the passenger side, only some on the driver's side made by
a smallish hiking boot, and some larger ones that Malcolm
would just bet were left by the park cop who had written the
tickets. They stood on the right side of the car, looking at the
leather briefcase and cellular phone. Malcolm motioned to the
officer.

"Get a slim and open the door." While they waited, Malcolm radioed for another team to meet him at the car. They
would check the area around the Mercedes, then tow it to the
police impound lot for fingerprint dusting, vacuuming for
fibers, and photographing.

Connor's voice beside him was quiet and strained. "I have a
key." The thought hadn't even occurred to him, and somehow
it seemed worse that way, more personal than he wanted it to
be. But it made sense. On Ariana's key ring they would probably find one to Connor's Lexus, not to mention Connor's
house. This thought he found unsettling in the extreme, but he
let it pass for the moment. He comforted himself with hope
that Ariana's keys were still in her pocket. Connor carefully

unlocked the door without touching the surface of the car, and watched as Malcolm slipped on a latex glove and very gingerly operated the door handle.

"Looks as if she drove it here herself, but I don't know. She may have been meeting someone." He looked around. "But why here?" If he expected Connor to have an answer, she didn't.

Tuesday evening

Later, as it was just growing dark, Connor pulled into her narrow driveway. She spotted the limo parked across the street, in complete defiance of posted parking regulations. The small decal on the right rear bumper, along with the somewhat unusual license plate number, would have told knowledgeable Washingtonians whose black stretch Cadillac lounged so nonchalantly in the tow-away zone. Its status was such that only the greenest of rookie cops or parking enforcement personnel (with no ambitions for advancement) would have dared to question the driver, let alone issue a citation. The rear door swung open and her father unfolded his lanky, 6'3" frame onto the pavement, pausing to say something to the interior of the car, which, with its very dark windows, yielded no clue as to its occupants. He closed the door and strode across the street.

To some people, Benjamin Jarrold Hawthorne was a ruthless and arrogant man who wielded power much as a home-run hitter wields a baseball bat. Others, who had some inkling of just how far his power reached, found him more than a little frightening. But whatever seemingly inhuman traits the intrigues of politics and national security had engendered within him, his closest friends and colleagues (of whom there were, by both choice and necessity, very few) knew Benjamin to be possessed of a great deal of humanity, perhaps too much for a person in whose hands the fate of large segments of humankind sometimes lay. It made his work over the years even more difficult than it might have been for a different sort of man, one with less conscience and more personal ambition. Despite his lofty status, his motivations were far more philanthropic and less political than most would have thought. He considered himself a patriot, a peacemaker, and an arbitrator. He was all these and more. But right now he was a father.

A few long strides took him across the street to where she stood. He looked at her face and without a moment's hesitation—and against all Washington standards of correct public behavior—he pulled her into his arms.

"I'm so sorry, honey." His words were soft, his voice charged with emotion.

The grief she had suppressed all day, at the crime scene and at the police station, welled up uncontrollably. But because Benjamin Hawthorne loved his daughter, he stood there on the busy Georgetown street, in full view of curious passersby, letting her cry on his $2,000 Saville Row suit and waiting for her tears to subside. Finally, feeling a bit foolish airing her emotions in public, she pulled away and asked him inside. He glanced at his watch, and for a moment her heart sank, thinking he would once again be rushing off to "business," that catchall euphemism her family had always employed where her father was concerned. Instead he smiled and answered firmly, "Sure, honey, let's go in and have some brandy."

Connor smiled despite herself. A glass of brandy or a cup of tea were her father's cure-alls for just about anything. One would think he had been from the British side of the family rather than her flighty, pretentious mother. They quickly mounted the steps to the front door, daughter anxious to be back inside her own haven, father just as anxious to comfort her, both supremely unaware of the thin, gray-clad figure that slipped out of the still-open door of Connor's garage and disappeared quickly into the deepening darkness. It was an unusual oversight for a man of Hawthorne's experience and one he would come to regret.

———◦◦◦———

He trotted through two back yards, and down two alleyways before stopping to catch his breath and remove the gray windbreaker. It was reversible, so he turned it inside out and put it back on. He removed the black baseball cap concealing his blonde hair and threw it in a nearby dumpster, then pulled a knitted tie from his pants pocket and quickly knotted it around the collar of his button-down, oxford cloth shirt. Donning a pair of round, horn-rimmed glasses, he started walking again.

Three more blocks brought him to M Street, where he faded into the crowd of bar-hoppers just starting their rounds. He looked for all the world like a self-conscious, nerdy GU grad student as he strolled to the parking garage near Wisconsin and M, and took the steps down to level four, where his innocuous Honda Accord sat undisturbed. He got in and started the engine. It had been a little too close, he thought. Who would have thought the great Benjamin Hawthorne would actually give a shit that his daughter's lesbo playmate had bought it? He shook his head at such a puzzling attitude. He smiled to himself because it didn't really make any difference. Everything was going to work out just the way he'd planned it.

———◦◦◦———

Back in the library, Connor was immediately struck by how different it all seemed from the night before, when every color had been harsh, every piece of furniture had loomed menacingly, every sound had echoed in emptiness. Now it seemed once more like the calm, comforting environment it had always been. The soft ivories and deep reds of the Oriental carpets, the warm glow of walnut veneer on the Queen Anne furniture, and the massive mahogany partners desk and high-backed chair where she sat almost every day to write and think. Her father was busily rebuilding the fire, and, once that was accomplished, he poured two brandies into crystal snifters, sitting them down on the hearth to warm a bit. He lowered himself down onto the leather couch and patted the seat beside him.

"Come sit down, sweetheart. You look as if you're freezing."

She obeyed without thinking, realizing that she was, indeed, trembling, both from the unseasonable chill in the air and the stress of maintaining her composure for so many hours.

"How did you get here so fast? I thought you were in Switzerland."

"Charter, flew out last night." Connor wondered if his leaving so abruptly had been detrimental to his work, but she didn't ask. She rarely delved into the nature of his true occupation. Right now she was just glad to have him here with her. She looked at her father for a moment, noting the fatigue lines etched into his handsome face. Had he quite that much gray in his hair the last time she saw him, she wondered, jolted into registering that he must be, what was it…almost 62. Funny how she hadn't noted the passage of time where he was concerned.

Neither spoke for many minutes. Tears occasionally coursed down Connor's face as she stared into the fire, but she made no audible sound. Her father silently handed her his large handkerchief, retrieved the two brandies, from which a delicious aroma now eddied, and settled himself to wait until she was ready to talk.

"What happened? Marty talked to a friend downtown, but he said the officer in charge hadn't reported in yet. Is Malcolm handling it?"

Connor nodded. "Yes, he was here...last night." The tears threatened again, but she choked them back. "This morning we went to where they...where they found Ariana. It was down by the Canal. Her car was there, and they impounded it for evidence..." She stopped, realizing it didn't matter about the stupid car. Ariana would never drive it again. She would never come dashing into the garage, tooting the horn to signal her lover that she was home, would never again come running up the steps from the den on the garage level, breathless with news of her day, her adventures, her ideas for forthcoming books. And because the here and now was so painful, Connor's memory was irresistibly drawn back to the day, not so long ago, that she had given the car to Ariana.

Knowing how much Ariana loved surprises, Connor planned a formal dinner party, well-staffed and superbly catered, attended by their closest friends, mostly other lesbians, a few gay men, and a handful of straight, but nonjudgmental friends. Of course, Malcolm had been there, accompanied by a charming female colleague with a wicked sense of humor. Connor's father had even managed a brief appearance, presenting Ariana with an overwhelming bouquet of roses and a lovely diamond bracelet.

After dinner was served and guests had gathered in the living room, Ariana opened her presents, enthusiastically praising each one and bestowing lavish hugs upon the gift-giver. But Connor saw her eyes flick over the array of gift boxes from time to time, curious as to which one contained her lover's birthday tribute. Soon, all the boxes were opened, and the floor was littered with the remnants of wrappings and ribbons. No packages remained.

With only the slightest of frowns, Ariana stood up and declared the birthday a success, inviting everyone to enjoy some champagne before the cake-cutting.

Ariana looked across the room at her handsome mate, clad in her trademark black and white, this particular evening rendered in a flowing silk jacket, slacks, and blouson shirt. A diamond choker was the only jewelry she wore aside from the twisted strands of gold and platinum that served as her wedding ring. Connor's eyes twinkled and she smiled at Ariana's barely concealed consternation. But even Connor couldn't wait any longer. Signaling her lover to follow, she led the way downstairs. Ariana looked puzzled but beside herself with anticipation as she followed. Connor stopped at the garage door, flung it wide, and snapped on all the lights.

There it sat, a gleaming 450 SEL, top down, wrapped up in the biggest yellow ribbon Ariana had ever seen. She was, for one of the few times in her life, speechless. The look on her face was worth every penny it had cost. She emitted a little scream and leaped into the front seat, then out again to kiss Connor soundly on the lips, then back into the car again. The keys were in it. They abandoned their guests and spent the next 30 minutes tooling along M Street, ribbon and all. Now, as she struggled to put the image of Ariana's unquenchable smile from her mind, Connor knew she never wanted to see that car again, ever.

"I'll have someone pick up the Mercedes when it's out of impound," Benjamin said quietly. Connor nodded. Her father had that uncanny knack for reading her thoughts. "I'll ask Marty to take care of it."

Marty was Julius Martinez, Senator Hawthorne's closest personal assistant, who, despite his cosmopolitan appearance and very articulate, almost effete manner of speaking, was also a one-time military intelligence officer and a very effective bodyguard. He was not a thug, but, as a few hapless individuals had discovered in the past, he could be quite deadly. Despite his finely honed martial arts skills and his proficiency with a variety of weapons, Marty's primary talent was truly his intellect. He anticipated every contingency, deciphered the coded words and ulterior motivations of those around him, saw patterns where others saw only randomness, and, most importantly, demonstrated a fierce personal loyalty to the man who had long ago thrown all good sense and proper procedure out the window to come back and save his life—one Benjamin Hawthorne.

"That's fine. I don't care. Just get rid of it," Connor said, dismissing the issue.

"Now, what information have you gathered?" Benjamin's attitude, on its face, might have seemed callous, but it was what Connor needed, to put some distance between herself and the image she had conjured up of Ariana lying there cold and wet and dead.

"There's not much physical evidence yet. Some footprints, the belt of her raincoat. The car had been parked there for three days...had three tickets on it."

Benjamin appreciated the irony, but declined to comment. "Do you have any idea why she was there? It's an odd place for Ariana to go. I don't recall her being much of a fan of the outdoors, and certainly not in the rain."

"That's just what Malcolm asked. I don't know, Dad. Damn it, I don't know why the hell she was wandering around down there alone. Except she wasn't alone, I guess." She paused and he sensed her awkwardness.

"I know you and Ariana were having some problems, honey, these things happen. It wasn't your fault she moved out. It wasn't your fault this happened to her. You can't take the blame for the choices that the people in your life make."

Connor suddenly thrust herself up off of the couch. In place of grief was anger, directed at herself, and at the woman whose life had been so brutally cut short.

"But it was all so stupid...we fought over something so stupid! I didn't know it meant that much to her."

"What meant that much to her?"

"That designer promotion thing...with Gerry Marchetti."

Benjamin's eyebrows raised a bit, indicating he was familiar with the name and with the flamboyant character who bore it. "The rather unusual fellow who wears all the silk jackets?"

Connor almost smiled. "That's okay, Dad, you don't have to be quite so politically correct around me. He's positively flaming, and he enjoys it. What I hate is that disgustingly ingratiating personality. Just oozes honey when he talks, pretending to be some kind of Italian nobility." She shuddered in mock distaste. "And hanging around here all the time, like some sort of weekly houseguest."

"So what does 'Count' Marchetti have to do with what happened between you two?"

"He's what started our last fight. That creep could always get to Ariana, so smooth, so full of the *'bellissima* Ariana'...and *'o, cara mia'*...more like full of crap if you ask me. But he has this idea for a whole new line of clothes, says he's going to name them 'Ariana', and all he wants her to do is convince me to plug the new line by mentioning it in my next book. Part of it takes place in Rome, and he figures I can just throw in the name a few times here and there. Like I'm going to do favors for this creep of a con artist." She sighed, her anger subsiding.

"So Ariana came to me a couple of months ago with this

bizarre plan, she even had a couple of paragraphs typed up that she is sure can be 'slipped in' wherever I'm talking about the main female character. She even announced that Gerry would be happy to spend even more time here so I could consult him on fashion, if you can believe that.

"Then, as if that weren't enough, he'd also convinced her that it was time I dedicated a book to her by name. And, just in case I was at a loss for words, he'd helped her draft this turgidly romantic dedication that would make anyone nauseous. Of course, Ariana assumed I would say, 'sure, why not?'"

"And you didn't react the way she expected?"

"Of course I didn't. I couldn't believe she would even ask me to do something like that. Turning my work into some sort of vehicle for corporate sponsorship. I told her this wasn't the movie business. I wasn't looking for advertising fees to mention trade names and I didn't want Gerry Marchetti in my house. I lost my temper. Then she got really angry."

"She didn't understand how you felt about your work?" Benjamin's tone implied he had already guessed what course that argument took. Ariana's tendency toward self-centeredness was common knowledge, even among those who adored her.

"That's just it. After all these years together, I thought she did, and the way she was acting seemed so out of character. All of a sudden she was shouting at me that I didn't love her because I wouldn't put her name in a book. I tried to tell her that it wasn't about her name...it didn't mean I didn't love her...it was about publicizing something private and intimate. And I wasn't about to let Marchetti use my book to promote some sleazy marketing scam."

"Knowing Ariana's temper, I imagine she didn't see it quite that way."

Connor sighed deeply. "No, she didn't. She said I didn't love her, that I was ashamed of her, that I didn't want to help her career, on and on. I just got angrier, too. I said, 'what career?' and that tore it. I guess I didn't realize how much it hurt her pride that the modeling jobs have dried up the past few years. I thought she understood that's the way it works in that ridiculous, heartless industry—no one looks at you when you're over 30 and stop looking like a prepubescent sex object or a prison camp survivor."

"You and I know that, and Ariana probably knew it, too, Connor. But she didn't want to admit it. And I imagine this Marchetti character played on her ego and her vanity. She wanted to be famous again; she wanted people to know her name, the way a lot of people know yours. She wanted her share of the limelight. She probably didn't even think about what it would mean to you."

"No, she didn't, and that's one reason I got so angry about it. It didn't even occur to her that there were *ethics* involved." Connor moved back to the couch and sat down heavily, defeated by the things she couldn't change. "So I wouldn't budge, and we said a lot of things I wish we hadn't. Then Ariana announced that if her friends weren't welcome in *my* home, then she wasn't either. So she stormed upstairs, packed all seventeen pieces of her Louis Vuitton luggage and left. She sent a hired driver for what she couldn't fit in the car. Next thing I knew she had rented an apartment at the Watergate, and I only found out about that because she had the manager send me the lease to sign."

"And you did?" Benjamin was smiling ever so slightly. "Obviously she wanted you to know where she was and she probably wanted you to make her come home."

"Yes, you're probably right. And even though I was still

angry, it kind of made me laugh that she'd had the chutzpah to have them bill me for the rent. But I just wasn't ready to go to her and try to work things out. I wanted her to come home on her own. Then…well…friends were telling me she was out partying, living it up, maybe even sleeping around." The pain of that betrayal made her voice rough.

"And you believed them? You really thought Ariana would be unfaithful to you after all these years?"

Connor had the good grace to be embarrassed. "I don't know. No, I don't think so. But you know how she could be sometimes, Dad, so impulsive and unthinking. The main thing is I just wanted her to come back and apologize and I waited and waited and…." Her words were choked off.

Gently, her father took her hand.

"And you waited too long." Connor nodded, her whole body hunched in misery. "But we all do that, honey. We all wait too long for something to happen, or for someone to do something we think they should, and one day we turn around and they're gone, or the moment is gone. It's a helluva hard lesson, sweetheart, but it's one we've all had. And sometimes you just can't change things, or people. You might have gone to her, forgiven her, but would you really have done what she asked? Put all that garbage in your book?"

"Maybe," she mumbled.

His voice grew a bit sharper. "No, you wouldn't have. Not in a million years, because you're Connor Hawthorne, and you know where to draw the line. No human being can ignore his principles if they really *are* principles. And all that has nothing to do with the fact that someone killed Ariana. Whether she were here, or at the Watergate, it doesn't matter."

He took her chin in his hand. "Do you understand?"

She nodded, her lips trembling with the effort to speak, and turned her face away. "Yes, but...."

"But what?"

"Don't you see, if she'd been here, I would have known she was missing. I would have known she didn't come home one night. She wouldn't have been...." Her voice cracked and her words were sandwiched between ragged sobs. "She wouldn't have been...lying out there...for three days...and three nights...in the rain...all alone." She crumbled before his eyes, and Benjamin Hawthorne, a man who had, without flinching, sent men and women to die in ways even more ugly than had Ariana, wrapped his little girl in his arms and let his own quiet tears fall gently into her hair.

CHAPTER THREE

—◈—

And constancy lives in realms above;
And life is thorny; and youth is vain;
And to be wroth with one we love,
Doth work like madness in the brain.
—Samuel Taylor Coleridge

—◈—

Wednesday, September 20
Washington, D.C.

At 6:00 a.m. Wednesday morning, Marty looked up as his boss came through the connecting door between their offices in the Old Executive Office Building adjoining the White House, and he was startled. He had known Benjamin long enough to interpret the expression on the man's face. This was a mixture of anger and worry. And while a lot of the pin-stripers in D.C. wore that face as part of their uniform (because they thought it demonstrated to the world they were serious, busy, and extraordinarily important), Hawthorne was known for his rigid equanimity under the most difficult circumstances. He didn't have to act important; he *was* important.

Now, however, his agitation was evident, and Marty had a fairly good idea why. The accounts of Ariana's death had made the front page of the *Washington Post* that morning. (The reprieve of almost a day was due to Malcolm's valiant efforts to keep a lid on things for a short while, and the fact the *Post* was a morning paper.) Even that relatively responsible organ of the fourth estate had not resisted the temptation to rub the aristocratic Hawthorne noses in the mud just a bit. The mainstream press had, until now, focused on Connor's work either as a district attorney or, later, as an author. Rarely had her lifestyle or sexual preference been an issue for them, if only out of an understanding of how the game was played. Mutual back-scratching was the order of the day. Benjamin Hawthorne was a valuable ally to certain reporters.

Now, with a murder in the family, the gloves were off. Connor's name had been mentioned throughout the story. She was identified as Ariana's longtime "companion." That was to be expected; it was common knowledge in certain circles. What rankled Benjamin, Marty assumed, was the focus on the couple's recent estrangement, Ariana's allegedly wild behavior, and the very vague implication that there might be more to this murder than met the eye. All of this was, of course, couched in carefully objective reporter lingo. But anyone with half a brain could draw the obvious conclusion that Connor might have had something to with her lover's death.

There were sidebar stories on the Hawthorne family, and on Benjamin, photos of the Georgetown house and of Ariana at a night club. It left the reader with a somewhat sordid impression of all of the people involved in this tragedy, rather than a sense of outrage that a woman had been brutally murdered in their fair city.

"I bet Amanda is ready to explode," Marty thought as he looked up from the paper into Benjamin's troubled eyes. "Sorry, B.J.," he said, employing the nickname he alone had always used. "What can I do?"

Benjamin swept aside the condolences with a tight gesture of his hand. "We need to know what's going on, Marty."

Marty reached for one of the phones on his desk. "Want me to call Morrison, goose him a little?"

"Yes, I do, but not right this minute." He sat down heavily in one of the leather armchairs. "Marty, this may not be just a random mugging or impulse murder." He looked directly at his subordinate, his eyes conveying more than the words themselves.

"You don't mean...."

"Yes, I *do* mean that. What if this is all part of someone's operational plan to get at me through Connor? They might not dare go after her, but killing Ariana would be close enough to really scare her, and send me a message."

"What sort of message?" Marty was instantly and intensely focused, mind gearing up, his finely tuned senses alerted to every nuance in Benjamin's words.

"That someone knows something he shouldn't." Benjamin's eyes were bleak as the Chesapeake Bay in midwinter. Obviously, the possible ramifications of that possibility shocked him.

Marty rocked back in his chair, seeking, with this casual movement, to allay his own rising sense of panic. "Can't be, boss. There hasn't been a hint of any leaks or any interest in any of the ongoing operations since we took care of that schmuck at the Pentagon who got too big for his gold stars." He leaned forward again and toyed with the fountain pen on his blotting pad. "Don't assume this has anything to do with any of our projects, B.J." His dark eyes bored into the older man, willing him to shake off the cloud of fear that appeared to have settled over him.

Benjamin sighed, then allowed the shadow of a smile to pass across his lips. "You're probably right, Marty. Maybe I'm just getting a little too old for all this."

His aide laughed. "Yeah, sure, and I'm the Queen of England." He paused and once again regarded his mentor with those intense eyes, his tone more serious. "You'll do what you have to do until it's time for someone else to take over. Don't borrow trouble, B.J."

The man opposite him relaxed just a bit and then stood with a gesture that said he had rediscovered his own sense of optimism and duty. "That's what you do best, Marty...remind me when I'm being an ass."

"I hope I do a little more than that," Marty said, smiling up at the man who had made it possible for the son of despised "wetbacks" to walk the halls of political power, and wield quite a bit himself.

For a moment, Benjamin looked at him with paternal fondness. "You do, Marty, you do. Now...get onto that jackass Morrison and light a fire under him. I don't want Malcolm's job to be any harder than it is." He left, pulling the door closed between their offices, signaling his need for privacy. Marty sat gazing at the closed door for a few moments, then got down to business. It was too early for his secretary to be at her desk in the outer office, so he pulled open a drawer and flipped through his own Rolodex before picking up the receiver and getting to work.

Later in the morning, the gray phone on Benjamin's desk buzzed quietly, indicating a call on his private line. He waited until it buzzed again before lifting the handset. The voice of his wife, Amanda, came through loud and clear, and immediately he knew she was in one of her more obstreperous moods.

"Benjamin, why haven't you called me about this situation?"

"What situation?" he asked, trying to keep the annoyance out of his voice.

"Have you seen the newspaper this morning?"

"Of course I've seen it, Amanda...and I've read every word. I assume you are talking about the reports of Ariana's death."

"No...although that certainly seems to have precipitated this humiliating coverage about our family."

Benjamin willed himself to hold his temper. "What are you talking about, Amanda? And why haven't you called your daughter? She's devastated."

Amanda didn't respond to his question, completely oblivious to anything but her well-fueled fury.

"I just want to know what you are going to *do* about it."

"*Do* about it? What on earth could I possibly do about a published newspaper report, Amanda?"

He listened to her sputtering on the other end of the line and could imagine how she probably looked at this moment, her face red-blotched with anger, the remnants of a hangover rendering her mood unusually vicious. Odd that he could no longer think of his wife as beautiful although, superficially, she was a handsome woman—a svelte 5'6" kept in fighting trim by a host of hairdressers, manicurists, fitness trainers, and plastic surgeons. Unfortunately, there was no longer anything beautiful about what was inside Amanda Hawthorne, a fact Benjamin discovered far too late in their marriage. Nowadays, her behavior made her ugly to behold, which saddened more than angered him.

"I want you to sue those bastards for god's sake...call the editor, demand a retraction, tell him you won't permit him to print any more of these disgusting lies and innuendos."

Benjamin took a moment to compose himself, trying to maintain a calm tone of voice. "Amanda, please calm down."

"Don't tell me what to do. You're hardly in a position to
dictate to me how I should behave."

Benjamin hoped this wasn't going to degenerate into yet another exhaustive lecture on her noble family heritage (which existed primarily in her mind), but his hopes were quickly dashed.

"I'll have you know that someone of my background and
breeding should never have to endure such disrespect and humiliation. You have never shown any understanding of my sen-
sitivities. If my father were alive, he would not permit the family name to be dragged into the gutter."

The mention of Amanda's father, a war veteran and a rather
kindly soul who, by chance, had earned himself a knighthood
and who rarely put himself forward, was one time too many for
Benjamin.

"I will have you know, Amanda, that the American press
could care less about your background. They would report on
this family even if you were a full-fledged member of the British
peerage, which, by the way, you are not!" She started to interrupt, and he raised his voice to override her protest. "I do not
control what is written in the newspapers," he continued. "And,
from what I can tell, aside from some regrettable insinuations,
there are no lies to retract. These articles contain nothing but the
truth."

This was too much for Amanda. "The truth! Are you bloody
well insane? Why they as much said in print that our daughter is
a pervert, and we can hardly have those sorts of things said about
our family even if...."

Her words were cut off instantly as Benjamin Hawthorne
raised his voice to its maximum volume. "That's *enough*! Do you
hear me, enough! I will not have this conversation with you ever

again. For the last time, our daughter is, and always has been, a lesbian. I may wish she had made an easier choice, but she had the guts to be honest, and it has not one goddamned thing to do with you, Amanda. The whole world is not about you and your petty snobbery and your delusions of nobility. The whole world does not revolve around Amanda Hawthorne. Don't you care that Connor has just lost the woman she loved, in a brutal, horrible way? Don't you care that she has been hurt, that she is in more pain than she's ever known in her life? Don't you give a damn about that beautiful, intelligent, loving, wonderful woman who is your own *daughter?*" Benjamin finally stopped to draw breath...and waited.

The words came back clipped and cold as stone. "As far as I am concerned, I *have* no daughter. I wasted 18 years of my life trying to raise a respectable, decent young woman and this is how I am repaid. She throws away her marriage, throws away her talent on prosecuting scum and writing trash. I won't have anything to do with it, do you understand? And you needn't bother coming home until you're prepared to apologize for your unconscionable behavior today."

There was a distinct pause while she waited for his capitulation, but it didn't come. He took another deep breath and reached a decision motivated not by regret or anger, but by a sense of integrity Amanda would never comprehend. "You need not expect me home at all." His tone of voice was implacable. And, without another word, he replaced the phone gently in its cradle.

A minute or so later, the interoffice door opened quietly behind him. Benjamin looked up at Marty. "I guess you heard that."

"Some, not all."

"I lost my temper, I probably shouldn't have."

"You should have lost it 30 years ago, B.J."

"Maybe if you'd been around to remind me, I wouldn't have let it go this far." Marty didn't bother to point out that he had never once offered personal advice to Benjamin, and never would, because it wasn't his place to interfere. He just shrugged a little and changed the subject.

"I talked to Morrison, gave him the hint, gently of course."

"Good. And, I almost forgot, I need you to get Ariana's car out of impound when they're done with it. See Malcolm if they give you any trouble."

"Do you want me to take it back to the townhouse?"

"No, definitely not. Connor doesn't want it there, she...."

Marty detected the slight huskiness in Benjamin's voice and immediately grasped the issue. Connor couldn't stand the sight of it, nor could she bring herself to go about the business of selling the car herself. Marty knew it wouldn't do to just take it back to the dealership to be sold. They would only end up calling Connor about the price, or to get her signature on the title. He would have it stored for a while.

"I'll take care of it, boss." He put his hand on Benjamin's shoulder for just an instant, then went back to his own office, shutting the door quietly.

Later on Wednesday morning

Despite an unusual degree of cooperation between the various law enforcement entities in Washington (including the FBI, the U.S. Park Police, the quasi-governmental Executive Protection

Service, and the D.C. Metropolitan Police), there were few, if any, leads in the Ariana Gennarro homicide. This displeased Malcolm even more than it displeased his superior, Deputy Chief Morrison, who had a keen eye for the politically sensitive cases in his division. Stanley Morrison wanted to see the title "Chief of Police" in front of his name some day, and pleasing powerful politicians was the best way to get it.

The District of Columbia was, after all, in the grip of the federal government because it was not a state. It was a federal district straddling the Potomac River, originally carved from the borders of Maryland and Virginia. As such, the status of its local government was always a question mark. Consistently poor management, graft, and allegations of shameless corruption had brought District officials under increasing scrutiny by the legislative committee charged with oversight. Most recently, the mayor's governing power had been severely curtailed, much of his authority delegated to a governing council. Reports of mismanagement and outright malfeasance were piling up every day. With violent-death statistics rivaling those of cities several times its size, D.C. had been referred to as the "murder capital of the country"—a fine moniker for the nation's capital. Pierre L'Enfant's dream city had become a nightmare for many of the people who lived in it.

The residents of the city itself were mostly black, and largely poor. They suffered most from the ravages of crime, particularly drug trafficking, and the rapid deterioration of city services. While police enforcement seemed to work rather better in some areas—mainly the NW sector of the city occupied primarily by upper-middle-class white professionals, government officials, and diplomats—large sections of the other "quadrants" of the grid-mapped capital had taken on the characteristics of a war zone—

battered, burned, and reeking of despair. Violence had become
so pervasive, in fact, that it took a crime such as the murder of a
friend of a powerful, wealthy, white socialite to catch Stanley
Morrison's interest. And it had his full and undivided attention.

A call from Julius Martinez, Senator Hawthorne's aide, had
awakened him at 7:00 A.M. that morning. He had snapped to attention, sitting there in his striped pajamas, his wife asking grog-
gily who was calling at that hour. Mr. Martinez had been most
polite, most apologetic for the early call. It was just that Senator
Hawthorne was so very concerned over the death of his daughter's friend. He wanted to be sure the top people were overseeing matters, and that the very competent police captain...Jeffer-
son, he thought the name was, would be handling the
investigation.

Morrison mostly said, "Yes, of course," and "I'll see to it personally," and "I understand." Before hanging up, Martinez casually mentioned he might be calling back for an update, if that was
all right. The question was purely rhetorical, because the message, shorn of all its careful propriety, was clear: "We're watching you from up here on the Hill, and we expect success."

It had taken Morrison fewer than 45 minutes to shower,
shave, dress, and race to his office. At 8:00 he was browbeating
the switchboard operator downstairs (simply because his own
secretary wasn't yet present to be browbeaten), demanding that
Captain Jefferson be found at once and told to report to the
deputy chief's office. He fumed until 9:08, when Captain Jefferson knocked on his inner-office door. He was not happy with
his subordinate's report.

"Sir, we've only been on this since Monday afternoon. We
have a victim of stabbing and very little forensic evidence. The
crime scene people worked out there all day yesterday, and the

results of the autopsy are due this afternoon. I've expedited everything as best I can, but you know how backed up they are."

"I'll take care of that." The deputy chief waved away these perfectly valid obstacles as if they were nothing more than obstinacy on the part of underlings. "This case is to have top priority."

"It already does as far as I'm concerned," Malcolm said grimly. Morrison looked up at him, the light dawning. "Aren't you a friend of that Hawthorne woman, the one who writes books?"

Malcolm grimaced at the way Morrison managed to reduce the life and career of an ex-district attorney turned brilliant author to "a woman who writes books," but he said nothing. He needed this man's good will, at least for the moment. He just nodded, mentioning casually that Ms. Hawthorne had been closely involved in solving the MacAllister case.

"I'd like two extra teams assigned to my office for canvassing and leg work," he ventured.

"Whatever...take the manpower you need." If Malcolm were surprised, he didn't let it show. In a flash of insight, not unusual for him, he realized that Deputy Chief Morrison had been "got to," and he was fairly sure by whom. He grinned inwardly and played his trump card.

"I also want to do a media blitz and set up a hotline for tips."

Morrison blanched a little at the damage this could do to his already inadequate budget, but he could still hear the soft, friendly, yet vaguely menacing tone of Julius Martinez's voice.

"All right, but try not to keep it open forever, okay? And I want daily progress reports, morning and afternoon." If anyone would report to Senator Hawthorne, Morrison wanted to make sure it would be him. Malcolm understood it, too, and suppressed another wry smile. He, himself, would talk to Marty and

Benjamin. Wouldn't the deputy chief seriously soil his boxer shorts if he knew how well-acquainted Malcolm Jefferson and Benjamin Hawthorne were?

He stood. "I'll have a report for you as soon as I see the autopsy results, sir." Morrison waved him out with that particularly offensive condescension with which insecure men treat their subordinates. Malcolm didn't care. He had long grown too thick-skinned and too practical to let himself be insulted by the Morrisons of the world. Being polite to the jackass was a matter of expedience. He closed the office door quietly and headed straight for the medical examiner's offices.

As he was reviewing the ME's findings with the technician on duty, his pager went off. He glanced at it, assuming it to be a nuisance page, but immediately recognized Connor's phone number.

"Mind if I use this phone?" he asked the tech. The young woman was surprised since few cops, especially high-ranking ones, ever bothered to ask anyone's permission to do anything, and least of all a lowly technician.

"Sure, I'll go get the reports on the gram stains."

Malcolm smiled at her as she left and quickly dialed Connor. He felt his chest constrict. It was a sensation he had never known until Marie Louise died, and now it happened whenever he felt anxiety over someone close to him. He hated it, saw it as a sign of weakness, but it wouldn't keep him from doing his job.

"Connor, it's Malcolm. What's up?"

"Maybe you'd better get over here." Her voice was tight, strained, barely in control. What the hell could have happened? "Bring your forensic people...my house has been demolished."

"What the hell do you mean? Demolished how?"

"Like I said, demolished, trashed, looks like a hurricane went through every room. All the books, the paintings, it's...." Her voice cracked ever so slightly, and he heard her take a deep breath to steady herself. "Just get over here and see for yourself."

"Okay, okay, just don't...."

"If you tell me not to touch anything, I'll scream."

"Sorry, just reflex, I know you know about...oh never mind, I'll be there in 20 minutes." He hung up, fuming. Once more, Connor's life had been invaded, damaged, her security threatened, and he hadn't been there. Just like with Marie Louise...he hadn't been there. He slammed through the swinging double doors at full force, nearly decking the technician who was just returning with more of the autopsy results, and causing her to drop the armload of folders she carried.

"Sorry," he barked, not bothering to help her pick up the papers scattered here and there on the linoleum. He dashed up the stairs three at a time. The woman just shrugged, thinking maybe he was as rude as the rest of them after all. They always acted as if their problems were total emergencies.

Unaware that he had been instantly reclassified as a rude, arrogant SOB, Malcolm was already pulling into traffic, slapping the flasher on top and hitting the siren. Excessive? Maybe. Necessary? Yes.

He keyed the radio and asked for the dispatcher to raise Leon and tell him to call Malcolm's cell phone. He wanted to keep this off the air and at least delay the press stampede.

Two minutes later the phone chirped and fell off the seat beside him as he rounded a corner far too fast. He slowed down and reached for it, punching the send key to answer. It was his sergeant.

"Leon, get a forensic team over to Connor's. Sounds like her house has been tossed big time." If Leon was surprised, it didn't show.

"Right on it, boss."

Malcolm pulled up in front of the Georgetown house in record time. To his surprise, he saw Benjamin's limousine parked outside. How could he have gotten here any sooner? What he didn't know was that he had not been the first one Connor called when she discovered her house had been torn apart. She called her father...for one vitally important reason. Even now, they were ascending from the lower level, having made sure that the most "sensitive" place in the house had escaped the intruders' notice.

Twenty minutes earlier, Benjamin had carefully swiveled four pieces of trim on the mahogany bar in the basement-level billiard room, then reached underneath to activate a switch that looked like nothing more than a wooden corner bracing beneath one of the bar's shelves. As he did this, the entire bar moved forward three feet into the room, revealing a metal door, laid flat into the surface. Then he placed the palm of his hand in the center of a faintly marked square near one end of the door. It hummed as the palm scanner activated, and, finally, the door slid back to reveal a set of steps going down. Connor did not join him. She was aware of the chamber's existence because it was in her home. In the event something happened to her father, she would reveal its whereabouts and its method of access to one of the names on a very short list stored in her safety deposit box.

Benjamin was back in a few moments, his expression of relief telling her that all was undisturbed. Despite the destruction all around them—broken bottles, glasses, pool cues—the vault had not been discovered. He returned the bar to its original position and the molding switches to theirs. He stopped as if wanting to say something more to Connor, but didn't. She knew he was worried, worried that somehow this "burglary" had something to do with what lay hidden beneath the floor. But she, herself, was not yet ready to make that leap. It might simply have been because of the news reports; they always attracted the weirdo element, the psychopaths. And besides, someone may have had Ariana's keys. That thought made her heart lurch for a moment; perhaps *he* had been here, the one who took Ariana's life. But she pushed the fear away and made a mental note to call a locksmith when the police were finished.

They heard him pounding on the door, and Connor marveled that anyone could get from there to here so quickly. Nonjudicious use of the siren, she surmised with some amusement as she went to let him in. He shook hands with her father and then looked around. The damage was beyond anything he could have imagined, even after 18 years on the police force. The suspect (or suspects) hadn't simply searched, they had willfully destroyed. From the hallway he could see the library. Every single book, even the leather-bound antiques and 20th century first editions, had been thrown down, the pages torn from many of them. A pair of Queen Anne wing chairs had been reduced to splintered remnants and piles of upholstery stuffing. Every drawer from Connor's antique Chippendale partners desk had been yanked out, emptied, and its bottom caved in. Paintings were flung to the floor, canvases torn from their frames. The beautiful old wooden wainscoting had been ripped from the walls in several places, probably with a crowbar.

Malcolm picked his way carefully through the first floor, paying attention to where he set his size 14 wingtips down. The scene was repeated in each room. Upholstery shredded, stuffing leaking out everywhere, a Haviland tea service smashed, a Rodin statue broken and crumbled on the stone tiles. The other marble sculptures had been reduced to shards. What had been a priceless treasury of art from every corner of the world lay in rubble around them.

The upstairs was even worse, perhaps because bedrooms are where personal things are kept and personal events take place. Malcolm knew that many victims found the invasion of this particular space the hardest to accept. The king-sized bed was an unrecognizable mass of disconnected springs and shredded fabric. Across the dressing room floor flowed a sea of expensive silks and wools—dresses, slacks, jackets, blouses—some torn, some merely trampled. The mirrored walls of the bathroom weren't mirrored anymore, a result apparently accomplished by the simple expedient of picking up the brass towel warming rack and heaving it into the glass, where it now lay amidst a sparkling rubble of slivers reflecting their shocked faces in odd prism-like fashion. Malcolm realized no one had yet spoken.

"What about the top floor?" he finally asked, looking at Connor. They left the master suite, and Malcolm followed father and daughter to the end of the hallway where a door led to another set of stairs. The door was closed, which immediately struck Malcolm as unusual. He had his own little voice that told him when something was wrong, though he would have been hard pressed to explain just what that voice was. Intuition? Good hunches? Maybe just brain cells that worked behind the scenes and arrived at conclusions a little more quickly than his conscious mind. Something was wrong here. What was it?

Every other door in the house had been flung open and left that way. As Connor reached for the handle, Malcolm suddenly slapped her hand away, startling her. The alarm bells were going off like Klaxon horns in his head now, and he would have felt foolish if he hadn't been so sure. But what was he so sure about?

Benjamin immediately interpreted Malcolm's expression and

his actions as he prevented Connor from turning the door handle. With a fierceness born of both fear and adrenaline-charged reflex, Benjamin reached out to thrust Connor into the adjoining guest room. In the same instant, Malcolm knew what "it" was—a sound, a click, a noise that had barely brushed the surface of his consciousness, yet still left its imprint. With every ounce of his considerable muscle and every reflex in his cop's body, Malcolm rushed Benjamin like a linebacker, hitting him just above the waist and knocking him backward into the guest room on top of Connor, the thud of body on body lost in the horrific thunder of an explosion that shook the floor and sent plaster dust raining down on them.

Malcolm was the first to recover, quickly rolling his weight off of Benjamin, and looking for Connor. Benjamin, too, was more concerned with his daughter than with himself, searching amidst the tangle of torn bedding and draperies. She came out of her momentary daze to see their faces looming largely over her. Benjamin had one hand cradling her head, the other on her cheek.

"Connor, are you okay?" She managed to move her lips. His voice seemed to come from much farther away than it should, the sound filtering through the momentary deafness the blast had caused.

"Hmm, I'm okay, what…what happened?" She could feel something warm trickling down her cheek. Her father pulled out his handkerchief, but she pushed his hand away. "Let me *up* for crying out loud! And tell me what the hell happened! You throw me into a pile of curtains," she said, looking sternly at them, "then you both land on top of me." She looked past them at the cloud of plaster dust in the hallway. "Jesus Christ!"

What was left of the door leading to the top floor of the townhouse now lay at the other end of the hall. That amounted to little more than an armload of kindling. Scattered all along the hall, and protruding from walls, woodwork, and carpet were scores of 10-penny nails and shards of what looked like safety razor blades, some driven halfway into solid wood. The three of them just stared, each lost in his or her own thoughts. Finally Connor looked at the two men. "What kind of bomb was this?"

Malcolm hesitated, then deferred to the older man. Benjamin, too, remained silent. The potential killing power of that bomb was almost beyond his comprehension, and he had seen people killed by explosives. But that had been a long time ago; he was not a field operative anymore, and life seemed more precious to him now than it had when he was a daring, brash, and perhaps callous 30-year-old. Besides, it was his daughter's life that had been put in jeopardy. But for the intervention of the stony-face man beside him, they would all be dead. Connor interpreted her father's silence as a refusal to answer the question.

"For god's sake, Dad, don't treat me like a child. What the hell was it?"

"Anti-personnel ordnance," he said, flatly.

"Anti-personnel...as in anti-person?" Her voice grew strident. "As in meant to kill us, kill me if I'd been here alone? Is that what you're saying?"

Benjamin could only nod in mute misery.

At that moment, the doorbell chimed. Malcolm was the first to react. "Probably Leon and the forensic team. I'd better check to be sure." But Connor shoved her way past both of them.

"I can answer my own door, if you don't mind." Malcolm started to mention the blood smeared on her face, then thought better of it. He just got out of the way. When he judged she was out of earshot, he looked Benjamin in the eye. "This is no burglary, and that bomb wasn't meant to destroy evidence. It was designed to be lethal, to shred anyone in front of that door. What is going on?"

Benjamin sidestepped the question. His own thoughts and emotions were so out of control, he knew he needed time to settle himself. "How did you know it was there?" he asked Malcolm.

"I didn't know. But first that door was closed. It's the only door in the house that is. Then I heard a click under the carpet, like metal on metal. It reminded me of basic training, working with mines. I just...reacted."

Benjamin nodded. "Two switches probably...one on the door, one under the carpet. Fail-safe." He looked up the stairs, a puzzled expression came over his face. "Why no fire?"

Malcolm shared Benjamin's curiosity on that question. After a few seconds consideration, he said, "I think it was designed that way...to kill, not to burn the house down." He paused, pondering the reasons why that had been the case. "But why not? Why not burn the evidence, make it that much harder to trace?"

Benjamin's face had gone completely pale. His voice came in almost a whisper, hoarse with anger and shock and fear. "They wanted her found, they wanted us to know. They expected Connor to come home alone, find all this," he waved his arm to encompass the vandalized house, "and they assumed she would be angry enough to go through the entire house herself, before she called anyone. She would have been here alone, she would have opened that door."

"But why, Benjamin? Jesus Christ, why Connor?"

"I have a feeling it was a message, Malcolm, a message for me." Before the cop could verbalize any of the questions racing through his head, Benjamin was downstairs, out the door and gone. He couldn't face his daughter. Connor was too intelligent a human being to avoid the conclusion he had already reached. Ariana's death might be his fault after all.

Malcolm shook himself to dislodge his own confusion and anger, and went down to speak to Leon. The forensic team was already well into its work, technicians bagging, dusting, photographing. Leon was examining the alarm panel.

"This wasn't tampered with, boss, as far as I can tell. And there aren't any obvious signs of forced entry. I've checked all the windows and three points of entry—the front door, the rear door, and the garage."

"Has your team reported in from the canal?"

"Yeah, twice."

"Did they find anything else?"

"No, nothing."

"And the victim's keys weren't in her coat pockets, right?"

"No, we would have found those right away." Malcolm stood silent for a moment. The perp (or perps) had used Ariana's keys. And they may have gotten the alarm codes from her, too, somehow. But the question remained...why? "Where's Connor?" he asked abruptly.

Leon jerked his chin toward the front door. "Outside, on the steps, staying out of the way." Clearly, Leon approved of civilians staying out of crime scenes. Malcolm looked through the leaded glass panes flanking the door. Connor sat, head on knees, shivering slightly. Leon's curiosity overcame his natural reticence. "What happened to her anyway? Did she surprise someone in the house?"

Malcolm didn't answer the question. He opened the hall closet and extracted a long, wool coat he recognized as Connor's. He felt Leon's frown in the center of his back.

"We haven't gone over that closet yet, boss."

"Don't worry about it, Leon, you're not going to find anything." He pulled open the front door, then stepped back into the foyer. "Leon, don't let anyone go upstairs, *no one*."

Leon immediately started to protest, but the look in his superior's eyes contained a message even the sergeant, for all his lack of sensitivity to people's emotions, couldn't fail to understand. This was no time to argue, although, being Leon, he couldn't resist at least *looking* argumentative and sullen.

On the steps of the townhouse, Malcolm knelt to put the coat around Connor's shoulders, then shifted himself to sit down beside her. He looked out toward the street. There were a few gawkers (even in this neighborhood where most residents primly minded their own business) and one clump of reporters being kept well back, almost half a block away behind a police cordon. He looked at the woman beside him, her hair full of plaster dust, the blood from the cut above her eyebrow dried to a rusty brown, her face still as death. "She's my best friend," he thought, wondering if it was odd that a man would think that of any woman, especially if the woman was not his wife. Then, almost as if he had been punched in the stomach, the realization hit him that he couldn't imagine losing her, couldn't fathom his life without a friend like her. After he'd lost Marie Louise, there'd been no one who had understood, no one but Connor. Tears, unbidden and unwelcome, coursed silently down his face. Connor turned and looked up at him, shocked out of her own despair by the pain in his eyes and the dampness on his cheeks. She reached for his hand.

"Hey...come on, it's okay. I'm okay. We all are. We're all pretty damned lucky, and you saved my life, you big lug." She squeezed his hand, watched him rally himself.

"Just doing my job, ma'am." They both laughed a little at the old joke. The tension lessened, but Connor grew serious again.

"Did my father say anything to you?"

"No, Benjamin didn't have much to say at all. What about you? Is there something you should tell me? Something about your father's work, or...." He trailed off, realizing he was getting into areas best left alone. He was no insider in the world of political or international intrigue; he knew just enough to stay away from it. On occasion, he had heard vague murmurings about Benjamin Hawthorne, had even wondered if Connor knew more about her father's various government jobs than she let on. But he was wise enough to avoid broaching the subject. Malcolm, unlike a lot of law enforcement people, was actually reluctant to pry into the personal affairs of other people. For him, it was a last resort in the course of an investigation. He was a respecter of privacy, and he wasn't stupid. Knowing things you weren't meant to know could get you in a whole bunch of trouble.

"There are some things I don't have the right to discuss with you unless my father agrees." He couldn't disguise his annoyance, and she put her hand on his arm. "It isn't that I don't trust you, please believe me. And it isn't as if I'm walking around with a lot of secrets. I'm not. I'm exactly the person you know me to be. But there are some circumstances that might be related to what's happened here, maybe even to what happened to Ariana." The last few words were spoken thickly, as if they had lodged in her throat and had to be forced out. Malcolm felt his momentary surge of indignation melt away. He put his arm around her shoulders.

"Hey...it's okay. I understand, sort of. I'm willing to wait and see and talk to Benjamin...Look, it's getting cold out here, and you can't stay in the house tonight."

"I know. I need to get some clothes, assuming there are any left in one piece, and go to a hotel."

"The hell you will." Malcolm was on firmer ground in this matter, and knew he would prevail. "We'll get your stuff and you're coming to my house. Besides, who would let you check into a hotel? You look like hell."

She allowed a wry smile to brighten her face for a moment and realized that she was too damn tired to argue. They both rose and went back into the house. They found Leon gazing intently up the broad staircase as if by sheer will he could gather evidence from the upstairs rooms without disobeying direct orders. Hearing the door open, he wheeled around, looking almost guilty. He covered his momentary embarrassment by gruffly reminding Malcolm that they would need Connor's fingerprints for elimination.

"I could have Kincaid do it right now," he volunteered, "and then we could get...."

Malcolm's eyes bored into him with the intensity of a laser. Leon, as his boss suspected, had been about to say, "we could get the Gennarro woman's prints off the body." A sudden, rare insight saved him from being throttled by his superior.

"...and then we could get started on comparisons," he finished, stammering just a bit.

"Her fingerprints are on file with the department, Sergeant. Or are you forgetting she was an assistant district attorney?" Malcolm waved the fingerprint man away. "I'm taking Connor with me. Page me if you find anything. And remember what I said."

Wednesday Evening

Malcolm lived in a pleasant, racially mixed, middle-class
neighborhood, composed primarily of working people and a few
professional types. The 1950s-era brick houses were roomy and
well-built, with broad porches and well-tended yards. Since
Marie Louise's death, Malcolm's elder sister, Eve, had come to
stay. She was as imposing a woman as Malcolm was a man. She
was tall, solidly built, and wore her hair in a cascade of dread
locks. No one dared give Eve any trouble or sass, as she was fond
of reminding people, and she embraced the world with a compassionate, but unstintingly no-nonsense attitude. Connor felt a
kinship with Eve, and was somehow relieved to be swept into a
gentle but firm bear hug that allowed her to cave in just a little
bit to the emotional onslaught of the past couple of days. Eve felt
Connor's body tremble, intuitively understood what was happening, and took charge.

"Malcolm, you take that suitcase upstairs, and tell them kids
to settle down." Eve led Connor to the comfortable overstuffed
sofa. "And you, young lady, you sit right down there. I'll be
back quicker'n you can say jambalaya." True to her word, Eve
returned to the living room in just a few minutes with a hot
steaming mug in hand. She sat down on the sofa, and handed the
mug to Connor. "Now you drink this right down. My daddy
swore by it, even if my momma did swear *about* it...real quiet-
like though, since momma said ladies didn't cuss." Eve grinned

and Connor couldn't help but follow suit. The combination of Eve's smile, her gentle humor, and her soft Louisiana drawl—something Malcolm had managed to lose—was more comforting than Connor could have imagined.

"Do I dare ask what's in this?" She peered into the mug of dark fluid.

"Like I said, it's an old family recipe. And it's a sure cure for what's ailin' you."

Connor took a sip and almost choked. "Jesus, Eve, this must be 150 proof."

"Now, now, young lady, don't you be takin' the Lord's name, and besides, it wasn't Jesus and Eve, it was Adam and Eve," she said, her eyes twinkling. "Don't they teach you white folk nothin'?" Connor smiled back. Eve was a devout believer in the "Lord" (though in her mouth it came out more like "Lawd"), but she wasn't prone to passing judgment on anyone and never felt compelled to make others join her in her faith. She had decided long ago, after living through more than one argument between her Baptist momma and her hell-raisin' daddy, that God did not mean for her, or anyone, to go around tellin' other folk what to believe. Overall, Eve had a fairly live-and-let-live attitude toward others, unless, of course, someone threatened her family, and rumor had it she was a tigress in that area.

At this particular moment, though, there was no fire and fury in Eve's voice. Her voice was soft. It came in low, comforting murmurs as she stroked Connor's hair and urged her to finish the potent "hot toddy." Connor finally began to feel warm, inside and out. Her tension dissolved, and with it, her self control. In three days she had lost her lover, lost her home, seen most of her possessions destroyed, and someone had tried to kill her. It was too much, even for a woman who had always faced life head-on.

She tried to blink back tears, tried to take a deep breath and fight it. But Eve was no stranger to grief. She didn't shy away from it, wasn't embarrassed by it. She pulled Connor's head down onto her ample bosom, enfolded her in strong, woman's arms.

"Just you let it go, child, just let it go. You cain't pretend it don't hurt." Connor did as she was told, giving in without protest. Somewhere in the back of her mind, it puzzled her, probably because she didn't realize that, for the first time in her life, someone was being a mother to her.

———◦◦◦———

She awoke the next morning in the comfortable guest room of Malcolm's house to the sound of children giggling and the aroma of breakfast cooking. It was all very odd, and also very wonderful. For an instant, the dream from which she had been suddenly snatched was real. Ariana was still alive. They were together on a gondola in Venice, traveling through Italy to celebrate their fifth anniversary. It had been a romantic journey, culminated by a lavish anniversary dinner at which Connor had presented Ariana with a diamond and lapis ring, a custom design of intertwined serpents set in platinum.

Ariana was thrilled with the gift, but even more thrilled with the care and planning that had caused it to be made. She looked at her lover with an adoration few human beings ever experience, and at that moment Connor believed that never in her life would she be any happier. They were undeniably in love, the two of them, and even if Connor wondered every now and then if she had chosen wisely in loving a mercurial, impulsive free spirit like Ariana, she wouldn't have traded a moment of their life together for anything on Earth.

Connor let herself drift between waking and sleeping. For a delicious, tempting moment, Ariana lay cradled in her arms, eyes closed, a tiny smile on her lips...then, too soon, it all dissolved. The hazy memories, the soft daydreams, the inner warmth...they fled from the harsh illumination of a starkly unpleasant reality. Ariana was gone, and there would be no more gifts, no more embraces, no more trips to Venice. What was gone, was gone.

Connor firmly put the fading images aside and burrowed down under the warmth of the quilt, letting herself savor the sensation of listening to everyday life happening all around her. Outside in the hall she could hear seven-year-old Brenda explaining in a very loud whisper that everyone was supposed to tiptoe because Auntie Connor was sleeping. Apparently her two brothers, 12-year-old Malcolm, Jr. and 10-year-old Isaac, were not impressed, for they began arguing loudly about who was being more noisy, which basically defeated the purpose. Connor wasn't annoyed. They were just being kids. A moment later, though, she heard Eve's voice in the hall. "What do you children reckon the word 'quiet' means?" Instantly, silence prevailed.

The peace and quiet was soothing to her spirit, but nagging thoughts about the world out there and her own responsibilities in it began to intrude. Reluctantly, she hauled herself out of bed, wondering about the mild headache, and then remembering the hot toddies. Her body ached, but, after having two grown men fall on her, it wasn't too bad. She went into the bathroom, noticed with a smile the fluffy towels and bubble bath placed there for her. On the sink was toothpaste and a new toothbrush still wrapped in cellophane.

Though a bubble bath was extraordinarily tempting, Connor

opted for a long, hot shower instead, soaping her hair twice to get all of the plaster grit out of it. She toweled off and examined the small gash on her forehead. It would probably heal just fine, she decided, and, besides, a small scar might give her a sort of rakish look. She could just imagine her mother's reaction; she would probably be on the phone summoning the world's top plastic surgeon, insisting it was a life-and-death emergency. Connor dried her hair, dressed, and repacked her suitcase. She knew Malcolm and Eve would want her to stay, but she needed to get on with the business at hand, which, she reflected, included making arrangements for Ariana's funeral.

From the look on his face, Malcolm was not happy when she descended the back stairs into the kitchen, suitcase in hand. She was ready to counter his objections. As it turned out, she didn't have to. Eve told him to mind his own business and let Connor mind hers. Malcolm immediately took on the demeanor of a frustrated little boy who's just been told he can't have everything his way, but Eve went right on serving up food. Malcolm, Jr. smiled knowingly upon hearing his father chastised, but his aunt's "look" effectively wiped the smirk off his face, and he immediately concentrated on his breakfast plate.

Connor gave Eve a grateful smile as she sat down at the table, announcing that she only wanted some coffee. Eve stopped dead in her tracks, looking down at Connor, spatula in one hand, coffee pot in the other. "Nobody leaves this house without hot food in his belly, child, and that goes for you, too. Cain't leave no way, no how. Now you just set there while I make you up a plate." And what a plate it was—thick ham, scrambled eggs, grits, and a side of biscuits and gravy.

"Eve, if I eat all this you'll have to roll me out the door, and I already called a cab."

"Better roll you than carry you, girl. No one starves in this house." Little Brenda giggled delightedly at the image of Connor being "rolled" out of the house.

"Well, I can tell Malcolm doesn't starve." The subject of this observation looked up from his second plate of food with such a sheepish expression, they all burst into laughter. It felt good, and for a moment the whole room seemed even brighter. But Malcolm's smile faded when he heard Connor's next words.

"I'm going to move into Ariana's apartment for a few days. I can't go back to my house for a while. You can reach me there...let me write down the number."

Malcolm dropped his fork onto his plate. "I don't think that's such a good idea."

Connor stared him. "What do you mean? The rent's paid up. Why shouldn't I stay there? I mean, if you're thinking it will remind me...." She paused, thinking of the children's presence. "It can't be any worse than being at my own home."

The muscle in Malcolm's jaw was working visibly. Connor could see he was struggling with some sort of difficult decision, but she couldn't imagine what it was. Finally Malcolm spoke through clenched teeth. "Connor, can we talk for a minute...please, outside on the porch."

She was thoroughly puzzled by his sudden change in attitude, but he was her friend. If he wanted to talk, fine. She led the way through the living room and out the screen door, seating herself in the glider. At the edge of the broad porch, Isaac knelt with his full array of toy cars, making appropriate "vroom" noises as he raced them back and forth.

"Son," Malcolm said gently, "go finish your breakfast and you can play with the cars later." Isaac frowned slightly, but, after a moment's hesitation, scooped up several cars to take with him and scampered into the house hollering, "Auntie Evie, Daddy says I gotta eat more biscuits and gravy."

Connor chuckled. "I take it he likes biscuits and gravy."

"Favorite food. Can't figure out why." The soft smile that Isaac's childlike opportunism had put on his father's face quickly faded as he turned to Connor, swinging gently back and forth on the glider. He couldn't hold her gaze and, for several seconds he stared over her head at the neighbor's yard.

"So what is it?" Connor's stomach felt suddenly very queasy as she wondered what else could possibly be wrong.

"During our routine investigation...." He stopped, still not willing to meet her eyes. Connor couldn't fathom why he was being so formal. He started again. "During our routine investigation of the...of the murder victim, that is, of Ariana, we searched her apartment for leads on her assailant."

After several more seconds, Connor prompted him to continue. "Yes?" The news hardly came as a surprise.

"I went there myself. I...uh...was hoping some of the details might not...well that you might not have to know."

"Know what?" Connor felt her stomach clench, and the hand that lay on the arm of the glider tightened visibly.

Malcolm finally looked directly at her. When she saw the expression on his face, she almost wished he hadn't.

"We found evidence that someone else was sharing the apartment."

"Sharing? What does that mean? With whom?"

"There was substantial evidence that another woman was living there."

A cold hand squeezed Connor's heart. What she was hearing from him had the quality of truth, but she wouldn't, *couldn't* accept it.

"How do you know she was living there? How do you know Ariana didn't just have a visitor? " Connor struggled to retain her composure. "Maybe even a one-night stand. I'm not going to fall apart just because Ariana might have had a fling with someone. After all, we were separated." She paused; he didn't answer. "Well? Tell me! How can you be so goddamn sure?"

His voice was devoid of emotion when he spoke, the words issuing from a face that appeared carved from ebony. "Among the evidence we removed were more than two dozen garments not belonging to the victim, plus numerous items of underwear and lingerie." He did not have to consult his notes. Every item they had found was engraved on his memory. "There was a full set of makeup and toilet articles also completely dissimilar to those used by the victim, and we recovered hair samples from the bathroom and…bedroom that did not belong to the victim." Connor realized he had ceased to use Ariana's name. She had become "the victim."

"The sum total of the evidence found forced us to conclude that this unidentified woman had been living in the apartment for…some time. We've lifted a good set of prints we believe belonged to the woman, but we haven't identified them…or her."

Connor sat perfectly still, trying to absorb all he had said. Anger surged through her, but she kept it in check. From the corner of her eye she could see Malcolm waiting for the storm. He had braced himself to absorb her fury and somehow mollify her pain. But the moment passed and there was only silence. Connor stood up quickly. "Thank you for telling me the truth," she said, and went into the house. She reappeared carrying her bag, going past him without a word to the cab waiting at the curb.

CHAPTER FOUR

Hast thou betrayed my credulous innocence
With vizor'd falsehood and base forgery?
—John Milton

Thursday, September 21
Washington, D.C.

When the cab deposited Connor on the sidewalk in front of the townhouse, she didn't bother going in, just got her car out of the garage and drove directly to the Watergate. When she had signed the lease for Ariana, the manager had sent her a key. She hesitated for only a moment at the door, which was still criss-crossed with police tape, then ripped the tape down, shoved the key into the lock, opened the door, and stepped into the foyer. She set her bag down and flipped on the light switch. Steeling herself, Connor continued into the living room, turning on lamps here and there.

The living room was done in the elegant modern style that Connor, an unapologetic traditionalist, generally detested—ribbons of chrome and leather masquerading as furniture, metal sculpture that jangled its sharp edges at the viewer, surreal paintings and cold glass everywhere. With the white carpet and white fabric walls, it was every bit the fairy tale ice palace, home to— Connor rebelled at the thought, but it was there in her mind anyway—the Ice Queen. Surely she could never think of Ariana in those terms. She had been warm and loving and...and what? Damn it! This was absurd. Her mind was behaving like an undisciplined child, running off in all directions.

Then she saw the picture on the end table beside the sofa. It was a framed photographic portrait of the two of them in Rome, at Trevi Fountain, acting like the quintessential American tourists, their glistening coins flashing in the air amidst the sparkles of water. Two coins in the fountain. Would it have turned out differently if they had indeed tossed in three? Would Ariana be alive to return to Rome as the legend promised? Would they again walk the Via Veneto, stop for tea at Babbington's, giggle at the gullible tourists buying fake Louis Vuitton purses on the Spanish Steps, and rush back to the Hotel Villa Medici simply because they had to make love? She surrendered briefly to the memories, but there was no joy in them—only sorrow for things that could never be again, and a horrible dread that she had been blind to some very crucial element of Ariana's character.

"Stop it," Connor chided herself firmly. "Just stop it."

The door to the bedroom loomed in front of her, both inviting and spurning her attention.

"Get hold of yourself, old girl," she muttered, sounding rather like her grandmother. "It's a room...it's only a room."

Once she stepped inside, though, she knew that was a lie. It wasn't just any room. It was Ariana's boudoir, because she was the sort of woman whose bedroom could only be called by its French equivalent. Lavish and soft and carelessly feminine, it smelled of Ariana's perfume, bath oil, and lotions. Her favorite silk robe was draped over the back of an upholstered chaise lounge, clothes decorated the floor, dumped here and there during one of her twice-daily attempts to select the perfect ensemble. Ariana had never been known for tidiness, a fact that kept BeLisia muttering under her breath on cleaning days.

Connor stepped into the bathroom. The scent of her lover was even stronger here. She felt her sorrow so keenly that for a moment she was unable to breathe. She reached out to the door jamb to support herself until the roaring in her head subsided. Maybe she couldn't stay here after all, now that she knew the truth about what Ariana had been doing; it hurt too much. This was a part of Ariana's life she hadn't shared. She could see the spaces on the counter where the confiscated cosmetics had stood, could actually imagine the presence of someone else here. Evidence, that's what Malcolm had called it…evidence. Her practiced eye surveyed the scene, just as she had reviewed a hundred crime scenes as a prosecutor, but in this instance, she could not find it in her to be dispassionate.

She stepped back into the bedroom. The hammering at the back of Connor's skull started again as she stood looking at the scattered pillows, the covers thrown back from either side, no longer tucked in at the foot. Almost against her will, Connor moved to the left side of the bed, stared down at the pillows where Malcolm and his detectives would have found the hair samples—another woman's hair. On the bedside table was a tortoiseshell hair comb. They must have overlooked that, must not have known that Ariana never wore hair combs. She looked across the bed at the open closet door. The racks were more than half-empty—another woman's clothes.

The tenuous composure Connor had managed to fabricate over the past four days suddenly dissolved in the face of one awful and inescapable truth she would never have accepted unless she had seen some proof of it for herself, had not believed even while Malcolm had tried to tell her. Before she died, Ariana had been living with another woman, making love to another woman.

In an instant, grief and denial were displaced by unmitigated fury at a love betrayed. Hot rage surged through Connor, and she surrendered to it. She tore the sheets from the bed, sending the lamp crashing to the floor. She trampled over the tangle of clothes and bedding to reach the closet, yanking Ariana's wardrobe, along with the hangers, off the rods.

Connor's mind was reeling. This was not just a fling, a one-night stand, a drunken error; no, a woman had been living here with Ariana. Living here, sleeping here, sharing her bed.

"No, goddammit," she roared out loud. "That's way too poetic, Connor. Not 'sharing her bed'...screwing, yes, screwing her goddamn brains out while you waited patiently for her to come to her senses and come home. She was having one hell of a good time! And you're the goddamn fool." Torrents of anger pulsated through her body. Her hands had a will of their own, sweeping the cosmetics from the bathroom vanity, tearing the shower curtain from its hooks. Then, back into the bedroom, shredding clothes, sheets, scarves, all of her will bent on destruction, until, finally, there was nothing. The rage was gone as abruptly as if a switch had been turned off. Perhaps it had just run its course. For whatever reason, the desire to destroy and obliterate was gone.

Connor looked into the mirror and saw her face twisted into a mask she didn't recognize. Without being aware of it, she had begun to cry during her outpouring of rage, but these were not the tears to which she was accustomed. She had cried often since Ariana died, but after that first horrifying night, her tears had been fairly restrained simply because they were only the surplus grief—

what was left over after Connor had clamped down on the emotions they truly represented. Now, in the wake of her destructive frenzy, ragged sobs came in huge gulps; her chest heaved, her lungs on the verge of hyperventilating. She sank down beside the bed, head resting on the mattress, her entire body trembling as she cried out a lifetime of hurts—injuries both real and imagined. Ariana's death, followed so quickly by the knowledge of Ariana's betrayal, had broken through the pretense, the carefully crafted fictions with which she had protected herself from too thoroughly examining her pain, her doubts, and her own sense of what was true. Seduced by circumstance into abandoning that control, Connor had loosed the demons—the dark denizens of that pit within her, where every hurt, every slight, every disappointment, loss, and humiliation had been locked away from consciousness. Those demons had not evaporated simply because they had been imprisoned by social convention or myopic denial. Connor's defenses had grown stronger over the years, her awareness of the shadow self foreshortened, but the demons still remained. And today they were running amok. Despite all the work she had done in therapy, despite all the insights she had gained into herself, she had never run thus headlong into her own inner hell and been forced to take inventory.

She was a woman who prided herself on emotional control, calm civility, moral certainty, and quiet strength. These had been stolen from her all at once. It was a shocking departure from standard procedure for Connor Hawthorne to cry and wail like an angry, wounded child. But then she had rarely been permitted to be a child, so perhaps it should not have come as such a surprise that the little girl inside the woman was really, really pissed off.

After a time, though, her physical body grew weary of these

paroxysms of anguish. Her breathing slowed to normal, her muscles began to relax. With a supreme effort of will, Connor finally managed to close Pandora's box, slamming the lid down firmly. As if recovering from a syncopal episode, she looked down, almost puzzled, at the wisps of torn silk in her hands. She let them fall to the floor. Her knees ached from the prolonged kneeling beside the bed; the muscles in her neck ached. Connor surveyed the destruction she had wrought as if encountering it for the first time. She had become, once again, the observer.

The pulse pounded in her temples as the walls closed in around her. There wasn't enough air in the room. She got up very slowly and went back into the bathroom, heels crunching on broken glass. Cupping her hands under the running faucet, she splashed cold water over her face, and dried off with a clean towel from the cabinet. She ran her fingers through her hair, tucked in her blouse, and straightened the collar over her jacket. Connor snapped off the bathroom light and did the same with the wall switch in the bedroom. In the foyer, she picked up her overnight bag, then sat it down again and went back into the living room. She retrieved the Rome photograph and tucked it under her arm. On the way to the elevator, she threw it down a trash chute without looking at it even once more.

———&oo&———

Later Thursday

"Val? Hi. It's Connor."

"Connor, honey, where are you? I've been worried sick. You haven't called, you weren't at the house. I couldn't get hold of Benjamin."

Connor knew the concern in her friend's voice was sincere. Val's "Jewish mother" persona was not an affectation, and she actually did, on occasion, come to sick beds armed with home-made chicken soup. She did not, perhaps, keep kosher in every facet of life, but she managed to keep alive the humor, tradition, and courage passed on to her by a mother and father who survived the Holocaust after two years in a Nazi death camp.

Val herself had survived two miscarriages and the death of her son and first husband in an automobile accident. She was not a stranger to tragedy, but she refused to join the ranks of the victimized. She had gone back to school with a vengeance, and now Dr. Valerie Morgenthal was one of the most sought-after psychotherapists in Washington. She had been called as an expert witness in one of Connor's court cases, and in the years since they had become fast friends.

"I'm sorry, Val. It's just that with everything...." Her voice trailed off, but she caught herself and took a deep breath. "My house was broken into yesterday. It was trashed and I couldn't stay there."

"So...where are you?" Val interrupted Connor's explanation.

"At the Four Seasons."

"And what may I ask does the Four Seasons have that I don't have?"

"What?"

"Don't give me 'what.' You heard me, chicky, what are you doing at the Four Seasons when you have friends who love you? Some martyr thing? Some victim thing? Or do you really hate the suburbs that much?" Connor started to interrupt the list of optional answers, but was rebuffed.

"Don't give me any back talk. I'll be at the lobby entrance in one hour and you know how I hate to schlep downtown, so I must love you." With that, she hung up. Connor didn't know whether to laugh or cry so instead she went downstairs to check out. After wandering the elegant lobby for a few minutes and realizing she had been too prompt to leave her room, she settled down in the comfortable lounge to order tea.

———⊶⊷———

Following her around wasn't doing any good as far as he could tell. She had gone to the other woman's apartment, but she hadn't been there long. He was puzzled by the sounds he'd heard as he eavesdropped outside the door, sounds like things being broken. It made him nervous even being there, and he had kept glancing up and down the hall. The security in the building was tight. He couldn't afford to get caught loitering.

Suddenly he heard her footsteps near the door. She was leaving! He had been forced to scamper headlong down the corridor, diving into a door marked "Refuse Disposal." Thinking himself safe, he was stunned when the door began to open. He slipped the stiletto from its sheath, gripping it firmly in a downward position. If she was the one opening the door, she must have seen him, must have come to investigate. Might as well take care of her now. Stop all this stupid chasing after her. But he was trapped behind the door, at least until she stepped all the way into the little room.

She didn't do that. Apparently bracing the door with one foot, she pulled down the small hatch, tossed something in, and left, the door swinging shut behind her. He stood there for a moment, letting the adrenaline rush subside. Moments later he was back out on the street, waiting for her car to emerge from the underground garage.

At the hotel, he was sure he could get to her once she was asleep that night, and, with luck, he could get her to talk before she died. Then, to his consternation, he had seen her at the desk, apparently checking out.

Now, he sat a few tables away, pondering whether to call for additional instructions. His car was handy. If she called a cab he was ready to follow.

———————◦•◦•◦———————

Fifty minutes later (the psychiatrist's version of an hour, Connor thought to herself, with the first real flash of humor she'd felt in days), Val's white Mazda Miata convertible barreled into the driveway of the Four Seasons and literally screeched to a halt. Connor reflected as she started through the glass doors that whether or not Val liked driving downtown, she certainly did like driving fast. Before Connor could clear the exit, Val had hurtled out of the car via some invisible ejector seat, waved aside the "You can't park here, ma'am," of the grandiose doorman, and swept Connor into a hug. This, of course, was somewhat of a feat given the sizable difference in height, Connor's 5'10" to Val's 5' 1/4"—Val refused to be just five feet tall; she said it was a matter of principle. Somehow, though, Val's hugs always seemed bigger than she was. Then she snatched Connor's bag as she observed, out of the corner of her eye, that the doorman was bearing down fast, determined to enforce the petty rules of his tiny fiefdom.

As he got within three feet, however, she swung around to confront him, shaking her finger in his face. "Boychik, I am a doctor. I can park anywhere I want, and besides, this woman is obviously having a baby. Now, if you will excuse us."

The doorman stared at her, then at Connor. Clearly, he was torn between being absolutely sure this woman was nuts, wondering if, indeed, she were a doctor, and if the fairly slim young woman beside her could actually be pregnant. But while he chewed on this and the data worked its way slowly through his brain, Val tossed the bag into the back of the car and hustled Connor into the passenger seat.

By the time the hapless doorman got around to saying, "But you still can't park here," they were nothing more than a white blur rounding the corner in third gear.

———

Damn! He hadn't anticipated that someone else would come to get her. When Connor, having paid her check and left the lounge, started for the door, he assumed she would hail a cab. He had rushed out ahead of her and brought his own car up close to the driveway entrance. He'd already noted the number of the lead taxi at the cabstand. As minutes ticked by, he began to panic.

What if she had gone out another entrance? But why? He began to edge his car away from the curb, trying to decide what to do when a white sports car almost sideswiped him. He started to honk, but thought better of drawing attention to himself. Then, without warning, she was coming out of the hotel, meeting the little woman driving the white car; she was getting in, leaving!

He stepped on the gas hard and pulled right out in front of a taxi taking its place in line. The cabbie, not given to courtesy or yielding to idiots, didn't even try to stop. The two cars met with a crunch of metal and tinkle of safety glass hitting the pavement. He saw the white car turn at the light. He hadn't even gotten the license number. He wrenched his door open, all the while venting a stream of obscenities. The cab driver, who did not particularly care for his attitude, punched him right in the mouth.

―――――◦◦◦◦◦―――――

Thursday,
later that afternoon

Malcolm Jefferson was angry. Or, at least, frustrated. No, he was *angry*. There were no leads to Ariana's killer, and none at all to the person or persons who had destroyed Connor's house. Worse, Malcolm knew there was a lot more to this situation and to these crimes than he had been able to discover, more than he had been told. Part of his annoyance was due to the fact that Connor was holding out on him, and so was Benjamin. Of that Malcolm was certain. He also guessed, however, that whatever was going on might not only be out of his jurisdiction, but exceedingly unhealthy for him and his career if he butted in where he wasn't wanted. Still, he had to do something.

Whether or not he was consciously aware of it, the need to do *something* had eaten away at his insides like a chronic ulcer ever since the night Marie Louise died. The woman he loved more than anyone in his life, or ever would love for that matter, had been taken from him, and he had not been there to help her, to save her, to stand between her and the scum who had killed her without a second thought. He had not been able to do anything as he paced through the hospital corridors, willing the doctors to save his wife, the fear they would fail tearing at his gut. The surgeon's expression had announced the outcome before the man spoke a single word to Malcolm.

Afterwards, it was months before he could do anything for

anyone. He took leave and drove to the shore alone. He stood on the sand at Rehoboth and tried to talk to Marie Louise, to explain, apologize, ask forgiveness for failing her when she most needed him. He heard nothing in reply but the breaking of the waves onshore. Perhaps he was a man too practical and too hardened by his life and his grief to hear her gentle words of consolation, but in his heart he felt she was near and trying to speak.

Finally, Malcolm went back to his home, his children, and his work. Thank God his sister, Eve, had been there, or what might have become of the kids while he floated through his days unfeeling, unaware that others grieved, too? He still remembered the night Eve had put the children to bed and then read him the riot act, told him to stop feeling sorry for himself and start being a father again. "Those kids lost their momma, and it's 'bout time you remembered that, 'stead a goin' round here like you was the only man ever lost a wife. She was a good woman, Malcolm, but she's gone to the Lord now, and your job is right here, right now—your job is them babies upstairs, you their daddy!"

Malcolm had been furious with her at first, but it didn't take him long to admit she was right. He'd wallowed, and wallowed big time. The following weekend, he took all of them, including Eve, to Ocean City, where he laughed for the first time in months while his sons splashed in the surf and his daughter toddled around him, covering him with sand. They were such remarkable creatures. How could he have ignored them? So bright and funny and full of life. They were the legacy Marie Louise had left him, and it was up to him to take care of them.

But one remnant of those times remained with Malcolm all his days—a fear of being helpless. Ariana's murder, and Connor's narrow escape from death, brought that anxiety full-blown to the forefront. It also made him angry. It was in that combative mood that he showed up at Benjamin Hawthorne's private club unannounced, after being told by Amanda, in tones chilly enough to freeze C&P Telephone's fiber optic cables, that *Mr.* Hawthorne was residing in town.

When he reached the building, he thought for a moment the skinny, beady-eyed doorman wouldn't stop backing up long enough to hear the purpose of Malcolm's visit. It never ceased to amaze the cop how much very large black men intimidated some white people. He wondered if it really was bigotry, or if some people were victims of a cultural conditioning they never got over. He was reluctant to flash his badge, knowing that police were hardly a welcome entity in the hallowed halls of this particular men's club. "Please announce me to Senator Hawthorne; I'm a friend."

The doorman's skepticism was written all over his face, underscored by the slight shake of his head and the reluctance with which he picked up the house phone. "There's a visitor here to see Senator Hawthorne." He looked at Malcolm again. "What'd you say your name was?"

"Jefferson, *Captain* Malcolm Jefferson." He didn't say captain of police, but the title did give the weaselly little man something to think about.

"Captain Jefferson." The reply at the other end must have been both curt and peremptory, for the man's face turned slightly red and he was even more humiliated when he realized he was stammering 'yes, sir' into a dead receiver. He hung it up, tried to regain some of his former arrogance, and failed miserably. He swung the wide door open, mumbling, "Go right in, sir. Mr. Martinez will meet you in the lobby."

Moments later, the brass doors of the middle elevator whispered open and Marty was striding toward him, hand extended.

"Malcolm, good to see you. I'm sorry about that jackass at the door." He motioned pointedly at the fellow who stood peering through the glass, and who quickly spun around to face the street again. "He has no experience as a doorman, and a lot of members want him canned, but he's some retired army guy, and the chairman has a soft spot for vets, no matter how surly and stupid this one is. Come on upstairs. Benjamin's waiting."

They met Senator Hawthorne in the study of the four-room bachelor apartment. Malcolm found it soothing, the creak of old leather, the reflection of the fire off wood paneling, the scent of good cigars. It was, in every respect a "man's" place, and he felt some solace in that, as if men could turn back the clock, fight all the battles, while the women stayed home, safe from the predators who walked the streets. Benjamin's voice interrupted this stream of odd and disjointed thoughts. "How about something to drink? Ginger ale? Club soda? Oh, wait, you're a Dr. Pepper fan, aren't you?"

Malcolm nodded. Benjamin remembered that he didn't drink liquor, and hadn't since Marie Louise died and he had almost offed himself. The Dr. Pepper was a holdover from his southern heritage.

"I keep it on hand because Connor likes it. Did she get that from you?"

Malcolm took the proffered glass. "Probably. Said she'd never even tasted it until a barbecue at my house."

"Please, sit down."

The two men stared at the fire from matching leather wing chairs. Marty had discreetly absented himself, and the study doors were closed.

"Benjamin."

"Malcolm."

They spoke at precisely the same moment, a fact which made them both smile.

"We both like getting to the point, don't we?"

Malcolm tilted his head to one side. "That's one of the things I've always respected about you, Benjamin. No bullshit beating around the bush. You know how to tell the truth, and you don't have to sugar-coat everything the way most people in this town do."

"I'm flattered, my friend, but don't get too carried away with admiration just yet. There's a lot you don't know."

"That's why I'm here. So I'll ask you again, what the hell is going on? Why did you tell me that bomb was a message? What message? That someone hates you enough to kill your daughter? Who sent it? Why?"

Benjamin held up his hand as if to stem the tide of questions.

"Malcolm, please, settle down…I promise I will tell you what I can. But you won't like it because it won't be enough, and it won't answer half your questions. You'll just have to believe that it's all I can do."

"Okay." Malcolm didn't look happy, but since he had expected nothing but a bum's rush, some information was better than none.

Benjamin took a long sip from his brandy snifter and took a moment to collect his thoughts, a process Malcolm chose not to interrupt.

"Most people in this town, or this country, think of me as an ex-Senator, ex-cabinet secretary, and current presidential adviser." He looked to Malcolm, who tilted his head in agreement with the obvious.

"The fact is, and these are statements not to go beyond this door"—another nod from his guest—"that I have long been involved with various government operations of a confidential nature. Some of these are what you would probably term 'covert' operations." He saw Malcolm's raised eyebrow. "I know, it sounds like all that cloak and dagger crap that the Company keeps foisting on the American public without their consent or knowledge. But what I do isn't quite like that.

"There are some individuals who feel there must be more checks and balances in place, to keep tabs on the military, on the intelligence agencies, and on the other 'bad guys' too—the terrorists, the extremists, the ones who really are a threat to peace." He smiled at Malcolm's puzzled expression. "No, I don't mean all of our guys fall into the category of bad guys. I just mean that might doesn't always make right, and wearing the uniform or carrying the badge doesn't always mean the person with that uniform or badge is automatically a good guy. Surely you understand that?"

Malcolm did. Though, as one of the many police officers who had never once dishonored the badge they carried, it bothered him a great deal. Still, things went on even in his own department that sickened him, and he knew corruption and double-dealing and private agendas could be found just about anywhere. He also believed the public would be outraged at some of the actions of their government if those actions came to light. He wasn't sure what all this had to do with the current situation. It sounded more like a lecture on elementary politics—the dirty kind. But he considered his answer carefully.

"I do see, Benjamin, but this all seems a little general. I don't need a civics lesson. Anyone in this town knows that the boys at the CIA and the NSA and the FBI are always up to something. Sometimes it's good and sometimes it's downright repugnant, but what has that got to do with Ariana, and Connor…and you? Specifically?"

The other man didn't answer for a long time, and Malcolm began to wonder if he would get any response at all. When he finally stole a look at Benjamin, Malcolm was stunned. It seemed as if the man had aged 20 years in the space of a few minutes. His face was haggard, colorless, and his usually piercing eyes appeared dim and filmy. Lines of fatigue were etched into his skin. "Why have I never noticed that this man is getting old?" Malcolm thought. What is he, 60? 65?

As if answering his guest's thoughts, Benjamin finally spoke. "I'm getting too old for this, I think. But the job's mine, and it isn't one I can bequeath to someone else, at least not for now." He refilled his brandy snifter and pressed a button on the desk. "I wish I could give you the answers to all of your questions, Malcolm. I respect you as much as Connor does, but I can't tell you as much as you deserve to know."

The door opened and Marty appeared.

"Pull a chair up to the fire and sit down, Marty, please." He looked once again at the somber policeman across from him. "I want Marty here because I hope he can help assure you that everything that can be done to track down the people responsible for that bomb, and probably for Ariana's death, is being done."

Malcolm felt a surge of anger, born of the frustration he always felt when the top brass started covering things up, treated him like a damn rookie, and politely told him to go away and play. He was used to it, but he didn't have to like it.

"Just what is that supposed to mean? I'm the officer in charge of this investigation, and if you're withholding evidence or information, Benjamin...." The words trailed off because, as they all knew, there was no real potency to his implied threat. A police captain trying to bully Benjamin Hawthorne was patently absurd. His threats were about as hollow as the promises of most politicians in this town. But he simply couldn't control the frustration any longer.

He was on his feet, leaning over Benjamin. "I mean, Jesus Christ, it's me, Malcolm. I'm Connor's friend, I care about what happens to her, I care that some piece of shit butchered Ariana. You didn't see your daughter that night." He leaned closer, pleading for understanding. "When I found her it was like...." He groped for the words. "It was like all the life had gone out of her. I have to *do* something, don't you understand?" His hands were clenched into fists. Marty slid unobtrusively to the edge of his seat, hands resting on his knees, muscles poised.

Benjamin was aware of the movement, though, and almost imperceptibly motioned with one hand, a gesture that communicated an "at ease, soldier." Then he looked up at the angry man, and in the quietest voice Malcolm had ever heard him use, he said, "I'm not the enemy. And I do understand how you feel. I love my daughter, too."

All the fight went out of Malcolm. Benjamin was right. The enemy, whoever it might be, was out there somewhere, killing with impunity, destroying people's lives, all for reasons he didn't understand. His shoulders slumped. "I'm sorry, I should go."

"No, please sit down...please." The tone was sincere. Malcolm lowered himself into the chair, staring into the fire as Benjamin continued. "I understand what it feels like, because I've lost people, good people, friends I've cared about and respected, and I couldn't do anything about it. Not one damn thing. I had to learn to live with being just a man, a fallible human being. I couldn't save everyone and I couldn't solve everything that was wrong." His voice grew more firm. "But just because I admit my basic human weaknesses does not mean that I won't do *anything and everything* within my power to keep my daughter safe. And there is a great deal more I can do than you can, it's as simple as that. You'll have to believe in me." He leaned forward, willing Malcolm to meet his eyes. "It doesn't make you worthless because you can't solve this crime. Fate dictated that you wouldn't be a part of what's happening here."

Malcolm blinked rapidly, choking down the emotions that rose in his throat. In just a few words, Benjamin had summed up everything that was still wrong, still unhealed inside Malcolm. "Worthless"—that's what he'd been, worthless, in a world that needed him to be of value.

The Senator regarded him closely for several moments, and when he spoke again it was with tremendous compassion. "You are a fine man and a fine police officer. You bring decency and humanity and integrity to a job where those qualities are hardly noticed anymore. Connor would not call you a friend, nor would I, if you were half the failure you think you are. The problem is that nothing I say will change how you feel about yourself. That's something you'll have to do when you're ready."

He sat back in his chair, but his spine had straightened, his eyes were clear once more. "Now, I want Marty to fill you in as much as he can on what is being done."

Marty leaned forward to let Malcolm see his face when he spoke.

"We now believe the attacks on Ariana and later on Connor are related to one of the ongoing matters in which the Senator is involved. With that in mind, I have initiated inquiries through our own network of people within the various agencies to try and get a line on whoever may have been responsible." He saw the questions that immediately sprang to Malcolm's cop mind.

They were written all over his face. But Marty held up his hand, palm out, to head them off.

"I can't tell you where these inquiries are being made. These are people you would never be allowed to question. And if, by some bizarre circumstance, you managed to interview any of them, not only would you get nowhere, but you would find yourself in a whole lot of trouble, trouble we could not get you out of without compromising our own work. Does that make sense to you?"

Malcolm nodded skeptically, still wanting to ask, still wanting more details. He hated double talk.

"The bottom line is that even if—and it's a pretty impossible 'if—you managed to track down the person or persons responsible for Ariana's death and for that device planted in Connor's house, there is absolutely no chance you would ever take anyone to trial."

Malcolm looked at him in disbelief. "This is still the United States, Marty, we still have laws here. It might be hard to get a conviction, but...."

Marty interrupted. "Not hard. Impossible. If any of our theories are correct, the people involved in this are beyond your reach, believe me, and that includes the ones right here in this town."

"Government people? Fed? Cops? What?" Malcolm wasn't quite prepared for what he was hearing.

"I can't say, I'm sorry. All I can say is that any of those things are possible. Besides, you don't have the resources that we do. We can look farther abroad than our own back yard. Do you know what I mean?" Malcolm nodded, at a loss for words. "And if it is close to home, you could jeopardize your job, your family, even your life, Malcolm, and none of us wants that, least of all Connor." This jogged something in the policeman's brain, something he hadn't considered much until now.

"Does Connor know whatever it is you won't tell me?"

Marty hesitated. He wasn't entirely sure how informed the Senator's daughter was. Benjamin correctly interpreted the hesitation and picked up the conversation.

"I've never wanted to involve my daughter in my work, Malcolm. But there are some things of which I needed to make her aware. She's a smart woman and she knows better than to give in to curiosity. She listens to what I tell her and refrains from asking questions. It's a wise approach, and one I sincerely wish you would take, please."

There was no condescension in Benjamin's voice. Malcolm had to admit that leaving this mess in someone else's hands did not sit well with him. On the other hand, he knew his exclusion was not out of any lack of respect for his capabilities. He stood up, holding out his hand to the Senator. Benjamin stood also, clasping Malcolm's hand in both of his own.

"One more thing," Connor's father said, "and you won't like this." Malcolm steeled himself for whatever revelation might be forthcoming.

"Ariana's death has to be put down to a mugging, nothing more. And Connor's house being ransacked was just the result of that same opportunistic criminal having stolen Ariana's keys." Benjamin saw the angry resistance in the cop's eyes. "It has to be that way, I'm sorry. The people we need to find have to believe that the case is closed."

"But I can't close the case without a suspect. You know as well as I do that Morrison's on this like flypaper, thanks to Marty here."

The Senator's assistant grimaced. "I talked to him before we knew what was involved, before the explosive device went off at the house."

Benjamin put his hand on Malcolm's shoulder. "Please, don't worry. It will be taken care of, I promise."

Marty walked him to the elevator. "Listen, I'm sorry this whole thing is turning out the way it is. I know how you feel, and so does the Senator. Don't think any less of him because he can't let you in." Malcolm nodded and shook his hand as the doors slid open. It was getting late, and the one place he wanted to be was home, the only place where life still made some sense.

---

*Thursday,
early evening*

If Connor had expected to be left alone to lick her wounds, she was mistaken. No sooner had they reached Val's house in Bethesda than Connor was ushered into the comfy den, assigned a seat in the big, overstuffed arm chair, and given hot tea. Val plopped down across from her in a leather sling back chair.

"So, what's going on in that great big brain of yours?" Val was not one to beat around the bush.

"My brain is fried, Val. I'm not thinking anything, I'm not feeling anything, and you don't need to worry about me."

"The hell I don't. What are you? Superwoman? Your life goes all to hell in the course of a couple of days and you're okay with that? My patients should be so lucky. I wouldn't even have a job." She looked shrewdly at Connor's drawn face, red eyes with dark circles under them. "So don't kid your old bubbe, okay?"

She sat back in her chair and waited.

The technique was transparent but effective. She knew that if Connor followed her usual m.o., she would give in, talk a little, grudgingly, of course, and eventually that would lead to more.

"All right, I'm upset. It's natural to grieve over someone you love. But I have to get past it, get on with my life."

"So soon? I didn't know we'd already been to the funeral and said the eulogies."

Something was odd here; Val knew it. Something unusual or unexpected had happened to alter the natural course of grief. True, Connor was an extraordinarily intelligent woman, and people like her were prone to intellectualize, detach from emotion, manufacture justifications for not showing a "weak" side. But, particularly since her relationship with Ariana had begun, Connor had demonstrated a remarkable and commendable willingness to plumb emotional depths, to give her heart to the woman she loved, and to let the whole world know how she felt about quite a few other things as well. The quiet, staid, terribly proper lawyer had discovered laughter, impulsiveness, and even silliness at times.

Now, some shift had taken place, one that Val didn't particularly like. It signaled a withdrawal. She had spoken briefly with Benjamin after he had first visited his daughter. The scene he described—the tears, the anger, the guilt—all that was normal and healthy. What she saw now was neither. There were no tears, no laughter, no reminiscing. Nothing. That was just it, there was nothing but a shell of a person seated across from her. What had made Connor choke off her grief so abruptly? What made a warm, loving woman cease to mourn and yet seem so completely lost?

An idea began to germinate in Val's mind, but she was too

good a therapist, and too good a friend, to steer Connor in any particular direction. If Val's supposition were correct, this was something that had to come from Connor, and no one else. The young woman was stubborn enough to deny it if backed into a corner.

"I hadn't really thought about the funeral." This clever side-stepping of the issue was not unusual for Connor. But Val was an old hand at chucking the ball back into the circle when it threatened to go astray. She didn't let anyone, friends or clients, get away with avoidance.

"We've got plenty of time for that later," she countered. "I wasn't talking about arrangements, and you know it. I'm just sitting here wondering if it might be better to mourn her *before* you bury her. Like we Jews usually say a Kaddish, the prayer for the dead."

"She won't be buried, she'll be cremated...it's what she wanted." Once again the evasion, the logical-sounding response. But Connor looked more miserable than ever, and there was hard, choking edge to her voice.

"Cremated, buried...whatever. Connor, don't play those games with me, sweetheart, I know you. This isn't about funerals, this is about you losing the woman you've loved for eleven years. This is about losing your lover, your mate, your...."As she searched for further words to remind Connor of the importance of this relationship to her, she saw the blaze of anger in the younger woman's eyes. "Uh, oh," she thought. "I was right."

Aloud, she only said, "What gives?"

Connor shrugged, mouth set in a tight line, hands gripping the arms of the chair, her entire body screaming "I'm angry" while her tongue remained stubbornly silent. Val took another tack. Direct questions weren't working.

"So, okay, you want to talk funerals. I would imagine you'd need a big place. Ariana had a lot of friends, a lot of people will probably want to be there."

"Yes, she was very popular." The tone belied the compliment. There was no admiration there, only biting sarcasm.

Val thought, "Oh my dear, if words could kill, I'd be dead."

"Of course she was popular, Connor, and I know you'll want to plan something appropriate. I mean, even though the two of you had been separated...." Here she paused. The next part was a bit brutal if what she suspected was true, but it needed to come out for Connor's sake. Val wished for a moment that she didn't have to be the one to do it. But it wasn't in her nature to evade the responsibilities of friendship.

"...still, you were a long-term couple. It was just a cooling off period for both of you."

Connor launched herself out of the chair with such force it startled even Val, and she had had some pretty unpredictable clients in her time. She didn't fear for her own or even Connor's safety, but she did find herself glancing about to see if there were any particularly valuable or important furnishings she might want to rescue. She also hoped Eli wouldn't get it into his head to come charging in to investigate if things got noisy.

But Connor didn't grab anything and hurl it. She'd done enough damage at the Watergate. Instead, she stood very still, looking at the lush, manicured lawn behind Val's house. It was so green, so beautiful, so alive. Her whole body trembled. Val didn't move from her chair, didn't urge Connor to sit down. Instead, she waited quietly, perhaps the hardest part of dealing with anyone in such pain. She knew that whatever Connor wanted to say must first be said in the direction of an inanimate object such as the window. Besides, Val wasn't sure she was quite ready to see the anguish in those eyes. "Must be getting soft," she thought, sighing quietly.

There was utter stillness for several long moments, measured out in soft ticks of the small brass clock, and punctuated with only the occasional soft thud indicating Eli was somewhere in the house. Val waited. When the words finally came they were spoken so quietly as to be inaudible, and she hated having to ask Connor to repeat them. But she had no choice.

"What, hon? I didn't hear you."

"She cheated."

"Ariana cheated?" It was just as she had surmised, but it would hardly do to say as much; mild surprise seemed more appropriate to the occasion.

"Yes." The word came out half-strangled, and Val's experienced eye took note of Connor's arms wrapped around herself in a classically self-protective position. Holding the pain in and keeping the world out.

"Are you quite sure?" Val asked.

"I'm not a fool, Val. I know. I saw the...evidence."

"Okay, for the moment we'll assume that Ariana slept with someone else."

"She did...she was...for a while."

"Any idea why?"

"How the hell am I supposed to know that?" Connor's arms fell to her sides, and she wheeled on Val, her face contorted with anger. "What are you saying, that it's my fault? It's my fault she was screwing around with some bitch from God knows where?"

"Now we're seeing it," Val thought. "Now it's surfacing." Aloud, she said, "I didn't say that, so you must be thinking it. I just meant that we all have ideas about why our lovers do certain things, because we know them pretty well."

"I thought I did know her, I thought we were together, I thought it was for life." Suddenly the irony of that statement seemed to hit Connor all at once, and she erupted into an odd laughter, choked with tears. "Isn't that a joke? For life? And there's no more life, no more Ariana, and it was all a stupid lie anyway."

"Don't do this to yourself, Connor." Val's voice was sharp. She realized she needed to start thinking like a friend, not a therapist, and she wasn't willing to let the distinction become blurred for either of them. If Connor wanted to see someone, Val would refer her to a colleague. For now, Val just needed to be herself, and that meant being not letting Connor drown in bitterness. "For heaven's sake, woman, you're smart enough to know better. Since when did you decide to wallow in self-pity and drama?"

Connor looked up, surprised at Val's tone.

"Don't look at me like that or pretend you don't understand what I'm saying. You know perfectly well that Ariana loved you dearly, as much as she was capable of loving anyone. You knew from the start she was impulsive and unpredictable, and at times self-absorbed. That was who she was and you accepted it." She raised her hand as Connor opened her mouth to speak. "Don't interrupt, I'm on a roll. The point is, people can love each other and do stupid, hurtful things anyway. That's how humans are— fallible. And you ought to know that better than anyone. You can be angry at her, and you can miss her, and you can mourn her, but you damn sure aren't going to turn Ariana's death into one huge betrayal of Connor Hawthorne, the poor, pathetic victim, at least not if I can help it. You're not a victim, and you're not the first person who found out that someone she loved was somewhat less than perfect. Dying doesn't make the dead into

saints and kvetching about Ariana's shortcomings won't make
you feel any better about losing her."

For a heartbeat Val wondered if she should have held her
tongue. Connor was clearly furious, standing as still as a stone
statue, eyes blinking rapidly, fists clenched at her sides. Then,
like a chalk sidewalk picture blurred by the first drops of rain, the
harsh lines of her brow and the rigid set of her jaw softened,
melted. All the fight went out of her.

"But why, Val, why?"

This time Val went to her, led her to a chair. "I don't know,
honey. I don't know why anything evil and sad happens. But I
know it does. And I know that, one way or another, we have to
deal with it and keep on living and breathing."

"Is that a therapist cliché, or your own advice?" Connor
smiled a little bit so Val would know the comment wasn't an
angry one. "Though I should be able to tell the difference by
now since your advice usually comes out in Yiddish."

Val shrugged. "Momma would call it Yinglish; she says I murder two perfectly good languages. But the point is, we can't
make idols of the people we love, and we can't let their faults
make us bitter. We can't let losing them make us hate life. If we
do, we end up sad, lonely, and pitiful. For me, well...." She
paused, swallowing hard, "When I get to feeling that way, even
a little, I think about my parents. I figure if they could survive
the horrors of a death camp and still look on life with hope and
faith and forgiveness...then I can, too."

Connor heaved a sigh. "I'm sorry, Val. I know you're right,
and this hardly compares with something like what happened to
your family, but...."

"I'm not saying your own pain isn't valid and significant to
you. But perspective is a good thing. It helps to take a step back

and not get too wrapped up in the drama. You can't lose sight of the good in your life, of the good in Ariana. Right now you're angry because of so many things. You argued, she left. And she had the temerity to sleep with someone else, and then the outright nerve to be murdered before she could apologize to you for doing it."

Connor's eyes told Val she was right on target. She decided to let her words sink in for a little while, and poured herself another cup of tea.

They sat silently for several minutes until Connor scrubbed her face with both hands and shook herself, as if to cast off some of the weight of her sadness. "I know what you're saying, Val. It's just that, coming on top of Ariana's dying, I couldn't bear the thought of her spending those last few weeks with someone else. It so goddamned unfair."

"*Oy gevalt,*" Val exclaimed with mock pity. "Ah, the old 'life's not fair' complaint. You know, you should have been a Jew; we have a certain talent for gloom." Val chuckled. "The fact is, life only seems fair when you're winning, when everything is just the way you think you want it. When the painful events happen, it's like someone changed the rules in the middle of the game. Unfortunately, that *is* the main rule—that the rules change. Some lessons are treats, some aren't."

"Is that a refinement of your 'Chinese restaurant' analogy?"

Val smiled. "You remember that? Yes, I still think we choose our lives from the very beginning, though my rabbi would take issue with me. But I think of it as 'one from column a, two from column b.' Sometimes we love it, sometimes we choke on it. We'd like to deny any responsibility for what we choose, but we can't. All we can do is learn from experience."

"Experience sucks!"

"Sometimes true, but what else is there? We could sit around on the grass meditating, but I, for one, have never been able to get both legs into the lotus position at the same time."

"I hate it that you can make me smile even when I don't want to, you and that pixieish face of yours."

"This face?" Val raised both eyebrows innocently. "My mother loves this face. Now, how about something to eat?"

"I didn't realize I was so hungry. What's for dinner? It had better include kreplach."

Val chuckled. "You'll have to ask Eli; he's the actual cook around here."

Connor immediately got up and went in search of Val's husband. But the older woman sat there for a few minutes, pondering. Her words had had the intended effect, but perhaps Connor's agreement had come a little too easily.

"She gave in too soon," Val mused. That worried her. Connor may have understood what was happening to her, may even have let herself and Ariana off the hook a little, but she had still clamped a lid on feelings that could be destructive if they were ignored. And she was still a long way from truly forgiving either Ariana or herself. There was something haunting her still. Val's Momma would have called it a *dybbuk*—a demon.

CHAPTER FIVE

———◁◈▷———

Sweetest love, I do not go,
For weariness of thee,
Nor in hope the world can show
A fitter love for me;
But since that I
Must die at last, 'tis best
To use myself in jest,
Thus by feigned deaths to die.
—John Donne

———◁◈▷———

Monday, September 25

One week after her body was discovered face down on the banks of the C&O Canal, Ariana Gennarro's funeral Mass was said over a closed casket at St. Stephen's Catholic Church on upper Connecticut Avenue in Washington. It was well attended by the press, who almost succeeded in outnumbering the mourners.

Connor sat in the frontmost pew, flanked by family—her father, her daughter, and her Aunt Jessica. The latter two had flown direct to Washington from London the previous day. Connor had been completely stunned when Val had summoned her to the living room, telling her with unusual vagueness that she had "visitors." There was 19-year-old Katy, trying to figure out whether to smile or look sad, and Aunt Jessica who went immediately to her niece and enfolded her in a great big "mother hug." At 5'11" and some 200 pounds of soft, womanly curves, Jessica Broadhurst was capable of bestowing world-class hugs; they were even rumored to possess curative powers.

"It's all right, dearie," she said in her briskly British accent. "It's been a bit of a shock to you, I know, but we shall all get through this together. Now come and give your lovely daughter a hug. She's missed you terribly."

Connor turned to Katy, who had moved closer, but still looked uncertain in that "not quite a grownup yet, but trying to be" sort of way. It was Connor's turn for mother hugging, and she was gratified to discover that Katy held onto her just as hard. They hadn't seen each other in over a year, partly because of conflicts in their schedules and partly because of disagreements they had both let get out of hand. But death adds perspective; their differences seemed rather petty now, and the embrace conveyed forgiveness on both sides.

"I'm so sorry, Mom. I can't believe that Ariana's...not here."

For a brief moment Connor reflected on the fact that death affects the young rather differently than the middle-aged, and differently still than the old. To a 19-year-old it must seem remote, unfathomable. They grieved, but their own mortality was rarely called into consideration when an older person died. Perhaps death was simply confusing to them, as if someone weren't playing by the rules.

"Mom...Mom...are you okay? I really am sorry about Ariana, honest."

"I know, honey, believe me, I know."

On impulse, Katy hugged her mother again. "I love you, Mom."

"Oh, God, I love you too, sweetheart."

"I'm so sorry about all the things I've said."

"Sshh, don't worry about that. It's gone and forgotten. What matters is that you're here now, and I didn't even know how much I needed you to be until right this minute."

Katy stepped back and smiled through her tears. The look of pride in her daughter's eyes made Connor suddenly very glad she had spoken the truth. She did need Katy, and it didn't seem like a bad idea at all. Besides, they shared something—a reluctance to believe that Ariana was actually and truly gone.

Now, today, at her funeral, there could be no suspension of belief. Death had taken center stage and all eyes were drawn to the oaken casket lying sleek and aloof before the assembled company of mourners and those who fed on mourning. Vague whispers and unintended noises echoed up along the lofty buttresses and bounced about in the stone vault far above them as they waited for the priest to begin.

Behind the immediate family sat Marty, looking unusually grave, and, beside him, Val and Eli, Malcolm, Connor's college roommate, MaryAnne Porter, and Eve Jefferson. Other friends of Connor's and Ariana's were scattered across other pews. Connor felt a rush of anger when Gerry Marchetti sashayed in, dabbing at his eyes with a silk hankie, acting for all the world like the chief mourner and causing a brief feeding frenzy in the media who were kept well back near the door.

None of Ariana's family was able to make the trip from Italy, although Senator Hawthorne had spoken to Ariana's father and had carefully offered, in fluent Italian, to "take care of" all travel expenses. But it soon became clear it was not so much a matter of money as a matter of health. Signore Gennarro was not well, nor was his wife. He seemed almost embarrassed that he was too old and ill to make the long journey, but he had little choice. His own priest had said a Mass for his *bambina;* that would have to be enough. Benjamin assured him that he had made a wise decision, and also promised he would have the service in Washington very discreetly videotaped, and a copy sent to the family. Even now two cameras were recording, one concealed near the altar and one taping from the choir loft at the west end.

Those few reporters allowed entry had not been permitted to bring any electronic equipment into the church. This restriction was enforced by four special agents at the door who turned a deaf ear to First Amendment protests and gave members of the fourth estate a choice: be "wanded" down with a metal detector, or stay outside.

Connor appreciated the security. She didn't want Ariana's funeral to become more of a media circus than it already had. On the other hand, the precautions seemed a little excessive. Her sixth sense offered up the vague inkling that more was involved in the security arrangements than simply preserving privacy. She was correct. The cameras were not recording just the Catholic funeral rites. Every person in the church was being carefully photographed in full close-up. It was not unknown for murderers to attend the funerals of their victims.

Later, when they reviewed the tapes, Benjamin and Marty would discover that two individuals in particular (a smallish, nondescript sort of man in wire-rimmed glasses, and a tall, dark-haired woman in a bulky trench coat) could not be identified as either acquaintances or members of the press. As a matter of fact, they could not be identified at all.

———•◦•———

Later that evening, Connor placed the urn containing Ariana's ashes squarely in the center of the mantelpiece in the library of the Georgetown house. That phase of the ritual had been the most difficult, standing witness as the slow conveyor belt moved the casket, inch by inch, into the crematory chamber. She didn't have to be there. She could have waited in one of the "chapels" with everyone else. But Connor was not one to shirk the unpleasant and the difficult, and she believed she owed it to Ariana to see this final task completed. Still, when she thought of the woman who had been so alive, who had loved and laughed and capered about, full of unquenchable hope and optimism, the woman she had held in her arms at night…it was still hard to watch what was left of her be reduced to nothing more than a handful of ashes. All Connor could say was, goodbye. It didn't seem adequate.

Now she stared at the urn, not knowing precisely what to do with it. What *did* one do? Connor and Ariana had never even discussed the subject. Death had seemed far too remote to require any plans for its arrival. She supposed there were those who carried urns about with them as they moved from place to place. And there were those who selected an appropriate spot and threw the ashes to the wind. She would likely take that course. Keeping the remains of a dead person in one's home indefinitely seemed morbid in the extreme.

There were only two chairs in the library now. The rest of the furniture had been sent for re-upholstery and repair, or had been discarded. She built a fire first, then sat down in one of the chairs.

Her gaze remained fixed on the flames for a long while as her thoughts ran in and out of her mind like the crazed bicycle messengers who frenetically raced about the streets of the city, first here, then there, never stopping to rest. There were so many images—not just of Ariana, but of the places they had been, the wonders they had shared. The kaleidoscopic movie of their life together, melding both the triumphant and the tragic into one swirling, moving picture, taunted her because it could not be captured and preserved in a still frame in her mind.

The sounds of something being dropped overhead, followed by the sound of laughter, brought her thoughts back to the living and to the present. Katy and Aunt Jessica were upstairs "arranging things."

When Connor had walked through the house the day before, the progress of the repair crews had been quite remarkable. It was a tribute to her father's ability to get things done; he had contracted for three full shifts of workmen around the clock. Little was left to indicate what had happened here, except for the fact that almost nothing remained of its interior decorations and furnishings. She had decided right then that she would return to her own house rather than continue staying with Val.

Katy and Aunt Jessica, after trying unsuccessfully to persuade Connor to stay at a hotel, had gone to a store and ordered three twin beds, three sets of bedding, several sets of towels, and had them all delivered while the funeral and cremation were taking place. When Connor had protested that no one need remain with her to baby-sit, the two women, though 40 years apart in age, had been of one voice and one mind.

"Forget it, Mom," Katy had said. "Where you go, we go."

Aunt Jessica had been equally firm. "Family is family, and we Broadhurst women stand together through anything." Overcome by their resolve, Connor had no choice but to agree. That was one reason for the early tour the day before, to assess whether any evidence of the explosive device remained. No one besides Malcolm and her father knew about it. She intended to keep it that way. Thus she assured herself that, unless you knew just where to look, most of the damage had been repaired.

Now, she heard Katy clattering down the stairs, calling some reminder back to her great-aunt who remained on the second floor. As she reached the entryway to the library, though, the sight of her mother sitting alone in the empty room with only the urn for company must have reminded her of the need for a more sober demeanor; her smile disappeared. Connor translated the awkward silence. Katy didn't know what to say. But then, even mature and worldly people often cannot handle the topic of death gracefully. In this case, Katy had more on her mind than just social discomfort. Connor suspected that guilt had finally reared its ugly head. The truth was that Katy had not been especially devoted to Ariana, though they had always been cordial to each other, and, when Katy was little, they had embarked on crazy, silly adventures together. But, as Katy grew up, she became less and less willing to accept Ariana's flamboyant Italian personality, which, in her adolescent wisdom, she decided was incompatible with her mother's quiet dignity.

There was a deeper issue, of course. Katy had been (and perhaps still was) dealing with the issue of lesbianism. As a younger teenager, she had hesitated to invite boyfriends to her home, dreading Ariana's overwhelming lack of tact and the ensuing embarrassment, though when friends did come to call, they were invariably charmed by both Connor and Ariana, and had nothing critical to say. But Katy had still been angry at her mother for not insisting that Ariana at least pretend to get back in the closet occasionally.

Connor, naturally, had recognized at the time that Katy was like any other adolescent, even if her household was rather out of the ordinary. Children, she reasoned, were invariably embarrassed by their parents, no matter what the parents were, or what they did. Connor's sexual preference just added to Katy's claim that life was *so* unfair.

Albeit that angst is a fairly common teen malady, those suffering from it take it very seriously. So Connor had worked hard at being fair to both her daughter and her partner. She had tried to mediate, show her support for Katy, and had even cajoled Ariana into being a little less obtrusive. The strategy had worked only sporadically, and the times it didn't were sheer hell. When Aunt Jessica suggested Katy finish prep school in England, Connor had been both relieved and distraught, imagining herself to have failed as a mother. But she let her go, missed her terribly, and visited frequently, always telling herself that the change was for the best.

Looking at the girl now, so grown up and dignified, Connor knew she had done the right thing. But it bothered her that there was as much penitence as grief in Katy's expression.

"Come over here, honey." Connor motioned to the other chair. "I know you may be feeling bad because you and Ariana didn't get always get along. When someone close to us dies, we always wish that we'd done things differently, been a little kinder, or more understanding, or whatever. But the fact is, you never did anything wrong. Ariana loved you, and you loved her. You two just didn't see eye to eye on things, and she wasn't the sort of person you felt comfortable having as a friend."

Huge tears welled up in the girl's eyes. "But I never got to tell her that I really did love her, and even though I said some pretty mean things, I thought she was great. It's just that I was so afraid of what people might think, and sometimes I even thought you cared more about her than you did about me, and when I was in high school, I even used to wish she would just go away, but...but not like this. I never meant like this."

"Oh, sweetheart." Connor knelt beside Katy and put her arms around the girl's shoulders. "I know you never wished Ariana ill, not really. But you have to believe that I never loved you any less, not for a moment, even when Ariana came into my life. You do know that, don't you?"

Katy sniffled and brushed her tears way. "I know that now. Aunt Jessica and Grandma Gwen had a lot to say about it when I first got to England. Grandma told me that I was being a 'right twit' about it. And you know how hard it is to disagree with her about anything."

Connor nodded, smiling. "Your Grandma Gwen is a pretty remarkable woman, and I doubt she'd approve of all this guilt you've saddled yourself with."

"But the thing is, I never got a chance to...." Katy began to cry again, her breath coming in huge sobs.

"A chance to do what, sweetheart?"

"I never...got to...tell Ariana I was sorry." Katy tried to calm herself. "I meant to write. I just didn't know what to say. And now I can't tell her and I hate that."

Connor's heart ached for her child and she wrapped her arms around Katy. "It's okay, honey, it's really, really okay. She knows. Wherever she is, she knows. She loved us both, and, you know what?"

"What?"

"We've still got each other."

Connor and Katy stayed that way for a while, mother and daughter healing old hurts and gently tending to fresh wounds.

Finally, though, Connor's knees protested against further contact with the hard floor, and she stood up and pulled Katy to her feet. If life were ever going to get back to some semblance of normality, Connor would have to give it a nudge.

"So, what's for dinner, young lady? Or haven't you and the terror of Trafalgar Square figured that out yet?"

Katy smiled, wiping the last tears from her cheeks with the backs of her hands. "Do you want to go out to that place by *The Tombs*." Katy was referring to a restaurant which earned its name for being a below-street-level hangout for Georgetown University students. Above it was the posh and considerably more formal *1789* restaurant. And next to it was the semi-glitzy, yet relatively intimate, *F. Scott's*, decorated, as the name implied, in a sort of chrome and flash neo-1920s decor, with music to match. The food and service were always excellent, the wine list more than adequate, and the booths, separated by plexiglass dividers threaded with tiny fiber-optic lights, assured a degree of privacy.

Connor wasn't entirely sure she was up for a night out, but her instincts told her that Katy needed it. While she had to admit that some voice in the back of her head was mewling for a solo pity party—trying to convince the person it inhabited to stay home and sulk—an even stronger voice, which sounded suspiciously like her Grandmother Gwendolyn, would have none of it. "Good Lord, woman, put your coat on and go have a hot meal and a good stiff drink. Enjoy your family." So that's precisely what she did.

<hr />

The morning after the Gennarro funeral, a 35-year-old career criminal by the name of Eddie Caldon was found shot to death in a tenement slum apartment. His rap sheet was long and violent—rape, armed robbery, grand theft auto, attempted murder, and a dozen lesser offenses, including pimping and fraud. In his apartment, detectives found three of Ariana Gennarro's credit cards, a set of keys to Connor Hawthorne's home, and a diamond necklace and ring that were among the items reported stolen during the burglary. In Eddie's boot was found a knife, which, though devoid of blood or any other forensic evidence, was structurally a perfect match for the wounds on Ariana's body. The Gennarro murder case was closed; the obvious suspect was dead and buried, unmourned and unforgiven, in a cheap plot in the far reaches of Prince Georges County.

Its outrage forgotten, the city went back to sleep—all but one man, who sat at his city-issue desk in the precinct house long into the night wondering how such a monstrous lie could put anything right.

―――――◦◦◦―――――

"There wasn't anything there." The man sounded both defensive and angry. His knuckles were blanched where they gripped the receiver. The voice at the other end was strident enough to be heard beyond the vicinity of the telephone, but no one else was present in the elaborate suite to eavesdrop.

"Utterly ridiculous! We know full well the material is in that townhouse. Clearly it is a question of you not having been sufficiently thorough in your search."

"I told you...."

"Do not interrupt me again. I expect you to follow through on the other phase of this assignment. After that, once the location is empty, you will return and find what you were sent to find. Am I being completely clear?"

*The man wanted nothing more than to leap through the phone, grab
this arrogant son-of-a-bitch by the throat, and choke him until his face
turned a pleasant shade of purple and his tongue swelled out of his
mouth. Unfortunately, he was in no position to accomplish the impossible, nor did he dare to let his anger and disgust show.*

"Yes, sir, quite clear. You wish me to effect the second phase and then
return to Washington."

"And when you do, you will take that goddamn house apart brick by
brick if you have to."

"Yes, sir. Should I check with Local before leaving."

"Since when does Local concern you?"

"I just thought that...."

"You just thought, you just thought. I'm sick of hearing that crap
from the likes of you. We aren't paying you for analysis or strategy;
we're paying you to follow orders and succeed. I'm hardly impressed with
your work so far. First this messy killing and a big media uproar, then
a futile search, and a device which doesn't eliminate anyone on the list
and instead arouses the suspicions of the very people on that list."

"I explained to you why I had to take care of the girlfriend that way."

"Which reminds me, make arrangements to get rid of that stupid Italian queer. He started this whole mess."

"But that will only arouse more suspicion, won't it?"

"Did I ask for your opinion?"

"No sir."

"Then think of something subtle—assuming, of course, that you are
capable of subtlety. An accident, a suicide, whatever."

"Whatever it is, that cop won't buy it."

"We can worry about the cop later. For now, deal with the Signore
and then get on with phase two."

"Yes, sir."

When the line went dead at the other end, he realized his hand hurt from gripping the phone. He took a deep breath and went to the bar to pour himself a generous three fingers of scotch, drank half of it and put the rest back on the counter. As with some men of less-than-average stature and slight build, being bullied by anyone else enraged him. Somewhere in his mind, it was his lack of bulk and height which gave others carte blanche to be abusive and arrogant toward him. He liked to think he made up for what he thought of as his physical deficiencies with brains and a complete lack of conscience. What others might quail at doing, he would do without a moment's hesitation. It had made him extremely effective as a mercenary. And the last 6'2" moron who'd called him "shorty" was now minus his tongue and various other parts of his anatomy. Fortunately for him, he was also dead.

Opening the walk-in closet, he carefully selected his evening's wardrobe: silk slacks, a shapeless silk jacket, tank top, expensive leather loafers, a gold chain, two gold rings, and a small gold stud earring in one ear. The effect was one of monied effeminacy, precisely as he intended. Before he left, he slipped the razor sharp stiletto into the sheath suspended inside the waistband of his trousers. He finished the scotch and went whistling and sashaying out into the corridor.

The Washington Post, September 27

Police officials revealed late last night that Gerri Marchetti, internationally known clothing designer, was found dead in his NW Washington home. While foul play has not been ruled out, inside sources said that Marchetti apparently hanged himself after unsuccessfully attempting to cut his wrists, as a result of a dispute with a homosexual lover. Police are still investigating Marchetti's whereabouts during the earlier hours of yesterday. They have learned he was present at several bars frequented primarily by gay men, and may have left one of those establishments in the company of an unidentified man.

CHAPTER SIX

Let the blow fall soon or late
Let what will be o'er me;
Give the face of earth around
And the road before me.
Wealth I seek not, hope, nor love,
Nor a friend to know me;
All I seek, the heaven above
And the road before me.
—Robert Louis Stevenson

Friday, November 29
12,000 feet over New Mexico

Connor's attention was fixed on the ground far below the plane. Beneath them, distinctly odd patterns of what she thought must be every possible shade of brown in the spectrum were interspersed with small bits of green in the undulating landscape. She wondered how people lived in a place that appeared devoid of life. Natives of the Southwest might have been offended by this assessment if they had not been aware that all of her frames of reference, as far as geography went, were decidedly green ones.

She was accustomed to the damp, humid lushness of D.C. and Maryland; the cool, misty, and equally damp environs of her grandmother's home in the English county of Sussex; the thriving vineyard regions of Northern Italy; and the aptly named Green Mountains of Vermont, where Connor kept a ski lodge. Except for a couple of plane trips to California to discuss the sale of movie rights based on one of her novels, and one pilgrimage to the gay mecca of San Francisco with Ariana, Connor's idea of going West meant driving to Leesburg, Virginia for dinner. Thus the whole idea of desert, let alone "high" desert, was utterly foreign to her, and equally forbidding. The settings for her novels were invariably urban. Her characters disported themselves in city restaurants, city clubs, and on city streets, with rare forays into suburbia. Thus her research, which was always thorough, had never touched on the great Southwest. The word "desert" conjured up fictional stories of cowboys and Indians, and movies starring the likes of John Wayne or Lorne Greene, possibly Barbara Stanwyck. Hot, dirty, dusty, barren—these were the sorts of adjectives she had expected would define her stay in New Mexico when she had decided to keep her commitment to speak at a writer's conference.

Passing through a thin layer of smoky clouds, the plane encountered pockets of turbulence that threw the 727 about like a toy for a few seconds. Connor didn't particularly mind; she flew a great deal. She noticed that her other seatmates in first class, however, viewed the upheaval with rather less equanimity. The gentleman next to her looked a bit pale, his arms clutching both armrests, and the woman behind Connor could be heard admonishing her husband, "I told you *three times* we should have taken the train, Justin. But you never listen."

Connor said to herself, "ah, a 'noodge' kvetching." She thought fondly of Val, who had come with Malcolm to see her off. What a pair those two made. Connor had barely been able

to suppress a grin when she saw them steaming across the terminal together, Val taking three steps for every one of Malcolm's—
the Mutt 'n' Jeff pair of all time.

"If you'd taken the Dramamine like I told you before we left,
you wouldn't look green, Justin."

Connor tuned out the whining behind her and went back to
the view outside her small window. She didn't actually understand air currents, inversion layers, and all that, but she was accustomed to their effects. She'd survived more than a few bumps
here and there, particularly on long flights over the Atlantic. She
felt the plane's momentum lessen as the pilot throttled back; the
whine of the jet engines came down a decibel or two. The
ground was much closer, and she could make out microscopic
cars and buildings. There was more vegetation now, parks and
playing fields perhaps, but not many large stands of trees, no sea
of green canopies such as the airline passenger approaching
Washington might find. On the other hand, the sky was a color
Connor had to admit she had never seen. The word "blue" was
in no way adequate. One would have to augment the description with "cerulean" or "aquamarine," or some as yet undiscov-
ered Crayola color.

A hard jarring, a thump, then another, followed by the esca-
lating roar of engines thrust into reverse, and the plane was
down. It began its taxi to the gate, and, as always, despite the ad-
monitions of the flight crew, the click of seat belt releases clat-
tered through the aircraft. The boldest of the airline-rule flouters
stood to open overhead compartments and retrieve their be-
longings long before the plane "came to a complete stop."

Connor, who never understood this sudden hysteria to push
and shove one's way off an airplane, was secretly pleased when
the man next to her, who had complained about one thing or

another throughout the flight, and wore his discontent as part of his wardrobe, was firmly thwarted in his efforts to be the first one off the plane. A steward told him, in no uncertain terms, to take his seat.

Once inside the terminal, and through the clutch of greeters at the gate, Connor took a look around. Albuquerque International Airport was a pleasant surprise—high-ceilinged and bright, almost quiet for an airport terminal. When she reached the intersection of the A and B wings, she came face to face, or, more accurately, face to base, with a towering sculpture of a Native American man who appeared about to take flight. The winged figure was counter-balanced in such a way as to give the viewer the sensation that he would succeed at leaning far, far out over the base of the piece. Other passengers elbowed by her brusquely as she stood there transfixed. The power of the sculpture took her breath away. "That is how art should make you feel," she thought, finally tearing herself away, marveling that she should have seen it in an airport of all places.

A moving sidewalk and two descending escalators took her to the baggage claim area. Nearing the base of the second escalator, she spotted a sign with the name "C. Hawthorne" printed neatly in block capitals. Then she focused on the person who held the sign chest high while carefully observing the arriving travelers. She was an attractive young woman neatly dressed in black jeans, a white button-down oxford-cloth shirt, and a short brown leather jacket. Her dark hair was pulled back off her face. When Connor was still more than a dozen feet away, the young woman smiled at her in recognition and hurried forward.

"Ms. Hawthorne. I'm Laura Nez. I'll be your driver. Welcome to New Mexico. I have your car waiting outside. If you'll just give me your bag checks, I'll see to your luggage."

Connor stared at her, not making any move to relinquish the carry-on to the woman's outstretched hand.

"I'm sorry if I seem confused, but I didn't order a car." Her tone was perhaps a little more curt than she intended.

"Yes, ma'am. But your father, Senator Hawthorne, did order one for you. Said he wanted you to have a pleasant stay here. And he left specific instructions to see that you had first-class service." She paused, uncertainly. "I hope that's okay. I've really been looking forward to meeting you."

Her look was plaintive enough that Connor could see no reason to refuse the courtesy or stubbornly hold on to her bag. Besides, it would save her reading road maps and finding her way to Santa Fe. She smiled to indicate that she was not as cross as she had perhaps sounded.

"Sorry to be so brusque. I'm just a little tired. Here."

"If you'll follow me, ma'am, I'll show you to the car, then I can get your suitcases. It usually takes a while for them to get to the terminal." She took the bag and the claim checks, and walked ahead of Connor to yet another escalator. As they descended, Connor couldn't help but note the thick braid sliding back and forth over the leather jacket and falling almost to the young woman's waist. Connor was utterly embarrassed to find herself thinking, "I wonder if that's a special Indian braid." Like many white people, she harbored a fascination with Native American culture, though she would have been the first to admit she knew little of it. Fortunately, unlike many white people, she also had the sensitivity and good manners not to regard them as if they were alien specimens. Thus, she also had the good grace to be embarrassed at thinking in clichés.

At the base of the moving stairs, a wide corridor opened out, through automatic doors, into the first level of the parking garage. Just beyond the sidewalk sat a long, silver Mercedes sedan. Even though the walk had taken less than a minute, Laura Nez apologized for the distance while opening the rear door for Connor.

"Sorry I didn't have the car right outside the arrival level, but with all the extra security these days, they'd have it on a tow truck before I could get back."

"That's okay," Connor smiled. "You should see the paranoia in Washington."

She got in, and the driver said, "I'll be right back with the bags…Oh, what do they look like?"

"Dark brown leather Pullman size suitcase with brass fittings and matching garment bag."

"Okay, please help yourself to the bar and there are copies of daily newspapers in the seat pocket in front of you."

The door closed and Connor heard a soft click as the automatic door locks engaged. Hmm, she thought. Extremely security conscious, I suppose. She pressed the door-lock switch on her own door. It clicked immediately to the "open" position. "Getting a little paranoid myself," she muttered. Not that it was unexpected considering the events of the last three months. But, given the facts that Ariana's funeral was behind her, and that all traces of the attempt on her own life had been thoroughly eradicated by the contractors and decorators in Washington, why did this sense of foreboding still weigh so heavily on Connor? Another instance, perhaps, of the "witch sense," her grandmother maintained was a hereditary gift to all the women descendants in her family. And Mrs. Broadhurst hadn't minced words during Connor's most recent visit. She'd spent most of October and November in England, both to see more of her family there and to get away from the memories and the publicity in Washington.

Besides, there was something indescribably soothing about her grandmother's cottage in Sussex, even if staying there did entail a mild lecture from time to time.

"All the Broadhurst women have it, child. And it's a gift, of that you can be quite sure. Don't raise that eyebrow at me, young lady, I know whereof I speak. You can pretend it's just guessing or 'women's intuition,' as gentlemen like to think. It's a gift of knowing, from deep inside, when things are right and things are wrong."

"You mean conscience?" Connor had grinned at her.

Grandmother Gwendolyn had not been amused. "No, I most certainly do not. And don't be insolent. You've been brought up to know the difference between right and wrong from a moral standpoint. I'm talking about life, Connor, about the events that shape our lives. Some of us just know when those events are proceeding correctly, when our part of the universe is in harmony. And we know when it is not. It is as if we are able to hear a false note in the midst of a piece of music others don't hear because they don't know how to listen properly."

Connor had mollified her grandmother by making a sincere effort to understand this so-called gift and the spiritual beliefs from which it arose. "But how does all this jibe with the rest of the world and with you going to church on Sunday?"

Mrs. Broadhurst looked at her granddaughter and sighed ever so softly. "My dear child, I go to church every Sunday because I enjoy it, because I like the hymns that we sing and I respect our rector. His sermons are soothing and generally kind and quite intelligent. The fact that I know there is more to creation and to spirituality than what is proffered by the Church of England does not require me to reject its contributions to humanity, or deny its traditional role in village life. Our church has a place and a purpose, as does every religious institution. Though frankly some of them puzzle me a great deal. I'm not asking you to pick one set of beliefs over another. I'm asking you to look within and become attuned to your gift of insight and potential for magic."

Coming from her grandmother, the mention of "magic" seemed almost absurd, but Connor could see the old girl was absolutely serious. And she had to admit there had been times in her life when she sensed things, or knew something was about to happen. And she recalled the vivid communications from her grandmother through dreams right after Ariana died. She had been tempted to dismiss them as the imaginings of a troubled, stressed mind, but, after listening to Grandma Gwen discuss psychic phenomena as if they were common household events, Connor began to wonder if she hadn't been unreasonably reluctant to embrace what her mind couldn't rationalize. On the other hand, what good was this gift if it hadn't saved Ariana's life? She had angrily confronted her grandmother with that very question. Mrs. Broadhurst had not been ruffled by it in the least.

"Has it occurred to you, Connor, that you may have had an inkling of a grievous event and not understood its meaning?"

With sudden clarity, Connor had remembered something she'd chosen to forget. One morning, a few days before they found Ariana, she had awakened with a crushing pain in her chest as if mortal fear were squeezing her heart. She'd felt the blood pounding in her ears. At the time, she'd dismissed it as nothing more than a bad nightmare. But that feeling had remained with her well into the next day. Was that the prescience her grandmother spoke of? Or just after-the-fact coincidence? Did the human mind simply play tricks, or was there something much larger at work? The power of the human spirit? Real magic?

Her mental debate was interrupted by the sound of the trunk

slamming shut. She hadn't even seen her driver return with the luggage. The door locks popped, and the driver's door swung open; in seconds they were maneuvering through traffic toward the airport's exit.

"My instructions are to take you directly to Santa Fe, Ms. Hawthorne, unless you have something to do in Albuquerque."

"First of all, it's Connor, not Ms. Hawthorne. And, second, I'm starved and I'm not ready for another long ride."

"Then please call me Laura and tell me what kind of food you're in the mood for."

"Okay, Laura, what do you recommend?"

The young woman smiled into the rearview mirror. "Probably not the broad selection you'd find back home, but we've got New Mexican, of course, and the standards—Italian, French, Greek...."

"Greek?"

"Sure, we're not all that backward, even if half the people in America think New Mexico is a foreign country."

Connor was instantly contrite. "I'm sorry, I didn't mean to imply...."

"No offense taken. A lot of tourists are surprised. They come here expecting Tex-Mex food on every corner."

As they took the curved ramp onto I-25, which bisected the city from north to south, Connor noted with approval the casual ease with which Laura handled the big car. Good. Nothing she hated worse than a bad driver.

"What's your favorite Greek place?"

"There aren't that many to choose from," she admitted with a tiny shrug. "But my personal favorite is near the University." She hesitated. "It isn't exactly fancy, though."

"I could care less about fancy," Connor assured her, returning the smile. "I do care about good food, though."

A few minutes' drive brought them to the UNM neighborhood and the *Olympia Cafe*, where Laura expertly parallel parked the Mercedes and jumped out to open the door for her passenger. But Connor was already on the pavement looking across Central Avenue at the campus. "Thanks for the courtesy, Laura, but you can forego the door-opening, okay? You don't need to wait on me." She started for the door and then realized Laura was not behind her. Instead, she had assumed a waiting posture, leaning against the car, arms folded across her chest.

"Aren't you coming?"

"Uh, no, ma'am, I'll wait for you here."

Connor spun around and went back to stand in front of Laura, arms akimbo. "Now, look, I appreciate you wanting to observe the formalities, but I don't put people, particularly people who work for me, into some separate subcategory of humanity."

Laura waited until a city bus had lurched away from the curb spewing diesel exhaust, then replied matter-of-factly, "Most people do."

"Well I'm not 'most people.' And I don't like eating alone if I have a choice. Clear?"

"Yes, ma'am!" The young woman gave her a mock salute.

"And enough with the ma'am already. You'd think I was ancient."

They went inside and ordered. By skillful planning, Connor was able to pay for both lunches while she sent Laura to hunt down a table amidst the hubbub of the small, student-mobbed restaurant. Taking her numbered receipt, she picked up their drinks and joined her companion, who had staked out a booth by the window.

Laura was right. The place wasn't the least bit fancy. The

booths had leatherette seats mended with strips of duct tape here
and there. The floor was linoleum tile, the table tops vintage
Formica. *Zorba the Greek* music played over a tinny speaker just
above them, and posters of the Greek Islands completed the du-
bious ambiance. But the aromas coming from the kitchen area,
just behind the ordering counter, were heavenly.

"What do I owe you for lunch, Ms...er, Connor?" The question was tentative.

"Nothing. Remember, you're on my time now, so meals are
on me."

"You're the boss." Her smile was wide, genuine, and perfectly attuned to the twinkle in her dark eyes. It was also contagious.
Connor realized her own face was finally falling into the habit of
smiling back.

"Number 87, number 87!" The deep, commanding, Greek-
accented voice of the owner/cook bellowed their order number
over the din. His tone left no doubt that he expected the cus-
tomers to pick up their orders promptly, if not sooner.

"That's us," Connor said, checking her receipt. "Be right
back." She returned with an overloaded tray.

"Did we order all this?" Laura asked in some amazement.

"I wanted to try more than one thing."

"I guess you did."

Laura helped unload the tray. Souvlaki, chicken kebabs, gyro
meat, hummus, rice, Greek salad, potatoes, and piping hot pitas.
They both dug in and ate in companionable silence for a few
minutes.

Connor paused after several bites from different plates. "This
is fabulous. I didn't know how hungry I was. Seems as if I
haven't been really hungry for a long time."

Laura nodded and responded to the first statement rather than the second. "It really is good, and he keeps the prices fair and the portions big enough to fill up starving students."

Connor took a sip of her soda. "I see I'm not the only Dr. Pepper fan."

"It's about all I drink other than water," Laura responded, grinning again. "It goes perfectly with green chile, sopaipillas, carne adovada, and breakfast burritos."

"Dare I ask what any of those are?"

"You might as well wait until you have them in front of you. It's easier to demonstrate than to explain."

Connor looked across the street. "That's the University of New Mexico?"

"Yes. New Mexico State is down in Las Cruces, the southern part. There's a community college in town, and there's the College of Santa Fe, which is a private school. And of course, there's St. John's College."

"There's a St. John's in Maryland, too."

"Same school, same curriculum, reading for a degree, studying the great literature of the world. But you would know all about that, you attended Oxford University, didn't you?"

"Yes, I did, but how did you know that?"

"I've been known to read a book or two, including the book jackets." The twinkle was back in her eyes.

"I'm sorry, Laura, I didn't mean for you to think...."

"Of course you didn't. I was just teasing. Fact is, the majority of the people I've driven seem to think that I must be stupid and lacking in ambition because of this job. Or, they 'take a great interest' in me, inquiring what it's like to be an Indian, oops, Native American."

Connor sat back in her booth, pushing the plates aside. "And what do you tell them?"

"I tell them it's like being a white person without all the accessories."

Connor stared at her for a moment, then burst out laughing. Others in the restaurant glanced over at the two women enjoying some private joke.

"You know, you're very...unexpected."

"I think I'll take that as a compliment," Laura said, raising her Dr. Pepper in a mock toast.

"You should. I like unpredictable, non-conforming people." Without warning, Ariana's face appeared in her mind. That was one reason she'd fallen in love with her—one never knew what to expect. Only too late had she discovered there was also a down-side to unpredictability. Connor shook herself ever so slightly to dislodge the image. If Laura noted the shadow that passed over the other woman's face, she did not comment. Instead she picked up her sunglasses.

"So, shall we be on our way, or is there somewhere else you'd like to go here?"

Connor thought for a moment. "Are there any good bookstores?" Wherever she traveled, she loved to indulge her passion for books.

"I don't know if there are really special ones, we have all the usual chains and there is...well, there is a good women's bookstore just around the block." She offered this information with careful diffidence, and Connor recognized and appreciated her discretion.

"Sounds great, let's take a look before we set out for Santa Fe."

Outside the cafe, Connor patted her stomach and announced that she would rather walk than drive the short distance to the women's bookstore.

Oddly, Laura looked less than pleased with the idea of walking. "Sure, but if you don't mind, I think I'll move the car, too. Just take a right at the corner, and a right at the next corner. I'll meet you there."

Connor was surprised. The car was legally parked and still had half an hour on the meter. Surely crime was not rampant in this sprawling Western city, and Laura did not appear the least bit lazy. But then perhaps the woman was responsible for damages or whatnot. If it made her feel better to keep the automobile in sight, so be it. Connor set off walking. Despite a chill edge to the air that promised a cold night, the sun was deliciously warm on her shoulders as she turned down a pleasant, tree-lined street with brick sidewalks. It had a residential neighborhood feel to it despite the numerous commercial concerns—a coffeehouse, a few small restaurants, a gallery of some sort, and, of all things, a piercing and tattoo parlor, the appearance of which completely debunked all the preconceived notions Connor had about the danger and seediness of such places. Further on down the street, Connor could see rows of homes and small apartment buildings, probably off-campus student housing, she assumed, and so different from her own university experience at Oxford.

Just as she reached the next corner, the Mercedes pulled up at the stop sign, Laura waved, and turned right. Connor followed suit, watching her driver pull the car up to the curb ahead. Laura was standing outside the bookstore examining a rolling cart of sale books when Connor came to stand beside her. "Full Circle Books" read the sign. Connor liked the name and the location; now it was left to discover if she liked what was in it.

She did. The store was warm and colorful and, as Connor wandered the aisles, she was genuinely impressed by the range of titles and genres. It was unexpectedly comprehensive for a relatively small retail space. A wealth of women's talent, spiritual essence, and experience was represented. Augmenting the book collection were jewelry, calendars, cards, gifts, all expressing a women's theme, but without rancor or bitterness. Connor rather appreciated that. Over the years, she had observed and endured the rabid militance and white-hot anger among some of her friends.

The only fruit of such anger, though, seemed to be a sad emptiness. Hating others didn't do much for the one doing the hating. But, on the other hand, she wondered if this might be just another rationalization to avoid direct conflict. While she had never been less than open about her sexual orientation, she still watched the Gay Pride marches from a distance. Her books contained no lesbian characters; she wrote no moving oratory to deliver at rallies; she had never even been to that Michigan Women's Festival. Connor had always felt that her openness was her contribution, but she was never quite sure. It was possible she was sidestepping the issue.

She was also intelligent enough to know that, despite being "out" as a lesbian, her wealth, social position, and successful career insulated her from the sorts of obstacles and discrimination against which many lesbians battled every day. Their lives were markedly different from her own. Perhaps that is why they were willing to fight, and perhaps anger was what sustained them. With a start, Connor realized she had been standing in one place for a long time. These philosophical binges in which she had indulged lately were beginning to worry her, particularly when she embarked on them while in public.

She looked up and noted that Laura was standing at the counter chatting amiably with a salesclerk. From their expressions and the words she caught here and there, it was clearly a conversation between people who already knew each other. Connor smiled to herself; she deduced that her initial hunch about Laura had been correct. Passing the mystery section, she experienced that tiny freshet of excitement she was almost embarrassed to acknowledge when she saw her titles prominently displayed. She still felt an almost childlike pleasure in seeing her work published and she was not yet jaded enough to pretend she didn't.

However, she wasn't quite prepared for the breathless enthusiasm of the young woman behind the counter when Connor set down the armload of books she had amassed during her browsing.

"You're Connor Hawthorne!" This could have been taken as either a question or a statement, so Connor simply smiled and nodded.

"I can't believe it. I just read *Truth on Trial*. It was great."

"Thank you, I'm glad you liked it." Connor had yet to come up with much that was original when responding to compliments. What was one supposed to say anyway?

"Wait, I've got to call Mary. She's the owner. She's upstairs. She's had two mysteries published...well of course they're real lesbian mysteries, so they're not quite like yours, but...." She was babbling now while dialing the phone, presumably an upstairs extension. Connor couldn't tell if her own work was being unfavorably compared with that of the bookstore owner, but she wasn't offended. She had, after all, just been wondering if perhaps her crime novels suffered for lack of lesbian consciousness.

A solidly built, smiling woman of moderate stature descended the rickety wooden stairs. She strode forward immediately and enfolded Connor's hand in a warm, two-palmed embrace.

"Ms. Hawthorne, I'm Mary Morell. It's a pleasure to have you here."

"It's a pleasure to be here, Ms. Morell."

"Please, call me Mary."

"Then you must call me Connor. And I have to tell you that I simply love this place." She waved at the tower of more than a dozen books she had stacked on the counter. "I'm not sure I can stop, even now."

"That's why I own a bookstore. I can't stop either."

"But your assistant tells me you are also an author. I'm sorry to say I haven't read your work, though I'm sure it's at Lammas in Washington. What house do you work with?"

"Spinsters Ink," Mary said. "I would be pleased if you would accept a copy of my first book as a gift."

"Only if you would consent to autograph it for me," Connor replied, responding easily to the owner's graciousness and warmth.

"In that case perhaps you would sign a couple of yours for the store. We'll be holding a special fund-raiser next month, and they would make excellent door prizes for the raffle."

"I'll do better than that," Connor replied. "I know you can't keep too many of any one title on hand. I'll be happy to sign all the copies you have here, and I'll have my publisher send you replacements for them, as my gift."

Mary didn't protest the gesture, nor did she gush with gratitude, a reaction Connor respected a great deal. The woman simply looked at her for a moment, said, "Thank you," and went off to gather up the books. Connor sat at a small folding table in the back of the store and signed the dozen or so novels. When she finished, she asked the sales clerk to ring up her purchases. As she signed the proffered credit card receipt, Mary appeared once more from the upstairs, book in hand.

"Here it is...a different kind of story than you write...."

"I know, I know," Connor smiled apologetically and held up

her hand, palm outward in a gesture of apology. "Mine don't have any real lesbians in them." The young woman behind the counter blushed a little. "I'll have to work on that." She tucked the autographed copy of Mary Morell's *Final Session* into her bulging bag and reached for Mary's hand once more. "Thank you so much. I can't tell you just why, but this has really made my day."

"Come back and see us," she said, her gesture taking in Laura, who nodded in agreement. Connor smiled and said, "I shall, indeed...you can count on it."

On the pavement, Laura reached for the sack of books. "I'll put that in the trunk." Once back in the car, Laura looked at Connor in the rearview mirror. "Sorry about all that. I didn't realize they'd make such a fuss."

"Don't apologize. It wasn't a fuss, and it was no bother. It's nice to know I have fans all the way out here in the Land of Enchantment."

Laura raised an eyebrow as if to ask how she knew the state's official nickname.

"It's on the license plates...I've been known to be observant a time or two."

"Touché," Laura said, smiling.

They slid back down Central to the interstate and the car accelerated smoothly into the traffic. Within twenty minutes they were on the outskirts of Albuquerque and Connor had fallen asleep.

Laura set the cruise control and found a niche in the right lane. Once on autopilot, she could relax a little and cast a glance every now and then toward the rearview mirror. She was beginning to rather like this multifaceted woman. Clearly, Connor had a sense of humor, she was very smart, and she was kind and courteous to other people. Laura was reminded how easy it was to develop preconceived notions about people, and how often those notions were false.

What she had expected was some version of an uptight, classconscious, money-waving celebrity who, though an avowed lesbian, had long since abandoned (or never possessed) any sensitivity to women's issues or people in general. Maybe it was partly that her books were peopled exclusively by heterosexual, fairly conformist characters. Or perhaps it was the face that appeared on the book jackets. Those eyes seemed distant, uninvolved, the mouth tight, the jaw a little clenched. That face was aloof and stony.

The face reflected in her rearview mirror was very different. This woman was sad, yes, and given the loss of her lover only a few months ago, that was natural. But her countenance was fluid and expressive, her all too fleeting smiles warm and genuine. She was certainly not the "cold-hearted bitch with a cash register where her heart should be"—as an ego-bruised young male writer had labeled her in response to Connor's unflattering, and perhaps harsh, review of his own novel.

Laura pondered just who the real-life Connor Hawthorne might be. What she saw initially, beneath all that reserve, was a human being with a great capacity for love and kindness and generosity. Oddly, this worried her. Laura had her own special ESP, partly based on extreme intelligence, partly on her heritage and the spiritual values of her family which, among other things, taught her to trust her own instincts and her own wisdom. There was much more to all of this than she had anticipated.

The last billboards and gas stations fell behind them and Laura let the car gather momentum. As she pulled out to pass a pokey old pickup truck, her passenger awoke.

"The speed limits are higher out here," Connor commented, as the powerful engine maintained an effortless 75 mph.

"They have to be or it would take forever to get anywhere."

Connor gazed out the window. To her left, the sun was going down in a...what? A blaze? A fiery torrent of colors? Why were there so many clichés associated with sunsets, and so few words that really conveyed the feeling they gave you? Even if she, the wordsmith, could not find them, however, there it was—bigger and more grand than anything she had ever seen. Part of the effect was produced by the sheer breadth of the horizon. When, after all, had she ever seen so much of the heavens at one time? And for the first time in her life, Connor knew what the person had in mind who first used the word "big" to describe the sky.

"Over to the west, on a nice, clear day, you can see Arizona," Laura said.

Connor looked amazed and a little skeptical. "But surely we aren't that close to the border?"

"Oh, a hundred miles or so."

Connor just shook her head in wonderment.

"Isn't this a clear day?" she asked, surveying the unrealistically blue sky, which looked for all the world like a giant postcard. Perhaps Laura was pulling her leg.

"No, it's been getting pretty cold at night, and when people are using their fireplaces, it gets kind of hazy. Up north, you'll notice the difference. That and the billboard jungle around the city kind of ruins the effect."

"If you think this is hazy, you should try Washington, D.C. in August."

"I have, wouldn't go back there for any amount of money."

"Smart woman."

They lapsed into silence and Connor returned to her study of the countryside. What had seemed only brownness viewed from the plane now revealed itself as much more than that—a curious mix of solemn earth tones, gray-green chamisa, twisted piñon pine, rabbit brush, and upthrust jumbles of stone. As they climbed toward Santa Fe, 2,000 feet higher in altitude than Albuquerque, they dipped in and out of shallow canyons cut by Mother Nature and highway construction engineers. Rock formations shaped like miniature plateaus were striated with rusty reds and soft browns and warm beiges. The last rays of sun lit up these walls of living stone until they glowed.

"This landscape doesn't seem as barren as I thought it would."

"Some people don't realize that this isn't really the desert, not like Death Valley or the Sahara. Here, we're on an enormous mesa, a tableland sitting between the Jemez Mountains and the Sangre de Cristo Mountains. They're like two arms of the Rockies. Once we reach Santa Fe, we'll be at about 7,000 feet and the mountains around the city are the Sangres. The Santa Fe Ski Basin tops out around 11,000 feet, I think."

"We must be climbing, my ears are popping," Connor said.

"We have been for a while, but more gradually. Here, it's steeper. This is the infamous La Bajada Hill where winter weather eats bad drivers for lunch, and is a general pain in the neck for people without snow tires or chains when a storm hits. When we get to the top, we're a little less than 20 miles from Santa Fe."

A minute later they crested the rise and there it was. In the twilight, stretched out ahead of them, the lights of Santa Fe sparkled against a backdrop of shadowy landscape and amidst the embrace of imposing mountains. It quite literally left Connor speechless.

As they began to pass Santa Fe exits, Laura explained they would take the scenic route. "Cerrillos Road has become one big strip shopping center," she said, her tone indicating that she regretted the evolution. "And St. Francis Drive is the main route north to Taos and Chama and the western part of Colorado. We'll take Old Pecos Trail, which becomes Old Santa Fe Trail, and be touristy about it."

Connor smiled and sat back to enjoy the view.

The two-lane road wound its way into the heart of Santa Fe. The houses were almost all adobe of one shade of brown or another, and clung to the landscape as if they had grown from it. It was easy to see why *Conde Nast* magazine had ranked this small town among the top tourist destinations in the United States. It fulfilled all the standard requirements: it was uniquely charming, old world in a frontier sort of way, and, from what Connor could see, chock full of shopping opportunities. It lived up to its Chamber of Commerce inspired nickname: The City Different.

Dodging self-absorbed tourists who wandered across streets as if automobiles were merely illusory, Laura turned right at San Francisco Street just before Old Santa Fe Trail joined the Plaza. She paused to let a family, who had chosen the very middle of the street to strike a pose, take a photograph.

"Do they even know we're here?" Connor said, imagining how dead these tourists would be if they had tried this in the middle of Pennsylvania Avenue.

"If you think this is bad, you should see it in the summer. The reason they're standing there is because that's Saint Francis Cathedral ahead of us, as in the Francis who gave the city its name."

"Am I missing something?" Connor asked. "My Spanish isn't all that good, but I thought St. Francis would translate something like San Francisco."

"That's because Santa Fe is the shorthand version of the name. The whole thing is quite a mouthful. It translates in English as 'The Royal City of Holy Faith of St. Francis of Assisi.' Santa Fe is the 'holy faith' part."

"One of the legacies of the Spanish conquistadors?"

"One of the least regrettable anyway." A shadow of a frown crossed Laura's face, but before Connor could ask her to elaborate, the tourists finally perfected their camera shot and vacated the street. Laura swung into a parking garage and announced, "We're here."

"Where's here?"

"La Fonda, the 'Inn at the end of the Santa Fe Trail.' The agency booked you in here. Your conference is at the Eldorado Hotel, just a couple blocks away. But it's fairly new. This place is more what visitors think of as 'authentic.'" She flashed a smile to let Connor know she was being facetious, and jumped out to summon a bellman and open the trunk.

"If you go right through that door," Laura pointed, "and follow the corridor, you'll find the front desk."

Connor did as she was told, but had only made it halfway down the hallway by the time Laura showed up with the bellman and the luggage. This was Connor's first taste of "Santa Fe Style," complete with adobe walls, high, round-beamed ceilings (she would later learn the beams were called *vigas*), and polished, Spanish tile floors. She focused with rapt attention on a display window for one of La Fonda's resident shops. The jewelry, fashioned of silver, turquoise, and various kinds of shell, was gorgeous and dramatic—bracelets, rings, necklaces, and what she supposed might be hat bands. Laura handed the bellman several dollars and sent him ahead to wait at the desk.

"Something else we're known for, we Indians that is."

"I'd heard of Indian jewelry, even seen some somewhere, but not like this."

"These are pieces of art, original designs signed by the artist. I think those are by Raymond George Tsosie."

"They're beautiful."

"True, but there's a lot to see. You might want to hold off your buying decisions for a day or two. It's a shame the flea market isn't still open this late in the year. You could get great stuff for half the money. Anyway, why don't we get checked in, and then you can decide what you want to look at first."

"We?"

"The agency booked a room for me as well. Your father asked that I be at your disposal while you're here. Sort of on 24-hour call."

"Is that something you usually do for clients?" Connor inquired, her intuition tickling at the back of her brain. Something wasn't quite right about this.

"Not too often. Most people can't afford it," she answered cheerfully and led the way to the lobby. At the front desk, which bore a strong resemblance to a sturdy saloon bar, Connor gave her name and handed over her credit card.

The pleasant young woman at the desk, who displayed a propensity for what would charitably be described as very dramatic makeup and alarmingly large hair, was prompt and friendly, immediately handing over two keys.

"You have rooms 204 and 206," she said, eyeing Laura for the first time. "One for you and one for...." She hesitated, not sure of the relationship between the two women.

"Just don't say 'daughter' please," Connor thought. "I can't be that much older." Aloud, she prompted the clerk. "My assistant."

Having tolerated the bellman's enthusiastic tour of her

painstakingly quaint, though somewhat small room, and having
rewarded his zeal appropriately, Connor opened the window,
which gave onto Old Santa Fe Trail and afforded her an angled
view of the Plaza. The very last trickles of golden orange light
surfed the horizon. The air felt clean and cool and dry. Everything—no matter the color, whether in sun or shadow—was
vivid, and cleanly delineated. It made her feel alive, made her
want to touch the buildings, the grass on the Plaza, the metal
sculptures, the wooden benches. After several minutes lost in
contemplation, she became aware that she was surprisingly hungry given the large lunch she had consumed. She looked at her
watch. It was only 6:30 or so. Perhaps it was the altitude causing
these hunger pangs.

Sitting down on the high-slung bed, she glanced at the telephone instructions and dialed 206. Laura answered immediately.

"Where do you recommend for dinner?"

"Depends. There are lots of restaurants. I think it's about one
restaurant or cafe for every 2.2 people in town. But if you're
tired, the one in the hotel is good, *La Plazuela*…has New Mexican specialties and some Anglo food if you're not up to adventure. Word has it the chef is exceptional."

"That sounds fine," Connor said, smiling. "How about 15
minutes or so to have a wash and brush up? I'll meet you in the
lobby or somewhere in between."

Laura hesitated. "You want me to join you?"

Connor thought they had settled the protocol question. But it
occurred to her that maybe she was thoughtlessly infringing on
Laura's personal time.

"Yes, but I shouldn't assume you don't have something else
to do."

"No, it isn't that at all, it's just that…."

"We're not doing that 'me boss, you serving girl' thing are we?" Laura laughed out loud. "No, we're not. See you in 15."

The dining room at La Fonda was more in the nature of an indoor courtyard, surrounded by scrollwork screens, trellises, plants, and furnished in a Spanish colonial style. Laura took her through an explanation of such delicacies as tamales, chile rellenos, blue corn tortillas, black bean soup, posole, and, most importantly, the distinction between green chile and red chile, both of which Connor tried, and both of which left her wishing the margarita glasses were bigger, or the water pitcher were nearer. She had to admit, though, that she really liked the food.

During dinner, Laura offered various bits of historical data about La Fonda and about Santa Fe. Connor, as always, mentally catalogued the bare facts, but proved more interested in people. A bit hesitantly, she said, "I don't know a lot about Native American culture. What, uh…what people do you come from?" She wasn't sure the word "tribe" was still acceptable and she wasn't even sure she should ask. But she found Laura intriguing, certainly outside whatever stereotypes Connor had absorbed over the years.

Laura did not appear the least bit offended. If anything, she seemed gently amused. As if pulling Connor's thoughts right out of the air, she said, "You can ask what tribe, although some Indians do not refer to themselves as a tribe. I happen to be Navajo, though I think there must have been some Anglo hankypanky in there somewhere. My facial structure is a little different than the generally accepted ethnological characteristics of the People."

As if sensing the capital "p" in the last word, Connor raised an eyebrow, a gesture Laura would come to recognize as usually interrogative, though occasionally skeptical.

"The People, the Dineh. Navajo is a name given to us by the Spaniards. The stories tell us where the People came from and how we must live in harmony with the world around us. The central theme, the Navajo Way, if you will, is about harmony. But that's a very long story and it's getting late for you."

"I'm fine. And I'd love to hear more. Are most of the Indians in New Mexico Navajo?"

"No. In northern New Mexico, there are mostly the Pueblo Indians—the Zuni, Acoma, Santo Domingo, Tesuque, Pojoaque, Taos, San Ildefonso and Nambe—what are called the Eight Northern Pueblos. Farther west from here are the Hopi, among the traditional enemies of the Navajo, and more to the south, several bands of Apaches, the Mescalero, the Jicarilla, and so on. And a lot of us are sort of mongrels I suppose, with intermarriage between the tribes."

"Where is your family?"

"On the rez. Up around the Four Corners where New Mexico, Colorado, Arizona, and Utah meet. Navajo Tribal lands straddle all four states. What we call Dinetah. It is our home between the four sacred mountains.

Laura looked at her watch.

"It's getting late. You're due at the Eldorado at 9:30...the keynote speaker, I believe."

Connor continued to be amazed at the preparation this woman had made for her arrival. Talk about doing one's homework. Apparently her entire schedule had been committed to Laura's memory. Looking at her own watch, Connor was amazed to discover that more than three hours had passed. And her body was still on Eastern Time. That translated to almost midnight as far as her internal clock was concerned. Most of the tables around them were already empty.

"You go ahead. I'll wait for the check," Laura offered.

"But...."

"Charged to your room, of course," Laura grinned mischievously.

"Good, then you should also know I'm a generous tipper."

"A full 20 percent it is. Good night, Connor."

Clad in her nightshirt, Connor took one more look at the night sky, now swollen with stars, then glanced across to the well-lit Plaza. She was surprised to see someone who looked like Laura striding purposefully away from the hotel, using the sidewalk diagonally bisecting the square of grass and trees. Same brown jacket, long braid. Or maybe not. It's just that she had had the distinct impression that Laura had been headed for her own room.

With this small mystery unsolved and filed for later consideration, Connor slipped in between the soft, cool sheets, pulled the fluffy quilt over her in deference to the crisp temperature, and went immediately and soundly to sleep.

———◦◦◦———

He saw the Indian woman come out of the side door of La Fonda. But she wasn't his concern. That dyke bitch in the hotel was. He'd waited weeks for her to get back from England because the big boss had said, 'not in Europe,' and then the fucking Senator had sprinkled bodyguards all over the place until she left again for New Mexico. It really annoyed him that she'd given him the slip at the airport. He had not been informed that someone had arranged a car and driver. Phone taps on her house and he still couldn't stay ahead of her. Fortunately, he knew where she'd be staying. He'd raced to Santa Fe in his rental car, then ended up waiting for hours until the silver Mercedes showed up.

He'd convinced himself there had been another change of plan and had started formulating excuses for his failure when he saw the car turn the corner and pause for some stupid tourists, just a half-dozen yards ahead of where he was parked at a meter.

Now, he was tired and hungry. He didn't like to be hanging around outside this long, but he had to be sure she didn't go anywhere, and he didn't dare wait inside the lobby. Considering his assignment, it would hardly do for some observant security guard to notice him, or worse, start wondering what he was doing there.

By 11:00 P.M. he was convinced she wouldn't be leaving the hotel until morning. And he knew perfectly well where she would be. He circled halfway around the Plaza, continued on Palace Avenue until it became Sandoval Street, then turned right on San Francisco and pulled into the parking garage under the Eldorado Hotel. Surrendering his keys to the night attendant, he took the elevator directly to the fifth floor, room 523. He let himself in, only slightly startled to discover that he wasn't alone.

CHAPTER SEVEN

———◦◦◦———

And oftentimes, to win us to our harm,
The instruments of darkness tell us truths;
Win us with honest trifles, to betray us
in deepest consequence.
—William Shakespeare

———◦◦◦———

Saturday, November 30
Santa Fe, New Mexico

The annual Society of Mystery Writers Conference was being held in Santa Fe this year primarily because the current president of the Society, Geoffrey Amyas Clarke, had visited the city two years earlier, become completely enamored of it, and thereafter been determined to stage some major event in this "iridescent jewel of the Southwest," as he put it. The phrase was as Clarkesian as was his verbose, flowery prose and his stilted pen-name, both indicative of Geoffrey's frustrated desire to be British rather than American. He was, in fact, a native of Harborville, Indiana, a biographical detail which never appeared on dust jackets or in press releases. His consistently predictable books about a British police officer's crime-solving adventures sold well in America, though Brits found them more comedic than suspenseful. As for Connor, she didn't particularly care for them, or for him. So it was with some irritation that she heard the sound of his voice behind her, raised in fulsome, gratuitous praise, as she entered the lobby of the Eldorado Hotel.

"Connor Hawthorne! How simply marvelous to have *the* most famous mystery writer in the country right here at our little conference. Look, everyone, it's Connor Hawthorne."

Connor knew there was as much sarcasm as flamboyance in this outburst, but she chose to hold her temper. Swinging around to face him, she said, "Geoffrey, how good to see you." He clasped her hands in both of his, looking approximately as sincere as a hyena smiling kindly at its dinner.

"It is so very good to see you, dear lady. I cannot tell you how devastated I was to hear about Ariana, absolutely devastated. You must be simply destroyed by it all. But, of course, you must put it behind you. And you must join us for lunch."

Connor, dumbfounded at the insensitivity with which this foppish fool could dismiss the death of her lover in four sentences, looked behind him to see whom this "us" might include. She recognized only Marsha Malitson, author of a successful series of books based on the character of an Italian-American cop in New York City. The two women behind Marsha were strangers to Connor.

Then she glanced toward the front door where Laura stood chatting with the concierge. "So sorry, Geoffrey, but I already have plans."

Always observant, and always on the lookout for juicy personal details of other people's lives, he swiveled both his eyes and his gossip radar in the direction Connor was looking. Spotting Laura, he emitted a high-pitched, girlish giggle (a sound that Connor, despite lifelong efforts at tolerance, could not stand to hear coming from a grown man...or woman).

"I see you do. Not letting any grass grow under our feet, are

we? Or should that be, not letting the sheets get cold?" He managed to invest this last tasteless comment with a leering malice
that both sickened and embarrassed Connor. Geoffrey, of course,
interpreted the rising color in her face to his having hit the mark.
"Not to worry, dear. Life does go on. We're none of us getting
any younger now, are we?"

The fact that Clarke was a 55-year-old man trying desperately
to look 25 belied his grasp of this wisdom, Connor thought,
firmly pulling her hand from his sweaty grasp. "If you'll excuse
me, I believe I'm due at the...." She looked down at the schedule "...Anasazi Room just about now." She turned on her heel
and left. Geoffrey, pleased with the encounter, transferred his attention to the young Indian woman who was looking at Connor's departing back.

"Robbing the cradle now, aren't we, ducks?" he said under
his breath. He was unpleasantly startled to see the young
woman's dark eyes fix directly on him. He looked away uncomfortably. Geoffrey Clarke was a poisonous snake, whose
conversations dripped with innuendo and sarcasm. But he was
also a coward who rarely looked anyone in the eye. Under
Laura's stern observation, he dropped his eyes again and felt a
twinge of fear he could not explain. When he looked up again,
she was gone.

Connor gave what she hoped was an interesting, informative,
and organized presentation on the challenges of incorporating
legal terminology and procedure into fictional stories and books,
after which she fielded questions from the audience of some 120
writers, questions ranging from the absurd, to the obvious, to the
occasionally perspicacious.

One dark-haired, olive-skinned woman in a white silk pants
suit offered several intelligent, thoughtful questions and observa-

tions. She spoke with an accent Connor thought might be French. It was difficult to tell over the buzz of voices in the room, and Connor could not place her until, after the question and answer period, the woman introduced herself.

"Ms. Hawthorne, I am Celestine Trouville." The name rang a bell, though the face did not. Connor had seen something in a literary publication. Celestine Trouville was a new young writer from France, and her work, a hybrid of mystery and romance, had become so popular there that an American publisher had undertaken to have English translations released in this country.

"C'est un plaisir de faire votre connaissance, Mademoiselle Trou-ville," Connor responded, dusting off her rusty but, she hoped, correctly pronounced French.

"Your accent, it is excellent," the woman said, both pleased and surprised. "But please, I must practice your language. Your French is much better than my English."

"I doubt that," said Connor graciously. "Your questions were very welcome. You understood what I was trying to say."

"But of course. It is important to you to have, how do you say, the authenticity, the reality, in your stories. I, too, believe that it is important. My work, though, is not about such intellectual topics. It is not very technical. Only romance and a bit of mystery perhaps. I admire very much your enormous skill."

Shaking her head as if to dismiss this somewhat excessive, though well-meaning praise, Connor laughed. "Now, remember, a writer has first to believe in herself. Comparing your work to that of others is the surest way to make yourself crazy."

There were others standing behind Celestine in an improvised waiting line, and when the French woman saw Connor's eyes flick toward those behind her, she instantly apologized.

"Oh, but I am keeping you from others who wish to speak

with you. Is it…perhaps it is too forward of me since we are not well acquainted, but is it possible that we might dine together at the lunch interval?"

The invitation was clearly sincere and entirely well-meant, unlike the one she'd received earlier in the morning, but Connor felt a need to get away from all of this for a while. A little hero worship went a long way even though this woman was rather more interesting and clearly less callow than some of the young, ambitious writers who had sought her advice and occasionally her bed. Still, Connor was courteous and kind. "I'm afraid I already have plans for lunch, Mademoiselle Trouville. Perhaps later."

The woman looked a bit disappointed, but smiled graciously in a manner that crinkled her nose with just a hint of flirtation. "But of course, Mademoiselle Hawthorne, a woman such as you is engaged always."

Not willing to play the part of the perpetually busy, sought-after celebrity, Connor reached for her arm as the young French woman turned away. "No, please, it's Connor first of all, and if you are free, we could have dinner later. I'm at La Fonda. Call me there."

Her invitation was received with what could almost be a grin. "*Merci beaucoup*, Connor. Until this evening, then."

An hour or so later, Connor had dealt, she hoped patiently, with admirers, detractors, competitors (they thought so, not she), and had declined three solicitations from would-be agents who were uniformly disappointed to find she was steadfastly committed to the woman who had loyally represented her since long before 'Connor Hawthorne' became a household name. Emerging from the meeting room, she was delighted to catch a glimpse of Laura, leaning against the glass wall separating the corridor from the open courtyard.

"How about some lunch?"

"Don't you have to lunch with your colleagues?" Laura's eyes took in the diverse, some might say colorful crowd milling about. Connor thought she detected a certain wry amusement in her tone.

"They're an odd lot," she said, smiling. "No reason I have to eat lunch with them. I've got two hours before the afternoon session. So we're off. You name the place."

"Whatever you say, boss." Laura grinned and picked up the leather briefcase Connor had set down.

"I can carry that," she protested.

"Of course you can. But I have to do something to earn my keep." She showed no signs of relinquishing the case, so Connor just shook her head in mock disgust and followed Laura out of the hotel.

After another green chile experience at a little place called Tia Sophia's, Connor returned to the Eldorado and the afternoon session. It dragged on in spots, but she wished to extend the same courtesy to her colleagues as they had shown her. Connor's keynote address had been very well-attended. She felt sorry for some of those whose workshops and presentations were only sparsely populated so she made a point of dropping in here and there to show her encouragement and support. Being a writer was difficult, getting published was a formidable challenge, and holding on to the public's interest was something that kept authors and their publishers awake nights. Even when she did not care for a particular book, Connor believed that the process of writing it deserved respect.

True, she was not very good at dissimulation. When specifically asked for her opinion, Connor tended to be honest. On the other hand, she never went out of her way to condemn someone else's work. She simply would not lie about it. She believed that for every person, there is some principle, some aspect of life which is of such fundamental importance or significance that dishonesty where it is concerned cannot be countenanced. For Connor, the written word was magical, or at least the right words put together in the right way was magical. Creating solidly literate and meaningful prose was, to her, the equivalent of worshipping at the altar of the mind. To know that millions, or thousands, or even just one other human being could be moved or mesmerized or tantalized by the words she put on paper was, for her, an awesome responsibility and a decided privilege.

She was in total agreement with a character (also a novelist) in a book by one of Connor's personal heroes, Dorothy L. Sayers, when she said, "At least, when you've got the thing dead right, and you know it's dead right, there's no excitement like it. It's marvelous. It makes you feel like God on the Seventh Day, for a bit anyhow." That is precisely how Connor felt about her work, though she had discovered her love of writing and her gift for it rather later in life than some of her professional peers. They were the most vocal critics initially simply because some didn't think she'd paid her dues; fame had come too easily, too quickly. It did no good for her to point out that her apprenticeship had been served in a different place—law school and the district attorney's office. She had spent years preparing cases and prosecuting accused criminals; she'd averaged 70 hours a week putting together evidence, testimony, and police reports. Few writers could boast of such experience.

Naturally, Connor recognized that some criticism was the product of envy. She had been successful with her first novel. On top of that, even if success had eluded her, she was a wealthy woman. Her fortunes did not rise or fall with the acceptance or rejection of her manuscripts. This some of her fellow writers found annoying in the extreme. As a result, Connor kept a fairly low profile. She didn't like squabbling with her colleagues, nor was she the sort to impose her own rigorous standards or her personal opinions on others. As far as she was concerned, there was an audience for every book, whether she personally cared for it or not.

What she could not tolerate, though, was sloppiness—whether it be in grammar, syntax, spelling, or proofreading. Those, as far as she was concerned were the tools of the trade. If you didn't have the tools, or the ability to acquire them, you oughtn't undertake to do the work. Students in the graduate seminars she taught at Georgetown had learned that dismissing English 101 as a joke when they were freshmen had probably been a mistake.

Connor herself was dismayed at the level of ignorance these students managed to maintain about their own language. Part of this, she understood, was due to the sharp contrast between American and British approaches to university-level education. But part of it was also the alarming deterioration of the public school system in the United States. It worried her that so many children could not read at all, and even young adults, raised on a steady diet of television commercials and billboard advertising thought "night" really was spelled "nite." One shuddered to think that some day the language might eventually be reduced to whatever was convenient to write or brief enough to fit on a sign.

All of this was running through Connor's mind as she waited for the speaker to answer a woman whom most of the audience had been unable to hear. She hoped she might be able to extrapolate the question from the answer. She couldn't, but she listened anyway. Finally, time was called and it was over, at least until the next day. Laura was waiting, as expected, and they walked back to La Fonda together.

As they rode the elevator up, Laura asked about dinner plans. Connor felt a wave of unexpected embarrassment when she realized she had promised to have dinner with the French author and hadn't given any thought to whether Laura had planned to dine with Connor. Thus, her tone wasn't quite as casual as she intended when she mentioned that fact to Laura as they approached their adjoining rooms.

"I'll be...uh...having dinner with one of the writers tonight. Maybe you've seen her books? Celestine Trouville, she's French, does mystery romances, or romantic mysteries, something like that. I've only glanced at one of them...of course only one has been translated and my French is pretty rusty." Connor realized she was babbling, which was absurd under the circumstances, but once one gets trapped on the babbling superhighway, it's hard to find an exit.

"Anyway, she's interested in getting some advice from me, or at least I imagine that's why she wants to buy me dinner. Usually that's the case with young writers—all curiosity. But I'll probably be in late, so I won't need you to drive or anything. Please have dinner here in the hotel if you'd like...on me." If she had anticipated any sort of negative reaction, she was pleasantly (or was it unpleasantly?) disappointed.

Laura only nodded, smiled, and said, "Catch you in the morning then. If you need me, just give a ring." And she was gone, the door clicking shut behind her.

The message light on the phone was blinking, and Connor retrieved a voice message from Celestine. The soft, almost shy voice, notable for its sibilant accents and sultry tone, suggested dinner at the *Old House*, the restaurant adjoining the Eldorado Hotel. Reservations had been made for 7:30, if that was not too presumptuous, and Celestine could be reached at the hotel. Connor smiled at the woman's Old World courtesy and left a message confirming the dinner engagement.

Over excellent wine and appetizers, the two women chatted comfortably about writing. Celestine still tended toward the role of admirer, but Connor insisted on spending most of the time discussing the other author's newest book. Celestine outlined the plot, throwing in some self-deprecating comments about improvements she had thought of only after the book went to press.

"That always happens," Connor assured her with a smile. "I can't tell you how much I hate rereading my own work. I see half a dozen changes I would make if I could do it all over again. But we just have to face the fact that nothing is ever going to be absolutely perfect."

These words, coming as they did from a best-selling author, appeared to reassure the young woman, who launched into yet another topic. Connor was trying to be attentive to the conversation, but her mind kept wandering away from the topic of whether romance and mystery could coexist effectively in one book. Overall, Connor doubted it; her own fiction kept very much to events and intricate plots. Her characters were well fleshed out, but they also did not dabble much in romance. Her preference for keeping personal and professional matters separate was reflected in her work. On the other hand, she would have to admit that at least one book, *Busman's Honeymoon*, by Dorothy L. Sayers, which had been described as a "love story with detective interruptions," was marvelously constructed and executed. While she pondered whether or not she might ever be able to produce a novel of that quality, she was startled into re-focusing on her dinner companion.

"But then what is sex but a most enjoyable recreation?"

Connor realized she had missed some vital conversational segue. The topic had strayed to more personal matters. Celestine was speaking about her lover, though in a rather elliptical way. She was, consciously or unconsciously, avoiding pronouns that would have revealed the gender of this person, something much easier to do in English than it would have been in French. She mentioned Michel. Or was it Michelle? Connor wasn't sure, but she suddenly had that flash of insight that told her what Celestine might be leading up to. Connor tuned back in as Celestine was saying,

"...and in France we are less tense—is that the word?— about making love. It is more natural to do it than not to do it. We make love because it is fun...if the moment is right, of course." The young woman laughed, a sound which was, if Connor admitted, extremely pleasing to the ear. But the direction of their conversation was taking a dangerous turn, at least as far as Connor was concerned, and Celestine's eyes were smoldering with an emotion that certainly had not been there earlier. Connor was pretty sure she could recognize lust, even in the eyes of a relative stranger.

These suspicions were confirmed by the expression of dismay on Celestine's face when Connor abruptly announced that the hour was late and she must be getting back. The disappointment was unmistakable, and, for the briefest moment, Connor thought she saw something else...a voracious hunger; in that instant she felt as if she were in the presence of a feline predator and the sensation made her recoil. But just as quickly the impression was gone, and Connor told herself she must be imagin-

ing things. Celestine was extremely cordial, insisting that she
would pay the dinner check. Connor assured her that the check
had already been taken care of. Now, she was anxious to extricate herself from a situation she should have anticipated much
sooner. She waited a few moments longer, then, taking the last
sip of her coffee, stood and offered her hand. Celestine stood
also, but ignored the proffered handshake.

"Ah, but you who have been to France should know better."
She quickly embraced Connor, then planted a kiss on both
cheeks, standing back to look at her affectionately. A quick
frown crossed her face, and she snatched up a napkin from the
table, brushing lightly at the lipstick smudges she had left behind.
Connor was instantly embarrassed by this vaguely intimate gesture and stepped back, away from the other woman's heady perfume and perfect lips. There it was again, that odd feeling of
something sinister. But Celestine quickly reverted to the uncertain, hesitant demeanor of her initial encounter that morning and
Connor felt foolish. "I must be tired," she thought. "I'm starting
to see threats everywhere I look."

"Ah, *bien.* You have many things to prepare for tomorrow,
and I have taken up too much of your time. Thank you so much
for dining with me."

The need to leave the dining room, which now seemed hot
and close rather than inviting and cozy, outweighed Connor's
desire to smooth over the awkwardness. She was upset and
honestly couldn't say why. This perfectly charming and beautiful woman had made flattering overtures, offering a night's pleasure with no strings attached. There was nothing wrong with
that. Celestine probably had not even heard of Ariana's death.
She may not have even known whether or not Connor had a
lover, though it seemed odd that she had not inquired, even

obliquely. Something about her, or just something about the situation, struck a discordant note. Was it intuition? Connor dismissed the notion as absurdly paranoid. She reminded herself that being as close to murder and attempted murder as she had been lately was bound to make the mind play tricks on her.

Celestine Trouville was just one more young, ambitious, emerging writer who wanted to find out about the "real" Connor Hawthorne, preferably from the vantage point of the neighboring pillow. For a fleeting moment, Connor wondered if she would ever again feel the soft embrace of a lover? Could there be anyone after Ariana? But even asking the question in her mind seemed disloyal. What she really needed was fresh air.

Connor forced a smile. "*Au revoir,* Celestine."

Laura tucked the book she had been pretending to read under her arm and looked up to see Connor leaving the *Old House,* exiting through the front door of the hotel. At the same time, she removed the tiny earpiece that attached to a cord looped through the collar of her jacket. The listening device under the table had worked perfectly. Admittedly, there had been nothing of consequence said as far as Laura could tell. Her experience told her this was nothing more than a chance encounter, nothing that had to be reported, at least not yet. But she would have to wait and see before she could act. And she had to be subtle. That was the most difficult part of being the "inside" person, she thought to herself with a small smile.

As she walked back to the hotel, only a flicker of her eyes indicated she was aware of the dark blue rental car, and the man inside of it.

Sunday, December 1
Santa Fe

Connor awoke to discover she had not drawn the curtains closed the evening before. The room was ablaze with light. It bounced off the whitewashed adobe and glinted from the polished surfaces of the furniture. The room was a veritable riot of color, and Connor's spirits soared with joy for a moment, only to be replaced with annoyance when she realized her day would be spent within the confines of conference rooms. Worse, it was unlikely the excitement level would increase on the second day. Usually, the best speakers and the most interesting topics were scheduled first on the agenda. She did not look forward to spending another day indoors when the world outside beckoned.

Then a thought struck her. "Who says I *have* to go?" But it was such a rebellious impulse, so out of keeping with her ordinarily responsible approach to life, that she almost abandoned the idea. Almost...but not quite. She rolled over and picked up the phone. Laura answered on the second ring.

"I want to go somewhere," she announced without preamble.

"Could you be a little more specific?" Laura chuckled.

"Out there, up north, some other state. I don't care."

"Okay," Laura said slowly, pondering. "But what about your conference?"

"To hell with it," Connor said with absolute conviction. "I

want to see places, not people."

"Do you want to check out of the hotel, or leave your things here and take a day trip?"

"Check out. I need to make a couple of phone calls, then I'll meet you downstairs. Say 45 minutes. And then I want something local for breakfast."

"No problem. I'll have the car around in 45 minutes." Before she could finish, Connor had rung off and started dialing the long series of numbers to use her phone card for a transatlantic call to Katy. She waited, listening to the uniquely European breep-breep buzzing of the phone ringing at Aunt Jessica's home in Oxfordshire where Katy would be spending the weekend. Just as she was about to give up, Katy herself snatched up the receiver.

"Hello?"

"Katy…it's Mom."

"Hi, Mom, are you back home?"

"No, I'm still in Santa Fe. But I'm headed up north to do some sightseeing, maybe Taos or someplace like that."

"Sounds great. What's it like out there?"

"Really different from Washington, or England. But I kind of like it. Talk about wide open spaces. You can see for a hundred miles in some places."

"Maybe sometime we could go there together."

Expressing a willingness to spend time with her mother was something new for Katy, and Connor avoided overreacting to it. She didn't want to sound like a starving person clutching at a proffered biscuit, so she kept her tone lighthearted. "I think that's a great idea. We could plan a trip during one of your breaks, and maybe do some horseback riding at one of these dude ranches I've read about."

"Sure, I'd like that. So when are you going back to D.C.?"

"Probably not for a couple of days."

"Well, you'd better send me a postcard."

"I'll do it today."

"Do you want to talk to Aunt Jessica?"

"Is she nearby?"

"Out in the garden."

"No, that's all right. Just give her my love."

"Oh, that reminds me. Grandma Gwen called and said we should tell you to get in touch with her right away."

"Did she say why?"

"No, but you know Grandma Gwen."

Connor sighed. "True. I'll try to give her a ring right now. If I don't connect with her, and you talk to her, you can report that the message was delivered and I'll keep trying."

"Sure thing. But don't forget. She seemed kind of intense about it."

"Will do. You take care of yourself, sweetheart. I know it's only been a couple of weeks, but I miss you like crazy."

"I kind of miss you too, Mom."

Connor could hear her daughter's smile across the thousands of miles that lay between them. "Gee, be careful with that mushy stuff or I'll get a swelled head. Bye, love!"

"Bye, Mom."

Connor hung up the phone and felt a surge of sheer happiness streak through her. It felt good, it made her smile, but in the next instant, it faded. She shouldn't be feeling happy, should she? How could she justify being joyous even for a moment? She was baffled by the contradiction and decided not to try and figure it out right that moment. So she started packing, forgetting about the request to call Grandmother Broadhurst, instead worrying that she might be late getting downstairs. Laura probably already had the car waiting in readiness. In this she was wrong.

Laura was still in her own room, engaged in a conversation that would have puzzled any eavesdropper.

"She wants to leave. Yes, leave here, leave Santa Fe...I don't know where yet, probably north...No, she isn't staying for the conference...Yes, I am aware that wasn't the plan...I'll just have to improvise...Yes...of course I'll stay in touch...I might need your help if anything crops up...No, not beyond what I've already reported. I'm not sure yet what the nature of that problem might be." She continued to speak for several minutes, giving a detailed and discreetly worded report. Then she put down the receiver, picked up her jacket and overnight bag, and headed for the parking garage.

Twenty minutes after a delightfully new experience known as smothered breakfast burritos at a locals hangout on Cerrillos Road called The Pantry, Connor and Laura were just cresting the "Opera Hill," a stretch of road so named because it climbed to the ridge where the world renowned Santa Fe Opera House stood overlooking New Mexico, or at least significant portions of it. The next rise, just past the flea market, which was closed for the season, brought Connor face to face with yet another view that stunned her. She was beginning to think this state had no shortage of magnificent panoramas, and she was not easily impressed by scenery. She had, after all, seen the Swiss Alps, the Scottish moors, the sunsets over Montego Bay.

But this land...it was immense and so utterly different from anything she had ever seen. There were few superlatives adequate to describe either the landscape or the feelings it aroused. Could anyone see this and not be moved by it? Connor asked the question out loud. Laura nodded in the affirmative.

"You would be amazed at how many people I've driven over

this rise who look up at it, say, 'oh, that's pretty,' and go right
back to whatever they were doing or saying."

"You're kidding, right?"

"Nope."

"Unbelievable! Would you mind pulling over for a minute? I
want to take it all in."

Before them the high desert seemed to stretch out forever.
Here and there towered mesas like layer cakes with horizontal
stripes of red clay and sandstone; clumps of pinon, chamisa, and
cactus hugged the hillsides and dotted the tableland. All around
them the mountains, white-dusted tops gleaming in the morning sun, protected the enormous valley, as if to keep one from
falling off the world. These were the fanciful thoughts that
crowded Connor's mind, so much so that she had not even noticed Laura signaling and pulling off to the side.

"It's one of my favorite places, too," she said quietly. "I love
coming over this rise and seeing it all over again."

Connor sat there for a moment longer. "Is it like this where
your family lives?"

"A little," Laura nodded. "But different, too. Less hospitable
perhaps, but then you wouldn't really want to be lost anywhere
in Northern New Mexico or Arizona. Not a lot of water. The
beauty here isn't about lushness or limitless abundance. Here you
find harsh beauty in a place that has grown old, and weathered
and still survives because Nature doesn't forget." She put the car
in gear, checked her mirror for traffic, and pulled back onto the
highway, leaving Connor to ponder whether the human being's
innate ability to forget was a self-protective mechanism or a serious shortcoming that would one day make the species extinct.

They stopped in Taos, famed for its ski resort, artists in residence, and its pueblo. Connor and Laura wandered here and

there for a while, but Connor's interest did not lie in shopping. They went on to the pueblo which, fortunately, was open to visitors that day. They traversed the plaza area, its silence broken only by Laura's quiet, brief explanations about feast days when celebrations and religious ceremonies brought the people of the pueblo together. Connor purchased several items from craftspeople, more to be kind than because she really wanted them. As they were leaving, Connor asked about the adobe church with its unobtrusive white cross. How did this jibe with Native American spiritual beliefs?

"Nowadays Catholicism is fairly prevalent. Back then they didn't have much choice really," Laura answered. "Just as my people didn't. The missionaries came with their unyielding determination to save the savages from eternal damnation." Laura kicked a small stone with the toe of her boot, sending a cloud of dust eddying into the light breeze.

"The Indians resisted, they even killed some of the missionaries or just sent them packing, but they kept coming back. Some of them were good men, no doubt, and sincere ministers who tried to teach their faith; others coerced the Indians with the help of Spanish soldiers to punish the nonbelievers. Some even tried bribing the Indians to bring the children to be baptized. Rumor has it that the bribes were so attractive, parents kept bringing the same children back over and over. The priests couldn't tell the difference...we all looked alike to them." Both women laughed, then Laura grew serious once more.

"Eventually the Indians gave in. They were a pretty tolerant people who didn't necessarily mind adding another deity to their constellation of gods. As time went on, though, the white men came from the east. They wanted gold, silver, and land...always the land. Once they pried the territory away from Mexico, they were intent on stamping out the Indian cultures, not to mention the Indians themselves. Thousands of my people were among those who were slaughtered, imprisoned, and eventually herded onto reservations. Big 'heroes' like Kit Carson helped the soldiers do that dirty work."

Connor nodded. "We're short on real heroes in this country. Too much of what we've learned is such bullshit."

"That's revisionist history for you, mold the story to suit the times in which you live."

"But more of the truth is coming out all the time. White society wanted nothing more than to obliterate Indian culture, didn't it?"

"Yes, the social workers stole our children, sent them to the white man's schools, usually Catholic-run, cut their long hair, beat them if they spoke Navajo or practiced any of our rituals. Some babies were just given to white people to raise, so they wouldn't turn out to be heathens." Laura's tone of voice had become ice cold, emotionless. Abruptly, she stopped talking.

"But why...?" Connor began.

"Why did we let them?" There was scorn in her tone.

"No, I didn't mean that."

"I'm sorry. After all these years, why should it matter? But the fact is all the tribes resisted until it became futile. The Indians here ejected the Spaniards once, but they came back. To this day, they hold a parade and a fiesta in Santa Fe every year celebrating the reconquering of Santa Fe by Don Diego de la Vargas."

Connor looked shocked. "But that's like...."

"Like what?"

"I don't know, it would be like the Germans holding a parade every year to celebrate Hitler overrunning Poland. How can you celebrate conquering a land where you had no right to be in the first place?"

"It's not really the same thing at all," Laura said with an edge of sarcasm. "There's a big difference. Hitler was slaughtering white people whose views on the Messiah were different from those of Gentiles. His acts were called heinous, which they certainly were. They were horrifying. And no one should ever be permitted to forget what happened in those death camps. That's why there's a Holocaust Museum. But there's no museum to remind people of Indian genocide, and there won't ever be one. At that time, it was perfectly acceptable to kill Indians. To some people, they weren't even human. They were just in the way of progress. That's the way of civilization. It doesn't matter who's there first, just who's there last."

Connor had not given a great deal of thought to the history of American Indians. She knew, or thought she knew, of the injustices, but the most basic injustice of all, that the natives who had roamed this land for century upon century were simply exterminated as a matter of economic convenience, had not completely sunk in until now. Unbridled human arrogance, combined with military mentalities and excess testosterone in decision making circles had prompted Europeans to sail to North America and blithely claim everything they saw without regard for those who already inhabited the land. But what gave them the right?

She did not realize she had uttered the last thought aloud.

"No one, unless it was God…or so they told my ancestors. Or it may have been those loud firesticks they kept shooting off. Fact is, the U.S. government had a dead Indian policy for well over a century. Indian scalps could be redeemed for cash. Sometimes they even brought more than beaver pelts." Laura took a deep breath. "I'm sorry. You've heard enough of this. I have to get off my soapbox. It isn't my job to saddle clients with a load of Anglo guilt while they're here."

"It's okay. It needed to be said. There are those who would have us believe that no one *ever* lynched black people, no one *ever* butchered Indian women and children, no one *ever* beat a slave to death. But that's bullshit. We have to remember." She thought about Val and her parents. "A friend of mine back home gets so furious when those twisted neo-Nazi white supremacists start yelling and screaming that the Holocaust never happened. Her parents were *there*. I can't even imagine how anyone could be so detached from reality, so filled with hate."

"Everyone has the potential to be that blind. But some of us hold on to the memory of those outrages, not in bitterness or anger, but because we know that by remembering we can avoid letting the same kind of thing happen again." They walked along in silence until they reached the car.

Laura stowed the purchases in the trunk and swung open the back door. "Well, how about we concentrate on present reality for the moment?"

Connor smiled at her. "It's a deal. But, you know, it feels strange sitting in the back seat. Do you mind if I ride up front?" She sensed Laura's hesitation. "It doesn't breach any codes of conduct, does it?"

"No, ma'am, of course not." She shut the back door and opened the front one on the passenger side.

"And you'll have to stop doing that, too."

"Opening the door, or calling you ma'am?"

"Both."

Laura just shook her head. "You're hopeless at being a pampered rich woman. So where to now?"

Connor had been considering that very question. "I think I'd like to go to Los Alamos." she said, anticipating Laura's comment, "*Not* to pay tribute to the builders of the bomb. There's an old friend of my father's who lives there. I haven't seen him in years."

CHAPTER EIGHT

Seek out—less often sought than found—
A soldier's grave, for thee the best;
Then look around, and choose thy ground,
And take thy rest.
—Lord Byron

Sunday Afternoon
Los Alamos, New Mexico

"Uncle John, it's me, Benjamin's daughter."

The old man peered through the top of his bifocals, then through the bottoms, and finally stepped forward a pace or two.

"Lydia? Is it Lydia Hawthorne?"

Connor grimaced, but refrained from correcting the elderly gentleman. It hadn't occurred to her he would be so old. Surely he wasn't a great deal older than her own father, who seemed vital and ageless. Perhaps it was only that so many years had passed between meetings. John Keneely looked 20 years older than Benjamin.

"Yes. I apologize for not calling first, but I couldn't find a listing for you."

He waved away her apology. "It's unlisted. Too many salesmen, too many eager beaver writers."

Connor blushed, thinking he was including her in that latter group, but then realized he might be completely unaware of her current profession, an assumption his next words confirmed.

"So, you're an attorney, aren't you? Prosecutor back in D.C.?"

"I was before I started writing."

He laughed. "Sorry about that writer crack, then. But they do get pretty damn tiresome. They keep coming back, doing those ridiculous retrospectives on science or digging up what they call background—something to add a touch of realism."

John Keneely had been a brilliant physicist in his time, beginning with his work on the atomic bomb. Granted, his contributions to weaponry were far less than those of the better-known scientists like Oppenheimer. But his youth at the time, and the fact that he had continued his career at Los Alamos National Labs for the next four decades made him the link of sorts between past and present. Now, of course, at almost 75, he was retired. But he had chosen to remain near the site of all of his accomplishments. At least that is what Connor assumed. She would never have had the impertinence to ask why he stayed on.

"That's just how it is, Uncle John. You're one of the only ones who remembers why this place started and what's happened since."

He looked up at his guest sharply, the smile fading. He regarded her with an almost alarming intensity. Connor thought she might have offended him by drawing attention to his age.

"I'm sorry, sir. I didn't mean for you to think...."

"It's all right, child. Don't apologize. I've gotten too sensitive in my dotage." His face relaxed once more, but something lurked in his eyes. His expression seemed more guarded, or perhaps it was her imagination. "So what brings you all the way to New Mexico?"

"Writer's conference in Santa Fe. Then I thought I'd travel around a bit, and I remembered you still lived here. My father would have wanted me to look you up, I'm sure, and I would have wanted to anyway. It seems like so many years since you've been to visit." Dr. Keneely had been a frequent and welcome visitor to the Potomac estate when Connor was growing up. She could remember seeing Uncle John and her father strolling the boundary fences, billows of pipe smoke trailing behind them.

"Benjamin doesn't know you're here?" It was almost an accusation. Connor was puzzled by his tone of voice; hers became defensive.

"I didn't plan to come up here. It was just an impulse. I thought that, well…perhaps it wasn't a good idea to call on you without ringing up first." This last was uttered stiffly, with more than a hint of Connor's British heritage in evidence. When she was ill-at-ease, the Broadhurst family traditions took over. They demanded stiff formality, courtesy, and an utterly calm demeanor in the face of social uncertainty. And Connor felt herself to be on very uncertain ground. She had expected more of a welcome, more cordiality from someone she had known since childhood, a man who had brought her odd, exotic gifts (which her mother detested) and taught her more about horses than any of her riding instructors. "Uncle" may have been only an honorary title, but it signified a relationship that had been very important to her. Now she was both hurt and baffled.

"I'd better go."

"No, please don't. I don't mean to be so crotchety. Goes with the snow on the roof," he said, patting his white hair, "and all these years of living alone. I've forgotten my manners." He gazed around the room as if puzzled. "Please, say you'll forgive me and stay for coffee, or would you rather have a drink? I keep forgetting you're all grown up now."

Mollified, Connor smiled at him. "Just coffee would be fine." Actually she had rather assumed she'd be invited to dine with him as the afternoon was waning rapidly. But she didn't want to push. Clearly, he didn't intend for her to stay long.

Over coffee and muffins, they chatted about insignificant matters—the weather, a little history of Los Alamos, what Connor thought of New Mexico—and John politely inquired about her novels. But nothing was said about Ariana, or about Benjamin's work, or about what John had been doing the last ten years or so since his retirement. Nor did it appear that he had kept in close touch with Benjamin, a fact she found extremely odd, if not disturbing.

They did not speak of the past. Connor already knew Uncle John's wife had died around 1975, and he had never remarried. There were pictures scattered here and there of John and Margaret Keneely, and one photograph of Uncle John's son, Paul, in Marine dress blues. He would have been in his late 40s now, Connor imagined. He had died in the waning months of the Vietnam war when the radioman for their unit had turned tail and run as snipers opened fire on the platoon, leaving his buddies without any way to summon the Hueys to evacuate them. All but two of the soldiers on that patrol had died, and the frightened soldier with the radio had been cut down less than a mile from where he had abandoned his post and his duty. Paul had, by all reports, met his fate with courage. John and Margaret had no other children.

Next to that photo stood a much older one, well-faded with time and exposure to sunlight. Three young men, brothers-in-arms in a sense. A very young John Keneely, dressed in dark suit, white shirt, and thin tie peered myopically into the lens. Next to him, kneeling in the center, Benjamin Hawthorne. The third man was David Keneely, John's younger brother. Connor knew about the photo, because its twin stood on her father's desk. It had been taken before Benjamin and David left for Korea. John could not go, because of his vision, and because he was needed more as a physicist for the Department of Defense than as a soldier.

Off the other two had gone, the older man, a newly commissioned Lieutenant, promising to look after his best friend's kid brother, a buck private. Six months later, Benjamin was wounded at Pusan and medivac'd to a MASH unit. After two months of rehab at a hospital on Guam, he came home. David came home, too—in a flag-draped coffin with a Purple Heart and the thanks of his country. Connor never knew the exact details of what had happened on that cold, bloody battlefield, but she knew Uncle John did not blame her father for it.

Instead, the loss of David and the loss of her father's two oldest brothers in World War II cemented a bond between the two men that she felt rather than understood. That bond had extended to include her as she was growing up. Knowing John had been like having an extra father. The way he distanced himself from her now was disheartening in the extreme, as if the man she thought of as "Uncle John" was some childish fantasy. Finally the small talk was as small as it could get and petered off into an incurable silence. Connor gathered up her bag, promising to send copies of her books if Uncle John would like to read them.

"Love to. Need something to take up the days, you know."

He walked her to the door, stopping abruptly and turning on his heel to face her. He put his hands on her shoulders and looked into her eyes as if searching for words to express his feelings. Somehow she was frightened, not of him, but of something she was irrationally sure he was about to say, something that might undermine her tenuous emotional stability, might completely change her life. She didn't even know what it might be, but the prospect terrified her. Then, just as quickly, the anxiety had passed. They were simply two old friends saying goodbye, and she scoffed inwardly at her apparently burgeoning tendency toward psychological melodrama. Uncle John hugged her and stepped back. His manner was so stiff she was surprised to see tears glistening in his eyes. So he *did* care. She hugged him again and felt how frail he had become. He was the first to pull away. He fumbled with the latch on the door, finally swinging it open.

"You take care of yourself, young lady." He put his hand on her arm. "I'm sorry I wasn't very good company, but I've spent the last ten years trying to get away from what's out there." He waved vaguely toward the street, his gesture perhaps encompassing the entire world. "Too many years of being responsible. The burden...too much for an old man. I told him. And now this."

Connor had no idea what he meant, but she did have an inkling he wasn't talking about just his work. There was more to it, but clearly she wasn't expected to ask, and he was not going to explain himself. Perhaps he was just wandering; he was an old man and there was unmistakable sadness in his eyes. Uncle John was a man in mourning. But for what, Connor wondered. His youth, his work, his family? Perhaps all of these, and with good reason considering the years he had spent alone. Yet never had she seen such complete surrender in another human being's eyes. It sent a shudder through her even as she stepped into the bright, warm afternoon sun.

"Goodbye, my dear." His voice was soft. As she turned away, she heard the door close behind, the latches being refastened. Laura stood leaning against the car staring at the street, having returned from filling up the tank and checking the oil. Now she waited patiently, eyes hidden behind mirrored sunglasses. Heeding her prior instructions, she didn't stop to open the passenger door, but took her place behind the wheel. All Connor said as she got in and slammed the door was, "Let's get out of here."

Laura started the car and pulled away from the curb.

From inside the house, Dr. Keneely watched them leave. Seating himself in a chair by the front window, he waited. From a drawer in the end table he retrieved a pair of binoculars. They weren't run of the mill equipment. The eyepieces had been ground to his prescription and were extremely powerful for their size. Using them gave him an illusion of sharp-eyed youth as he focused on the dark blue sedan that had pulled up just across the street and a couple of houses down.

"Amateurs," he muttered to himself in disgust. He heaved himself up and went to the utility closet in the kitchen. Using both hands, he manipulated two almost invisible sliding bolts on either side of the circuit breaker panel protruding from the wall. He had to yank at the panel hard until it pulled free, swinging reluctantly outward on its recessed hinges. Behind it were a small lever and two toggle switches. He pulled the lever to its lowermost position, heard a small hiss. He flipped both switches. Lights above each now glowed red. He looked at his watch, paying close attention to the sweep second hand.

He picked up the cordless phone next to him and dialed a long-distance number, one which few people possessed.

"Benjamin, it's John."

There was a slight pause.

"I know, I never call much anymore, but I had to tell you that she was here...Lydia, your daughter, she was here, at the house...I don't know why. She said she was down in Santa Fe, suddenly decided to visit...No, it wouldn't matter at all except that someone else is here, too...right outside, across the street— one man, dark sedan. It looks like a rental, can't make out the tag, covered with mud...No, I don't know what it means, but I can guess." He sighed deeply, listening to the voice of his old friend, but not really listening. He looked at his watch again.

"Benjamin, please. There's no time for that. I'm too old to fight this...Yes, I *am*. I'm old and I'm tired. I never was a soldier like you or David. I can't be sure I could deal with him even though I know he's coming and where he's coming from."

He allowed his old friend to talk some more. Anyone else in the room could have heard the other end of the conversation, heard the anger and panic in Benjamin's voice. John interrupted him again.

"It isn't anyone's fault, Benjamin. You can't blame Lydia. She couldn't have known she was leading anyone here. Besides, it's better that you know how close they are. You've got to take every precaution. You know what the stakes are, what hangs in the balance. We gave our word." He paused again.

"If there is any future for this world at all, Benjamin, you've got to continue...Yes...you have to keep going. And you have to find someone else to carry it through. I'm done now, and we both know it. We can't let those damn fools exploit what's there, now can we?" There was an empty silence at both ends of the conversation as two lifelong friends, closer than brothers yet separated by 2,000 miles, sharing a burden so great that neither was sure he could go on, pondered death. Finally, John spoke again.

"Benjamin, all my life I've wondered about the work I did

here, about the bombs we kept building, about what happened to the world after that. I wondered if we were to blame." He paused to take a deep breath, then went on. "When David died, I decided in some twisted logic that more and better weapons would mean no more Davids would have to die. War wouldn't happen that way anymore. It would all be one big Mexican standoff. But that isn't how it turned out, Benjamin. The boys still die, and we can still annihilate the planet and everyone on it. Paul died and Margaret didn't care about living anymore because I was so filled with anger I couldn't help her get through it." He paused again, but he was not interrupted. A man had a right to say what he wanted at the end, and Benjamin knew it.

"What we found out there, that's the only really positive thing I've ever encountered, maybe the only real truth either of us will ever know, and I won't jeopardize it by clinging to what little is left of an old man's life. Haven't we both learned how pointless that is? And I'm not afraid. I didn't see what you saw, but still, I'm not afraid." His voice quavered with emotion and he took another deep breath. He wouldn't snivel and sob his way out of this existence.

The voice at the other end spoke again, pleading in its tones, but the elderly man interrupted.

"No, Benjamin, how many times must I tell you? You've always respected my decisions, don't stop now. You're a good man, and you're the best friend I ever had. I'm glad we did this together."

John hung up. It rang again in moments, but he ignored it. He looked at his watch one last time. Just a very few minutes now. His eyes wandered over the photographs on the mantelpiece. He couldn't really see them at this distance, but he knew each one by heart. Odd, perhaps, that he had no recent pictures of Benjamin. Just as well; he and David would remain forever those idealistic young men, just as Paul would always be that sweet 19-year-old, trying so hard to look serious but not quite succeeding. And Margaret, dearest Margaret, the only woman he had ever considered loving.

John lit his pipe and moved to his favorite chair. There was no need to watch at the window any longer. If the stranger came close to the house, that was his own bad luck, and all the better for the world at large.

He was torn. Following the silver Mercedes was his assignment, but why had she come here? Why had she visited this house? The name on the mailbox was Keneely, which rang a bell somewhere in his mind. This might be important, might be worth checking out. Besides, the transmitter had a long range, it was hooked into a global positioning satellite. He could track little Ms. Hawthorne just about anywhere within a hundred miles with his receiver. There was time to report in, get instructions, see if a phone tap could be set up for the location. Unfortunately, the number he dialed on his cellular phone was busy. He would wait. He tried for more than 25 minutes.

Finally, unwilling to let his quarry get too far, he decided to make a quick survey of the house, see who was there, and then be on his way. He took another look around. The neighborhood was quiet; people were probably at work. He got out of the car, closed the door, and looked up and down the street. Before he could take more than one step, an enormous explosion flung him backward over the hood. He felt the impact of heat and light in his face, and scrambled to the ground on the other side of the car. Pieces of burning wood, roof shingles, shards of glass, and bits of metal showered over him. He crouched, hands over his head, terrified.

"Jesus, holy Jesus Christ," he kept saying over and again. Finally objects stopped falling from the sky, and he dared to look over the edge of the fender.

The Keneely house was...gone. Where it had been only seconds before, there was only fire and wreckage and a shallow hole of sub-basement. Nothing and no one could have survived, although the houses on either side seemed untouched. The force of the blast had traveled upward and outward toward the street. But why?

He crouched there, completely baffled. What the hell was going on? Did the Hawthorne woman have something to do with this? His train of thought was interrupted by the sound of sirens. Damn, the last thing he needed was to get tied into this. He acted quickly, got back in his car. Neighbors farther down the street were coming out of their houses. Backing slowly and deliberately, he turned the sedan around and headed away, staying scrupulously at the speed limit until he was several blocks from the fire, then parked at a small shopping center and got out to survey the damage.

Both windows on the driver's side were cracked. The body was pitted along the left side, and the roof and hood were scorched in spots. He would have to ditch the car very soon. A glance in the mirror told him that he didn't look much better himself.

He needed to check in, at least, with his control in Santa Fe, but when he reached into his jacket pocket, his hand came away with bits and pieces of plastic and electrical wiring that had once been a cell phone and now were sharp enough to draw blood. He licked at a cut and took stock of his surroundings. There were no pay phones in sight. Jesus, how did people live in towns like this? He got back behind the wheel and opened the briefcase. The tracking receiver bleeped softly, showed his quarry headed west again instead of back to Santa Fe. Now where the hell was she going?

When John Keneely's home collapsed in on itself, the contents almost vaporized by the heat of an explosion produced by a combination of natural gas and strategically placed blocks of C-4 plastic explosive, Connor and Laura were too far away to be alarmed by the muffled boom and the accompanying shock wave. If anything, it resembled the sound produced by a jet breaking the sound barrier.

After leaving Uncle John's, Connor had abruptly announced that she wanted to go somewhere quiet, somewhere far from civilization. Laura didn't answer immediately since she wasn't entirely sure what Connor envisioned as being far from civilization. So she remained silent, driving in a westerly direction while Connor studied the road map. After a few moments, Connor announced that she wanted to see Navajo country, Shiprock or Farmington or, what was that place, Canyon de Chelly (which Laura reminded her was pronounced like "shay" not "shelly"). She wanted to get there quickly, too, and had already picked out a likely route. Laura pulled over to the side of the road and followed the direction of Connor's finger along the map.

"But those dotted lines mean no pavement, Connor, just dirt."

"So what? The weather's good. This is a good car."

Before they reached the turnoff for Route 126, there were significant rain clouds on the horizon, the temperature was falling slightly, and Laura knew this Mercedes was not designed for the off-road experience. Yet she was disinclined to argue with Connor in her current mood. Her instincts told her that trouble was brewing all around them. No sense in starting some right here in the car. The route Connor had chosen was good enough, as long as it didn't rain *much*. West of Los Alamos they paused at the turnoff and pondered the large, orange warning sign: ROAD CLOSED FROM DECEMBER TO MARCH. Laura sighed softly.

"Well, it's just barely December, I suppose." She shrugged, gave the car some gas, and tried to ignore a quiver of anxiety as the wheels left that nice, firm asphalt. Fifteen very long, slow miles later Laura's anxiety had blossomed into worry. It was raining gently but steadily. The road surface, hard-packed in dry weather, was getting slimier by the minute. The heavy car still held the road, but she could feel the tires lose purchase from time to time. Their tedious progress made it seem as if hours passed between mile markers. Connor had been very quiet for the last hour, whether out of concern for their safety, or because she was lost in thought, Laura wasn't sure, and she hesitated to shatter the silence. An hour earlier she had noted a flash of headlights in the gloom behind them, and she checked for them regularly, doing so discreetly enough to avoid arousing Connor's suspicions.

The area through which they were slowly passing was heavily wooded, very unlike the terrain near Santa Fe. Tree limbs drooped overhead and crowded the sides of the road, weaving a green shroud that blocked out any potential rays of sunlight. Peering into the woods, Connor occasionally caught glimpses of cottages and cabins, presumably summer homes now locked up and temporarily deserted. She looked over at Laura whose hands, she noticed, were gripped rather firmly about the steering wheel, while her mouth was set in a thin line of concentration.

"I'm sorry. This wasn't a very good idea for a shortcut, was it?"

She sounded so apologetic Laura had to smile. "No, it probably wasn't, but it's bound to be over soon. And it's too late to
turn back. We're closer to the end than the beginning."

"It's kind of spooky here, no one around. We haven't even
passed another car."

"This area's mostly summer people, hunters, like that. They
don't spend any time up here in the winter. Road's not very
good." She said this last with just enough tongue in cheek to
make Connor laugh.

"No, it isn't. But you're doing just fine. You drive well."

"Maybe there's a career in it," Laura retorted.

At that moment, the car slid slightly sideways, and Laura's attention was once more riveted on the road. "I hope we don't
have to pass any cars going the other way. This road is getting a
little too narrow." What had been a generous two lane's worth
of graded surface now appeared able to accommodate only the
Mercedes and perhaps half of another car. On either side of the
roadbed, the water runoff ditches got progressively deeper.

"I think we're only about 5 miles from Cuba."

"Meaning the town or Fidel's island?" Connor joked. "We've
been out here so long we could come out anywhere."

"In this case, the town. Take a look at the map."

Sure enough, this road from hell ended, or became more civ-
ilized, at Cuba where it crossed Route 44. Connor's perusal of
the map was abruptly cut short by the first expletive she had
heard Laura utter. The road had taken a sharp curve to the right
and suddenly the short stretch ahead of them was even narrower.
Worse, the roadbed was built up so high here that the embank-
ments on either side fell a good six or eight feet, steeply graded.
Getting even one wheel over that edge would certainly mean
rolling the car over.

The very center was the only safe place to be. Unfortunately, the car, now inches deep in red, slippery, clinging mud, was developing an unpleasantly independent personality. Laura needed every bit of her driving skill as she fought to keep their vehicle on the road without making any sudden movements or changes that might upset their tenuous equilibrium. With small turns of the wheel, she deliberately and precisely matched the rear-end slew of the car. Still, it was as if the car were hydroplaning. They were going so slowly the speedometer barely flickered, but stopping would be as dangerous as speeding up. Foot by foot, the heavy car closed the distance between itself and the safety of hard-pack dirt and gravel where the road re-entered the forest. The Mercedes was traveling at an angle now, the nose pointed northeast, though the car itself was moving north. It was disorienting, one long, slow, controlled skid.

"You're doing a great job, you know," Connor said quietly.

The encouragement was appreciated, but Laura could not break her concentration for even the moment it would take to respond. She kept trying to loosen her grip on the steering wheel, knowing it didn't help matters to be that tense, but two tons of metal moving around under her, almost out of control, was just plain scary. Besides, she had worries far more serious than simply being stranded, far more even than rolling the car. They would both survive that.

A very long two minutes later, the front wheels caught the edge of a surface that seemed almost as good as pavement, and both women exhaled, looked at each, and laughed. The tension was broken.

"Were you holding your breath, too?" Connor asked, unable to suppress a nervous giggle.

"Damn right I was. And I believe this was *your* idea."

"Never again, Laura, never again. The next time I suggest a shortcut, well...just say no." This oft-quoted cliche produced more laughter. "After all, we could have starved out there."

"No, not really. I always carry Slim Jims in the glove compartment."

"What on earth is a Slim Jim?"

Laura looked at her with exaggerated disbelief. "You don't know what a Slim Jim is? Where have you been all your life?"

"In the city I guess."

"I think they have these in the city, too. Open up the glove box."

Connor did as she was told, and several long, thin objects, shaped like drinking straws and wrapped in red and yellow cellophane, fell out.

"Now, tear it at the notch there on top," Laura instructed, "and pull the wrapper down." Connor saw a shriveled stick of what could have been loosely described as meat. "Okay, now take a bite." Connor did, and her expression was pretty much indescribable. Laura supposed she had not been much exposed to American junk food.

All she could say was, "What *is* that?"

"I don't know exactly, I've never wanted to inquire too closely. I just like 'em. Maybe it's an acquired taste, sort of like caviar."

Connor chuckled softly. "Uh huh, caviar. I can see the resemblance." She handed Laura one to munch.

"Besides," Laura added, "I figured between the Slim Jims and that fully stocked bar back there, we could survive until March."

Taking her cue, Connor climbed over the seat to the back and returned with two ice-cold Dr. Peppers. Laura had to smile when Connor finished one "Slim" and reached for another.

A short time later they broke free from the grasp of the Santa
Fe National Forest and reached the metropolis of Cuba, bulging
at the seams with commerce—a tiny restaurant with bar, an
abandoned filling station, and a Circle J convenience store. Laura
pulled up to the gas pump and went in to pay. While she was
pumping, Connor made her own foray, which included stops at
the rest room and the snack counter. She emerged a few minutes
later with a paper sack and what appeared to be a five-gallon soft
drink. She looked so pleased with herself when she got back in
the car that Laura looked at her quizzically. Connor upended the
sack, spilling out a cascade of red and yellow wrappers.

"What did you do, buy every Slim Jim in the store?"

"Pretty much. I also have two burritos, two things called
chimichangas, two tamales, and the largest Dr. Pepper on earth.
I am thinking of reporting it to the Guinness people."

"Is this a junk food binge?"

"No, just broadening my horizons."

Laura eyed the selection skeptically. "I'm not sure this is the
way to do it. Have you ever had food that's been cooked continuously for hours?"

"Sure. My grandmother's venison and kidney stew."

Laura wrinkled her nose and gave a slight shudder. "Then
maybe you *will* like this stuff. Apparently there's more to you
than meets the eye."

"I should certainly hope there is. Now, which one do you
want to try first?"

"I think I'll stay with the well-preserved beef sticks, thanks."

"Coward."

"So where to now, Ms. Navigator?"

Connor was studying the map. It was getting dark. The
"shortcut" had cost them a couple of hours. "I don't suppose

these roads marked in grey would be very good ones," she said half to herself.

"Let's try and avoid the dark gray, the light gray, and especially the dotted lines," Laura said, with only a slight tinge of sarcasm.

"But those are the only kind that go directly to Canyon de Chelly."

"True, but it's getting late. There's really nowhere to stay unless we go up to Farmington. And with the rain, all the dirt roads could be risky. Caliche mud is like sticky ice."

"Then on to Farmington it is," Connor said, folding the map away. "Route 44, with stops at Counselor, Nageezi, the Blanco Trading Post, and Bloomfield."

Laura swiveled her head in the direction of her passenger. "But you're not even looking at the map. You remember all those junctions?"

"Sure, why not? Photographic memory. I'm smarter than the average yuppie, and definitely smarter than I look."

"I think you look plenty smart and you're...." Laura stopped abruptly, appalled at what she had almost said. Telling a client she was attractive—how stupid could she be? She glanced over and saw that Connor was staring straight ahead, waiting for the end of the sentence. "...and you're obviously talented," she finished lamely.

"My memory was a godsend at school. I remembered almost everything I'd read. Of course there were a few proctors who suspected me of smuggling crib sheets into class during exams because I kept quoting accurately from the text. As if I'd have been that stupid. Then, when I went up to Oxford, it made all the difference between a First and a Second."

Laura mused aloud. "I never really liked school. It was a long bus ride, started out before dawn every morning. Got home after dark in the winter. And no one seemed to care much if I did well at book work. My grandmother said it was necessary because the law made us go, but that there were many more important things to learn about the world, and I would never find them in books."

"Did she teach you?"

"Some, but at the time I was young and rebellious like any adolescent. Later, I left the rez, wanted to see the world out there, the white man's world where all the glitter and excitement were. Ended up marrying an artist who was all hung up on the inherent nobility of Indians. Of course, I didn't realize at the time that I was some sort of sought-after cultural prize. But he painted me a lot, and sent me to college where I actually did learn a few things."

Laura kept talking although she had detected the almost imperceptible tightening in Connor's face when she mentioned her marriage. And she was smart enough to figure out why. She supposed she should drop the other shoe.

"But one day my husband-slash-patron came home and found me with someone else…one of his models." Out of the corner of her eye, she saw Connor's eyes flicker, waiting for a pronoun that would answer the unspoken question. "What's kind of funny is that instead of being outraged, he just wanted to paint the two of us. He was going to call it *Woman—In Bronze and Alabaster*. He made this huge pretense of wanting to create art, but, frankly, I think he was like any other guy. They don't mind two women getting it on, as long as they can watch."

Connor favored Laura with a rueful smile of agreement and waited for the rest of the story.

"So, anyway, off I went, armed with my degree and ready to

storm the bastions of the white, male world. Joined the police force in Santa Monica, and since everyone thought I was hired only because I was both nonwhite and a woman, I put up with lots of crap from my colleagues. Those were the days of rampant affirmative action. Half the people were trying to at least pretend to be forward-thinking, and the other half were being dragged, kicking and screaming, into the 20th century. After a while, it got old."

"So what happened?" Connor was completely focused on Laura's story. She was, for the first time in many weeks, thinking about someone else's life besides her own, and it felt good.

"Oh, not much. I thought about joining the Air Force, decided that was taking affirmative action a little too seriously since I really didn't want to be anything but a pilot, and they hadn't gotten to the point where they'd give a woman, an Indian woman at that, a 40-million dollar jet to play with. Those were toys for the boys only. So I knocked around here and there, picking up, what is it, life experience. And, then, I ended up right back here. My grandmother was right about a lot of things, and one of them was that I would come back because I would never be happy away from the People, away from my home."

"I'd like very much to see your home."

"You may not really like what you see. The beauty isn't always obvious to visitors. The land seems barren, unfriendly. But it is sacred to us."

"Why?"

Laura paused and began to speak as if reciting the lessons of childhood. Yet there was no sensation of rote repetition; in her mind and heart, the legends were alive.

"Once First Man and First Woman had prepared the Fifth World for the People, they set in place the Four Sacred Mountains. To the East, where the sun rises, they put Sisnajini. In the South, Tsodzil, the mountain of Female Rain. In the West, they placed the twin-peaked mountain, Dokaoslid. At the place of emergence, where the People escaped from the Fourth World to the Fifth World, they set the Mountain Dibentsa. Within the Four Sacred Mountains is Dinetah."

Connor was silent, absorbing the rhythm of the words and their meaning. After a few moments, she spoke. "That's a beautiful story. Do you still believe the things you were taught as a child?"

"Once I did. Then I scorned them as fairy tales. Later, when I got..." she held up two fingers in the shape of quotation marks, "...educated, I relented a little and condescended to categorize my people's history as cultural mythology. But after I came home, let's just say I learned a lot more here than I did at Berkeley."

She looked over at Connor. "And what about you? Now that I've done all the self-revelation." She reached down and flipped on the headlight switch. The sun was down now, but the last colors still lingered in the sky.

"Oh, you know, privileged upbringing, good schools, lots of travel, law career, and here I am, the writer." She looked over at Laura, who remained impassive, saying nothing. There was a long stretch of silence. It was not until several miles later that Connor finally spoke again, in a quiet voice.

"I guess that isn't what you wanted to hear."

"Only if the *Cliff Notes* version is what you want to give me."

"I'm sorry. I'm not used to talking about myself, except at the superficial level. Every time those wretched columnists and interviewers get hold of me, all they want is either juicy gossip or pure fluff. No one really wants to know about your life, do they?"

"I do," Laura said, her voice gentle.

"But it always seems so absurd and boorish to whine about a life that most people want. How can you complain about having all the material things you desire, going anyplace you choose, doing precisely as you wish?"

"Did you always do precisely as you wished?"

"Yes...well, when I got older, when I was all grown up, assuming, of course, I am grown up."

Laura smiled. "We'll assume we both are, more or less. What about before that?"

Connor smiled ruefully. "Then I did what Mother wanted. It was a case of Amanda getting what Amanda wanted, although I fought her every step of the way."

"What did Amanda want?"

"Just about everything I wasn't. She wanted a socially adept, graceful daughter who emulated Mom. She wanted cotillions and ball gowns and long white gloves and admiring suitors and tea parties and the Junior League. She wanted a beautiful daughter to peer out at her from the society pages."

Laura could hear the vestiges of long-suppressed emotion in Connor's tone and opted for a few minutes of silence. When she finally did speak, she chose the question that was uppermost in her mind. "Why do think you aren't beautiful? I would have to disagree."

Connor looked as if she didn't know how to answer the compliment. Finally, she said, "The image I've always seen in the mirror seems plain in comparison to those of women the rest of the world generally calls 'beautiful.' I never knew what my lover saw in it. I guess I just counted my blessings and kept my fingers crossed that she wouldn't find someone else."

Then the tears came. Laura's only reaction was to pluck tissues from the center console and hand them to Connor, who hurriedly dried her face and blew her nose.

"Sorry, don't know what came over me. Silly."

"That would be the 'stiff upper lip' thing I suppose?"

"Of course."

"It really isn't necessary right now. I'm okay with other people's emotions, but suit yourself. So is there more to the story?" Laura was not going to let her off the hook easily.

"Let's see. Growing up I tried to be the right kind of daughter. I got married to a man who was a good catch, according to my mother. He was, I suppose, for someone completely different. Amanda got me all dressed up like a dog's dinner.

"A what?"

Connor laughed. "Sorry. It's a sarcastic Brit saying. In this case it means I was absurdly decked out in silk, satin, and lace, and low heels, of course, so I wouldn't look taller than Alex." She grimaced at the memory. "And Dad marched me down the aisle, though I think he was as uncomfortable as I was. He knew I wasn't doing what was right for me." She took a deep breath. "But, in those days, Queen Amanda ruled. Even my father, who could be overseeing the fate of half the free world at any given time, could not seem to withstand her steamroller tactics. He usually settled for just getting out of the way."

"Always?"

"He did put his foot down on occasion, particularly where I was concerned. When I was growing up, he insisted I spend a lot of time in England with my aunt and my grandmother. I think he knew they were the sane members of his wife's family. And he sent me there to attend university, when Amanda wanted me to go to some glorified finishing school." Connor knitted her brows. "You know, I think if I'd stood up to her about marrying Alex, my father would have backed me up. But I just caved in, trying so hard to be...to be normal I suppose."

"You mean, not gay?"

"Yes, not gay, not a queer...not different. I thought marrying Alex would make everything all right. I'd slept with a few men before him, usually when I was drunk, and it wasn't so bad, except that I felt incredibly cheap afterwards, cheap and used. But I figured it was just a matter of practice makes perfect. I could be straight."

"And you couldn't?"

"No, I couldn't. All my life I was drawn to other girls, from grade school right on through university. I tried to hide it. God, I was scared to death someone would find out or read my mind or something. But I knew what I wanted was more than simple friendship, and I think Amanda suspected as much. She hated it when I acted 'masculine,' wore trousers, rode horses, played sports, cut my hair short. It just confirmed her worst fears, I think. All her hopes were tied up in my being a 'real' woman. I couldn't fit the bill. The only good thing that came of being married was Katy, my daughter. She's...well, all mothers brag, but she's an amazing young woman."

"Does that surprise you?"

"Sometimes. I think how screwed up I was at her age and I wonder."

"How so?"

"Katy seems so much wiser, so much more aware of herself and the world. I guess I'm just impressed."

"So what happened to her father, Mr. Wonderful?"

"He remarried very soon after our divorce and went straight to New Zealand to run his family's holdings there."

"So he never saw much of Katy."

"No, and I wish he'd taken more of an interest. Even though she doesn't discuss it much, I think it has always hurt her that he doesn't call or write very often, and that Alex's parents have all but pretended their first granddaughter never happened."

"Probably because they want to pretend the big wedding never happened."

"I once tried to explain that to Katy, but at the time she seemed more intent on blaming me for the failed marriage than being angry with her father for his neglect."

"I'm sure she'll come around, if she hasn't already. There's every chance you've been a better mother than you assume. So...what happened after the marriage that wasn't?"

"I went to law school, then joined the District Attorney's office. I experimented with women, little secret affairs here and there. I still felt as if I should hide it though. Eventually, I couldn't stand that life anymore. I became a writer. My life was my own, and I had no reason to stay in the closet anymore. Then I met someone and settled down."

"Ariana?"

The single word hung in the air between them. Connor had not spoken it aloud, or even heard it, since the funeral.

"Yes." Connor's voice was barely audible.

"I'm sorry, Connor. I shouldn't have mentioned her name. But I read about what happened. I'm sorry."

Connor stared out into the night at the stretch of blacktop visible in the path of the headlights. When she spoke again, her voice was under control, though the pain was still there. "Yes, I met Ariana, and we fell in love. Or I guess I fell in love first, and she was kind enough to do likewise."

"You really put yourself down a lot, don't you?"

Connor was startled into asking, "I do?"

"Seems that way to me, but, please, continue."

"We fell in love, my father gave me a house in Georgetown, and I made a serious career out of writing. We traveled everywhere, we had good friends, we entertained, we...we made love." Her voice trailed off.

"It sounds like the part of your life with Ariana was very good, kind of made up for some of the other parts."

"It did. It made up for a lot. I still can't, I don't know, I can't seem to completely believe she's gone. I keep thinking maybe she isn't. Foolish thing to imagine, I know."

"It isn't foolish at all. I know how it feels. It's what makes being human such a pain in the caboose. When Jocelyn died, I walked around as if nothing were wrong, as if I were just waiting until she got back from some errand that had taken longer than expected. But eventually I stopped waiting."

"She was your lover?"

"For three and a half years. Not long enough. We met at a women's conference in Albuquerque. She worked at the Air Force base. That's one reason I took a job there."

"What happened, if it's okay to ask?"

"Considering that I've been interrogating you about your life, it seems only fair." Laura ran her hand over her face, then smoothed back her hair, a gesture she often used when she was thinking.

"What neither of us knew when we fell in love and thought that life would be one endless adventure, was that Jocelyn had cancer. She wasn't fond of doctors, I'm not either for that matter. So she hadn't gone for checkups in a long time and...." Laura paused, then began again.

"When she finally did go, the cancer was all through her. They suggested a radical mastectomy, a complete hysterectomy, and aggressive chemotherapy. It might have given her a 50% chance, maybe even less. Jocelyn listened to them and said 'no'." I respected her decision. I didn't want to lose her, but I respected her right to die in peace and in one piece."

"It must have been awful to stand by and watch someone you love die, day by day, never knowing which time you saw her might be the last." She reached out and briefly touched Laura's arm. "I don't know if I could do that."

"Do what? Jocelyn's the one who had to do the dying. I just had to hold her hand, and fortunately for her, it didn't take long." Her voice was harsh, as if with the effort of concealing powerful emotion. "The thing I hate most is that I couldn't stay until the very end, that I wasn't the last thing she saw."

"It's difficult to be around death, Laura. Some people simply can't do it."

"No, I should have been there. I wanted to be there. But old habits are hard to break. I couldn't abandon my beliefs. In the end, I was still a Navajo."

Laura could sense Connor's puzzlement. She was no doubt wondering what being a Navajo to do with staying with a dying person? But she didn't ask. Maybe she was too polite. Instead she sat quietly. Laura took a long, deep breath.

"My people believe we are beings created from all things in the world. That means there is good and evil within each of us. The evil part is where the bad thoughts and deeds come from. When we die, the good part of us, the good spirit, I suppose, returns to the pool of life energy, some say to the sky, to Father Sun. But the evil part, the *chindi,* stays around for days, right here on earth.

"If a person dies indoors, the *chindi* is trapped there and can infect the living with evil, or with ghost sickness. So when a

Navajo is about to die, his family members carry him outside the hogan. Otherwise, the hogan is cursed. If it happens by accident, a sudden, unexpected death, then a door is cut in the North side of the hogan to release the *chindi*. Then the hogan is burned to the ground."

"I take it the same holds true of dying in hospital room?"

"Yes, any place that is not outdoors. As a child I was taught this. I tried not to believe in it, but there it was in my head. And when I knew—and I really did know—that Jocelyn was about to die, I left. No, I didn't just leave. I ran. I ran down the corridors, down three flights of stairs and across the parking lot. The nurses, Jocelyn's parents, they all thought I was crazy. I never went back."

There was a long pause while Laura took several gulps of the now watered-down soda.

"Before long, I went home. Grandmother arranged a sing for me."

"You mean a ceremony, a chant, right?"

"Yes. How did you know that?"

"I've read a few Tony Hillerman novels, like several million other people."

Laura managed a small smile. "We owe that man a lot. He's made us Injuns seem pretty darned romantic, hasn't he?"

But Connor was serious. "I don't think he romanticized. It seemed more like he was teaching about the Navajo, and using fiction to do it."

"I suppose you're right. Before I know it, you'll be teaching *me* about Navajo spirits."

"I wouldn't dare! So, did the chant…work?"

"I don't know if you can say something like that works."

"Poor choice of words?"

"No, I don't know if there *is* a word. The purpose of a sing is to return the patient to harmony, to ask the assistance of the gods. It isn't something that happens all at once, and it isn't something you can put your finger on, or a stethoscope on and say, 'see, it's cured.' But I do know that the pain slipped away from me, the world looked beautiful again. It took a while, but that's where the process began."

The two women retreated into their own thoughts for a long while until Connor asked an unexpected question.

"Did you ever find anyone else? Anyone else to love?"

"No, I never did." Laura thought that probably wasn't enough of an answer, or that it wasn't the real point of the inquiry, so she waited for Connor to elaborate.

"But did you want to? I mean, was it a long time that you mourned her?"

Sensing for the first time that this line of questioning was not simply born of curiosity, but rather constituted a desperate effort to understand the process of losing someone you loved, Laura glanced over at Connor before speaking. "I don't know what really counts as 'a long time.' I didn't care about anything at all for weeks, and then my life gradually began to draw me in again. Learning to live my life was a process. There wasn't any particular day when I woke up and said, 'I'm over it now.' Instead there were more and more moments in which I allowed myself to be happy, to be alive, to be joyful. The sing they arranged for me was part of that process. In some ways I will always miss Jocelyn because she was my first true love, the first woman who loved me back, really and truly." Tears glistened in Laura's eyes.

"You don't have to talk about this," Connor said apologetically, reaching out to touch Laura's shoulder. "I shouldn't have asked."

"Why not? It's what you're going through this very minute. If I were in your shoes, I'd want to know what was in store for me. And all I can tell you is that it does get better, it does get easier, and, if you're wise enough to listen to people who care about you, it isn't necessary to spend too many precious moments of your life wallowing in guilt and grief and anger."

"But it's awfully tempting, isn't it?"

"That it is, my friend. That it is." Laura nodded to emphasize the point and then gestured through the windshield. "And I believe we're just coming up on our destination now— Farmington, New Mexico, which I think you'll find fairly well-equipped with shopping centers and chain motels, considering its sort of in the middle of nowhere. Holiday Inn okay?"

"Sounds just fine. I'm ready to be stationary for several hours."

In Cuba, he realized they were at least 30 miles ahead of him, traveling toward Farmington. Their seemingly aimless wandering was wearing his patience thin. He had been sure he could catch up to them in the forest, had spotted the taillights ahead of him several times. But the road sucked, and the stupid rental car was all over it. Driving skill was not something he possessed in great measure.

He had crawled over the road in places, almost losing control and plunging the car down an embankment. Now, here he was in some goddamn hick town looking for a pay phone. He ended up at the Circle J parking lot, unaware that the woman he pursued had been there only an hour or so earlier. He pumped quarters into the pay phone and dialed a number in Santa Fe.

"Where are you?" Her voice was sharp and angry.

"*Some place called Cuba.*"

"*What the hell are you doing there?*"

"*Following her. What do you think I'd be doing?*"

"*You were supposed to have taken care of her by now.*"

"*She keeps getting ahead of me. I thought she'd slow down on that damn dirt road in the forest so I could get close enough. But she just kept going.*"

"*Where is she now?*"

"*Northeast of me. Toward Farmington I think.*"

"*You think! You'd better start being sure. And what happened in Los Alamos?*"

"*I don't know. She came out of the house, and I waited around to see who was there, then the house blew sky high.*"

"*The news said it was a gas leak.*"

"*I don't know…it was one hell of an explosion. Almost fucking killed me.*"

"*I suppose we should be grateful we don't have to explain your body on the scene.*"

He scowled. *Goddamn it, he hated women like her—bossy and bitchy.*

"*Hey, this isn't my fault. And this wouldn't be necessary if you'd done your thing in Santa Fe.*"

"*Silence,* vous etes un idiot complet! Allez! *Get back in your car and start driving. I will call you with further instructions if there are any. For now, assume your assignment is active.*"

He felt his face flush, both with anger and embarrassment because he then had to admit that the cellular phone had been destroyed.

"*What!*"

"*It got damaged in the explosion. It wasn't my goddamn fault.*"

"*The satellite tracking receiver is unharmed?*"

"*It's working fine.*"

"Then start using it! Pretend you have a brain." She hung up.

"Bitch!" he muttered to himself as he got back into his mud-encrusted car. He was for damned sure going to get some dinner first.

CHAPTER NINE

———◦◦◦———

The reason firm, the temperate will,
Endurance, foresight, strength, and skill;
A perfect woman, nobly planned,
To warn, to comfort, and command;
And yet a spirit still, and bright
With something of angelic light.
—William Wordsworth

———◦◦◦———

Sunday night
Washington, D.C.

Malcolm had not been able to reach Connor since she left. He hadn't wanted to call her the day she arrived, and, although he'd left a message at her hotel on Saturday, there had been no reply. This morning, the hotel operator had told him that Ms. Hawthorne had checked out. Yet she had not been aboard her return flight. He had enough pull to find out about passenger manifests. There was no sign of her. He called Benjamin's office and spoke to Marty. No, the Senator had not heard from his daughter, but he would certainly let Malcolm know if she checked in.

Malcolm paced his office, fear nagging at the pit of his stomach. Why was he so worried? What could happen at some writer's conference? But why wasn't she *at* the conference? He knew somehow that something was wrong, and, over the years, he had learned to trust his instincts. But how did you look for someone in a state the size of New Mexico?

———————

Monday morning, December 2
Farmington, New Mexico

Unaware that her impulsive and seemingly aimless wandering had set off alarm bells in several quarters, Connor awoke to yet another New Mexico sunrise. She wrestled the window open and stood in the crystalline light inhaling the sharp, clean air, devoid of aromas of vehicle exhaust and human decay that spiced the atmosphere back home. "Hmm," she sighed. "I could get used to this."

They stopped for a quick diner breakfast before leaving Farmington. Connor once more astounded Laura with her capacity for food—steak and eggs, and a tall stack of pancakes. "It's the air, makes me hungry," she'd grinned when Laura raised an eyebrow.

By nine the two women were on their way. Connor wanted to see Shiprock, or, more specifically, the rock whose shape gave the town its name.

"So you want the Tony Hillerman tour?" Laura asked in mock seriousness.

"Yes, I want to see all those places I've read about—Many Farms, Tuba City, Kayenta, Window Rock, Navajo Mountain...."

"Whoa, you're talking about the entire Navajo Reservation. That could take days."

"I'm in absolutely no hurry. Does that phone work out here?" She gestured toward the console in the back seat.

"Just until we get out of range of Farmington."

"Then you keep driving and I'll be right back. Connor swung herself over into the back seat and picked up the phone. Laura eyed her in the mirror as she began dialing. There was no answer at her father's office, so she hit the END key and dialed Malcolm's office from memory. She checked her watch, it should be after lunch in D.C. She was delighted when Malcolm picked up on the third ring.

"Malcolm, it's Connor, how are you?"

"Where the hell *are* you?" The unexpected vehemence of his question took her aback.

"Well, gee, and I'm fine, too, thanks."

Malcolm paused to get himself under control.

"I'm sorry, Connor. I was worried. I couldn't reach you. You didn't return my call. I left word at the hotel Saturday night. Here it is Monday."

"I didn't get your message, and I'm sorry, too. I didn't mean to worry you. But I'm fine. I'm on an adventure into Indian country." She caught Laura's eye in the rearview mirror and flashed her a conspiratorial wink.

"Indian country? Where exactly?"

"The Navajo Nation, if you must know. I'm off to see the homeland of the People."

"Well, be careful."

"It's okay, Malcolm. Calm yourself. I have a very competent driver," she flashed Laura a grin, "and a good, sound automobile, and I'm enjoying some peace of mind."

"A driver?" Alarm, or at least disapproval, was evident in his tone.

"Yes, a driver. What is *with* you?"

Suddenly, the phone bleated out a series of high-pitched tones and went dead. They had lost the cellular tower in Farmington. Connor tried again to reestablish the connection with no luck. She sighed, but wasn't particularly concerned.

"I'll call him later," she said, climbing back up front.

At the other end of the severed connection, Malcolm growled with frustration. He sat tapping his pencil on the desk blotter for a few minutes then picked up the phone, stabbing the intercom button. "Marguerite, get hold of local police on the Navajo Reservation. Yes, the Navajo Reservation. Probably the Navajo Tribal Police. I don't know which office exactly. Just get me someone."

⁃⁓◦◦◦⁓⁃

At Shiprock, Connor and Laura discussed prospective destinations. Turning south onto Route 666 (a numerical designation which deeply offended certain local members of the religious Right, but didn't faze the Navajo) would take them either all the way to Gallup or to a turn off at Sheep Springs, which would eventually bring them to Canyon de Chelly. On the other hand, continuing more or less due west on 64/160 would take them past Mexican Water and Kayenta and on to Tuba City. After that, they could then loop back through the Hopi Indian Reservation, a sort of enclave in the midst of Navajo land, and make their way back to Canyon de Chelly from the west. The route was circuitous, but Connor was not worried about time, a decidedly unusual attitude for her. Perhaps the land itself was affecting her. Everything here seemed outside the stream of time and haughtily unconcerned with the haste and impatience of human beings. The horizons stretched out behind them and before them, so far away as to make the average human being seem minuscule by comparison. Connor did not feel insignificant; instead she felt less self-important. The things in which she ordinarily believed to be of consequence had shrunk to lesser proportions. One could not avoid the conclusion that when the humans were all gone, this land—these mesas and ridges and mountains—would still be here.

Connor had chosen west as their direction, so west they drove. After Beclabito, they passed into that portion of the reservation which lay in Arizona. Connor debated a detour to the Four Corners Monument, but decided that, for the time being, she would just imagine the novelty of standing in one spot where you were in four states all at once. The car sped along the pavement, and they passed little in the way of "civilization."

As the day wore on, Laura glanced periodically in the rearview mirror, her attention drawn by the glint of sunlight on chrome. Just within view, the blue sedan followed in their wake. Some 75 miles into Arizona they reached Black Mesa, where the decision to head toward Navajo Mountain must be made. For the first time, Laura resisted going along with Connor's impulses.

"That's a dotted line. The road isn't improved. That means lots of dirt and more than a few potholes."

"Do you really think we can't make it?"

"I don't know. But it's pretty desolate out there. We could get stranded."

"Stranded? When we still have eight Slim Jims and two six-packs of Dr. Pepper? Won't happen. And, besides, this is *my* adventure. I refuse to play it safe."

Laura forced a smile. This wasn't going well. She felt as if she were stuck in slow motion, waiting for events to unfold. It made her inexplicably irritable, something she certainly preferred to conceal. Why hadn't the blue sedan approached, made some move? What was the delay? Why did it seem as if no one was in charge? Some of Laura's questions were answered much sooner than she expected.

Three miles up Route 564, where the road was still nominally paved, it happened. Connor was asking questions about Navajo ceremonials, and Laura's concentration had faltered for a few moments. She was startled to see that the blue sedan had almost closed the gap between them. Did the driver know they were only a few miles from dirt road? Had he chosen to make his run while they were still on pavement?

She quickly checked to see that both of their seatbelts were secure and slowed ever so slightly, allowing the other car to pull even with the left rear fender of the Mercedes. She would be able to use the greater weight of their own car to their advantage.

At that moment, Connor must have sensed something was happening. She looked over her shoulder and started to comment about impatient people when the impact flung her against the passenger door. Laura spun the steering wheel hard to the left, slamming the big Mercedes into the sedan. The rebound from the impact sent Laura's car lurching toward the right side of the road. She felt the right wheels slip off the edge of the black top for a moment.

As Laura swung the wheel back to the left again, the driver of the sedan swerved wildly away to avoid her. Laura could see his face clearly for a moment in her side mirror as he struggled to

control his car, which was skidding on dirt that had blown across
the road. In an instant, she read his intention, his anger, and his
confusion. He hadn't expected an offensive strategy, that she
would make the first move.

Stomping on the accelerator, he began another deadly run at
them. Pulling almost even, he rammed the sedan hard into the
side of the Mercedes. Metal screamed as the two cars caromed
off of each other over and over, the two drivers battling for position on the narrow road. Pieces of trim fell away, tumbling
over and over in their wake.

The German import was the better car. It was heavier, more
powerful, and more maneuverable. It should have emerged the
winner and it would have, but for the unexpected interference
of Mother Nature. Wind and rain erode even hard rock. Out in
the open desert, sandstone was much more vulnerable. Pieces
tended to break away, roll, and end up where they were not supposed to be. As they topped the next rise, still side by side, Laura
was horrified to see a substantial boulder sitting squarely in her
lane. They would be on it in seconds. Try as she might, Laura
could not force the sedan out of her way to the left. She had no
more road on the right. There was nowhere to go but off the
pavement. She swerved to the right, but even her lightning re-
flexes did not give them enough time. The left front apron, and
then the tire of the Mercedes caught the edge of the boulder.
The peculiar shape of the stone gave the car, traveling at over 80
miles per hour, just enough lift to become airborne.

Nose up, and barrel-rolling right, the big automobile spiraled
into space as if it had been launched from a cannon. The tires
came up to greet the sky, then completed a 360–degree roll as
the desert floor came rushing up to meet them. Miraculously,
the Mercedes landed on four tires, gravity taking over before it

had time to begin another roll, which might have landed the car on its top or side.

Laura heard the tires explode when they hit. The back end slewed around hard, the metal rims of the wheels digging twin ruts in the desert floor as the automobile tried to adhere to that law of physics stating that an object in motion tends to stay in motion until acted upon by an outside force. In this case the outside force was an outcropping of sandstone that snagged the rear bumper and tore it loose before uniting its molecules with those of the right rear fender. The car finally came to rest with its nose facing the road.

It ended as suddenly as it had began. Laura could see that Connor was dazed but still secure in her seatbelt. A moment later she realized the attacker had not given up. As if near-death by vehicle wasn't enough, she heard popping noises, then loud cracks, metal on metal, metal on glass. Something hit the windshield in front of her eyes. She ducked instinctively, then looked up. The windshield glass had cracked, spidered upon impact, but it hadn't broken through. Peering through the only clear part, she saw a man standing at the edge of the highway, with a gun in his hands. He raked the Mercedes with large caliber bullets. Fortunately, none of these deadly projectiles were penetrating either the metal or the glass, and Laura knew Connor was trying to make sense of that fact.

"What is he doing? Why aren't the…?"

"Even this car won't stand up to that kind of assault indefinitely. I have to get out." Connor tried to peer through the windshield and Laura pulled her down hard into the seat.

"Stay down, for god's sake!"

Laura yanked at plastic retaining hooks on one side of a center console that rode piggy back on the hump between the floorboards. Connor had assumed it was just a drink holder, drinks which were now scattered everywhere throughout the interior. But Laura yanked, then kicked at the cover until it gave way, slamming into Connor's legs. From underneath, Laura withdrew a wicked looking piece of blue steel weaponry, a hand-held machine gun. Then, without another second's hesitation, Laura grabbed the handle of the driver's door and pushed against it. The door was jammed. She swiveled around and kicked it hard until it flung open.

"Stay put, no matter what," she called over her shoulder. "Close the door when I'm out." She rolled out of her seat onto the ground and gauged that the wrecked car sat at just enough of an angle that the open door protected her for a moment, giving her time to scramble into the rocks. The sporadic gunfire stopped for a moment.

———◦◦◦———

The sudden movement outside the car confused him. He had a brief thought that he probably should have picked a better spot to make his move. But he had grown impatient. He was sick to death of following Connor Hawthorne all over the freaking countryside. True, he hadn't been specifically told to kill the Indian woman, but he lived in a world in which most people were expendable. So who cared? One dead body more or less.

He felt pretty cocky about the whole deal when he started shooting up that goddamn car—until he saw the Indian woman roll out of the car like a government-trained commando. And she was armed. His self-assurance dissolved into panic.

"Shit!" He wasn't going to wait around out here in the open. He would finish the job later. He set out on a dead run across the 50 or so

yards between him and the spot where the blue sedan had skidded to a stop. Had he been as intelligent as he thought, or even reasonably brave, he would have sought cover, tried to make a fight of it. He might have even gotten lucky and made it to the higher ground to his left, which would have put him above the rock outcropping.

But he was a coward and not much of an open-field strategist. He might have been a vicious, efficient killer at close range, a deft hand at stalking his prey over city streets, but here he was on someone else's turf, and that someone else scared the daylights out of him. All he could focus on was getting away from the goddamn bitch with what looked like an Uzi in her hand. He died with this rather uncharitable thought on his mind and one hand on the door of his car. He had chosen incorrectly.

For her part, Laura was surprised to see the killer cut and run when she had expected a battle of wits and strategy. Thus, she didn't react for a split second. Then she, too, was up and running, abandoning the cover of rocks. She not only ran faster than he did, but she read his state of mind. The assailant was on the defensive! "Some hit man," she thought. He wasn't going to turn and fire, he just wanted to get away, and he was almost to his car. Laura couldn't let him do that. They'd be sitting ducks if he escaped and came back with reinforcements.

She dropped to her belly, steadied the automatic weapon in both hands, took aim, and cut him in half as he reached for the door. The window in front of him shattered as some of the bullets went through his soft tissue. As he started to fall, the car exploded. From her prone position, some of Laura's shots had gone low, hitting the fuel tank. She instinctively turned away, curling into a ball to protect her face and head as pieces of metal, glass, and plastic shot into the sky, and the shock wave hit her back.

A few seconds later she raised her head to look. There was not much left of the once-elegant Crown Victoria. The would-be assassin lay on his back in a pool of burning gasoline. "Not much hope of identifying him," thought Laura, "but maybe, for the moment, that's just as well."

The surge of adrenaline that had propelled her from the car and into the firefight that never quite happened was all gone now. She picked herself up wearily and walked back to the battered Mercedes, which was now pockmarked with bullet dents in addition to the damage done in the accident. Connor just sat there, unmoving, and watched Laura's slow progress. She was limping a little. And Connor saw, with some alarm, a streak of blood on her face. Laura opened the driver's door.

"It's over." She pulled the clip out of the gun, cleared the breech, and tossed it in the back. Then she sat behind the wheel, her head tilted back on the headrest, eyes closed, letting her heartbeat return to normal.

Connor looked at her in disbelief. "What's over? My God, are you okay?" Connor pointed at Laura's cheek.

"I'm fine. Must be from my hand. I cut it when I was getting my gun."

"Which begs the question…why do you have a gun? I mean, what in the name of God is going on? That man was trying to kill us?"

"Well, you, actually."

"Me?"

"I generally don't warrant that kind of attention, Connor. I would have to assume you were the target all along."

"All along? Since when?"

"I don't know exactly, but certainly since you've been in

New Mexico he's had his eye on you."

"You knew that?"

"Yes."

"And you didn't do anything about it?"

"Like what exactly? He hadn't done anything illegal. He hadn't threatened you. All I could do was wait and try to figure out what he had in mind or whom he was tied in with."

"Tied in with? Are you suggesting he's part of some conspiracy?"

"Possibly." Laura was thinking of the woman in Santa Fe with whom Connor had dined.

"So what am I, some kind of bait?" All of Connor's panic and shock was expressing itself as anger.

"No, if you were just bait, you'd be dead. My only job was to keep you alive. Need I remind you that you were the one who insisted on coming out here? You were the one who just had to see the wide open spaces. All I could do was try to minimize the risk. But there's no way to do that in a place like this." She waved her arm to encompass the empty landscape. "Then, since he kept holding back, I had to assume his assignment was just to keep you under surveillance. When he made that run at us all of a sudden I almost wasn't ready for it. I screwed up."

"You didn't screw up, Laura. I can't help but notice that we're both still alive."

"True," Laura answered in a noncommittal tone.

"Who are you exactly? Whom do you work for?"

"My name *is* Laura Nez, and I'm a part-time driver for hire. But I'm also a special agent."

"For what agency?"

"Let's just say I'm on the Benjamin Hawthorne team."

"You work for my father?"

"That's right."

"But why are you here? Did he actually send you to keep an eye on me?"

"Yes, and not because he doesn't think you can take care of yourself," she said, anticipating Connor's defensiveness. "He was afraid you might be in danger after what happened to Ariana." She said the name easily. "Then I uhderstand there was some sort of explosive device detonated in your home. When you decided to come here, well, there are lots of other complications about you being here, but your father's first concern was your safety."

Connor stared at the craters in the windshield.

"This is an armored car, isn't it?"

"Yes, and you should be damn glad it is. I wouldn't have had time to get to him first if it hadn't been."

Connor was silent for a long moment, her attention drawn to the smoldering body on the pavement.

"Is that something you have to do very often?"

Laura's face was grim, her jaw clenched. "No. And if you want to know if I enjoy playing cops and robbers, the answer is also no. Killing is still killing, even when you don't have any choice." She flung herself out of the car and went to stand looking out toward the desert, away from the carnage in the road. Laura was obviously very angry; Connor was sensitive enough to leave her alone for a while. Besides, it gave Connor some time to sit quietly, think, and try to sort out what was happening.

The violence of the last half hour was appalling. Death was something to which she had never become really inured, and there had been more than enough violence in her life of late; in one sense, this just seemed like the next installment in a very unpleasant serial. Certainly that man, whoever he was, would have killed her had she been alone, or had they been traveling in an unprotected car, or had Laura not proved to be a formidable adversary. The question that nagged at her was *why* he tried to kill them, and why here? She tended to think it might pertain to whatever material lay hidden in her townhouse in Washington. That could be the only possible element that linked her to the kind of people who set up "hits" on other people. Granted, she'd made her share of enemies as a prosecutor and fielded her quota of death threats. But that was a long time ago. She doubted any of her literary colleagues were sufficiently threatened by her success to put out a contract on her life, though she had the wryly humorous thought that Geoffrey Clarke might want to see her hanged in effigy. But this spate of violence all led back to Benjamin somehow. Her father's work had to be at the center of this bizarre chain of events. Yet, ironically, she still did not know the exact nature of this secret which people seemed willing to kill or be killed for.

Her train of thought was interrupted by the sound of Laura trying to wrench the trunk open. The force of the collision had jammed the fender against the edge of the trunk lid. Connor found she could not open her own door, so she crawled across to the driver's side and went to help. Together they worked at the trunk, one turning the key in the latch, the other yanking, until it popped open.

Laura reached for a black leather case behind the right wheel well. Sitting it on the ground, she unstrapped the top and flipped it back to reveal a satellite communications unit. From other compartments she pulled various components and began assembling the device. Connor was fascinated by the gadget. She watched Laura's deft hands complete the task in under a minute. But when she had finished and flipped three sequential toggle switches, the unit remained silent and dark. No lights came to life, no speakers hummed. Just silence. Laura worked with it for several more minutes, then sighed and began disassembling it.

"What's wrong with it?"

"I don't know exactly. Must have been damaged in the crash. I checked the battery pack last night and it was working fine. But we don't have time for me to take it apart."

She finished wrapping up the equipment and refastened the case straps. Then she did something that Connor found rather odd. She picked up the device, along with a shovel from the trunk and a large plastic bag, and circled around behind the outcropping. There she quickly dug a hole, some two feet by two feet and about a foot deep. She placed the leather case in the bag, and the bag into the shallow trench. Then she refilled the hole, tamped down the loose dirt, and, using a piece of brush, erased all traces of what she had done. She looked up to see Connor watching her curiously.

"The car's had it, the front axle's broken. We couldn't carry that equipment very far, and I don't want it falling into the wrong hands. It has some coding and decoding equipment built into it. Besides, at some point I can come back and get it. You'd be amazed at what something like that costs."

Connor had to smile at this bit of fiscal prudence in the face of extreme peril. It did not escape her attention that they were nowhere near a telephone or a service station, and the cell phone wouldn't work out here. However, she recalled that it wasn't all that far back to Black Mesa and the small trading post they'd passed. Not a pleasant walk, but not difficult either.

Laura pulled up the soft partition that formed the floor of the trunk. Underneath, where a spare tire would have been stored, was a sizable compartment. From this she removed two large canteens and two backpacks on ultra light frames. Then she dug into her overnight bag, extracting a pair of sturdy hiking boots. She looked at Connor.

"Please tell me you brought something like these," she said, holding out the boots. "Mine would be too small for you."

Connor looked at them, blinking in some confusion. Absurdly, her first reaction was to be mildly offended that Laura assumed Connor's feet were large, though actually, they were. She wore a nine and a half and, despite the fact the Indian woman was no more than an inch or two shorter than Connor, one look at her feet would confirm no more than a size eight or so. But what on earth was she thinking of? Worrying about comparative shoe sizes? Was she, God forbid, turning into her mother?

Connor looked down at her own leather walking shoes. "I think these will be just fine for, what is it, three or four miles back to the junction."

"We aren't going back to the junction."

"What? But why not?"

"We can't, Connor. I don't know who or what is back there. He may have someone close by, checking up on him. When he doesn't report in, they'll come looking, and the only way to get here is down that road. We could walk right into something I can't handle. And, out in the open like this...." Her words trailed off, but Connor understood. They wouldn't have a chance without the protection of the car.

"Why don't we just stay here and wait? Someone else is bound to come along, someone who *isn't* looking to kill us."

"That's possible, though this road isn't all that well-traveled, especially at this time of year. But just how are we supposed to know who is a threat and who isn't? It will take a lot of explaining if I start waving a gun in some innocent person's face. No, it's more likely that anyone who comes along will be looking for us, and they won't be friendly. We have to head that way." She pointed toward the northeast.

Connor followed the direction of Laura's outstretched arm. There was nothing out there but rocks and dirt and scrub. The idea of willingly walking into that barren wilderness was ridiculous. Her city-girl senses rebelled at the thought.

"Great, so we just go out there and get lost. No one will shoot us, but we'll still end up skeletons. Forget it! I'll stay here and take my chances with Mr. Anonymous' friends."

"The hell you will!"

Connor was stunned at Laura's outburst. Up to now, she had pretty much deferred to Connor. But before she could muster the appropriately indignant response, Laura was in front of her, grasping Connor's upper arms, looking right into her face, eyes flashing with anger.

"You listen to me, *Ms.* Hawthorne, this isn't a vacation anymore. And it sure as hell isn't a game. So you don't get to call the shots. My job is to keep you alive. And, frankly, I'd like to stay that way, too. Everything I decide is with that object in mind. This isn't downtown Washington, this isn't Central Park. The rules are different here, and you won't last one day unless you listen to me. Is that clear?"

Connor stood very still, trying to get her temper under control. No one she knew ever talked to her like that, mostly because, when there was haranguing to be done, Connor was the one who did it. Hers wasn't the sort of personality that responded well to orders. She was more accustomed to giving them. Role reversal had her off balance. And, on top of that, she was just plain scared. It was all too much for anyone to absorb.

Ariana's murder, the bomb in the townhouse, all the weird dreams she was having, the smoldering body over there on the pavement, and miles and miles of nothing all around them.

"But we can't just walk off, Laura. What if no one ever finds us? What if we do get lost in the middle of nowhere? We'll die anyway." Her tone was angry and more than a little panicked.

"Connor, stop it!"

There was a long silence as Connor stood there trembling in Laura's viselike grip. Then she took a deep breath and she knew her next comment caught Laura completely off guard. "You weren't going to slap me, were you?" A ghost of a smile played over Connor's lips.

Laura grinned at her and stepped back. "Not unless you got completely out of hand."

"I apologize. I don't know what got into me. I really don't usually lose my cool that way."

"I don't blame you for being frightened. You'll be fine if you don't let it cloud your judgment. See that guy over there? Well, never mind, you don't actually have to look at him. But the point is that if he'd stood his ground and not run like a scared rabbit, he'd probably be alive. He had the advantage, but he let fear take over."

"And you didn't?"

"Are you asking if I was scared?"

"Yes."

" We all get scared"

"Even you?"

"Hell yes, I get scared all the time. But it isn't useful to give in to fear, so I've learned not to, at least not if I can help it. And I can tell you're not the kind of woman to give into it either." Connor nodded thoughtfully. Laura looked at her for a moment and said, "I'm sorry I sounded so overbearing. But I'm worried and I'm tired. Most of all, I promised your father I wouldn't let anything happen to you, and I almost failed to keep that promise, which is very much against my principles."

"You know my Dad?"

"Yes, I know him as well as anyone gets to know him, I suppose. He isn't exactly a big talker. But I know he's a good man, with a strong sense of honor, and, besides that, he loves you a lot."

Laura's words, spoken from the heart, touched Connor deeply. She suddenly missed Benjamin very much. "I wish my father were here. He'd help us."

"Of course he would, but he isn't. I told him you would be safe, and you will be, no matter what." The statement was so firm, so final, that Connor understood what had prompted Laura to leave the safety of the car, rush out into the open, and face the assassin head-on. She had risked her own life without a moment's hesitation. She was willing to die if the situation demanded it. It bespoke courage and commitment beyond anything Connor had ever witnessed in her life.

It occurred to her that, in her work as a writer, she had carelessly written about acts of bravery or heroism without truly understanding them. That was because the people in her novels weren't real. This, on the other hand, *was* real. The body on the road was real. The blood on Laura's face was real. Death...was real. Connor wondered if she, herself, possessed Laura's sort of courage. She tended to doubt it, although she was wise enough to know that only in the most difficult tests of themselves do human beings discover their true depths. Perhaps she had not yet encountered her own harshest test. For the moment, Connor was prepared to go along with Laura's plan without asking a lot of stupid questions or throwing up a lot of pointless objections.

She pulled her hiking boots out of her suitcase, put them on, and began lacing them up.

"So, what do we do first?" she asked.

"Put your warmest clothes in this pack. It's going to get really cold. I've got a down parka that will fit you. And don't pack anything you don't absolutely need. But be sure to take your wallet and all of your identification. Don't leave anything in the car with your name on it."

Connor complied, selecting a wool sweater, extra socks, underwear, jeans, a couple of turtlenecks, and a pair of gloves. She was loath to abandon some of her favorite clothes, but then she chided herself for being silly. After all, staying alive was a little more important than not abandoning her favorite leather jacket, however perfectly broken in it might be.

While Connor finished packing, Laura got back in the car and fished the registration and several receipts out of the glove box, stuffing them in the pocket of her jacket. Reaching into the back seat, she retrieved her weapon and Connor's briefcase. From a compartment under the front seat she extracted a half dozen clips for the Uzi. When she came back around the car, Connor eyed the gun and the ammunition without comment. Laura handed her the briefcase.

"We'll need to get rid of this, too. Your books and notes are in it."

Connor stood there staring at the object dangling in Laura's hand, her face as still as the desert around them, her cheeks suddenly quite pale. "No, I won't."

Laura's face was a model of poorly concealed impatience. "Look, Connor, I've already explained to you...."

"No! Ariana gave me that. It was the last thing she ever gave me."

Connor's blue eyes glistened; she choked on the words. Laura's expression changed at once and her tone was much softer. "I didn't know and I'm sorry. Believe it or not, I understand exactly how you feel. I carried Jocelyn's silver key ring around for months in my pocket, as if it were some magical talisman that would keep us united across the chasm between the living and the dead. The day I lost it, I sat in my apartment sobbing uncontrollably over a tiny chunk of metal." She looked down at the handsome leather case in her hand. "We'll take it with us. When we get far enough from here, we'll dump the contents and burn them, okay? It won't weigh as much once its empty."

Connor nodded numbly, still unable to speak. Then Laura did something purely unexpected. She sat the bag down gently, stepped forward, and put her arms around Connor. "It's going to be all right, believe me."

Connor hugged her back, knowing full well that Laura was not just talking about this day's events. It was obvious she had been in that place from which Connor was trying to escape—a personally crafted hell of fear and despair and sheer loneliness. Laura had made it back. Maybe she could, too.

A few minutes later they set out, each carrying a pack and canteen. The Uzi was fastened to Laura's belt, along with one of the ammunition clips. But she wasn't the only one armed. Laura had retrieved a small automatic pistol in a leather holster from the trunk of the car and, after ascertaining that Connor was conversant with its mechanism, insisted she clip it to her belt. "Wear it in the back; it won't be uncomfortable. Please…just in case…."

Connor didn't feel any need to ask, "in case of what?" Instead, she attached the gun to her belt and picked up the briefcase, looping its strap over her shoulder. "So, where exactly are we going?"

"Finally decided to ask, eh?"

"Only if I'm allowed. Or is this a 'need-to-know' situation?"

Laura smiled at Connor's obvious attempts to lighten up a little. "Well, we're going thataway," she said. "And by Wednesday night, with any luck, you will get to meet my grandmother. But we'd better get started. We have a long way to go."

Connor's eyebrow did its quizzical acrobatics at the mention of Wednesday, which meant three days and two nights of roughing it, but she made no other comment.

The two women walked long into the night, putting miles between themselves and the scene of the "accident." Anyone with any brains would quickly figure out that a lot of shooting had gone on back there, but by the time any outside authorities were called in, they would both be out harm's way, at least that was the plan.

———✦———

Monday evening
Washington, D.C.

Benjamin Hawthorne sat in the dark. The sun had long since set, but he had made no move to switch on the desk lamp. He had never felt more alone.

John was dead.

He did not need confirmation of the explosion in Los Alamos, but he'd still checked the wire services first thing this morning and discovered the brief news item. That gentle old man was the closest thing he'd ever had to a best friend or brother. Now he was gone, obliterated, and, along with John had gone most of Benjamin's hope. As long as there had been the two of them, and the old woman, there was a chance. Now, who else could he turn to?

He could not quite convince himself that Marty was ready for this level of responsibility. No matter how competent he had shown himself to be, he was too young, still learning about realities. Connor? No. He had already endangered his daughter's life. The bomb at the townhouse had demonstrated that. He couldn't bear to see her harmed. Ariana's death had visited so much pain on the person he loved most in this world, and it was his fault. He should have been more careful. But who was after this secret he had held in trust for so many years? Who? Did they know what they were seeking, or was it simply suspicion? And why did they move now?

It seemed as if the weight of his years and the weight of a lifetime spent protecting secrets and holding the lives of other people in his hands was crushing him. It was not the first time Benjamin had felt despair, but it was the first time he seriously considered surrendering to it. He slipped open the center drawer of his desk. There, tucked into a custom-made cradle, was a gun, a Glock 9mm, on the small side perhaps, but equal to its purpose. He picked it up, weighing it in the palm of his hand, absorbing its promise of death through his skin. Cold, sleek, ugly, final. It was loaded of course, nine shells in the clip, one in the chamber, the only one that would count. He clicked off the safety. He knew how to do this properly; he just needed to steady his nerves for a moment.

But, as he stared at the gun in his hand and listened to the clock gently ticking away what could be the last few seconds of his life, Benjamin knew he could not do this thing. He could not abandon his daughter, a gentle, loving woman, so wounded as a child, now so wounded as an adult. How could he add to that pain? And how could he end his own life until he was absolutely sure she was safe? He thought of Amanda, though not with the same affection, at least not anymore. In his heart, pity now reigned where love for her had once held sway. But still, he would not wish to hurt her. Finally, he thought of the old woman, still keeping faith with her own, sacred oath. How could he relinquish his responsibility when there was yet so much to be done?

All at once, an entirely unexpected image came into his mind— his mother-in-law, Gwendolyn Broadhurst. Her presence was almost palpable and infused him with new hope. He put the Glock back into the drawer and closed it. He felt her smile and heard the voice in his head, "Now is not the time to quit, Benjamin." He repeated the words aloud, as if to firmly convince himself and to mollify the unseen ghosts gathered around him.

Marty knocked softly on the boss' door and, as usual, went in without waiting for a response. If Benjamin wanted absolute and undisturbed privacy (which he did on certain rare occasions), he had only to activate a switch on the desk panel beside his knee. Electrically activated deadbolts on both doors would slide home, ensuring complete security. Otherwise, Benjamin's reluctance to stand on ceremony meant that visitors only need knock and then enter. He greeted his young assistant with a tired look of inquiry.

"It seems that your daughter may have simply gone sightseeing, B.J."

"Seems? That's not a report, Marty, that's a guess." His tone was sharp.

Marty remained outwardly unruffled. "Not exactly a guess,

sir." Tacking on the word "sir" was the only indication he was offended.

"According to the car hire agency, their driver reported from Santa Fe that the client was leaving there for an unknown destination in the northern part of the state. Unfortunately, their employee was no more specific."

Benjamin knew more of the specifics than that. He had spoken to Laura Nez while Connor was still in Santa Fe. And he knew Connor had been in Los Alamos, seeing John. But he chose not to share this information for the time being. Instead he slammed his fist down on the desk. "Don't tell me that no one can spot a silver Mercedes sedan somewhere in a half-deserted state. She must be somewhere!"

Marty was genuinely offended. It sounded as if he were being accused of not doing his job. He rose and spoke stiffly. "I understood that you did not wish to make a more public issue of your daughter's whereabouts, sir. It is hardly possible to make contact with local law enforcement agencies without creating some speculation and, possibly publicity. We, personally, have few assets in place there, certainly not enough to perform a full-scale search over several thousand square miles."

Benjamin looked up at his assistant. "I'm sorry, Marty. Right now I'm worried and I'm frustrated because I don't know what the hell is going on."

"I know, B.J. We'll keep looking. I'm sure she's fine."

After he left, Benjamin turned to the matters before him, matters that had, at one time, seemed vitally important. But even as he opened the first file, marked, "Top Secret, Eyes Only," his attention wandered again. The assets in place...Marty was right, they were minimal. And now there was only one that really counted. He hoped he had guessed right.

CHAPTER TEN

———◦◦◦———

God offers to every mind
its choice
between truth and repose.
—Ralph Waldo Emerson

———◦◦◦———

Tuesday morning, December 3
Washington, D.C.

T he phone was ringing when Malcolm returned to his office from his regular biweekly meeting with other precinct captains. He snatched it up, hoping it would be Connor. It wasn't. Instead, it was Lieutenant Albert Tsosie of the Navajo Tribal Police.

"This Captain Jefferson?" the voice inquired.

"Yes, it is. Have you found out anything about Ms. Hawthorne?"

"Not exactly."

"What do you mean, 'not exactly'?" Malcolm tried to hide his impatience.

"Just that we haven't found any trace of the girl you're looking for, but we think we might have found her car." Malcolm felt the bottom drop out of his stomach.

"*Might* have found her car?"

"Can't be certain, but it looks that way. One of Agnes Yazzie's boys found it last night and...."

"Last night! And you're just now calling me?"

"Now hold on, Captain. Out where that car was sitting there aren't any phones. Kid had to hitch a ride into a trading post at Black Mesa and call the Tuba City station from there. I sent someone up there this morning, but it's still a good 60 miles from here."

Malcolm tried desperately to calm his voice as he began taking rapid notes. "Okay, I'm sorry. But could you please tell me what happened exactly? Is the car abandoned?"

"That's one way of putting it. We traced the tags back to a chauffeur service down in Albuquerque. It was signed out to a woman named Laura Nez, who was assigned to Connor Hawthorne supposedly through Monday afternoon. The other car...."

"What other car?"

"Well, there were two cars out there. The uh, let's see, the Mercedes, which we assume your friend was in, and another car, a Ford sedan, rental car. The Ford was still burning when the kid found it."

"Burning?" Malcolm's voice was barely above a whisper.

"Yes, pretty much gutted. There was one victim...."

Malcolm's entire body clenched.

"...male, hard to tell the age, probably Caucasian, pretty badly burned, and my officer thinks shot to death beforehand." Malcolm exhaled. It wasn't Connor. But, dear sweet Jesus, what had happened?

"Is there any sign of Ms. Hawthorne or her driver?"

"No sign of anyone besides the dead man. The Mercedes was all shot up, someone fired a lot of bullets at it, and it had apparently been involved in some kind of accident. The tire tracks indicate it went off the road at a high rate of speed. But there weren't any bloodstains, and apparently none of the bullets went through the windows or the body of the car. Kind of odd. Frank says it looks like the glass was bulletproof, maybe the car itself, too."

The curiosity in the policeman's voice was obvious. He was waiting for Malcolm to fill him in on what sort of situation had developed in Albert Tsosie's jurisdiction. The problem was, Malcolm didn't know. But he was beginning to get an idea.

"Was there any indication of what happened to Ms. Hawthorne or...what did you say the driver's name was?"

"Laura Nez. And, no, we can't really tell what's happened to them. But there were a lot of footprints around the Mercedes. Looks as if the two of them left on foot, headed north, though I can't see why they'd do that."

They'd do it if they were running, Malcolm thought. Damn it, he couldn't stand sitting here on his butt while Connor was out there somewhere evading a killer. He wondered if the dead man had been just that. His gut reaction was yes.

"Have you requested any search and rescue units?" Malcolm asked, wondering if they had that sort of thing on an Indian reservation. His question was answered immediately.

"We're not equipped for major search and rescue, Captain Jefferson, and besides, we really didn't know who might be missing, or why. If you hadn't called me yesterday, we'd still be pretty much in the dark about this. As it is, I called the Feds. Murder on the reservation falls under their jurisdiction."

"Murder?"

"Well, the dead man didn't shoot himself, did he? They've already got an agent coming up from Gallup."

Malcolm's mind was spinning. He had to talk to Benjamin.

He interrupted the further musings of the Navajo officer concerning the length of time it took to get a response from the Feds.

"Thank you, Lieutenant. Please keep me informed of whatever you do find. I'd really appreciate it. And don't hesitate to call my office collect." He hung up without waiting for a goodbye and fumbled in his bottom desk drawer for a road atlas of the U.S.

His dialed Benjamin's office. No answer. Next he called the club. Marty picked up. "Marty, this is Malcolm. I need to talk to Benjamin."

"Hey, Malcolm, listen he's really up to his neck right now. Could he call you back this evening?"

"No! I need to talk to him right now, Marty. It's about Connor."

There was a lengthy silence on the other end. "Is something wrong, has something happened?"

"Just let me talk to Benjamin, please, now!"

"Okay, okay...hold on."

It still took what seemed like an unreasonable amount of time for the Senator to get on the phone, but, when he did, he came right to the point.

"Marty says something's happened to Connor." Malcolm could hear the strain of marginal self-control in his voice.

"That isn't what I said, Benjamin. I don't know where she is, but I *think* she's probably all right."

"Probably? What the hell does probably mean?"

"Just calm down and listen."

Benjamin took a deep breath. "All right. Go ahead."

"I got a call from Connor yesterday on a cell phone. All she said was that she was driving around the Navajo reservation, sightseeing I guess. Did you know she'd hired a car and driver?"

"I did that for her. So she wouldn't have to worry about any of the arrangements."

"Anyway, before I could ask her anything, she must have lost the signal. The phone went out. So I put in a call to the Tribal Police there."

"You what?"

"Look, Benjamin, I know all about your privacy and discretion and all that secret bullshit, but right now I don't particularly care. I asked them to keep an eye out for her. Just said I was worried because she hadn't checked in at home."

"Okay, I'm sorry...again."

Ten minutes ago, I got a call from a Navajo Tribal Police officer in Tuba City...I looked at a map, that's in the Arizona part of the reservation. They found Connor's car on some deserted stretch of road...."

"Hold on just a minute, Malcolm. Marty, get on the other extension, take notes." Malcolm heard the extension click. "Okay, what else?" Benjamin was all business now, the professional at work.

"They found her car. The tribal cop said his officer reported that there had been some kind of accident, and Connor's car was, and this is how he put it, 'all shot up.' But there weren't any bloodstains in it, and he also said the car appeared to be customized with bulletproof glass and armor plate of some kind. Do you know anything about that?"

"Yes, I do, but go on."

Malcolm swallowed his irritation at having his question ignored.

"There was another car involved somehow, but it had burned, and there was a body beside that car...a *male*," he hastened to add when he heard the sharp intake of breath, "apparently dead from gunshot wounds. It apparently burned when the car burned. They haven't yet identified the body." Malcolm paused. "Thing is, there's no sign of Connor or her driver. And they had to run the tags to find out about the Mercedes. There were no papers in it."

Benjamin's mind was working like a computer now, weighing each bit of information, sifting, coming to conclusions. Someone had attacked the armored Mercedes and failed to kill its occupants. Laura Nez had killed the assailant, but her own car was disabled. Presumably the satellite phone had been damaged or she would have already checked in. The two women were on foot, headed for an unknown destination. Benjamin's voice sounded calm when he spoke, much more so than Malcolm's. But the Senator had the advantage of inside knowledge to ease his worry. He knew Laura Nez. He knew that, other than Malcolm, Connor could not have been in safer hands.

"Did the local law enforcement contact the FBI?"

"Yes. He said an agent was being sent from somewhere else, Gallup I think."

"I'll have to take care of that."

"You mean you'll have them send extra agents?"

"No, I mean I'll make sure they don't send any agents."

"Jesus Christ, Benjamin, what are you talking about? We need as many people as possible to start searching. I let you get away with that crap with framing Eddie Caldon because you told me it was vital and he was your basic piece of crud. But I'm not playing your little spy games anymore. I'm going to make sure every available law enforcement officer is combing every square inch of that damned reservation. Do you hear me? I am getting on the horn right now."

The silence on the line was deafening.

"No, Malcolm, you're not." The words fell like ice cubes dropped, one by one, into an empty glass. They sent an involuntary shudder through the angry cop. "If you care what happens to Connor, you are going to listen to me."

"So talk," came the sullen reply. "But don't you dare question whether or not I care what happens to her."

"I'm not, Malcolm, believe me. But you have to calm down. First of all, the woman who is Connor's driver works for me."

Benjamin saw Marty's eyebrow rise slightly. No doubt the younger man was surprised to discover that his boss had plans and schemes he shared with no one, not even his good right hand. Benjamin continued speaking softly but firmly.

"I assure you Laura will not let anything happen to my daughter. Believe me, she is as safe as if you were right there protecting her. If she weren't, I'd call in the Marines. But right now that could endanger her far, far more. And I cannot give you a better explanation as to why. You're going to have to have faith in me, have faith that I would rather die this very minute than see my daughter hurt any more than she already has been."

Malcolm listened, but he hated what he heard. He respected Benjamin, and, deep down, he knew how much the old man loved his daughter. Still, it was the same old cloak and dagger crap, the "need-to-know" bullshit. And that left Malcolm twiddling his thumbs while Connor was in jeopardy. He retorted, "Then why hasn't this hotshot bodyguard of yours checked in? The cop said this happened yesterday."

"You have to understand what it's like in that part of the world. There isn't a phone on every corner. Where did he say the cars were found?"

Malcolm consulted his notes.

"Near some place called, uh, Black Mesa, about five miles off the main road."

Benjamin felt a chill pass through him, but he gave no visible or audible indication. "That explains it, Malcolm. I've been out there a few times with Amanda, not that she liked it. It's pretty remote. And I was on assignment in New Mexico back in the 60s. Believe me, even now, it's a long way between telephones and gas stations. Obviously Laura decided it was safer to take a different route than the way they came in. Knowing her, she was well-equipped for a hike, and Connor is fully capable of keeping up."

Hearing another incipient argument in Malcolm's sigh, Benjamin hastened to end the conversation.

"Look, just sit tight. I'll let you know as soon as they check in with me." He hung up and sat for a moment, head in hands, swearing softly to himself. Marty approached his desk.

"B.J., look. I'm sure she's okay. But what is going on? Isn't it about time you filled me in on the total picture?"

Benjamin looked up at his eager face, the concern in his dark eyes. As always, Marty was there when needed, always at his side. Maybe it was time, but no, not yet. Soon, but not yet. No reason to risk yet another life. Benjamin evaded the question by changing the subject.

"What time is the meeting scheduled for in New York?"

"Seven a.m. day after tomorrow."

"I don't suppose we can delay it."

"Not if we are going to have any chance of striking a deal with our Colombian friend. He's willing to help us out with inserting the search and destroy teams, but he's nervous. The drug bosses can sniff out just about anything, and he doesn't want to end up in small pieces."

Benjamin nodded. They'd been working on this particular assault on the cocaine pipeline for months. He couldn't foul it up now. But then he had a thought. Marty was ready for the responsibility. Benjamin knew he was.

"Can you handle this alone, Marty?"

"What, the Colombian?"

"Yes."

"I can handle it, sir. But don't you think he will expect you? If you want, I could stay here and monitor the satellite receiver, let you know when Connor checks in."

"No. I've made up my mind. You'll leave tonight and set up the security procedures. Choose your own team from our pool and send them ahead this afternoon."

"Yes, sir."

"If you need me, page me."

"I won't let you down, B.J. We'll have ourselves a couple of roasted cocaine kingpins before Christmas." He smiled and, after checking over the communications console to make sure everything was in order, let himself out of the apartment.

Malcolm sat at his desk for a long time, thinking over what Benjamin had said. It made sense, mostly. And the logical course of action for him was simply to do nothing, get back to his own caseload, and take his mind off Connor. Benjamin said she would be okay. Why couldn't he believe it? He wondered what really nagged at him? His personal hunch mechanism? Or was it his ego? Did he resent the fact that someone else was looking after his friend? Was it nothing more than arrogance that made him feel no one could protect her as well as he could? Then there was the fact so many of the pieces didn't fit. First Ariana, then the bomb planted at the house, then some sleazebag felon takes the rap for murder and burglary, and is also conveniently dead.

Finally, that Italian jerk just happens to hang himself. No, it was all wrong, and Malcolm had the nagging feeling that even Connor didn't know what was going on. It wasn't fair. She was out on a long limb and someone had put her there, probably Benjamin. He felt another surge of anger at the career politician, or soldier, or spy, or whatever the hell he was. How dare he manipulate the situation? Back and forth his mind went, trying to settle on a course of action.

Suddenly an image of Connor came into his mind. She stood alone on a high cliff. A shadow moved behind her, closing in, stalking her. Then the image was gone, so abruptly he couldn't be sure it had been there at all. But Malcolm was sweating even as icy little fingers clutched at his stomach. He reached for the phone, his mind was made up. No matter how illogical, how pointless, and no matter what the reasons, he couldn't stand by and just do nothing. He pulled the dog-eared road atlas out of his desk once more. A pre-recorded "thank you for calling, but all of our agents are busy" message whined in his ear as he flipped to the map of New Mexico. Finally an actual person came on the line.

"This is D.C. Police Captain Malcolm Jefferson. I need a seat on the next available flight to Albuquerque, New Mexico, and a connection to…" his fingers traced over the map in front of him "…a town called Farmington, if they have an airport. Yes, I'll hold." He waited, calmer now that he had come to some sort of decision, right or wrong.

"Yes…uh huh…no? How about just to Albuquerque then. I

can't wait that long for a connection. Yes...it'll have to be in first class." Malcolm was too big a man to travel in coach.

"How much?" He sighed. This was also going to be an expensive impulse. "Yes, that's fine. I'll give you my credit card number now. I need the tickets to be waiting at the counter."

His next call was to Eve. "I need you to pack a bag for me, just a suit and a couple of shirts and my shaving gear...I'm going to New Mexico. I think Connor's in trouble." There was no protest from Eve's end, for which he was grateful. She just asked him how soon he had to leave.

"Flight's in a couple of hours from National. I'll be right home to pick up my stuff and say goodbye to the kids."

Tuesday afternoon
Navajo Reservation

She could not recall ever having been this thirsty. They did have water, but it was in limited supply, and Laura insisted on rationing from the very start. "There are only one or two natural springs between here and where we're going," she'd explained patiently. "This time of year, after a dry summer and fall, they may not even be running at all."

Connor didn't whine, though she really wanted to. The night before had been unpleasant at best, camped in a shallow canyon where Laura was fairly sure their campfire would not be visible. After a long hike in relatively warm sunshine, she had been shocked by how quickly and how much the temperature dropped. The sweater and parka had done little more than keep her from freezing. Only the campfire had made it bearable.

Now, trudging along once more, with Laura in the lead, her feet were blistering, she was hungry, and she thought there wasn't much she wouldn't give for a long, long drink of water. Better yet, an ice-cold Dr. Pepper, or a beer in a frosty mug. She shook her head to rid her mind of these tantalizing and frustrating daydreams, and ordered her body to keep putting one foot in front of the other. She forced her mind out of wishful-thinking mode, which might also lead to self-pity mode, and instead replayed the events of the previous night.

Despite the misery of the cold after the sun had gone down and surges of fear over their predicament, Connor could not deny this impromptu excursion had a purpose. It was not logical, but she had the very distinct feeling that all Grandmother Broadhurst's talk of "witch sense" was absolutely true, and that being here had somehow strengthened that element of Connor, or called to it in an intangible way. At first she had tried to ignore the sensations. Leaning back against a rock beside the campfire the night before, she waited for Laura to return with more scrub wood. Above her, framed by the canyon walls, an expanse of sky stretched, so riddled with stars it didn't seem entirely real. Who knew there *were* that many stars?

As she looked up, trying to take it all in, she could have sworn the ground actually shifted beneath her. The sensation was so real, in fact, that she flung herself to one side, clutching at the sandy bottom of the canyon, just as a dream in which you think you are falling may awaken you with a startled flinch. But she was awake, not asleep. As she lay there, listening to her heart pound, she felt herself sinking, not quickly, not dangerously, just softly sinking into…? Into the earth itself, into Mother Earth.

Thoughts completely foreign to the ex-district attorney turned crime novelist suddenly blazed up in her mind. Concepts like infinity, eternity, destiny, the size of the universe were entertained all at once. In some sort of vision, she saw herself for a moment, as if from above, as if through the eyes of a bird—a hawk or an eagle—soaring high overheard.

Her mortal body was but a speck below, riding the heaving surface of the planet as it inhaled and exhaled, a child cocooned in the strong embrace of a living entity which hurtled through space carrying along on its back billions of its children. The universe became so vast it frightened her.

Then, without thinking or wondering why, she stood up, raised her arms to the sky, reaching, reaching, her fingertips stroking the velvet blackness, the tiny diamond studs that sprinkled down through her fingers, the stars falling into her eyes, her mind alight with knowledge, understanding. Fire seemed to emanate from her fingertips

Gravity was but a hoax, a pretense at understanding the rules of the universe. With this awareness, she felt herself lift, rise, growing taller, stronger, feet no longer touching the ground, in flight through some other dimension of time or space. She was immortal, a warrior, a traveler all at once. The walls of the canyon grew hazy, the outlines no longer sharp. She was on the other side of...?

A piece of piñon in the fire exploded like a tiny cherry bomb and she was back, curled up in the sand beside the small blaze. But back from where? She wasn't sure she wanted to know. A soft rustling announced Laura's return. She tossed the armload of wood on the stack and flopped down beside the campfire. Glancing at Connor, her face grew suddenly grave.

"Are you all right?" she asked.

"Sure, why do you ask?"

Laura took note of the paleness of her face, the slight trembling, the vaguely glassy-eyed look in her eyes.

"Just checking...being a competent sidekick," she smiled.

"I think at this point I'm the sidekick, *kemosabe*." Connor felt her face warm with embarrassment. "Sorry, another Indian stereotype."

"Hey, don't take everything so seriously. Tonto wasn't a bad guy. He definitely was second banana, and his dialogue was moronic, but he didn't act like an idiot, didn't scalp innocent settlers, just used his 'injun' skills to help his boss track down the bad guys."

"I don't know, seems like there was a lot of Sambo in Tonto."

Laura laughed. "I hadn't thought of it quite that way, but I guess you're right. I suppose I just wanted to see the positives— I'm like that sometimes. On good days, the Navajo version of Pollyanna."

"That doesn't seem to jibe with the work you do. I thought all government spy types had to be dyed-in-the-wool pessimists, looking for plots and conspiracies under every rock."

"Caution isn't necessarily cynicism, Connor. I'm very careful, that's true, but, on the other hand, I'm just as likely to trust as I am to suspect. I try to keep it even. And I have a surprisingly good batting average when it comes to evaluating people. At least your father finds it surprising. Just that old Indian magic," she added, with a self-deprecating smirk.

"How did you get to know my father?"

Laura was silent for a moment. "Considering you're his daughter, I don't suppose he would mind you knowing. Remember, I told you I came back to the rez finally, and I didn't know what I wanted to do with my life anymore. I thought of joining the Tribal cops, but I'd had enough of that in California. One day my grandmother's sister came to me and said she'd had a vision...." She looked up to see if there were any signs of in-credulity in her listener, but Connor looked perfectly serious and completely attentive. "You see, old Agnes was a crystal gazer...we have all sorts of different kinds of magic. Different people do different things, use different kinds of medicine. Any-way, she told me about Jocelyn, about meeting her, I mean. Not about the cancer. She told me that a woman waited for me to join her. And after the woman, a man would come to walk be-side me for a while, then he would make me his messenger." She looked up at Connor again and then continued with a sigh of what might have been reluctance.

"Anyway, I didn't think much of it. But a few days later, there was Jocelyn. And a few years later, she wasn't." Laura swallowed hard enough to be heard in the stillness of the desert.

"But your grandmother's sister didn't tell you that?"

"No, it wouldn't be ethical in that sort of situation. And it would have changed everything between us, even before our first date." Laura's voice had thickened with emotion. Connor looked up at her, concerned, but Laura just shook her head.

"Not long after that, a man came to see me—your father. I'm still not sure why. He said he'd heard a lot of good things about me from my ex-supervisor when I was a cop. That didn't make a lot of sense. But we talked for a long time. He asked me the oddest questions, but I found myself answering them anyway."

"Odd how?"

"Just things like how I felt about the state of the world. Whether I thought there really was a right side and wrong side to be on. All pretty philosophical, not the sort of questions one usually hears in a job interview. Finally he told me he wanted to hire me. I'd already recognized who he was, naturally. But I couldn't imagine what I would do for a retired U.S. senator

turned presidential advisor. I thought it must have been some affirmative action ploy or something political like that. That's what
I told him.

"I remember he laughed. Said, 'that's one reason I want you
to work for me...you're honest. And I'll be just as honest. Two
of the several reasons I'm here are because you're a woman and
you're a Navajo. Does that bother you?'"

Laura smiled at the memory.

"At first I thought it did. But there was something about the
way he said it that made me realize it wasn't about tokenism. It
was about being special because of who I am. He didn't say that
exactly, but I knew it was what he meant. And I liked that. But
the situation still seemed odd, so I told him I wanted to think
about it for a while. He seemed to expect that. And then he said
a really strange thing. He said, 'Speak with your grandmother
before you make any decision.'"

Connor could see, on Laura's face, an instant replay of the
puzzlement Laura felt at the time. Her brows were knitted together, remembering.

"I couldn't figure out if he *assumed* that I had a grandmother,
and, since we are by tradition a matriarchal society, I would want
to ask her advice, or if he actually knew her. So I asked him, 'Do
you know my grandmother?' and he smiled and said, 'What's
important is that your grandmother knows *me*,' and he left.

"I puzzled over that for a while and concluded that there was
no arrogance in his comment, just the opposite really. Instead of
saying it was important for my grandmother to know someone
as important as he was, he was saying that her opinion of him
was the deciding factor. I was impressed, so...to Grandmother's
house I went." She paused, smiling. "You know, I had to catch
up on white people's nursery rhymes years after the fact."

"I missed out on some of the American versions myself. Used to be vaguely embarrassed at cocktail parties."

"I can only thank the gods that I've never been faced with a cocktail party. But, anyway, to try and make this long story a bit shorter, I went to my grandmother. She was, and still is, one of the least talkative people I've ever known. She just doesn't waste words, almost as if she believes there were a certain number allotted to each person and she doesn't want to find herself running out before she's ready to leave."

Laura began feeding more wood into the fire, pondering, Connor guessed, the idea of her grandmother dying. Laura stirred up the fire and continued. "So Grandmother looked at me and said, 'What do you think of this man?' And I thought about it for a minute or two, until she poked me in the chest, here." Laura put her palm over her heart. "She poked pretty hard actually. I was surprised, but she didn't change expression. 'Not here,' she said, pointing to my head, 'but, here,' poking me in the chest again. I got the message. This wasn't about weighing words and promises and pros and cons, it was about what my heart believed. I had the answer instantly. I trusted him, and I knew there was something important I must do for him. I hadn't even gotten the words out when she smiled and turned away. She already knew."

"She sounds like my grandmother. Gwendolyn always knows what's in my heart, too. Calls it the Broadhurst 'witch sense,' a sort of family gift."

"And do you have it?"

From force of habit, Connor started to give some dismissive response. But she couldn't. For the first time in her life, she knew the things her grandmother taught her were part of her heritage, something valuable, rather than just the quaint super-

stitions of an old lady. She no longer wanted to reject the notion
of special gifts she might have. What had happened this very
evening was enough to make her bite back any and all offhand-
ed jokes about ESP and the spirit world. As a result, her answer
to Laura's question was thoughtful and honest.

"I'm not sure. Recently I've been having these incredible
dreams, and my Grandmother Gwendolyn is usually in them,
talking to me just as if she were standing right there in the room.
And sometimes I do sense things, even know things I shouldn't
know. I used to pass it off as coincidence, luck, intelligent deduction, you know, rationalizations. I know this probably
sounds silly, but before you came back with the wood..." She
paused, looking at Laura for signs of impending ridicule or disbelief. But the young woman stared at the fire, listening quietly
and intently to Connor's explanation. "...I had the strangest experience. I thought maybe it was a dream, but I don't think so.
I was up there somewhere..." Connor pointed heavenward,
"...looking down at myself and the desert and the whole earth.
I seemed small, and the universe was so enormous it frightened
me at first. Then I saw patterns to it all. Patterns I thought I
knew. Now I can't remember them or what they meant. But it
just seemed like I wasn't really *here*, if you know what I mean."

Laura nodded solemnly. "I know. Some people call it the dreamtime, or another dimension, a place out of this time and space. Everything there is very unusual and very different from what you see or
what you perceive in this reality. And this reality looks different, too,
when you're seeing it from that place, like music being played in an
unfamiliar key, or colors that don't look the way they should." Connor was startled by this apt description of what she had seen.

"You've been there?"

"In my own way. Everyone's journey appears to her

differently. Or so my grandmother says. And she should be right. She's the head of our clan. I was born to the Standing House Dineh." Laura noticed Connor's interrogative eyebrow. "The clans are subgroups of the Navajo People. We are born *to* the clans of our mothers, and *for* the clans of our fathers. We generally remain part of our mothers' clan."

"Interesting concept," said Connor smiling. "Didn't I hear somewhere that a Navajo woman can divorce her husband simply by putting his personal possessions out on the porch?"

Laura laughed. "That's a bit of an oversimplification, not to mention that the average hogan doesn't have a porch, but that was the general idea at one time. Traditionally, women are the property owners, real property that is. Though, nowadays, with Christian marriage rites and *belagaana* customs like wife-beating and drunkenness sprouting up all over, the old ways are fading."

"*Belagaana?* I've seen that word before, but I've forgotten what it means."

"Sort of a general, all-purpose term for white folk."

"Hmm. You know what you said about the old ways fading?"

"They are."

"That seems like the greatest tragedy of all, when a people lose their culture. And some of the old ways seem so much more desirable, a lot simpler."

"Not always," Laura said, shaking her head. "It's easy to get into that nostalgia mindset, but don't forget witch-burning, slavery, and institutions like the Catholic church declaring that women had no souls just a few centuries back. And, even today, in some Arabic cultures all a man has to do is say, 'I divorce you' three times to his wife, in front of witnesses, and she's history. Also fairly simple, if not very fair. Some of the so-called 'old ways' had to go."

"I'd have to agree."

"But even back then, Navajos didn't assume that the women owned the men or vice versa. The Navajos didn't even have a word that meant 'slave' before the Spanish came and taught them the meaning up close and personal."

"How do Navajos feel about gay people?" Connor let the question fall into the dense silence around them, where it lay for a while, awkwardly.

"They have no taboo against gay people, if that's what you mean. On the other hand, they have very specific taboos related to just about every activity in life. When it comes to acceptable sexual partners, Navajos have a complex system of family and clan interrelationships that must be respected. For a man and woman from the same clan or related clans to lie together, as they put it, is extremely taboo, brings evil and sickness, even though they might be what you would consider very distant cousins or not related at all.

"In some Native American tribes, a gay man was considered a holy being, a sacred clown perhaps, or a seer. Same for hermaphrodites who were thought to represent the wisdom of both the male and the female. We have hangups about things, just not the same hangups as most of the world out there."

"What do you think is the biggest difference between your people and mine?" Connor asked.

Laura pondered the question for several moments. "I think the biggest difference is that the Navajo don't see their spirituality as separate from their lives."

"I'm not sure I know what you mean."

"From what I've seen, the practice of religion for a lot of people is just one part of their life, sometimes an inconsequential part. The traditional Navajo *lives* his religion, every single day, from the moment he arises until he sleeps. There are rituals and prayers for even the most simple activities—planting, building, slaughtering sheep, hunting."

"So the Navajo do hunt?"

"Yes, but not for sport or trophies. We hunt for food. And we ask the animal's forgiveness when we kill it. We believe all creatures have a spirit that must be acknowledged and honored. And we believe that Mother Earth is a being to be respected."

Connor shook her head and sighed. "It's a shame that more people don't feel that way. To a lot of them this planet is just one big chunk of real estate with oil and mineral rights and trees to cut down." She looked up at the star-studded night sky and the gibbous moon that rode high above them. "I imagine they're already wondering who gets to pillage whatever there is on the moon."

"They have to look ahead, Connor. Someday there won't be anything left here."

Both women sat for a while, each absorbed in her own thoughts. Finally, Connor yawned. "Okay, no more soap boxes for either of us. I could have sworn I didn't bring mine with me."

Laura chuckled. "We need to get some sleep. Tomorrow will be a long day."

Connor smiled. "Speaking of sleep, I don't suppose you have a camp cot and a pillow folded up in that knapsack of yours?"

"If I did, I'd already be sleeping on it."

"Gee, thanks."

Connor curled up once more, as close to the fire as possible. Several times in the night she heard Laura moving about, feeding the fire, gathering more wood. Once, she opened her eyes and realized that Laura was not lying down at all, but rather she was sitting against a rock, watching. For what Connor did not know, but it gave her a distinct feeling of security, and, perhaps, a twinge of guilt, too, that Laura was missing a chance to sleep. But the twinge was not quite painful enough to rouse her out of her fetal position. She was cold, she was sore, and she was uncomfortable, but still she had slept.

They had risen at dawn, and now, hours later, trudging along behind her guide, Connor puzzled over the events of the night before. She wondered if she were delusional. Had she simply been so tired that the unreal seemed real? On the other hand, did it matter? Once upon a time, not so long ago, she would have said, "Of course it matters." But her perspective had changed. What everyone agreed on as being "reality" no longer seemed an unassailable absolute. Nor was it that attractive or compelling. What her mind automatically rejected, her heart, or perhaps her soul, was embracing with unusual and slightly unnerving enthusiasm. This was odd for two reasons. Connor was a person who lived by her intellect, and she was also someone whose heart was deeply scarred. She had always been more comfortable with thought than with feeling. Ariana, with her wide-eyed willingness to accept the possibility that there really was magic in the world, had been able to sway Connor occasionally from her strictly rational views. But bereft of her lover, Connor had begun a retreat to the sanctity and safety of her mind. She didn't want to feel, or question, or strike out into unfamiliar territory. At least she thought she didn't. Now she wasn't sure. Out here, in this strange and slightly forbidding land, a place to which she had chosen to come, her heart and spirit were breaking free of their restraints. She could almost feel the indignant rebellion of her grey cells against this abrupt change of policy. Her mind was fighting the unknown, the unquantifiable, the inexplicable, but it was losing the battle.

"Time for a rest." Laura's announcement caught Connor off guard as the Indian woman stopped abruptly and unfastened her pack straps. Connor, while riding her complex train of thought, had not really noticed the miles they had covered. She was surprised to see that the sun was already setting. How far had they come? Laura answered the unspoken question, a habit Connor still thought uncanny, but to which she was becoming accustomed.

"We've made good time. As much as 20 miles maybe. There should be water about a mile ahead of us, near that rock outcropping. It's the top of a narrow canyon. At the head of the canyon there's a pool and a spring, if they're not dried up." Connor must have shown her alarm, for Laura added, "Don't worry, though. We've been careful." She shook her own canteen. "I've still got about a third of a gallon here. And you've still got some. We'll make camp again just before dark. We'll be eating my grandmother's fry bread and mutton stew for dinner tomorrow."

"Is that a good thing?" Connor asked.

"She thinks so," Laura said with a smile. "And you had better think so, too."

The women each took a cautious drink from their canteens and sat for a while in silence, watching the sunset spread itself like liquid fire across the horizon on their left. Connor found herself looking more at Laura than at the sunset, but if her companion noticed, she did not appear self-conscious. Connor saw the tiny squint lines around Laura's eyes with companion laugh lines at the corners of her mouth. Hers was a memorable profile, Connor thought—strong jaw line, finely sculptured nose, long eyelashes, full lips, and smooth forehead surmounted by just a small widow's peak where strands of her dark hair, having won their bid for freedom from the confining braid, curled ever so slightly downward. Inexplicably, she seemed like a stranger, and, with a flash of insight, Connor knew why. The most striking of Laura's features were her eyes. They were eyes that kept secrets, yet opened wide in wonder. They were eyes that invited you to stay, yet frightened you just a little with their unfathomable depth. But in profile they were hidden. Connor found herself wishing she could look into them again.

As if on cue, Laura turned to Connor, who blushed slightly. Staring was so rude. What had she been thinking? Laura smiled gently and put her hand on Connor's shoulder. "I think we had better get going." The unexpected touch was like electricity that sent a tremor running through Connor. Tiny goosebumps prickled to life down her arms. Not knowing what else to do, she jumped to her feet with surprising vigor (considering the long march behind them) and swung her pack onto her back with as much nonchalance as she could muster. But as they resumed their trek, her mind shifted into overdrive. How dare she react like that to a relative stranger! Faithless, that's what it was. Faithless, disloyal, traitorous. Ariana had been gone only a few months. Then another voice in her head said, "Slow down, Connor. You're making too much of this." She trudged on, unable to still the maelstrom in her head.

Connor gradually realized that her psyche was having a fire sale, dumping everything out for examination, and this was something she *never* did. So what in heaven's name was happening to her? She preferred to believe she was the same person she had always been. But then, no matter what the answer, it still begged the question...who *was* that? Like most people who finally get around to asking themselves that question, she thought of herself only in terms of her roles, her jobs, her relationships to others. Connor Hawthorne, woman about town, writer of mysteries, prosecutor of malefactors, ex-wife, daughter, mother? All of those and, of course...widow? She wondered if that was quite the right word for it? Sort of mainstream heterosexual really, but she couldn't think of a substitute. Ariana wasn't her "ex," after all. Ex-lovers were alive and well somewhere, usually living and loving with someone new. Ex-lovers might pass you on the street someday, might invite you to their new home if the breakup had been amicable. Ex-lovers might even come back. But she would never see Ariana again, ever. She couldn't come back.

Then another thought struck Connor, an unpleasant question really, one for which she had no answer. "Was Ariana my ex-lover before she died, only I didn't know yet?" she asked herself. "Or was it just a fling she was having?" She grimaced at the word. "Fling" sounded so playful and happy. What could be happy or playful about betraying someone who loves you? Maybe it was just the bitterness talking. She couldn't decide if it was worse or better to have discovered Ariana's other life. Must it change the way she grieved? She knew it would be infinitely better if she could remember those many bright years without letting the past few weeks of Ariana's life poison the memories. But she didn't feel strong enough to let go of the anger, the images of Ariana in the arms of a stranger. A week ago, Connor had been quite sure she would never be able to forgive. But here, in this unsettling place, walking under a clear, blue sky, she felt differently about that, and a host of other things she thought she'd settled long ago.

Connor tried to reach out with her mind and reclaim her long list of acceptable values, her standards of rational thought. She was frustrated to discover that it was extremely difficult, if not impossible. Maybe it really was something in the air, or something not in it, like the amount of oxygen she was used to. She just didn't know, so she kept walking. And with every step, despite the uncertainty of events, she grew stronger and more assured that she was very much alive.

Laura looked back over her shoulder with that uncanny half-smile that spoke volumes. Connor found herself wishing she knew what the hell was in those volumes.

Tuesday evening
Washington, D.C.

Benjamin Hawthorne stared at the documents on his desk. It was late; the club's public rooms downstairs had long since closed. He was in the process of doing what has come to be called, "getting one's affairs in order." Not that they weren't generally in order anyway. He had reached an age, as well as a level of involvement in dangerous situations, that made estate planning a necessity rather than a luxury. He reviewed his will, in which he anticipated few changes. Despite his separation from Amanda, he was not the least bit inclined to punish her. She had done her best by her own lights.

The Potomac farm, the cars, the chalet in Switzerland, the beach home in Florida, all these would be hers, along with a sizable trust to maintain her style of living. As for Connor, the townhouse was already hers. He knew she didn't lust after money or possessions the way her mother did, but still he wanted to provide, as any father does. Her trust was equal to that of Amanda's, and Connor was given title to the horses at the farm, as well as permanent rights of visitation to the stable. And, be-

cause he trusted his daughter's judgment, he left her sole posses-
sion of controlling interest in a handful of small, but very successful business enterprises. She could do with them as she
wished.

Naturally, Connor was also the residual legatee; should
Amanda predecease Connor, all would go to Benjamin's daughter. There were other bequests. He had not forgotten Marty, and
generous scholarship trusts had been established for Malcolm Jefferson's children in Marie Louise's name. Arrangements for substantial contributions to several charities concluded the terms.

He jotted a few notes and put them in an envelope addressed
to his attorney. If Benjamin came back, he could sign a new will.
If not, the old one would suffice. He returned the documents to
his safe and closed it. Then he picked up the phone and dialed
American Airlines. It was a menial task, one more often left to
an assistant. But there would be no security risks now. He made
a reservation for a first-class seat to New Mexico the next morning, in the name of Burton Hamilton.

He had sets of perfectly valid identification in several names.
Each of the aliases he might have chosen had at least one thing
in common—the initials B.H.—a standard technique to avoid
potential awkwardness over clothing and luggage monograms.
This particular name always reminded him of the infamous duel
between Alexander Hamilton and Aaron Burr. Perhaps that is
why he had chosen it. It was beginning to feel very much like a
duel between two people with a debt to settle, even if the identity of his adversary still eluded him. So, for the moment, Burton Hamilton he would be.

He packed an overnight bag, including several items and
pieces of clothing not necessary for the average business trip—a
sturdy, warm jacket, denim jeans, a heavy sweater, field glasses,

a topographical chart, a golf hat with a visor, and the Glock 9mm. Into a specially constructed, detachable compartment, went his laptop.

Lastly, he scooped up the week's work—reports, surveillance summaries, and phone tap results—and shoved them into a slim attaché case. He left the club by the rear door, carefully surveying the street. It appeared empty, but, after all these years, he had learned just how deceiving appearances could be. He stood in the doorway and used his cellular telephone to summon a cab. If cellular frequencies were being scanned, all the better. He clearly announced his destination to the dispatcher—Union Station. Ten minutes later, a Diamond cab pulled to the curb.

The station was relatively quiet in deference to the late hour. Benjamin sought out the only open kiosk and purchased newspapers, magazines, and a paperback book. The departure board listed an Amtrak train leaving for New York in fewer than 30 minutes. Still, he did not yet purchase a ticket.

He strolled the cavernous hall, appearing supremely nonchalant, yet his glances took in every detail—the old woman with a cane, the baggage attendant leaning on his trolley, the clerk behind the ticket window, the teenaged couple sharing a bench and fawning over each other, the tired-looking woman and child surrounded by carry-ons and infant paraphernalia, and, there, the youngish man in jeans and a khaki jacket just coming through the revolving doors.

He could be the one, Benjamin thought. But then again, it could be any of them, or none of them. He kept to that fine line between caution and paranoia. From the corner of his eye, he saw the newly arrived man glance around, then head for the newsstand.

Just 20 minutes now, and still Benjamin steered clear of the ticket window. He sat down nearby and scanned the paper. Seven minutes. He rose quickly, but without seeming to hurry, and strolled to the ticket window.

"Private compartment to New York," he said, extracting his wallet. Paying cash was quick and left no traces.

The clerk handed over the ticket and change, and admonished him to hurry. The train would be leaving from Track 2 in five minutes. Benjamin still took his time gathering up the change and replacing it carefully in his wallet. With only three minutes to spare he walked briskly toward the corridor for Track 2. A quick glance over his shoulder told him all he needed to know.

The man in the khaki jacket had broken into a trot toward the ticket window. Benjamin smiled to himself. A well-trained operative would have purchased tickets to all potential destinations immediately upon entering the station and observing Benjamin waiting. That way, he would have been prepared for any contingency. As it was, he had to ask questions, or, if he were really trying to be discreet, make up some story about why he wanted to go where that other gentleman was going. Then he had to buy the ticket.

On the platform, Benjamin looked behind him. Still no sign of the follower. Maybe he'd been wrong, but no, there he was, running hard now, advertising his intentions. But he was still a long way from the platform. Benjamin boarded the train and quickly found the compartment. He stood at an angle inside the door to the roomette car, watching the man's progress.

He had two plans in readiness, depending on whether the pursuer caught the train. If he did, Benjamin was fully prepared to step off, and had selected a place of concealment behind a cement pillar. While the man was struggling to get aboard the train, which was even now beginning to move, he would not be focused on his quarry. And, since Benjamin had reserved a private compartment, the man could hardly ascertain if the occupant was inside of it. He would ride all the way to New York, unless he managed to bribe a porter to investigate.

That plan was not put into action, however. The fellow didn't run very fast, and, peering around the corner of the doorway, Benjamin was gratified to see him standing on the platform, winded and clearly frustrated, as the train eluded him. "Chalk one up for my side," Benjamin thought as he settled himself into his compartment, summoning the porter immediately. "But that's just round one."

He gave the attendant instructions, along with a $20 tip, asking not to be disturbed under any circumstances until they reached New York. He was tired, he said, and needed sleep before a big meeting. The attendant pocketed the twenty and assured him with a smile that Benjamin would not be bothered until they were half an hour out of Grand Central.

When he left, Benjamin pulled down the window shade, turned on the small reading lamp, and, opening the door, peered out. The attendant had continued on to the other cars. Benjamin let himself out of the compartment, locked the door, and took up a position on the platform between his car and the next one ahead. Before long, the train slowed, making its suburban Maryland stop.

There were few passengers waiting, but Benjamin eyed them carefully as they boarded. Not enough time really for them to have gotten someone here, but still, no chances. Just as the train lurched, getting its footing on the track in preparation to depart, Benjamin stepped off, slamming the door behind him. No one was left on the platform, and no one else tried to get off the train. The porter was in a car ahead of him and wouldn't see his unscheduled departure. The train rumbled away as he moved quickly down the stairs and out into the parking lot. Using a pay phone, he called a taxi, then waited in the darkness of a bus stop shelter until it came. No other cars entered the lot, no one loitered within view. Finely honed instincts told him he had eluded his pursuers, whoever they were, at least for the time being.

CHAPTER ELEVEN

All that we see or seem
Is but a dream within a dream.
—Edgar Allen Poe

Wednesday, December 4
Window Rock, Arizona
The Navajo Reservation

Malcolm waited impatiently. He was so keyed up there was no other way he could wait. He sat in the bright lobby of the Tuba City Station and tried to will the office door into opening. The past 18 hours were a blur he was still trying to straighten out in his mind. He had rented a car in Albuquerque when he arrived, intending to make it all the way to Tuba City. Unfortunately, the distances in the "great Southwest" were just that—great. By the time he'd reached Gallup on I-40, he was fighting to stay awake and keep the car on the road. Good sense and years of cleaning up the bloody aftermath of traffic accidents, prevailed over the anxiety gnawing at him.

In Window Rock, just over the border into Arizona, he stopped at a small motel. He slept only fitfully, his dreams filled with images he couldn't understand. Connor was in them, as was Benjamin. But there were other figures, dark and ill-formed. His instincts told him they were somehow evil. They lurked in shadows. He was oddly certain that he knew one of them, one of those shadow figures. He just couldn't figure out who it was. A bright flash of light illuminated the landscape of his dream, then another, and yet another. It produced a strobe effect, causing the people around him to move jerkily and unpredictably. One figure stood in the center of his view, between two upthrust arms of rock. A split second of illumination revealed the face of an old, old woman. Then he was completely alone except for birds, which might be hawks, flying far overhead, calling to him; he stood on a narrow cliff edge, listening, waiting, but he did not know for what. There were footsteps behind him.

He awakened from the dream in a sweat even though there was a definite chill in the room. Out of the corner of his eye he saw something move, there, by the dresser. Startled, he reached for his weapon, swinging the nose around to face...nothing. There was *nothing* there. He could feel his heart pounding and immediately looked at the luminous dial on his watch. Six-thirty. In the morning? Evening? Surely he had not slept all day. Yet it was pitch dark out. He was experiencing that panic some travelers feel upon waking in a strange place, their internal clocks out of synch with their surroundings. He picked up the bedside phone. Finally, after several rings, a sleepy voice answered. "Yeah."

"Could you tell me what time it is?"

That the question was absurd to the voice on the other end was obvious from its tone. "It's 4:30 in the morning." Click. Malcolm was listening to a dial tone.

That explained it. How could he have been so stupid? He hadn't reset his watch from Eastern Time. It was 6:30 in Washington, a little past his usual rising time. He laid back on the bed for a while and thought about going back to sleep, but there was little chance of that. The adrenaline his dreams and half-dreams had sent surging through his body was receding, but it left him wide awake. He was ready to get going, and he was hungry. He doubted there was much chance of getting food at this hour; he would just have to find something on the way. Malcolm took a long shower. The water pressure was hardly vigorous, but the temperature was hot. While he lathered up a second time, he had tried not to think about the dreams. Somewhere in them was a threat, though whether it was Connor or himself who was threatened, he couldn't be sure. It might also be a warning. But Malcolm didn't put much stock in dreams. If God, or the angels, or the good fairy for that matter, were in the habit of warning people in dreams, he thought they should have sent him a dream about Marie Louise. He could have been warned that his wife was going to die that day.

He turned the hot tap off and shocked his skin with ice cold spray for a few seconds. As he briskly toweled himself, he was reminded that he had a job to do. In his mind, this took the form of a pep talk of sorts. "Enough of this bullshit, Jefferson. You're a cop. Act like one. Start dealing with reality, or you'll never find her."

Now, some three hours later, he sat waiting outside Lieutenant Albert Tsosie's office. It had really only been a few minutes; it felt like hours. Malcolm was in the position men of action deplore most—enforced inactivity. Here he was, ready to ride to the rescue, take charge, make things happen, take the ridge, so to speak, and instead he was sitting on his butt.

He was, however, smart enough to know that he couldn't go wandering around the 25,000 or so square miles of the Navajo Reservation haphazardly searching for one person without some sort of guide. He also knew that he was out of his jurisdiction,

way out. He couldn't demand cooperation from the local authorities; he had to ask for it nicely. Problem was, he wasn't *feeling* nice right now; he was frustrated and supremely impatient.
He also felt distinctly out of place. To his increasing annoyance,
the receptionist/dispatcher kept staring at him. He was beginning to get that impression that black people were rare around
these parts. On top of everything else, it was too quiet. Police
stations weren't supposed to be quiet. They were supposed to be
busy, loud, bursting at the seams with activity. He wondered if
there were any crime around here at all. "Probably nothing
much to do," he thought uncharitably. "No wonder they sound
so goddamn laid back."

In this assumption he was wrong, though perhaps he could be
forgiven his lack of understanding. The Navajo Tribal police
were actually fairly busy all the time, particularly since they were
chronically understaffed and covered a very sizable jurisdiction,
if not an exceptionally large population. They had their share of
crimes, although murder and certain other felonies fell to the investigative offices of the FBI. True, they did not approach their
jobs with the visible urgency and tension common to most law
enforcement officers, but they were Navajo, and their methods
and attitudes were different.

Malcolm got up for the third time, and paced up and down
the short corridor. He was about ready to explode when the office door finally opened and a bespectacled Navajo in uniform
motioned him to enter. The two men shook hands and Malcolm
sat in the indicated visitor's chair. Albert Tsosie seemed both
young and old. His hair was gray at the temples, yet his face was
almost smooth, with mostly squint lines around his eyes from
hours under the fierce sun. He was not much over 5'10" and
getting noticeably round at the middle. Malcolm supposed that

might be why the man's gun belt hung on the coat rack behind the desk.

"Sorry to keep you waiting, uh, Captain, isn't it?"

Malcolm took out his badge and ID folder, and passed it across the desk. The police officer barely glanced at it, smiling at the formality.

"I would have recognized your voice anyway," he said. "But thanks." He pulled a file folder from the pile in front of him. "I figure you'd like to get right down to business. Here's the report from my deputy about the accident scene, or the crime scene," he added, with a shrewdly questioning glance at Malcolm. "And we have photos and the witness reports, just one report really, from the Yazzie kid, Jimmy Yazzie. Agnes is pretty annoyed with my deputy for coming up to her place to take a statement from Jimmy. She hates cops." He handed the entire folder across the desk. Malcolm was utterly, but very pleasantly, surprised. He had expected the runaround, lots of static and stonewalling and jurisdictional debate. That's pretty much how it worked where he came from, where cops fought zealously to protect their "turf" and their "collars." He had been prepared to beg if necessary for the right to look at whatever information the department had. And this soft-spoken cop handed it over without being asked. Tsosie leaned back in his chair to let Malcolm read the contents of the folder.

There wasn't much in it. The deputy's report was on top. It was fairly standard, although the location description would have amused Malcolm at some other, less tense moment. Rather than the standard address lines found on most police forms, this space was much larger, leaving room for all manner of geographical description. In this case—"Vehicles found 4.8 miles north by northeast of Black Mesa, on SR 564, approx. 4 miles due west of Tsegi. Witness: James Yazzie: son of Agnes Yazzie, 2 mi. south of Keet Seel Ruin."

The facts of the scene were as Tsosie had described them over the phone. The deputy had drawn a diagram showing the positions of the two vehicles in reference to the road. Attached to the diagram were a half dozen black-and-white photographs. Malcolm shuddered when he saw the condition of the Mercedes. It was riddled with bullets. He had to take the deputy's word that there was no blood, and no sign of violent death in that car.

On the other hand, death took center stage in the photos of the burned-out rental car. The roughly human shaped lump on the ground bore little resemblance to a person, but Malcolm had seen enough burned bodies to know it was.

"Any ID on this guy?"

"We ran down the license plates. It was rented on Friday to a fellow in Albuquerque." he shuffled scraps of paper on his desk. "Here it is. Name was Horace Black. Gave a Virginia driver's license." He raised an eyebrow, gazing at Malcolm for a moment. "Apparently he's from your part of the country. Paid cash, bought the extra insurance, probably to avoid an argument, and he left a $1,000 cash deposit."

"That made sense," Malcolm thought. A standard MO for avoiding being traced back to anyone else.

"I had my duty officer call around to some hotels in Albuquerque and Santa Fe, just a long shot really. But she had some luck. Fellow named Horace Black checked into the Eldorado Hotel in Santa Fe on Friday night, left Sunday morning. Maid told the desk clerk he might have had someone staying with him. But that's about all we got. No sign of him since then, until this." He nodded at the photo in Malcolm's hand.

Tsosie sat back in his chair again, waiting. Malcolm read

through the report again, looked at the photos, and finally put everything back in the folder.

"So, maybe you'd like to tell me what's going on here?" the Lieutenant asked in a tone balanced precisely between outright insistence and polite inquiry.

Malcolm looked up at him, hesitating. He didn't know much, and what he did know, at least part of it he had promised to keep confidential. "It's not that I don't want to tell you. I need your help and I know it. And there's no reason why you should help me if you're in the dark. But the honest truth is that I don't really know just what is going on. Connor Hawthorne is a friend of mine."

"Writer, isn't she? Used to be a D.A. or something?"

Malcolm did not let his surprise show. "Yes, that's the one."

"Isn't she the daughter of some important politician, used to be a Senator?"

This man was no uninformed hick, and Malcolm was rapidly discarding every preconceived notion he had formulated during his trip out here. Had he known that Albert Tsosie possessed both a bachelor's degree in business administration and a master's degree in criminology, he would have further regretted his cavalier assumptions.

"Yes, she is."

"Kind of makes me wonder why we don't have the Feds crawling all over every square inch of that area," he said, nodding at the map on the wall. The statement was shrewd, and Tsosie just let it hang there. Malcolm did not yet know that Navajos were generally not the chattering sort, that they didn't try to fill up silence or elaborate unnecessarily. He took it for a well-honed interrogation technique and squirmed in his chair. The fact there was no all-out law enforcement response rankled him severely. But Benjamin had called off the troops, and there wasn't a chance in hell Malcolm could overrule him. It was also hard to explain to the Lieutenant why a powerful man such as the Senator would not exercise every ounce of his authority to ensure a massive and exhaustive search. It didn't make a lot of sense to him, which made it hard to explain it to someone else. He wrestled with it for quite a while, but Tsosie didn't encourage him, didn't repeat the question, didn't do anything except sit there and wait.

"It's hard to explain, Lieutenant."

"Just call me Albert."

"It's hard to explain, Albert. The situation is sort of delicate."

"This Ms. Hawthorne doing something she shouldn't be doing?"

"No, no, it's nothing like that." Malcolm shook his head firmly. "A friend of hers was murdered in Washington early last September. Then someone broke into her house. We're just worried she might be in some kind of trouble...." Malcolm's voice trailed off uncertainly. This wasn't going very well; he still hadn't answered the real question. But the Navajo cop didn't press. He followed Malcolm's lead.

"So you couldn't get a line on the suspect who murdered this friend?"

"Well, actually, the case is closed. Found a guy dead who had Connor's house keys, a weapon that was a good match." Malcolm wished he sounded more convincing.

"So what makes you think she's still in some sort of danger?" Tsosie's tone of voice and the expression on his face said it all. He wasn't buying this story because it didn't make sense. Unless, of course, something was being intentionally omitted, something which left a hole you could drive a truck through. He watched Malcolm fidget.

"Look, Albert. I honestly don't know all the details. I only know that it might have something to do with national security." Even as he said it, he realized how absurdly melodramatic it sounded, even to him, although he was fairly sure it was true in some sense. The Lieutenant didn't change expression. "Okay. I know how that sounds," Malcolm continued. "I hate it when the Feds start throwing that security stuff around. Hell, they do it to me all the time. But Senator Hawthorne believes that calling in the cavalry..." oh, God, what a bad choice of words, he thought, "...that calling in the FBI or other agencies might actually jeopardize his daughter's life. And, actually, she is supposed to be with someone who is acting as a bodyguard."

"This..." Albert consulted his notes, "...Laura Nez is a *bodyguard*? People she works for seem to think she's a chauffeur."

"I know, but Senator Hawthorne specifically told me that she is known to him and that he arranged for her to stick with Connor while she was here."

"I don't suppose you have any idea what she's doing here on the reservation."

"I talked to her for just a minute or so on Monday. All I got was that she was going adventuring, sightseeing."

"As in tourist?"

"I guess so."

"Well, Captain," Tsosie said, leaning back in his chair and steepling his fingers over his chest, "I guess what I'm wondering is just how this national security issue, as you put it, may affect people here. You tell me that this missing woman is in some kind of jeopardy, but she's just out here playing tourist and is apparently wandering around the reservation on foot with a bodyguard. We find her car with too many bullet holes to count, along with a dead body, and you can't quite explain what might be going on." He paused. "You'll forgive me if I seem a skeptical."

Malcolm did understand. He was even more annoyed, more frustrated, and he had to figure out how to get this man to help him without being able to give him a good reason. "Look, I know how you feel. In your shoes, I'd feel the same way. But I've told you just about everything I know, in fact, it really *is* everything. But she's my friend, and I owe her. I've got to do something." He stopped, then started again. "This woman I told you about, who was murdered in Washington, she was...."

Malcolm hesitated, wondering if this were necessary, but something in Albert's eyes told him the truth was the only thing that would work here. He went on hurriedly tumbling out the words before he could regret saying them. "This woman was Ms. Hawthorne's lover, her partner, for over 10 years. Connor's been despondent and angry, and she hasn't really cared about anything. I couldn't imagine what would make her start wandering around out here. She was supposed to be in Santa Fe for a writer's conference over the weekend, then come back to D.C. All of sudden I get a phone call from her, it only lasts maybe 30 seconds. Then you tell me what happened to her car. I talked to her father. There wasn't much he could, or would, tell me. Just that he would 'handle' it somehow. But I couldn't leave it at that. I had to come here myself."

The Navajo cop didn't speak for several moments. He gazed at the map on the wall. Finally, he stood up. Malcolm was sure his appeal for help had fallen on unwilling ears, but he was wrong. Tsosie ran a finger over the northwestern section of the map. "We'll have to start here, where the cars were found. There was no trace of them to the south, so we'll head north." He looked over at Malcolm. "I assume from what you've said that we can't call up the 'cavalry.'" He smiled to let Malcolm know he had not been offended. "Besides, I can't spare my own people if it isn't official. And I'm assuming this isn't."

Malcolm nodded in agreement.

"Then it looks like it's just you and me." He reached for his gunbelt and strapped it on. "I've got just about everything we need in my carryall. That's the four-wheel drive parked by the door. Why don't you get your stuff and meet me outside? Then we'll go by my place so I can get some extra clothes."

It began to dawn on Malcolm that the sort of search they were undertaking was radically different than anything he had ever experienced. He'd searched for people—lost people, kidnapped people, suspects—but on familiar territory, the streets and alleys of a city. And after a full shift, or even a double shift, you still went home because it was just a few miles. He had a funny feeling they wouldn't be going home until they'd succeeded in finding Connor, one way or the other.

At Albert's house, the Navajo officer politely suggested that Malcolm was not dressed for this assignment. He looked skeptically at the D.C. cop's three-piece suit. "Did you happen to bring anything a little more rugged with you?" he inquired. "Work pants? Jeans? Maybe some boots?"

Malcolm was a little puzzled. "Are we going to be walking a lot?"

"Could be. Depends on where their trail leads us. Some places even the carryall can't make it."

Malcolm looked down at his urban outfit and felt a little foolish. What had he been thinking of? "I guess I wasn't planning very well. Is there a store around here?" He grinned ruefully. "Preferably one with big sizes."

"There's a store sells western clothes, cowboy stuff. They might have what you need. I'd borrow an outfit for you, but I don't know anyone as big as you."

An hour and a half later, they left Tuba City. Malcolm felt sheepish in his stiff new jeans, western shirt, and work boots. A western hat—a cowboy hat, for god's sake—lay on the seat beside him. Albert had insisted that the sun was very strong here, even in early December; a hat was a sensible precaution. It still seemed pretty damn silly. These weren't the sort of clothes he would ever go to work in, partly because it wasn't his habit and partly because, as a black man in a largely white bureaucracy, his suit was part of his personal armor, a symbol announcing to anyone who might challenge him that he was playing in their league.

He'd also purchased the only jacket they had that more or less fit him. Wearing his suit jacket, or even his trench coat, would have looked absurd, even to Malcolm, who was no clothes horse to begin with. But he wasn't comfortable wearing his shoulder holster in plain sight while out in public—another habit of longstanding. Not that it would have mattered. He realized there probably wouldn't be a lot of public where they were going, but he felt more secure with the short leather coat on and his weapon out of sight. He was only grateful that the new jacket, which had put yet another solid dent in his credit limit, had no fringe hanging off of it. He could just see Connor's reaction to Malcolm Jefferson turned Buffalo Bill. The smile that played across his face as he thought of how tickled she would be at the look of him faded quickly. Where the hell was she? He made a private vow—if he could just find Connor, if he could see her alive and well, she could laugh at him all she wanted.

———◦◦◦———

Wednesday morning
Arlington, VA

While Malcolm sat cooling his heels in the Tuba City Station, Benjamin was checking out of the Key Bridge Marriott, just across the Potomac from Georgetown. He took the first available hotel airport shuttle and looked for all the world like an aging tourist. He had exchanged his well-cut suit for the jeans and sweater. He had donned the golf cap and sunglasses.

At the American Airlines entrance, he graciously assisted an elderly woman to alight and even carried her bags into the terminal for her. Benjamin picked up his tickets at the counter and checked his bag with his weapon locked inside. He could hardly get the Glock through the security checkpoint, and he did not wish to draw unnecessary attention to himself by flashing credentials showing he was permitted to carry it.

As he took his seat in first class, the flight attendant smiled at him, handing him a pillow and taking his drink order immediately. She was solicitous in the extreme, and Benjamin could not help feeling he had been swiftly categorized, assigned to the codger bench. He settled back in his seat as the plane lumbered down the runway, gathering speed and finally heaving itself, almost unwillingly, off the ground.

He had not slept well. He was troubled by shapeless fears that wandered in and out of his restless dream like uninvited guests who could not be turned away. Finally, the old woman came and her mouth moved, speaking words he could not understand.

Despite his fatigue, though, his tension was gone; in its place remained a calm certainty.

He wondered why he had waited so long to go back. Perhaps he had become so obsessed with protecting the secret that he was afraid to jeopardize it. Yet he had to admit he was also frightened of the secret itself, or at least of getting any closer to it. What he had seen was forever engraved on his mind, yet he understood so little of it. Fear of the unknown—such a pedestrian human reaction. He was almost embarrassed to acknowledge that even he, Senator Benjamin Hawthorne, would succumb to it. Then he laughed to himself. "Such arrogance," he thought. "What am I? The powerful and wonderful Oz? How absurd to imagine that I am not capable of being afraid of what I don't understand."

He had to change planes in Houston. He went directly to the designated departure gate only to discover his connection would be delayed. Equipment failure, they said. Three to four hours wait. Benjamin scowled at the agent, but held his temper. He didn't want to draw attention to himself. He went back to the main terminal, checking his surroundings carefully as he strolled to the nearest lounge. The situation seemed secure. His altered identity had done the trick for the moment. It wouldn't last long, but at least whoever might be waiting for him in New Mexico would not get much warning that he was coming.

Wednesday evening
Navajo Reservation

Only a few miles from their destination, as Connor and Laura continued to trudge along in the growing darkness, Connor let her mind wander more and more from the monotonous task at hand. As a result, she let her foot wander into a deep hole. The loss of normal equilibrium was so unexpected she couldn't figure out quite which way to fall. By default, it was backward, in the direction of the weight of her backpack. The errant foot, still caught, did not follow the direction its parent leg wished to go. Connor saw a galaxy of stars as her ankle twisted in a direction it was not designed to go, and she sought the comfort of a string of expletives.

Laura, who happened to be several feet ahead looking for familiar landmarks, rushed back at the first sound of trouble to find Connor lying on the ground, with her foot in a hole and uttering distinctly unladylike language. The scene was just funny enough and incongruous enough that Laura was torn between her instant concern for Connor and the urge to laugh at the very undignified picture she presented. The laughter won out, and Connor looked up indignantly into the mirthful face of her would-be guide.

"Well I don't see what's so goddamn funny," she barked. "I think I broke something."

"I'm sorry. I'm sorry. I'm just tired. And seeing you up to your knee in a prairie dog den...." She stopped and made a visible effort to be serious. "You'd probably see more humor in it if you were standing here looking down at yourself right now. And I have it on good authority that you didn't break anything, although you did sprain something."

"What, you have prairie dog helpers who talk to you, make a diagnosis on the spot?" Connor looked suspiciously at the hole. "Hey, just how big is a prairie dog? And do they bite?"

"Not very, and not as a rule, unless you annoy them by dropping in unexpectedly." While delivering these brief answers, she began digging away the dirt around Connor's leg, then started lifting her by the shoulders.

Connor looked up at her to determine how serious this bit of anthropological information on the habits of prairie dogs was and, seeing the twinkle in Laura's eyes, found herself suddenly hiccuping with laughter. The sound of it was so strange that it completely neutralized whatever control Laura had achieved over her own amusement. She lost her grip on Connor and fell backward, unceremoniously landing on her behind.

For the next several minutes, denizens of the desert were treated to an altogether unfamiliar sound—the unbridled laughter of women—echoing and bouncing off the rock formations and trickling through the arroyo, where a curious little mouse raised its head in wonder. When they finally settled down and caught their breath, Laura extricated Connor from the prairie dog's home. She took a step to test the ankle with some weight on it. She couldn't hide the wince of pain, but she expressed her determination to stoically limp the last few miles. Laura just shook her head at such foolhardiness and scouted ahead for a campsite. She came back in a few minutes.

"There's a fairly deep arroyo about a hundred yards away. Ordinarily it isn't the safest place to camp, but with this weather we aren't at much risk of being swept away by a flash flood. And there's enough dry wood to feed a campfire."

Connor, who was standing and leaning against a boulder, tested her weight on the sprain, grimacing just a little. "It really isn't bad," she asserted, though her certainty wavered a bit under Laura's doubtful expression (conveyed by one raised eyebrow). "Well, not as bad as I thought anyway. But I still want to know why you were so sure nothing was broken."

"Trade secret. I'll tell you someday. Now, put your arm around my shoulder."

"Hey, I can walk on it."

"I didn't ask if you could. I'm sure you'd be glad to crawl all the way, but humor me, please? That's right, lean on me, put as little weight as possible on your foot. Good. Now, start off with me, right foot first. No, the *other* right."

Connor laughed. "Sorry, I've always had a foot and hand dyslexia problem."

"Now you tell me. All right, one more time."

Though Connor was tall, Laura was not that much shorter, perhaps an inch, two at the most. And the arm that Laura had around her waist felt strong. It was an odd sensation she analyzed as they hobbled along; her writer's mind turned the question over and over, and sorted out possibilities. Rarely had any woman been strong for Connor, rather it was she who was always the strong one, in relationships, even in friendships for the most part. Connor was physically more imposing than her lovers, and more prone to adopt the leadership role. She supposed some would call it more "butch," but she detested labels and stereotypes. To her mind, it was more a matter of her natural tendency to take the lead—in love, in her careers, in life. She'd felt compelled to do so, as if by being in charge of most things she could control her own destiny and, if she admitted it to herself, keep from being hurt. Unfortunately, it didn't always work out that way. Now, as she felt Laura's solid strength buoying her up, her heart was even more puzzled than her mind. A new sensation had come to call, but was experiencing a communication gap with the current resident. It was most unsettling to have one's philosophical foundations shaken.

Once campfire building, ankle wrapping, and dinner were dispensed with, the two women once again shared the night sky. Tonight, however, rather than metaphysical issues, Connor's investigative mind worried at the problem of who was trying to kill her. She could not really believe in an old grudge rearing its ugly head. The situation must be connected to her father. Unfortunately, she did not know enough about his everyday business to even guess intelligently.

"You're frowning," Laura said, looking at her curiously. "Any particular reason?"

"Other than wondering who's trying to kill me, or rather kill us. Do you have any thoughts on that? You probably know more about my father's activities than I do."

"I doubt it. Benjamin doesn't share much information, keeps everything compartmentalized."

"Good spy technique?" There was more than a hint of bitterness in Connor's tone, but Laura evaluated the question simply on its merits, without responding to the implied judgment about her choice of career.

"I imagine so, but then I'm not exactly a spy. I'm more of a useful asset. But since you're trying to work this out, let's look at what we do know."

Connor pursed her lips. "All right. One, whoever murdered Ariana must be connected with that guy back there. Two, someone went to a lot of trouble to follow us here."

"Or they already knew you were coming," Laura amended.

"True." Connor allowed that to sink in. "I didn't make any real secret of my plan to attend the conference. The part that's odd is that he managed to follow us all the way from Santa Fe when I was making impulsive decisions about where to go rather than following an itinerary."

"That's the element in this that bothers me most," Laura said, shaking her head. "I immediately suspected an electronic tracking device, but I swept the car with a detector every morning before we set out."

"Are you always that efficient and that cautious?"

Laura shook her head. "I'm nowhere near perfect, hardly the Navajo version of Emma Peel." Connor smiled at the reference; she'd always loved *The Avengers*. "But I do pay attention to my job, especially when it could mean the difference between someone's life or death. Sweeping for bugs was a basic precaution."

"Is that why you didn't like having the car out of your sight?" Connor said with sudden comprehension.

"Mostly, although I also knew that you were safer inside of it than outside."

"We've seen a practical demonstration of that," Connor replied, thinking of the dozens of bullets slapping into the windshield.

"The other odd thing about what happened on the road is why he seemed so unprepared for me to make an offensive maneuver."

Connor saw the answer to that instantly. "It had to be because he didn't know about *you*. He assumed you were a paid driver who'd panic and not know what to do when he came up alongside us. It didn't occur to him you were trained to react to that sort of threat."

"Which means his intelligence isn't very good, after all," mused Laura. "And that is inconsistent with the other events, where someone is getting very good information. I don't suppose we should consider the person you called on the cell phone, your friend, Malcolm."

Connor started to be offended, then backed off. Laura didn't know him. "No, that would be a case of barking up the wrong tree. He's a good friend, has been for a lot of years."

Laura shrugged and yawned. "I'll take your word for it. We don't know much for sure at this point. And, for the time being,

I don't think all our supposing will do us much good. Sleep might be a better idea."

Connor had to admit that her mind was worn out. She once more curled herself up as near the fire as possible, reaching behind her to unclip the automatic pistol from her belt. "Why don't you just keep that on until we get where we're going," Laura said softly. "You never know." Connor half-shrugged and, despite the throbbing in her foot and all the unanswered questions buzzing through her head, she finally fell asleep.

She did not know that she dreamed, that she chased the receding shadow of Ariana's killer through dark tunnels and foreboding caverns, or that she cried aloud in her sleep. Nor was she aware that Laura, keeping watch long into the night, knew what paths Connor walked in her dreams and went with her, following a few paces behind, ready to bring her back should she wander too far. When it was time for her own sleep, Laura carefully and gently lay down beside Connor and wrapped the troubled woman in her strong arms, chasing away the monsters and the shadows.

CHAPTER TWELVE

Our torments also may, in length of time
Become our elements.
—John Milton

Wednesday Night
Brussels, Belgium
NATO Headquarters

The staff officer stood, hands clasped behind his back, staring out of the large window that permitted a prized view reserved for those with sufficient rank. Brussels was a lovely city, particularly at night. It had been a long time, however, since he had stopped to consider the beauty in anything, be it a landscape or a woman. He had no time for such considerations now; for that matter, he had not been blessed with the sensitivity required to appreciate harmony, beauty, or diversity.

To him, life was simple, ordered, either/or. It was society's misfits who tried to make it otherwise. He, himself, had long ago discarded philosophical gray areas—they annoyed him. Ethical debates were for the bleeding hearts, the cowards, the sneaks, the con-men looking for an angle, always trying to avoid conflict. He, on the other hand, reveled in conflict because, whenever there was conflict, he was smart enough to choose the correct side, the winning side.

To the colonel, the world was divided into clearly delineated camps: right and wrong, his way or someone else's way, win or lose, and, of course, underlying it all, fascism or communism— democracy having been relegated to the slag heap of failed experiments in the colonel's estimation. If he had to choose a label, he was a fascist. All this talk of the will of the people. Hah! Sheep! They were all stupid sheep, waiting for the strong hand of a good shepherd. That he continued to wear the uniform of the world's strongest democracy was a matter of expediency, nothing more.

The colonel's greatest frustration at this point in his life was his inability to sway the world to his way of thinking, a failure he usually attributed to the bunch of sniveling Communists running the media. His message, carefully promoted by his small cadre of loyal soldiers around the world, through both word and deed, was repeatedly ignored, or worse, ridiculed. These morons did not understand the need for imposed order. They should abhor the violence of terrorists and mistrust the rhetoric of the left wing? Of course, in truth, his "group" had been responsible for some of that violence and some of the more extreme rhetoric, but that was a strategic maneuver. The more chaos he could create, the more someone of his outlook and military experience would be appreciated. People would turn to him eventually to put an end to chaos, an end to disorder, an end to puerile attempts at democracy for all human beings. A few more well-placed explosives, a few hundred more women and school children dead, a few more planes falling from the sky, and even the most obtuse citizen must see that all this violence and tragedy was simply the result of permissiveness, of letting the enemies run amok—the commies, the niggers, the spics, the Jews, the chinks, the redskins, the wetbacks, the rag heads, all of them try-

ing to wrest control of the world from those to whom it right-
fully belonged—the white men—the soldiers of God, of whom
he was the pre-ordained leader. This was a role for which he had
prepared, for which he was suited.

The colonel was a good-sized man at 6'2", and his uniform
was expertly tailored to accentuate broad shoulders and disguise
an incipient middle-age spread. It aggravated him that, despite
daily exercise and a spartan diet regimen, he no longer possessed
the physique of the 22-year-old lieutenant he had been 40 years
ago. Nor did he possess the same good health. A private physi-
cian in Berne (he had gone outside of Belgium to protect his privacy) had confirmed what he already knew. Thirty years of chain
smoking and heavy drinking were finally taking their toll. He
didn't have a lot of time left to make his visions a reality, and,
much to his anger and frustration, he did not yet have the military power. He had been passed over three times for promotion.
Fawning idiots who followed the party line and unqualified col-
oreds with their pitiful sob stories had kept him a mere colonel
for 12 years, while undeserving ass-licking puppets wore the
general's stars and sat in the seats of power and royally fucked up
the world.

It was small comfort that he was the commander of his own
special force. He was not so far immersed in his own megalo-
mania that he imagined his handful of terrorists to be a private
army. He was born to command hundreds of thousands, even
millions of fighting men, his own legions, and the colonel knew
he had but one chance left. Toward this end he had bent all his
efforts.

Six months ago, he had been approached by an American, a
man who spoke convincingly of a secret, something so powerful, so unimaginable, that the one who controlled it would in-

deed control the world. The colonel had been skeptical at first (he automatically disliked the informant), but the man's credentials were unquestionable, so he set about trying to confirm any hint of this secret. Time and again he hit dead ends, and, so effective were these red herrings, they seemed, in themselves, to confirm the existence of something out of the ordinary. At no time since undertaking his mission had he been able to unearth any solid piece of the information he sought. Until now. But still he was being thwarted, and it made him furious. He tried to calm himself as he waited in his office, expecting a report that had better, by God, be favorable. So far, almost nothing had gone according to plan, a circumstance which would have deeply offended his ego had he not blamed everyone besides himself. As he saw it, he was at the mercy of the imbeciles who worked for him.

The secure phone line on his desk rang twice, then stopped. Possibly a faulty routing on transatlantic cable. Some information was far too sensitive to discuss via satellite transmission, and he did not expect his underlings to be foolish enough to try it. They used a "hard" connection since his position at NATO put him above suspicion and made his communications sacrosanct. When it rang again, he picked it up and barked into the receiver. "Speak!"

"Sir! This is Marlena."

"Report!"

There was hesitation. That, too, annoyed him.

"Report! Is Phase II complete?"

"No, sir. It is not."

The colonel could feel his pulse pounding in his temples, rage boiling up inside of him. He wanted to scream, strike out at the voice on the other end, put his hands around her throat and...He tried to get control of his voice.

"I want to know why."

"Ferret has been compromised...permanently."

Goddamn it, the fucking stupid son of a bitch was dead.

"How?"

"Not clear, sir. The target had assistance in place."

So he must be getting close. There was sufficient pleasure in this thought to calm him for a moment. If she had protection, then wherever she was, that was it—the Holy Grail, the secret weapon, for surely that is what it must be, some device or technology so powerful, even that jackass in the Oval Office didn't know about it, nor did the Joint Chiefs. Only that sleazy spymaster, Hawthorne, his lesbo daughter, and someone else, someone on-site probably.

"Sir?" The tinny voice interrupted him in mid-gloat.

"What?"

"Your orders, sir?"

"Get to the target immediately and replace Ferret. It's," he consulted his watch, "7:00 p.m. here. You're eight hours behind, it's still morning there. You have ample time to catch up with the target."

"But, sir, the exact location is unknown."

"Then you'd better get your ass in gear and find out. I'll expect positive results in 24 hours, at your next report."

"Yes, sir, uh...there's more."

"Then spit it out."

"Ferret's last report indicated an unusually destructive explosion at a private home in A-town."

A-town! Atomic town. That meant Los Alamos. Damn! He knew it. There was someone there who knew about the weapon, maybe even the person who had helped develop it.

"Anyone in the kill zone?"

"Yes, sir. An employee of A-town."

Bingo. He was so close now he could taste it, he could see the world at his feet, his soldiers bringing about a new order. "Transmit details via DP."

"Sir, there are no resources for that at my current location."

"Then take care of your assignment and return to available resource."

"Yes, sir, but...."

"I don't want to hear anything further from you except that you have succeeded."

He slammed down the receiver so hard that the framed photograph on his desk fell over. He picked it up, taking a moment to admire the handsome face of his dead son. The colonel's expression softened as his fingers stroked the surface of the picture.

"I would have shared this moment with you, Robert," he said. "You would have been the heir to my power, my conquest." The lump in his throat choked him. Grief for his slain son had burned in the colonel's soul for 25 years, just as the cancer was now burning away his body. The betrayal of his son's memory by those he served had transformed the father's pursuit of power from overweening ambition to holy cause. He would make them pay, all the do-gooders, the peacemongers, the slime who had made a war unwinnable, and taken his beautiful boy. He knew that Robert's so-called buddies had betrayed him, had retreated under cowardly orders, leaving his son alone with the radio, alone in the jungle, without his unit, without protection, standing his ground until he died.

If that weren't horrible enough—to lose your only son. But then the lies started, the unforgivable lies. Robert wasn't given the honors he deserved—no Purple Heart, no Silver Star, no Congressional

Medal—the least he deserved for his bravery. No, the goddamn motherfucking sonsabitches at the Pentagon, so apologetic and concerned, telling him they didn't want to make a public issue of it, but Robert hadn't been a hero at all, they said. They had investigated very carefully, they said. Robert had been a deserter, a coward; he'd abandoned his post, had let his unit down, had been responsible for their deaths, all except two survivors who had testified about what happened during the patrol.

"Liars! Goddamn filthy liars!" The words slipped out between his gritted teeth. He knew they were just covering up, trying to shift the blame. Robert's teachers and his commanding officers, they had all been liars. The colonel had known better; he had ignored their absurd accusations. They had actually tried to convince him his son was disturbed, for god's sake, that Robert tried to hurt people and animals, that Robert lied. Well, they were the goddamn liars, just like those two soldiers who'd said Robert was to blame. They were trying to avoid the court-martial they deserved. They ran away and put all the blame on Robert, poor, dead Robert, who couldn't defend himself. Every time he thought of it, pain knifed through his heart. He'd lost his only son, and those bastards had dishonored the boy and shunned the father. They would all come to regret the day his son had been left to die.

The colonel reverently returned the picture to its appointed place, at the precise angle he had chosen for it on every desk he had ever occupied over the years. It went with him to each new command, both as a reminder and a talisman. He opened the safe behind his desk and withdrew the Book—the Master Plan for ending the chaos in the world. Within the well-thumbed leaves of the worn, black leather binder, he found solace. It comprised 230 pages of carefully handwritten plans and procedures and new

laws—laws he would enact and enforce, laws which would punish the cowards and reward the righteous. Naturally, many people would die. His soldiers would cleanse the earth of vermin, at
least two-thirds of the population, perhaps more. He smiled as
he turned the pages. It was as if God, Himself, had given these
words to the colonel. He wondered if they were intended to
somehow recompense the loss of his son.

———

Wednesday
Santa Fe

Her face was considerably less attractive when she was angry.
Of course, that is true of most people. But, in her case, the fes-
tering evil dwelling inside her twisted what might have been described as an aristocratic visage into something as frightening as
it was ugly. Fortunately, no one was present to witness the transformation. She muttered to herself as she strode back and forth,
violently yanking clothing off of hangers and stuffing them haphazardly into a suitcase. She detested that pompous, arrogant,
self-righteous bully, and she rankled at the way he ordered her
about. He made her skin crawl. On the other hand, she believed
in the so-called cause, or at least in that part of the cause that
promised her power. A life that had begun in wretched poverty
and complete helplessness had taught her the advantages of being
in charge. Of course, had she been more conversant with the
colonel's views on the role of women in his new society, she
might have reconsidered her loyalty. But she wasn't, and her
own lust for power clouded an otherwise intelligent, if morally
bankrupt mind.

To her, power over others was salvation, aphrodisiac, and narcotic, all wrapped into one. Its aroma excited her; exercising it made her quiver with pleasure. To her, the power to decide between life and death for another human being was the ultimate proof of her own ascendancy. Having long since abandoned whatever remnants of humanity her harsh upbringing had left intact, she was, in the vernacular of the day, a stone killer, without a single vestige of conscience. For this reason, she was a valuable tool to anyone who sought to dominate with violence, because she liked killing and she liked to watch killing. She liked to decide that someone would die. She often daydreamed about that. Had she ruled during the glorious days of the Roman Empire, no gladiator could have expected her royal thumb to turn upward in a vote for life. Her vote would always be for death, and that included the pompous ass colonel.

She saw him as being little different from the succession of "uncles" in her life, the men who pretended to desire her mother, but were usually more eager for the forbidden pleasures to be had with the young daughter. Yes, they'd used her. But she had used them also—to learn how to wield this power over such pathetic excuses for men. They may have thought they were in charge, but they weren't. Occasionally, when one of them accidentally looked at her face while he pawed at her, he would invariably stop cold when he saw her eyes. The expression in them was enough to frighten even the most insensitive and shallow of those stupid pigs who had mistaken her silent acquiescence for submission.

In the depths of her eyes dwelt sheer malice, and her condescending smile mocked their desperate attempts to satisfy forbidden desires. Indeed, those pedophiles who had been foolish enough to really look at her usually recoiled in horror, so startled they would pull away, mouths agape, penises wilting absurdly. It amused her to see that, their precious manhood dangling limp and useless.

Thus she had learned about the power she could wield over men, or women. It didn't really matter which. Lust and stupidity might be more blatant in men, more common, but they were present in the female gender as well. Seducing men was child's play. The old aphorism made her smile since she had honed her skills long before most girls even thought about their sexuality. In all fairness, she would admit that seducing women was more complicated, required more subtlety and caution, more patience. But in the end, the result was always the same. Except for that goddamn Hawthorne bitch. How dare she refuse to play the game? Her body convulsed with anger once more, but she reminded herself to breathe deeply and dissociate from the emotion. Anger was not useful in her line of work. Besides, the game was still in progress. The last move would be hers. The last victory grin before the thumb was turned downward.

Ultimate control, ultimate power. She smiled. That is what had made this assignment so delicious, at least until now. Back in Washington she had basked in the puerile adoration of that stupid bitch, had manipulated her, used her, seduced her, screwed her, and then watched her die. She would have preferred to do it herself—killing was a visceral pleasure to be savored—but Ferret had so wanted to do it. He enjoyed it, too, but, she reminded herself, at a much less refined level. For him it was more of an animal instinct, psychopath that he was, though she doubted he possessed sufficient intelligence to merit the status of psychopath.

She, on the other hand, did. A carefully honed intellect, a brilliant deductive mind, an excellent education, seductive charm,

social grace, a perfect body, and—underneath it all—a soul so
dead that no hint of warmth or love would ever find a foothold
within it. She hated as reflexively as other human beings breathe.
She hungered for the smell and taste of fear as others hunger for
food, which was why she'd watched from the opposite bank of
the canal that day, her binoculars trained on Ariana's lovely face
as it was suffused with blood. Ferret's hands tightened around
that delicate neck, choking her unconscious before he finished
her off with his knife. She watched it all, shuddering with pleasure as he straddled her hips and buried the thin knife in her
chest. God, how she wished Ferret would rape the woman, right
there in the mud where she could watch it all. But apparently he
didn't do that sort of thing, the little prick. She thought it probably *was* little, and limp.

She abandoned her packing as a sudden urge surfaced to dis-
obey the bastard in Belgium. To hell with him. She would follow her own timetable. She opened the doors to the terrace and
sat down in one of the chairs, pondering her next move. She regretted that she hadn't been able to seduce the target. She had so
enjoyed taking the girlfriend away from that smug bitch, all
puffed up with so-called talent. It had been a most pleasant game
to play. It would be even more amusing to get her hands on the
"widow" just to see the look on her face when she learned the
truth. But the orders were clear and concise—Connor
Hawthorne was to die immediately. It didn't occur to her for a
moment that she could fail, or that anyone on earth was clever
enough to penetrate her cover or discern her plans.

CHAPTER THIRTEEN

Though nothing can bring back the hour
Of splendour in the grass, of glory in the flower;
We will grieve not, rather find
Strength in what remains behind;
In that primal sympathy
Which having been must ever be;
In the soothing thoughts that spring
Out of human suffering;
In the faith that looks through death
In years that bring the philosophic mind.
—William Wordsworth

Wednesday night
The Navajo Reservation

Malcolm and Police Chief Tsosie made good time to the site of Monday's accident near Black Mesa. They did not linger. All Malcolm needed to know was already contained in the report. Albert quickly identified the tracks of the two women heading north.

"What is there in that direction?" Malcolm asked, pointing northward.

"That's what puzzles me. No towns, no trading posts, no substations."

"What about private homes?"

"Hard to say. The Yazzie outfit is more in that direction," he pointed with his chin toward the east. "And old Joseph Yabenny's place is more to the west. But I don't know of any places offhand that line up with these tracks." He frowned at the footprints.

"Does this Laura Nez have family around here?"

A smile played over Albert's lips. "You probably don't realize this, but here, the name "Nez" is like Smith or Jones back where you come from. Navajos don't go so much by surname as by family connections, clan membership. Without knowing who she's related to, or finding someone who knows her, it would be almost impossible to track down her family."

Malcolm looked glum, but Albert shrugged and said, "Even if we don't know exactly where they're headed eventually, we know which way they went. And we'd better get started, we've only got a few hours of light left."

They lurched and bumped across the desert, rarely getting over 20 miles an hour, but still making good time according to the Navajo cop. Albert kept his window down and periodically checked the tracks as they went. Malcolm was silent, having nothing to contribute in the way of expertise. He was completely out of his element now and he shuddered to think how hard he would find it to survive in a place like this. To him, the face of the land was decidedly unfriendly.

It was some time before Albert broke into Malcolm's reverie.

"This person we're looking for, your friend. Mind telling me why you're feeling so protective?"

Malcolm gave the question serious consideration before he answered.

"It isn't like she's helpless or anything. I don't want you to get that impression. She's incredibly strong and capable. She's a smart lady who can take care of herself. Though I guess it wouldn't seem that way to you, with me riding to the rescue like some white knight," he paused, grinning, "or black knight as the case may be. It's more that I owe her."

Albert raised one eyebrow slightly. "You mentioned that before. Must be some debt if it brings you all the way out here."

"It is. When my wife died a few years ago—she was killed in a bank robbery—I didn't think I could make it. We had three kids and life was so good. One day we were a family, the next day we weren't. Marie Louise was the most important thing in the world to me." He paused. Albert waited out the silence until Malcolm was ready to go on.

"Anyway, I thought about..." Malcolm swallowed hard, "...about killing myself, but Connor stopped me. And she helped me find the people who were responsible for Marie Louise's murder. Connor and my sister, Eve, they made me come back."

He didn't explain what he meant by "back," but Albert nodded.

"I know about that place where you end up when someone you love is taken from you. For my people, that kind of grief takes you out of harmony with the external world and into a place where it's impossible to experience the joy of being alive."

"That's exactly what it felt like," Malcolm agreed, thinking about how hard it had been to feel anything at all back then.

Albert continued. "I lost my wife, Gloria, almost 20 years ago. I'm glad it wasn't a violent death, or a long, drawn-out painful one." He paused to light a cigarette, cracking open the window in deference to his passenger.

"She loved horses more than anything. She had been riding

since her Uncle put her on a pony when she was about five years old. She had a way with them. I'd swear they listened to her, even the ones that were wild." He took a long drag from his cigarette.

"We were down near Phoenix one winter, and Gloria was teaching at a riding academy there. I came by to pick her up in the afternoon, and I saw she was in one of the corrals working with a horse who'd been badly mistreated by some idiot who thought he knew how to break horses. Anyway, Gloria had been making a lot of progress with this colt. I was about 50, 60 feet away, leaning on the railing watching her. It always amazed me, the way she'd look them in the eye, talk to them real low, just like they understood every word she said." He cleared his throat quietly.

"That day I guess one of the riding students wanted to ask her something. The little boy came dashing down one of the herding chutes right up behind this horse. The animal heard him and panicked. I saw it wheel around and rear up. Poor kid was so shocked he fell backward, and the horse was about to come down right on top of that child with his front hooves. It would have killed him probably.

"Next thing I see is Gloria ramming her shoulder up under his withers, trying to knock that horse sideways while she grabbed at the kid and shoved him toward the fence. Then she turned to face the horse to give the boy time to get out, but the animal was so terrified, she couldn't calm him down. The next time he reared up she backed away, tried to duck. One of his hooves caught her in the side of the head, crushed her skull.

"It happened so fast, seconds I guess, and I stood there, frozen to the spot. It was like a bad dream where I couldn't make myself move. But when I saw her go down, I scrambled through the fence and chased the horse down the chute. The little boy was crying, sitting on the ground on the other side. And Gloria just lay there. I took her hand, I tried to talk to her. I remember I was screaming for someone to help us. But she just smiled the most beautiful smile at me, and then she was gone." Albert took a last drag off his cigarette and ground it out in the ashtray. "So I brought her back here and had the proper things done for her."

Both men were silent for a while.

Malcolm said quietly, "That must have been very hard, to see it happen."

"Yes, in a way it was, and yet, you know, I'm glad I was there. That last smile kept me going for a long time, until I could begin to conceive of a life that didn't have Gloria in it. Her uncle was good to me, too. He came and sat with me for hours, not talking, but he helped me all the same, showing me the way back. Eventually, the world was beautiful again."

"You never remarried?"

"No. In the old days, it would have been expected of me to marry one of my wife's sisters. But I couldn't. Gloria was too close to my heart, too close to my spirit. I couldn't share that with anyone else."

"I know," said Malcolm. "I know." A thought occurred to him. He looked over at Albert. "What happened to the horse? Did you...?"

"Shoot him?"

"Yeah, I'd have wanted to if I'd been in your shoes."

"No. The stable owner wanted to. Went straight into his office for a rifle when the ambulance left. But I had just watched them pull the blanket over Gloria's face. I couldn't stand the thought of any more death. And I knew she wouldn't want that either. She didn't blame the horse. Why should I? So I begged him not to do it. I don't think he understood, but he gave me his word that he wouldn't destroy the animal."

"You were more forgiving than I would have been."

"What was to forgive? A terrified animal struck out blindly. There was no malice, no intent to kill." His voice softened slightly. "Your wife died at the hands of men whose hearts were dark, men who had ceased to value human life. They were killers. It's beyond most of us to forgive such people when they take those we love."

"I can't."

Albert was silent for a while, checking the ground alongside them to be sure they had not strayed from their path.

"So you said you caught the guys. Your friend helped you find them?"

"She's a smart woman, had a 90 percent conviction rate when she was a D.A." Albert nodded appreciatively. "She helped me analyze the evidence we had accumulated on a series of bank robberies. She found a pattern, a link that tied these guys in with almost all of them. We had some forensic evidence from two of the crime scenes, and she put it all together."

"What did you do when you found them?"

Malcolm squirmed a little in his seat. "What do you mean?"

"Did you kill them?" Albert's choice of words was blunt, but honest.

"No."

"But you wanted to."

"I did want to. But Connor was with me that night. She shouldn't have been, but she's hard to say no to."

"And she wouldn't let you do it?"

"No, she wouldn't. It was the second time she was there at a turning point in my life. It's not like she grabbed my gun or anything. She just talked and talked. Hell, she wouldn't *stop* talking."

Malcolm closed his eyes for the briefest moment, remembering that horrible night, the sweat running in his eyes, his finger poised on the trigger of his gun, the three defiant, snarling faces staring back at him. And through it all, Connor's voice. She pleaded, demanded, cajoled, reasoned, never stopping long enough to let him make that decision to commit murder. And suddenly his backup was there, and there was no decision to make. It was over.

"Sounds like quite a woman. I'd say she was pretty intent on not letting you become like the men who killed your wife." Malcolm thought about that for a moment.

"Yes, she was," he replied at last.

"I believe there's a capacity for evil in all of us. It seems to be greater in some than in others. Sometimes it comes down to whether or not we give in to it."

Malcolm looked at him. "Do you really believe in evil?"

"Yes, I do. My people believe there is an evil part within each of us. We were taught that from the beginning. And we were taught to believe in witches, and skinwalkers, and even curses."

"Do you accept all that? Aren't some of those things old superstition?" Malcolm tried to keep skepticism from his voice.

"Maybe. Then again, maybe not. But I've lived here all my life, and I've seen a lot of things that encourage me to keep an open mind." Malcolm sensed that Albert was not going to elaborate further so he let the subject drop.

A few minutes later, Albert stopped the carryall and got out. Malcolm was summoned from his own thoughts and joined Albert at the edge of a shallow canyon. Tracks led down into it and milled about a scorched patch, which marked the remains of a campfire.

"They stopped here the first night I imagine. They made a good distance. We've come about 20 miles. So that would have been Monday night. This is Wednesday. If they keep up this pace, they could be 40 or more miles ahead."

"Then let's get going." Malcolm started back to the vehicle.

"I don't suppose you can just pick up that carryall and lug it over to the other side of this little canyon?"

Malcolm surveyed the landscape sheepishly. "No, sorry. I wasn't thinking. But we can't continue on foot. We don't have time." There was an added note of urgency in his voice and Albert looked at him curiously.

"Why are you so worried? We'll catch up to them sooner or later. They're leaving clear signs. I can follow it by moonlight."

"Something tells me we have to find them tonight." He hesitated, reluctant to sound foolish, but he had no choice. "I had a dream about Connor and about someone trying to kill her, at least it seemed that way." He looked at the older man, his eyes pleading for understanding.

Albert was thoughtful for a long moment, then he turned his gaze northward. "Dreams are powerful. They usually have a purpose. Do you remember if there were any animal messengers in your dream?"

"Animal messengers? You mean...? Well, there were hawks or some kind of birds circling overhead."

"Hmm. I can't say I always know what dreams mean, but I've learned they bring us messages we need. If you think your friend is in trouble and we have to get to her tonight, that's what we'll do. But we need to go down canyon a couple of miles where it really shallows out and we can get across."

After the detour, they continued their pursuit of Connor and Laura at a speed barely safe given the terrain. And, as darkness seeped its way across the desert, they had only the headlights and a three-quarter moon by which to see. They proceeded more slowly; to Malcolm it was excruciatingly slow. He had to keep reminding himself that Connor was on foot. They could catch up with her any time, though his patience wore thin as Albert had to stop more frequently to check the trail. After one halt, the right front wheel sank as they started forward again, possibly indicating an underground stream which had loosened the soil above it. Malcolm was ready to panic, but Albert calmly rocked the carryall back and forth until they were free. Malcolm gritted his teeth. More time lost.

The moon rode high above the earth, draping the rocks and sand and piñon trees with a silvery shroud, and casting deep shadows through which they passed. Malcolm checked his watch. It was after midnight; Wednesday had become Thursday. Two hours ago they'd found the second campsight where the two women had been the night before. They apparently hadn't covered as much ground Tuesday. Maybe they were getting tired. That gave Malcolm hope. He might find her any minute.

Albert had driven as fast as conditions permitted, trusting to luck and to the fact that whoever was leading this hike had an unerring sense of direction. She hadn't strayed from her course by a degree and her followers were closing rapidly, of that Albert was sure. He coasted to a stop again. The tracks he examined in the illumination from the headlights were fresher. The wind had done little to erode them. If he was right, they couldn't be much more than a couple of hours old. The women could be anywhere from four to maybe as much as ten miles ahead, though he was betting on the shorter side. He'd seen signs of two rest breaks in the last ten miles. The distance was beginning to tell on them, or at least one of them.

He swung himself back into the driver's seat, rubbing his eyes. He was tired, his eyes felt gritty and hot, but he had a feeling they were close. He told Malcolm his opinion about the tracks and had to smile at the eager reaction.

"Then let's get going. We're almost there."

Albert shifted into first gear and let out the clutch. The carryall crept forward, wheels spinning slightly in the sand, then they both heard a loud, metallic snap. The engine was roaring but the vehicle wasn't moving. Albert took his foot off the accelerator and the engine throttled down to a normal idle.

"Damn."

"What? What's wrong?" Malcolm had avoided stick-shift cars and anything sporting a 4WD insignia on its fender for most of his life. He knew how to drive them if need be, but he was generally mistrustful of any auto that didn't come from a U.S. car maker, and didn't have four doors, a bench seat, and an automatic transmission. So now he looked at Albert in horror. Why wasn't this goddamn tin can moving?

Albert sighed and thumped the steering wheel. "Pretty sure the clutch cable's gone. No way to fix it. I can call for someone to come out here, but it's going to take a long time, which you tell me we don't have."

"How far away do you think they are?"

"Like I said, could be four, five miles, could be ten. I can't tell for certain. But I know they've been here within the last couple hours."

Malcolm got out and walked several paces away from the car. He stared up at the sky, fists balled in frustration. He couldn't believe they were this close and there was nothing he could do. The night stars glittered above him, the only sound was the quiet ticking of the carryall's engine as it cooled down. Malcolm felt himself standing on a precipice, afraid, alone, and out of options. His lips moved with silent words.

"Okay, God, you and I haven't seen eye to eye on much of anything these past few years. I still don't understand why Marie Louise died. And maybe I never will. But, if there's anything you can do to help me, I've gotta find Connor. I know it isn't fair to start in praying right when I need something really bad, and I haven't talked to you in a long time. But don't hold it against Connor, okay? Please."

Having said his piece, Malcolm's mind was made up. He went back to the carryall and picked up a canteen and a small knapsack. He stuffed a flashlight and a small first aid kit into the pack and slung it over his shoulder. Albert eyed him solemnly. "You can't wait, can you?"

"No, I can't. And I've got to hurry. I'm not in very good shape any more. I don't know how far I can run, but I'm damn sure gonna give it my best shot."

Albert smiled at him. "You're really something, you know that?" He came to stand beside Malcolm. "I know I can't cover as much ground as you can in the next couple of hours. I'd never keep up. Here." He took a battered compass from his pocket. "These two ladies are following a steady course." He pointed to the NW mark on the compass. "First you put the line on N and then see what direction the northwest mark points. Then pick out a landmark in the distance, not too far away, like that big finger of rock sticking up out there, that's pretty much in line with the mark so you can go right for it. Check the compass every time you reach a landmark. At the same time, you've got to keep watching for these tracks...see, here...these two sets of tracks made by hiking boots. One set's a little smaller than the other. If you don't see the tracks for a while, double back on your own tracks until you pick up their trail again. And…" he hesitated, "if you really get lost, stay put. I'll find you. I'm going to radio for a chopper out of the airport at Farmington to be here at first light."

He held out his hand to Malcolm, who grasped it warmly in both of his own huge ones. "Thank you, Albert, thanks for going along with this whole thing. I know it must seem crazy to you but…." Albert held up his hand to silence Malcolm.

"Nothing about this seems crazy to me. If I were in your shoes, I'd do the same thing. Now get moving. If that hawk is any indication, you may be on a deadline. Head for that tall rock first."

Malcolm turned and looked out into the pitch black beyond the headlights. If he were to give this idea any thought at all, he would have to admit it frightened him. He'd rather chase a street punk down back alleys than go out into that empty darkness alone, but there was no choice. He quelled the panic he felt and began walking away. He paused, waved once at Albert, and broke into a trot. He wondered how long he could run.

CHAPTER FOURTEEN

And therefore never send to
know for whom the bell tolls;
It tolls for thee.
—John Donne

Thursday, Two hours before dawn
The Navajo Reservation

It was a tiny sound, such as any small, scurrying animal might make in the dry desert. But it was enough to wake Laura, whose senses were keen and attuned to her surroundings. She waited, barely breathing and completely unmoving, for the sound to repeat itself. Several seconds later, it did—a soft scrape. It came from the up canyon direction, and her intuition told her the sound was not made by any animal. It was human-made and it signaled her a warning. There could be no benign reason for stealth out here. A friend, or even a friendly stranger, would call from a polite distance and announce his presence, or make significant noise so as to alert those whose camp he approached. Laura regretted she had built up the fire a couple hours earlier. It still glowed red-hot and illuminated the two women clearly. They were easy targets.

Carefully disengaging herself from Connor's still form, Laura began to inch backward toward the canyon wall behind her,

where her pack stood. Just beside it was her gun. It baffled her
that she hadn't sensed the presence of anyone nearby as they
hiked. But then Connor's nightmares had seemed so troubling,
Laura had shifted her psychic focus to a different plane and had
taken her mind off what it should have been on—her damn job!
She was reminded, not for the first time, that human beings were
remarkably fallible, despite even the best training and the best
education. But she forced her mind to clear itself of random
thoughts. Even if she had only moments to act, patience was
essential.

In between her tiny, crabwise movements she paused to listen, but heard nothing. For a moment, she was relieved. Perhaps
she had been mistaken, perhaps her paranoia was acting up again.
On the other hand, perhaps the person out there was simply
watching and moving as she moved. That would be the most
sensible strategy. Remembering the lessons of her childhood, she
reached out into the darkness with her mind, feeling for the
presence of another person. At first there was emptiness, and
then it came to her all at once—a presence, no more than that,
a malevolence so focused, so cold it pierced her mind like a shaft
of ice. And it was very close. She was out of time.

Her mind reeling from the contact, Laura reacted with pure
instinct. She rolled hard to her left, hands reaching for the
weapon. But just as her fingers closed on the grip, shards of rock
exploded next to her face. She heard the bullet ricochet off the
wall, followed closely by another. She tucked and rolled, the gun
cradled in her arm, as she scrambled to put herself between Connor and the unknown assailant. Another bullet exploded into the
wall.

At the very instant Laura tried to get over and past Connor,
the sleeping woman suddenly wakened and sat up. The unex-

pected movement tripped Laura, throwing her completely off balance. Instead of landing in a partial crouch, weapon up and firing, she ended up half-standing, her right foot caught behind Connor, her left extended too far out in front to regain her balance. As she tried to recover, tried to bring the Uzi to firing position and sweep the foreground in front of her, a single bullet pierced her upper chest; the impact flung her backward. The weapon in her hand swung into an upward arc, the spasm of Laura's finger on the trigger spraying the heavens instead of her assailant.

The sound of the shots abruptly awakened Connor, but, coming from an almost drugged sleep, she couldn't get her bearings. Suddenly she felt Laura hurtle over her, heard yet another shot, then a thud. She tried to get to her feet, remembering too late her swollen ankle, which crumpled under her. She cried out as she fell to her knees, and then she saw Laura's body face up on the other side of the fire.

Connor was frozen to the spot. Awakened so abruptly from her sleep, and taken from the dreams through which she alternately flew and struggled, the scene in front of her was, for a moment, beyond her immediate comprehension. Laura lay there, unmoving, as a red stain spread slowly over the front of her white shirt like some horrible parody of a blooming poppy. Then Connor smelled something burning and realized the sleeve of Laura's jacket, resting at the edge of the campfire, was smoldering. Reality hit her like a blow to the stomach. She scrambled on her hands and knees to her friend and yanked her arm back from the fire, grabbing a blanket to smother the tiny sparks around the burned holes in the jacket. She grasped Laura's hand, looking wildly about her for the source of the bullet that had done this. Everything was silent.

Part of her mind screamed, "Run!" But, looking down at Laura's face so deathly pale, she knew she wouldn't leave. "Please, God, don't let her be dead...don't let her be dead. Please." Her shaking fingers groped for a pulse at Laura's neck. For a moment she felt nothing and her heart felt as if it were being crushed by some huge fist. But wait. There it was, a faint fluttering. Some voice in her head overrode her fear. "Calm down, Connor. You have to help her quickly. You have to stop the bleeding now!"

Connor dived toward her pack and yanked out a thick pair of cotton socks and a couple of T-shirts. She tore open Laura's shirt, shocked at the amount of blood she saw. The bullet had entered Laura just above her right breast. For a moment, the sight threatened the equanimity of Connor's stomach. She fought back the nausea that rose up in her throat and pressed one of the folded socks against the hole in Laura's chest, putting firm pressure on it. She ripped one of the T-shirts into strips to hold the sock in place. Laura moved slightly, probably responding to the new pain. Her lips opened partially, almost as if she were trying to speak. Connor leaned over her, stroking her hair.

"Sshh. It's okay Laura, it's okay. You're going to be okay."

"I seriously doubt it." The voice that came from just outside the ring of firelight was familiar. For the second time in as many minutes she was overwhelmed with utter disbelief.

Albert was still waiting for a confirmation from Tuba City that a helicopter would be dispatched from Farmington when he heard the popping noises far in the distance. He knew immediately what the sounds were, but he had no idea how far away.

Two or three miles, considering how dull and faint they were. The sound of gunfire could echo over great distances in this terrain. He was torn. His first urge was to grab his shotgun and run in the direction Malcolm had taken. His second was to stay there and maintain radio contact. His portable unit probably didn't have the range to contact a base station. On the other hand, if Malcolm or his friends were injured, he could talk the incoming chopper in once it got close to his original position, where the carryall was stranded.

He keyed the microphone of the built-in transmitter in the vehicle. "Tuba City, Tuba City, this is Tsosie. Inform helicopter to contact me on channel seven when they reach the coordinates I gave you earlier. I will not be at vehicle, repeat, I will not be at vehicle." He paused, wondering if he should also report the shots he had heard. His hunch was against it, and Albert Tsosie was never one to quarrel with hunches, which is probably why, instead of staying where he was, he took his shotgun, his portable radio, and his canteen, and trotted away.

———

Malcolm also heard the shots. They sounded very close. The first two reports, only seconds apart, were sharp and he could hear the whine of the ricochets. Ten or 15 seconds later, he heard another shot, but this time there was no echo of a bullet caroming off of rock, and it was followed by a burst of automatic weapons fire. It sounded as if a war were in progress. He took several running steps in the direction from which he thought the sounds had come, but as the waves of vibrations began colliding with hard surfaces, they circled all around him. He had lost his bearings. The moon hid itself behind a cloud while his eyes sought in vain for the landmark in the distance he had chosen for a guide. He stood there, breathing hard from the alternating jog/run/walk which had brought him this far.

Switching on the flashlight, Malcolm scanned the ground for signs of Connor's and Laura's tracks. They were nowhere within his little circle of light. He'd lost them. His only chance to finally be where he was needed at the right time, in the right place, and he'd blown it. Anger and frustration boiled up inside him, displacing the hope to which he had been clinging. He sank to his knees, pounding the dry sand with the butt of the flashlight. Tears coursed down his face. "Dammit, dammit, dammit to hell. Goddamn it, Connor, where are you?"

A sharp screech startled him as he knelt there, and sent his adrenaline surging. He swung around, jumped to his feet, and yanked his service revolver from under his jacket. There, perched with great dignity on a sharp edge of rock sat a bird. Since Malcolm's knowledge of birds was generally limited to those found within the city, all he could say for sure was that this large feathered creature was certainly not a pigeon. It was huge, standing perhaps two feet tall. Like the bird in his dream? A hawk? Whatever the species, it had appeared out of nowhere and was solemnly engaged in regarding Malcolm with an intense and unwavering stare. It gave him the creeps, the way it looked at him. Then it occurred to him just how foolish he looked, standing there in the middle of an Indian reservation holding a gun on a bird.

Malcolm holstered the weapon and waited, not knowing what to do. Within seconds, he felt an odd tingling sensation up and down his spine, one he'd had from time to time in his life, a feeling that told him something was up, something unusual was happening. He'd had it when each of his children was born.

He'd had it when he'd met Connor Hawthorne. He'd had it the day Marie Louise died, and here it was again. He didn't care much for the sensation, because he never knew what it meant— sometimes it heralded a good thing, sometimes a very bad one. He had no idea which it was this time. Then there was this damn bird just sitting there. It showed no sign of fear, which seemed odd for a wild animal confronting a human.

Then he heard something. Not the bird; it couldn't have been the bird. It was more like a voice, and it was in his head, not outside of it. Oddly, it didn't sound like his own little voice. It was familiar and yet not familiar.

"Go, and go now!" The voice was peremptory if nothing else.

"But where?" his mind countered.

"Your guide is there, Malcolm. Follow him."

At that instant, the moon slid from behind its cloak of clouds. The immense hawk unfolded its broad wings and took flight, circling twice over Malcolm's head, some 50 feet above. Then it wheeled and shot straight toward the three jagged pinnacles Malcolm had seen earlier. Without hesitation, he dropped both the flashlight and the canteen, and began to run—as fast as he had ever run in his life. The hawk stayed low, circling periodically, then darting ahead of him. His eyes never strayed from it. He didn't look down, didn't pick his way, didn't for an instant worry about tripping or falling. A strength that was not his own flooded his limbs, pumping his legs faster and faster. Huge waves of energy surged through him, as if his lungs were filling and re- filling with something other than oxygen. Deep down, Malcolm knew he was playing for all the marbles, win or lose. Connor's life, his life, his own redemption, all hung precariously in the balance. Tonight, everything depended on faith alone.

———◦∞◦———

"I seriously doubt it."

At the sound of the voice, Connor whirled around to confirm with her eyes what her ears could not believe. In the dull glow of the fire stood the trusted right hand man of Benjamin Hawthorne—Mr. Julius Martinez. A .45 automatic was in his right hand, Laura's Uzi, flung from her grasp as she went down, dangled in his left.

"Marty! What in God's name are you doing here?"

Her mind was reeling, trying to arrange facts, draw conclusions, propose some kind of action. Nothing made sense. But there were two indisputable facts. Laura was lying on the sandy floor of the arroyo bleeding to death and Marty was holding a gun. But why would *he* shoot Laura?

"Surprised to see me, Connor?"

"Of course I am. No one even knows where I am. How did you...?

"How did I find you? Well, that was easy enough."

"But *why*? What are you doing all the way out here?"

"Let's just say I'm cleaning up after some people...incompetent people. After all, that's what I do best."

Connor looked once more at the gun firmly clenched in his fist. "Marty, my God. Did you shoot Laura? She was here to protect me. Did you think she was going to hurt me?"

"No, and it would have made things easier if she'd been on our side."

"Our side?"

"Well, not yours, Connor." He smiled at his little joke. "I'm afraid you are on the losing side, you and Benjamin. And your friend there," he gestured toward Laura's prone figure, "who has, by the way, wasted a great deal of my time by interfering with our plans."

"Interfering?"

"She insisted on keeping such close tabs on you in Santa Fe, and then, of course, there was that incident where she terminated the Ferret."

"Ferret?" She knew she sounded idiotic, repeating the ends of sentences, but she was thoroughly baffled, still trying to make sense of this surreal situation in which she found herself.

"That unfortunate, though admittedly stupid fellow your little friend here blew away on Monday."

"The man in the blue car. How do you know about him?"

"How? Because I sent him in the first place. And I am in the habit of keeping track of my operatives, unlike your dear father."

"You sent him to *kill* me?"

"That was the general idea, and I must say I was extremely disappointed. He was much more successful in dealing with your girlfriend, the lovely and extremely fickle Ariana. But then he always did have a flair when it came to close-quarters knife work."

The import of his words gained a foothold in Connor's mind slowly, chillingly. Ariana. The man Laura had killed, the man who was going to kill them—he had murdered Ariana, and Marty knew it. No, Marty had ordered it. Anger rose in her throat. She could hardly see him through the blood-red mist in front of her eyes. She felt herself start to rise and the sharp pain from her ankle only added to her fury. "You son of a bitch!" She lunged at him.

Marty fired. The bullet whistled just past Connor's right ear. She fell backward against Laura.

"The only reason you're not dead is because we haven't finished our conversation."

Connor trembled with fury, but she stayed where she was. "Why Ariana? Why? She didn't have anything to do with this. She couldn't have done anything to hurt you."

"She was *your* girlfriend, wasn't she? More or less." Connor was too angry to reply. "And she was useful in her own way, after we put Count Marchetti up to all those shenanigans with Ariana, promising her a clothing line and endless fame. At the time, we just needed more access to your house, in case the information we wanted was there."

Connor thoughts went immediately to the hidden chamber in her home, but she kept her face expressionless. Marty was warming to his story, enjoying the account of how he had manipulated Ariana, and then Connor. "And then when the impetuous woman moved out, what an opportunity. One of my operatives moved in, rather literally. Your Ariana wasn't averse to sharing her bed."

Connor willed herself not to react. She saw that he was trying to get her angry, out of control so she would blurt out something of use to him. He waited. She said nothing. He finally spoke again, his voice dripping with contempt. "Your friends in high places never caught on to the mystery woman. Ironically enough, you've met her. She wanted to get you into bed, too. Strange woman. Can't see the attraction myself. She was supposed to kill you, not seduce you."

Connor's confusion showed on her face. Marty's next words came out with a distinctly French accent. "Oh, Ms. Hawthorne, it is such a *plaisir* to meet the great author. You will have dinner with me, no?"

A cold fire burned in Connor's gut. Celestine Trouville, the woman in Santa Fe. *She* had been Ariana's lover and she had intended to kill Connor. "My God," she murmured, just loud enough for Marty to hear.

"Even after all those years as a lawyer, you're still gullible. Just like your father. All those years of experience and I managed to completely deceive the master spy himself." Anger spasmed across Marty's face for a moment, but he regained his composure quickly. "He wasn't willing to share, wouldn't take even me, his ever so competent protégé, into his confidence. So I had to find a different way." He moved closer. "Let's not waste time. I *want* what's out here, Connor." A grim determination settled over his features. The gun was aimed at Connor's chest. "I *want* the secret your father has been keeping."

She felt as if she were slowly sinking into an abyss. Her father's friend and closest associate was standing here in the middle of the desert holding a gun on her. He was looking for a secret about which she knew absolutely nothing beyond the combination to a safe back in Washington. To obtain this secret, he had had Ariana killed; he had shot Laura, who even now was probably dying. "And he's planning to kill me, too" she thought, "unless I do something about it." Somewhere in her head she heard a familiar voice, the one from her dreams. "Take courage, my child, and act!"

Connor looked up at Marty. His expression was cold, but a certain impatience could be detected. He had the look of a man who knows he is about to win and is eager for the victory celebration. Her mind was suddenly clear, no longer clouded by fear and anger. Marty might think she was a helpless, beaten woman, but that was an error she would make him pay for. There was one chance to save Laura and herself, and it was clipped to the back of her belt. With her back against Laura's leg, she could feel the gun pressing into her spine. She had to think of a way to get it out of its holster and the safety off before he could kill her. That would require a little sleight-of-hand—some sort of misdirection. She winced and shifted her weight as if to take the pressure off of her injured ankle, then took a deep breath, and turned slightly sideways, making it appear that she was assessing Laura's condition.

Connor knew criminals. She'd spent years prosecuting them, interrogating them, and writing about them. She'd probed their minds, their motives. Marty was no different. He might be brilliant in his own way, but he wasn't superhuman. He was a criminal, a murderer. And he was driven by an enormous ego and overpowering greed. This knowledge might just give her an edge, however tiny, if she could carry out a bluff, if she could make some pretense at giving him what he wanted.

"I won't tell you anything unless you let me help her."

"I won't let either of you live unless you provide answers."

Connor reached behind her, giving the impression she was trying to get enough leverage to rise.

His reaction, as she expected, was a step forward and the instant order, "Don't move." This allowed her to leave her right arm behind her back. She let herself look supremely annoyed.

"All right, all right." She shook her head. "I still can't figure out how the hell you found us out here."

He shrugged. "That was the easiest part. What's the one thing you take with you everywhere? You never leave it behind. I was counting on that, even after the Ferret failed so miserably."

Connor cast her eyes about, puzzled, frowning, until they came to rest on the briefcase, Ariana's gift. Marty's eyes followed the direction of her gaze.

"The tracking beacon is sewn into the lining, and you kept it with you all the way across the desert. Too bad your father didn't have the same idea. As it is, I'm in a position to take control of his little project out here, and I intend to make better use of it. Power is only worth having if one is willing to wield it."

Connor still had no clear idea what he meant, but admitting ignorance could be fatal. She adopted what might be construed as a condescending expression. "And what makes you think you're prepared to wield that kind of power?"

He smiled. "You're too transparent, Connor. I'd have given you more credit. Your stalling tactics aren't going to get very far, because I don't have time to indulge them. Tell me where it is. The location can't be far from here."

"How would you know that?"

"A long time ago your father's old friend, John Keneely, came to call. I didn't get to hear everything, just enough to convince me that this was a secret I would have, no matter what the cost."

The mention of John Keneely jogged something in her mind. He and her father had been avid hikers. They'd been to the desert, the mountains, all over the world. Surely they had been here in Arizona, too. An idea suddenly came to her. She let her eyes flick to the backpack Laura had carried for three days. The gesture wasn't lost on him.

"What's in there, Connor? A weapon, or perhaps documents that might provide me with answers?"

She didn't consider herself much of an actor, but she would give it her best. Feigning dismay, she said, "All right. Laura has some sort of map or chart she's been following. She consulted it several times a day. But there's nothing special marked on it. She must know the place you're looking for, but now she can't tell you."

He focused his attention on Laura's still form. Connor used the moment to wrap her fingers around the butt of the gun and slide her finger down the edge of the trigger guard to deactivate the safety.

"She doesn't look good, does she? But I have my drug kit here," he patted his knapsack. "I could probably bring her around long enough to get some answers. Might be painful, but that's one of the drawbacks of choosing the wrong side." He sighed with resignation, as if his time were still being wasted. "As for you, well, you're of no value to me. Besides, I've never really cared for you." He pulled back the hammer of the automatic and stepped around the fire toward her.

There was no more time. Connor threw herself at Marty with every ounce of strength she had left, ignoring the white-hot pain that coursed through her ankle. She caught him off guard and, in the fraction of a second he needed to regain his balance, she drew the gun from her holster and rolled away from him as he struck out at her with his left fist. Bringing the weapon up between them, she fired point-blank. Marty staggered several feet back, the bullet having caught him in the left shoulder. Connor tried to steady herself and fired again. But her marksmanship wasn't equal to her desire to kill. The next shot went wide. She tried to fire again too quickly, and the slide jammed, a cartridge stuck halfway between magazine and firing chamber.

Marty looked at her, anger blazing in his eyes, blood running down his left sleeve. "You stupid bitch," he snarled, raising his right hand with the gun still in it. "You're going to pay for that."

Connor looked him in the eye. She'd failed. She only hoped the son of a bitch would bleed to death. What she regretted most was that Laura would suffer even more. "You're probably right," she said quietly, as much to herself as to him. Her voice was level, there was no fear in her eyes, even though her mind and her heart and her soul were railing against the thought of dying. She wanted to live, God how she wanted to live! But there didn't seem to be any way for her to accomplish that feat. She took a deep breath and said, "Get it over with, you bastard."

For the briefest of moments, Marty paused, and then the canyon echoed again with the sound of the gunshot.

———————————

The orange red glow just ahead told Malcolm he was close. Where there was light from a fire, there were people. As he rushed toward it, though, the voice came to him again.

"Go softly, Malcolm, softly." It was against his nature to be cautious, especially now, when so much might hang in the balance. But he reduced his pace, letting his breathing slow and his heart return to normal rhythm. He could no longer see the hawk above him. Malcolm fought with the desire to break into a run once more. What if he were too late? That was what tore at his gut—guilt. He'd never told anyone that he was supposed to meet Marie Louise at the subway station before she went to the bank. He was supposed to go with her and they would have dinner together. But he'd been busy *again*, he'd missed the appointment *again*. She had died because he'd been too late. Ariana had died and her killer had gone free because he was too late figuring out why. This was one time he wasn't going to be too late.

He was closer now and could hear snatches of sound. Voices? Yes, they were voices, coming from in front of him. The closer he got, the more certain he was that one of the voices was Connor's. Suddenly he felt foolish. What if she were sitting by a campfire with her guide, discussing the day's hike? Could it be

that simple? No! He wasn't wrong about this. Malcolm stepped
briskly but quietly, pulling his gun from its holster as he went,
each stride taking him closer to what he now saw was a narrow
canyon. The light came from within that canyon. The other
voice was male.

He broke into a run, covering the remaining yards as if he
flew. He skidded to stop at the very edge of the shallow chasm.
There was no time to think, no time to question the weird
tableau which lay beneath him, lit only by the remains of a
campfire. In the dim glow, a man stood with his back to Malcolm. Half-kneeling on the ground with a gun in her hand was
Connor, and beside her lay a woman whose chest was covered
with blood. All this Malcolm saw in a heartbeat, and he saw the
gun, its ugly barrel pointed at Connor's head.

———

Connor heard the shot and flinched involuntarily, but there
was no pain, no impact. She opened her eyes and looked into
Marty's face. His expression was one of surprise, with his mouth
open wide, as if about to utter some shocked exclamation that
had become caught in his throat. To her astonishment, the gun
fell from his hand, thudding into the dirt. More blood spouted
from his arm. He leaned over, trying to pick up his weapon. Another shot rang out, kicking up dust just beyond where Marty's
head had been before he bent over. Connor yanked at the slide
on her gun, a rush of adrenaline shooting through her veins. She
felt it snap forward, then snap back. She raised it once more and
fired at his chest.

Slowly, as if strings holding him up were severed, one by one,
his body crumpled and fell. He came to rest face-down. She looked

behind him, then upward. There, above her, towered the enormous bulk of Malcolm Jefferson, outlined against the moon, smoke trailing from the barrel of his revolver. It was the most unexpected and most wonderful sight she had ever seen in her life.

CHAPTER FIFTEEN

Revenge triumphs over death;
love slights it;
honor aspireth to it;
grief flies to it.
—Francis Bacon

Thursday morning
Albuquerque, NM

Benjamin arose early and packed his luggage into the rear compartment of the four-wheel drive Nissan Pathfinder he had rented. The night before he had visited an electronics store where he purchased, for cash, a top-of-the-line radio transmitter/receiver, as powerful as most ham radio operators used, and other equipment that would have been awkward to carry aboard the plane.

Once out of the city, he stopped at a rest area and set up the radio on the front seat next to him. Quickly wiring its power supply into the accessory panel near the floorboard, Benjamin tuned it to the proper frequency, reducing the volume for the time being. Next to that, he opened his laptop, plugged the power cord into the cigarette lighter, and connected the modem to the car's cellular telephone. He turned the computer on, and dialed into a secure satellite data channel. He needed to leave an encrypted message for Marty, but first he wanted a progress report of the security arrangements in New York.

Benjamin had tried until well after midnight to connect through his office. Finally, he'd had to contact his confidential secretary to go down to his office and reboot his system. Now he was relieved to see that the log-on was successful. He quickly checked his own secure electronic mail. Odd that there was nothing from Marty. There were, however, two reports from the team leader. As word after word of the second message was decrypted and scrolled across the screen, they sent a wave of cold fear through his body. David Breen reported that, given Marty's absence, and having received no specific instructions, he had proceeded with all preliminary arrangements on his own. Would Senator Hawthorne please contact him to confirm?

Benjamin's mind whirled in confusion. What could possibly have kept Marty from his assignment? He shook his head. Marty wasn't the type of person who would shirk this kind of responsibility unless the reasons were pressing. Benjamin switched to his news-clipping service, ran a search for Marty's name and his own, for the past 24 hours on all wire services. Within two minutes, the results of the search popped up. Nothing. He pounded on the steering wheel in frustration.

His mind swiftly began to catalogue and analyze the available information. Various possibilities presented themselves and were then rejected based on other known factors. But a small nugget of suspicion kept rising to the surface. Each time he immediately dismissed it; the idea was absurd, it was beyond absurd. How could he imagine for a moment...? But that kernel of doubt would not be denied. Benjamin had not achieved his position nor stayed alive this long by ignoring any real possibility. Oddly shaped pieces of this bizarre puzzle began to fall into place even

as Benjamin fought against accepting the emerging picture.
Whoever the enemy was, he was very familiar with Benjamin's
and Connor's routines, their habits, their homes, their daily activities. The unnamed adversary appeared intent on discovering
something of which no one could have any real inkling—the
secret Benjamin protected. Someone had followed Connor to
New Mexico and attacked her on the Navajo reservation. Who
knew where she would be? Who was close enough to the family to anticipate each step? There was only one possible answer
to all of these questions, and Benjamin hated himself for uttering
it aloud. But there it was.

"Marty."

He sat for a long moment, anger, fear, and doubt churning in
his stomach. It made him physically sick. It couldn't be, yet it
must be. There had to be some other explanation, but he
couldn't think of one, because there wasn't one. He fought
down his burgeoning rage and tried to blot out the hot shame of
betrayal at the hands of someone to whom he had offered total
trust. He needed a clear head right now. He needed to find out
a great deal and he had to do it very quickly. He looked down
at his laptop, and then Benjamin did something he had never, in
all the years he had known Marty, even contemplated doing—
spying on a man who was his friend. He punched several keys
and changed back to the encryption/decryption program, using
a master override password to access a complete record of Julius
Martinez's electronic communications.

The screen blinked twice, then rolled a column of garbled
characters down the screen. The data was not accessible. It had
been reencrypted via some other logarithm. The only explanation was that Marty didn't want it accessible to anyone, including his boss. The prompt "Enter password" blinked at him from

the screen. He tried his own master password, which would give him access to any and all databases connected to the system, then watched as the words "Checking Password" flashed slowly. What the hell was taking so long? Then, instead of a screen of unencrypted information, a warning flashed on the screen. "Password entry invalid, enter correct password now!" Benjamin typed in the password Marty had been assigned. The response was faster this time. "Password invalid. Unauthorized access has been attempted."

Immediately, a different program, apparently triggered by the incorrect password, began running. It was performing a global file-delete routine. One after another, the coded message headers in Marty's correspondence file were wiped out and replaced with "message deleted." Benjamin recognized the strategy, and it frightened him. It bespoke a degree of careful planning, which meant Marty was up to something much bigger and more dangerous. As he watched the mass deletions, he also realized that if Marty's program were to activate something more destructive, like a virus, he could be completely shut out of his own system. His fingers were a blur on the keyboard as he tried to terminate his access link. He couldn't, and he suspected that, unless he broke the connection immediately, the virus could copy itself to his own laptop, or even help someone identify his location— though there was every possibility that had already happened during the lengthy password check.

Benjamin yanked the cord out of the modem jack and stabbed the power switch. Not a recommended exit perhaps, but necessary. He slid the removable hard drive out of its slot, and took an identically configured one from its case. It contained a mirror image of all the programs and files on the primary drive, but had not been exposed to any potential infection. Once the backup drive was seated, he reactivated the laptop. It booted up, went through its own virus checks quickly. If there had been a seek and destroy virus, it hadn't made it as far as the ROM chip or the onboard RAM. He breathed a sigh of relief and reestablished his connection with the satellite. He didn't dare log back into the system, though, at either his office or his apartment, so he routed a connection through a server in McLean, Virginia, that was known to but a very few individuals.

His first task was to scan telephone records. Even if Marty had wiped out e-mail and coded transmissions sent to his own office, he would find it difficult to do the same thing to other kinds of records, specifically long-distance telephone calls. He would be smart enough not to make outgoing calls he didn't want traced, but he might receive incoming calls. And if he had routed calls through dummy locations, there was just a chance Benjamin might find a repetitive pattern. One of his greatest strengths was analysis. He understood most kinds of information systems and how to get them to answer his inquiries. Still, it was almost two hours and an entire legal pad of notes later that he found the pattern he was looking for. He had backtracked for almost three months, scanned Telsat records, transatlantic cable calls, and picked out repetitive numbers and their locations.

One number stood out—Benjamin had seen a pattern of calls from Marty's office to a number in California, which, if he remembered correctly, was where Marty's family still lived. A quick check of the records for that number turned up dozens of calls to the main switchboard at NATO headquarters in Brussels. The times for those calls corresponded exactly with the times of incoming calls from the Washington office. It was obvious that the California number was blind, a relay switch that routed calls to other destinations such as Brussels. But there was no reason for

Marty to be in constant contact with someone at NATO. Surely it had nothing to do with any project of which Benjamin had knowledge. That could only mean one thing—Marty was running an operation outside Benjamin's knowledge, and chances were it had something to do with infiltrating Benjamin's own project. That meant Marty was the enemy, or at least one face of the enemy. He had been pretty arrogant to use such an easily traced method of communication. But why shouldn't he? Benjamin trusted him implicitly.

With barely controlled anger seething inside him, he dug further into communications logs. The calls from the California number had gone directly to a particular extension within the NATO building on a "straight-through" priority. That kind of setup meant that the person on the other end was expecting these calls. On a hunch, Benjamin pulled up the logs on incoming satellite calls to Brussels during the past week. He scanned down the list and then he saw it—area code 505—New Mexico. Damn! He checked the number against reverse listings—the Eldorado Hotel in Santa Fe. There were two calls, one on Tuesday, one Wednesday. None today. Not yet.

As all these new facts coalesced in Benjamin's brain, his hands were already busy on the keyboard. He accessed the manifest of staff office assignments at the NATO building. Within moments, he had a name—Colonel Franklin Ulysses Bordman—and the man's service record. The officer's name sounded familiar, and it took only a few seconds to remember why. Colonel Bordman's son, Robert, had been killed in action in Vietnam, but had not received the usual posthumous commendations. Benjamin remembered it because John Keneely's own son, Paul, had been involved in that incident. It had been determined by a review board that the colonel's son had been directly responsible for the loss of all but two men in his unit. Robert Bordman had died a coward's death. Rumor had it that the colonel had been apoplectic with fury when informed of the findings of the review board. Benjamin himself had fielded an angry letter from the man, demanding further investigation. Benjamin didn't need to investigate. In deference to John, he had looked into the matter carefully when Paul was killed. Some years later, Benjamin heard one of the Joint Chiefs make a sarcastic, yet somewhat pitying comment about Franklin Bordman's crusade to clear his son's name. Apparently he had never given up the cause. And now Benjamin's closest aide was in regular communication with the colonel.

"He's still angry," Benjamin said to himself. "That kind of anger could easily turn into something much more sinister. He wants revenge. And somehow, he's gotten to Marty, or vice versa. How else could he guess that there is a secret worth uncovering? He probably thinks it's some sort of weapon, thinks he'll get even for his son. He had to have found out from Marty." The image of Julius Martinez, his friend and companion, coalesced in his mind; then his anger shattered it into a thousand pieces. In its place was the picture of a man Benjamin didn't know. His heart still rebelled, because he was a loyal man. But his mind was calling the shots now. Everything, not just the project, but his daughter's life, was at stake. Benjamin knew he must act quickly and decisively before this particular conspiracy went any further. But first, on yet another hunch, he scanned the wire services for stories related to events in Santa Fe. He was about to give up when he saw the item just being added to the database.

From the *Santa Fe New Mexican*, Thursday, December 5:

Visiting Writer
Killed in Hit and Run

According to police sources, French writer Celestine Trouville, a participant at the Annual Society of Mystery Writers Conference, was the victim of a hit and run accident outside the Eldorado Hotel Wednesday just before noon. The victim was taken to St. Vincent's Hospital and pronounced dead upon arrival.

Hospital staff declined to comment on the cause of death, but sources close to the police indicated severe trauma to the head, neck, and back of the victim. Police are seeking a late model black sedan, possibly a Chevrolet or Oldsmobile with New Mexico plates.

Benjamin did not know the Trouville woman. She certainly was not one of his people. Therefore, if this were not a coincidence, and he knew in his heart that it wasn't, then she might be one of Marty's people. But why would she be dead? Who ran her down? And if she was at the conference, had she intended to harm Connor? That seemed likely, and yet her death didn't fit. "I can't waste time speculating," he said to himself. He shut down his computer and disconnected the modem so he could use the phone. He put in a call, punching in the long series of numbers from memory. While he waited for the connection to go through, he reviewed his options and came to swift decisions. He was an excellent strategist, whether on the battlefield, or in the back alleys of espionage. When a voice answered, Benjamin identified himself by a code name.

The Senator's instructions to the man at the other end of the line were clear, concise, and detailed, and issued without a hint of the wrath he felt. He left no room for misinterpretation. If the individual at the other end was surprised by any part of what he was told to do, there was no indication of it. The ability to follow orders without asking unnecessary questions was a requisite skill in his line of work. Only questions of who, what, where, and when were the man's priorities. The word, "why," rarely, if ever, crossed his mind, let alone his lips. Thus, he listened carefully to Benjamin, interjecting only those inquiries vital to successful completion of the assignment.

One of the few "perks" (if one could, in all good conscience, even call them that) of the type of power Benjamin wielded in the world of covert operations was the right to make life and death decisions without being questioned. He was one of perhaps half a dozen individuals who could do so, though he did not see it as a privilege to be coveted. To him, it was a heavy burden, one he bore unwillingly; his conscience never fully acclimatized to the world in which he moved, a world in which death was a fairly routine sanction. But there were times when the absolute necessity of moving quickly could not be denied. Some few must be trusted with decisions, and he had proved himself worthy of that trust time and again. He had shown his loyalty, his intelligence, and his wisdom. He had also shown compassion, although that particular attribute was not quite as valued among his peers. If anything, he might be suspected of being a trifle soft these days. But not today, not on this day.

The substance of Benjamin's phone call was neither soft nor compassionate. When he was done, he had not only imparted specific tactical instructions and orders, he had also issued death warrants, and he felt no qualms about them. He knew his directives would immediately be carried out to the letter. Otherwise, the quarry might escape, and that was unacceptable. Right now, he had a much more immediate concern. Where was Marty? There was every chance he was in New Mexico, perhaps had even been responsible for that writer's death in Santa Fe yesterday. If so, he was ahead of Benjamin. And Marty knew approximately where Connor was.

Driving to the reservation would take too long. He needed other, quicker transportation. Under different circumstances, he would have gone to Kirtland Air Force Base, right there in Albuquerque, and commandeered a helicopter and pilot. He had the power to do it. But that could prove disastrous if Marty had his hand in every pie, as it appeared he did. The news of Benjamin's presence would leak quickly from a military installation. Warnings might even reach the targeted individuals in Belgium before his own people in Paris could get to Brussels, and Benjamin was determined they would not escape. Thus, a lower profile was called for. He turned the rental car around and headed back to the airport.

Two hours later, having presented credentials in yet another name to the air charter service (credentials that included a chopper pilot's license), he was requesting clearance for takeoff. It had been a long time since he'd been checked out in one of these. He just hoped the bicycle theory held true.

———≈◇◇≈———

Navajo Reservation
Thursday Morning

Albert made good time. He was still moving pretty fast considering his age and degree of fitness, the lapse in which he rather
regretted as he huffed and puffed his way over a short rise. He
paused for breath and heard a single shot reverberate off the
rocks; he was getting close. Off to his right, the sun was just rising. It's soft light spilled over the eastern horizon and flowed
quietly across the desert floor. Albert removed his binoculars
from the case at his waist and scanned the field ahead of him. He
saw no signs of movement, but he knew that dozens of arroyos
and small canyons had been carved into what appeared to be flat
land when seen from a distance. The big cop could be in any one
of them, along with whoever was doing all the shooting earlier.
If this had been a simple rescue operation, he would have fired
his own sidearm as a signal to those awaiting help. But this situation was one big question mark as far as he was concerned.
Thus, he was careful not to advertise his presence; he continued
walking briskly yet quietly along Malcolm's trail.

Albert smiled to himself; following the detective's path was
hardly an admirable tracking feat, since the man's sizable footprints were hard to miss. Even one of those duded-up Feds they
sent here from time to time could follow it. He was puzzled and
a little worried, though, about one set of signs he had tried to interpret a ways back. Malcolm's tracks had stopped, moved

around as if in confusion, and there were marks of what might have been a man's knees on the ground. Beside them were numerous indentations in the hard soil, not footprints, but small cylindrical impressions, half a dozen or so. Even more worrisome was that he'd found Malcolm's canteen a few feet away, and, just beyond that, his flashlight. Yet the tracks had unerringly led away on the same heading he had been following all along. The spacing and shape of the footprints told Albert that Malcolm was running again, fast. The length of his strides was pretty damned impressive. He couldn't imagine how had he managed to run like that in the dark, without his light.

Albert turned these questions over in his mind as he walked along, eyes alert for any change in the tracks. He was a man who liked answers to questions, firm answers. He would, he hoped, find them up ahead. Instead, he heard a shot, this one from a different gun, if his senses were accurate. He kept going and when he heard the sound of voices, he slowed his pace. Just ahead was one of the many arroyos he would expect to see out here. Albert had every intention of assessing the situation before announcing his presence, so he silently approached from the south, taking extra minutes to move softly. He concealed himself behind a large boulder and slowly crept around it to peer into the arroyo. He saw Malcolm bending over someone who lay on the ground. Beside him was a woman. Albert deduced from her appearance that this was the missing Connor Hawthorne. The person on the ground would presumably be her driver, Laura Nez. He stood up and called out.

"Ya-ta-hey, Malcolm."

The big man wheeled around toward the sound, gun in hand. As he recognized Albert, relief flooded his face.

"How did you get here? I thought you were staying with the car."

Albert picked his way down the short, steep pathway, his shotgun broken and cradled in one arm. "Gunfights in the desert in the middle of the night always make me nervous, my friend. I thought you might need some help." He looked down at Laura. "And it looks like you do."

Malcolm knelt again beside the prone young woman. "She's lost a lot of blood, and this first aid kit doesn't have much in it. Oh," he said, remembering his manners, "Connor, this is Lieutenant Albert Tsosie. Albert, this is Connor Hawthorne."

Albert nodded and smiled briefly. "I've heard a lot about you, ma'am, from your friend here. And he's a pretty good friend, too. Runnin' off into the middle of the desert in the dark."

Connor returned the smile and nod, then looked at Malcolm, who was doing his best to bandage Laura's wound. "I know he is, I'm a lucky woman. If he hadn't been here...." Her eyes flicked unwillingly at the body lying only a few feet away. Albert wondered about that, but he was patient. He knew he would get all the information eventually. Let them tell it in their own time. Not as if they were going to be interrupted any time soon. Amidst the static and chatter of his hand-held radio, there had been no mention of Albert's name, nor of any air support being dispatched. He suspected that the chopper from Farmington had not even left yet. It was either grounded by weather— he could see the storm clouds far to the east—or mechanical failure, not uncommon.

Malcolm murmured something to Connor, then walked over to Albert, who was looking curiously at the man lying face-down in the dirt. The bullet that had killed him must have gone straight through his heart judging from the location of the wound. Albert assumed it came from Malcolm's gun. "Hell of a shot to make in the dark from 40 yards away with a service revolver," he said, gazing up at the edge of the ravine where he assumed the cop must have been standing.

"It would have been, but I only winged him. Connor finished the job herself. But how did you know how far away I was?"

"Well, I don't imagine this gentleman would let you climb down that path there while he waited. So you must have taken your shot from up there. And since I saw your tracks near that boulder, it just seems that way."

"You're right about that." He stood staring for a moment. "He was about to drop the hammer on Connor. A few more seconds...."

His voice trailed off, not wanting to verbalize what would have happened if his steps had not taken him to the edge of the arroyo at that very moment, if his shot had not given Connor just enough time. He looked at Albert, suddenly remembering that he, Malcolm, had no jurisdiction here and had just discharged his weapon, wounding another human being. He assumed the procedures following such an action on the part of a police officer would be much the same here as they were back home—an investigation, a suspension. There might be more penalties because he was acting outside his own jurisdiction.

Malcolm pulled his weapon from the shoulder holster, broke it open to exhibit the cylinder, then shook the cartridges into his hand, extending his closed fist to Albert, who held his palm up almost on reflex as Malcolm let go of the five bullets and one empty shell casing. Then Malcolm handed his revolver to Albert, butt first. Albert eyed him skeptically.

"Why are you giving me your gun?"

"Back home, I'd have to surrender my weapon to another officer, and you're the only other officer here."

Albert ignored the gun and took the big man's wrist, turned

it over, palm up, and transferred the ammunition back to Malcolm's hand. "Look, I know you do things a certain way back where you come from. And we have procedures, too. If you were one of my cops and you just shot a suspect, we'd pretty much do what you're trying to do. But, Malcolm, first of all, you aren't one of my cops. Second, you fired to save those two women. And third, we're in kind of a jam here. We don't know what's going on; at least I don't. You might need that sidearm before we're done. So put it away, and let's worry about the formalities later."

He squatted beside the dead man and turned him over. Malcolm was surprised. That was something the forensics people should do. Everything should be left undisturbed. Then he shook his head. 'What are you thinking?" he said to himself. "This is no crime scene on 13th Street. We're 40 miles from a damn phone." Besides, they'd trampled all over the campsite. There wasn't much crime scene to preserve.

"You know who this guy is?" Albert asked.

"Name's Julius Martinez, the son of a bitch." The fury in Malcolm's voice was obvious. "The aide, the *former* aide and right hand man to Senator Benjamin Hawthorne, Connor's father."

Albert raised an eyebrow. This situation was getting more and more complicated. "Any idea what he was doing here?" Both men looked at Connor, who still knelt at Laura's side, talking softly to her, begging her to hold on. She felt the intense gazes of the two law officers and turned her face halfway in their direction.

"Marty just showed up out of nowhere," she said. "I don't know what he was after, and I didn't have the answers he wanted. He shot Laura when he first arrived, while I was asleep.

She was trying to defend me." Connor choked back the lump in her throat.

"I take it your friend here killed that man we found back on the road near Black Mesa?" Albert asked.

"Yes. He tried to run us off the road. After we crashed, he started shooting at us. Laura shot back and then his car blew up. Marty told me that he sent that man to kill me, and he was going to finish the job. I had a gun that Laura had given me. It was in a holster behind my back. I tried to shoot him and I only wounded him. Then I missed a shot and the gun jammed." She pointed at the spot where the automatic still lay in the dirt. "That's when Malcolm came, right when Marty was going to kill me. I had to shoot him." Her eyes strayed to the body near-by. Then she looked back and forth from one man to the other. "What are we going to *do*? We've got to get her to a hospital."

Albert shook his head. "The carryall your friend and I came in is about three miles back that way," he nodded toward the south, "and it's broken down."

"What about the chopper?" Malcolm involuntarily looked skyward, as if it might miraculously appear.

"I haven't heard anything on the radio. We're out of range. I don't even know if they're on the way."

Suddenly there was a sound from Laura, who was trying to raise her shoulders off the ground. Connor leaned over her, gently restraining the young woman.

"Don't try to talk, Laura, we'll get help for you. It's okay, just be still."

"...Grandmother...." the rest was unintelligible.

"What is it? What about your grandmother?"

Albert joined Connor, who looked at him in confusion. "I can't make out what she's saying. I can hear it, but I don't understand." Laura spoke again, looking directly at Albert. Her words came out between groans and gasps, but he nodded in comprehension.

"She's speaking in Navajo, ma'am. Says we need to get her to her grandmother's place. But I don't know who her grandmother is."

Laura spoke again, more clearly this time. Albert patted her arm. "Don't you worry about that. He's out of the way and we'll take care of her. It's you who needs the help." Connor looked at Albert questioningly. He smiled. "She's really something. You may not believe this, but all she's concerned about is your safety. Wanted to know if the man who attacked you is still around."

"I can believe it," Connor softly replied, and she looked into Laura's eyes. There she saw pain, but no fear. There was something else, too. Connor suspected it was something akin to love. But the mere thought frightened her. Love was dangerous and disappointing. And losing someone you loved hurt like hell. But she was going to do everything in her power to save this woman's life.

She reached for Laura's hand, held it tightly in her own, then pressed it against her cheek. Warm tears trickled over the slender fingers she clung to so tightly. Those fingers tightened around hers with a solid, unyielding strength. She looked up, startled, at Laura's face. Where before she had seen only ashen skin, now there was color. It seemed impossible, yet it was true. Connor was filled with an almost irrational hope. They had come this far, maybe they could make it all the way. Then she felt something akin to electricity course through her body; it felt warm and healing. And, without preamble, the voice of her Grandmother Broadhurst was right beside her, telling her to take heart, that help would arrive, that all was indeed not lost. She closed her eyes and felt the loving embrace. Her tears flowed freely and then the moment passed. Her grandmother was not there anymore. And yet someone else was, a similar presence, yet different. For a split second she thought she saw someone else standing beside them. But it must have been only a shadow, she told herself, just a shadow.

Albert stood up, then retreated a few paces to where Malcolm sat, his face glum and frustrated. "I couldn't get her to explain exactly where her grandmother's place is. I think we can assume, though, that it's in the direction they were traveling." He paused, frowning. "I just can't think of anyone who lives that way." He sighed, resigned to the only possible course of action. "But it's all we've got, so we'd better get going. We can use these pack frames to make a stretcher. She told me she can make it. I believe her." Something else was puzzling him though. "Funny thing is, she also told me her grandmother can make her well. I just hope she's right about that, too. Though it beats me how even the best medicine woman could do much with a bullet wound that bad. Still, you never know." He shrugged and picked up one of the packs.

Malcolm took another of the packs over to a rock and began to unlace the lashings. He watched his old friend, who still knelt beside the Indian woman, and knew that Connor's survival was dependent on the outcome of this nightmare. Not her physical survival, maybe, but what was left of her heart, her spirit. He could see that somehow it had gotten all tied up with this Laura Nez. He didn't dare to speculate what the consequences might be if Laura died out here, simply because she had been doing her job—protecting Connor. It was a lot of guilt for anyone, let alone a person who had just spent the last three months trying to regain some equilibrium. He felt a tug and realized that Albert had finished preparing one pack frame and was trying to extricate the other one from Malcolm's hands. He grinned sheepishly. "Sorry, mind wandered."

"Well, bring it back here for now. We need it."

Malcolm watched as Albert, with swift, economical movements, used the cording from the packs, his own belt, Malcolm's belt, and the dead man's boot laces to fashion a stretcher of sorts.

"This should hold all right," the Navajo cop said. "I figure if you take one side and the lady and I take the other side, it shouldn't be too hard. It'll be a lot easier on her than dragging it like a travois. And maybe you can carry one of the canteens, too."

It was not the first time in Malcolm's life that he was glad to be big and strong. And it was one of those occasions when he did not have to worry and ponder his role in the grand scheme of things. Two of his gifts—his size and strength—were needed. Very uncomplicated and very useful. He looked over at Connor who, despite the pain of her reinjured ankle, was gathering up the remains of the packs. He saw her stop and pick up her briefcase. Malcolm recognized it. He was surprised she had carried it so far, and his expression conveyed that curiosity as she turned around to look at him.

"This is how he found us, how Marty kept track. He put a homing beacon of some sort in it. He said he knew I would never leave it behind." She looked as mortified as she must have felt. Her own stubbornness, her own refusal to let go of that tangible link to the past had almost cost Connor her life, and could yet cost Laura hers. Connor's arm came back as she prepared to fling the bag down the canyon, but Malcolm stopped her.

"Don't. You'll regret it. None of this was Ariana's fault. Let me see that for a minute."

He took the case and carefully felt along the edges until his fingers encountered a subtle variation in the smooth leather. "Albert, let me borrow your knife."

The Navajo cop unsnapped the small case on his gunbelt and produced a three-inch lock-blade. Malcolm sat down on the ground and carefully slit the case at the seam nearest the suspect lump. Sure enough, a small glass and metal disc rolled into his palm. "There it is." He handed the case back to Connor and placed the disc on a flat rock. With one large foot, he ground it into dust. Then he turned away and almost stumbled over Marty's body.

"What do we do about him?" he asked Albert.

"Nothing much we can do. We don't have digging tools, and there aren't enough rocks we can lift to completely cover him. He'll just have to stay here until we can get someone to come back for the body, or what's left of it." There was no sympathy in his voice, and he obviously had no intention of wasting effort in preserving a dead body whose former occupant warranted little in the way of respect. "We need to get going." His chin pointed in Connor's direction. "Are you sure she can make it? She looks pretty hurt."

"She won't give up. She's a fighter."

"Okay, why don't you check the dressings on Laura's wound while I look for the best way out of this arroyo to the northeast."

Albert found a path about 15 yards up-canyon. They carefully moved Laura onto the makeshift stretcher and all three picked it up. The woman's eyes opened again for a moment, fixed on Connor, then closed again. But she smiled, and Connor smiled back. They walked slowly and deliberately out of the canyon, beginning the final leg of the journey. High overhead a hawk circled, its keen eyes taking in the forlorn little party creeping slowly north.

CHAPTER SIXTEEN

—◆◆◆—

We live by admiration, hope, and love;
And even as these are well and wisely fixed,
In dignity of being we ascend.
　—William Wordsworth

—◆◆◆—

Thursday afternoon
St. Giles on Wyndle
Sussex, England

Gwendolyn Broadhurst did not sleep well Wednesday night. Her dreams had been filled with various symbols experience had taught her boded ill for someone to whom she was close. Her special instincts told her the threat of danger was directed at her granddaughter. Prior inklings of something negative had prompted her to ask Katy to have Connor call Gwendolyn, but there had been no word. Mrs. Broadhurst knew Connor was on some sort of business trip in the western part of the U.S., what was it? New something? New Mexico? Yes, that was it. She'd always found that an odd name for a state, but then there was much about the former colonies she did not quite understand— from their politics, to their obsession with Hollywood actors, to their generally bad manners.

Not that she didn't admire the spirit of some Americans she'd come to know on various visits across the Atlantic, and she found some of the landscape quite lovely. But Gwendolyn was, above all else, a respecter of tradition. Under this heading she would probably have filed subjects such as manners, education, respect for one's elders, propriety, social grace, and dignity. In her experience, she found that Americans generally did not share that tendency toward tradition...at least not her traditions. And the way they named their states! She shook her head and went through to the library. There she consulted a world atlas, thumbing quickly to the "United States" heading. She traced her finger from east to west, remembering that the state she sought was in the vicinity of the very large one called Texas.

Grumbling ever so slightly, she reached for the half-lens reading glasses hanging from a chain around her neck. "The text on these maps is absurdly tiny," she thought, preferring that explanation to the more logical one of deteriorating eyesight. Although she could make out that the city of Santa Fe was the capital of the state, every other detail was microscopic, given the scale of the map. She dropped the atlas on the library table and scanned the shelves in what she thought of as her "Geography Section." There it was, a map book she had purchased several years earlier on a trip to New York City. It contained a detailed map of each individual American state and the provinces of Canada. She switched on a reading lamp and settled herself in a deep wing chair beside the fire.

Locating the plate for New Mexico, she studied the terrain and topographical features of the almost square-shaped subdivision. The largest city appeared to be Albuquerque. Gwendolyn found the name intriguing, mostly because it was unfamiliar to her and she was not at all sure how it might be pronounced. She preferred to pronounce words correctly, particularly proper nouns, because one demonstrated respect for others by accurately speaking their surnames and the monikers of their cities and streets. As a former teacher and foreign language aficionado, she presumed it must come from some Spanish word. Unfortunately, this did not help her come up with the Americanized "albukerkee." Her version of the name would have baffled any native New Mexican.

Finally, she put aside the linguistic issue and continued searching, staring at the map for a full five minutes—waiting. She frowned. Usually it was a fairly simple matter to put herself in touch with her granddaughter, but nothing was coming to her. She sat back, closed her eyes, cleared her mind, and focused on her breathing. Then she went back to staring at the map. People who did not know Gwendolyn Broadhurst well might have considered this activity odd, if not downright eccentric. All that staring and then looking off into space, then waiting. Others, however, more familiar with the ancient Celtic traditions of the unbroken line of Gwendolyn's female ancestors would have recognized this ritual for what it was—Listening. That was one word for it, anyway, and it was perhaps too simple a word to explain the skill, or the talent, or the gift, some people possessed. But it served in place of explanations too complex and sometimes too far beyond the understanding of those who asked about it.

She had always been able to send her mind (or her spirit) to other places and could see the perils of those far away. The ability had startled her when she was young, but she wouldn't dare to question her creator's wisdom in awakening the gift in her. She accepted what was and didn't waste time wondering about it. Gwendolyn Broadhurst was a great traditionalist, whose favorite toast with a glass of sherry was "God Save the Queen." It just happened that some of her traditions were very ancient indeed, and they included skills at which many others would choose to scoff. She dismissed their skepticism as the product of ignorance and fear, something they might get over someday.

Thus, Gwendolyn listened. But nothing of any significance came to her. Clearly, Connor was not in this state of New Mexico. She was as sure of that as if she had received a telegram confirming the fact. She flipped back to the front of the book, to the full United States map, and studied the states in the vicinity of New Mexico. The word "west" came unbidden into her mind. The state bordering New Mexico on the west—Arizona. As the name began with A, it was close to the front of the book. She pondered this somewhat similar configuration, closed her eyes, and concentrated on the image of her granddaughter.

Slowly, the room around her, even the warmth of the fireplace, faded from her consciousness. With different senses entirely, she saw her standing somewhere in the open. The air was crisp and cold. She heard the vague murmurings of animals, or perhaps other beings, passing near her. She focused more determinedly on Connor. Then, as if traveling at more than the speed of light, she felt her astral body sucked instantly into a vortex and released somewhere else, somewhere much more light, yet surrounded on all sides by pale grayness. Taking a moment to gather her own energy around her, Gwendolyn looked all about. Before her stood three portals. She let her inner guide choose the leftmost door. As she stepped through that door, she was immediately somewhere quite different. Looking slightly downward, she saw her granddaughter crouched beside another woman who lay upon the ground, a woman who was obviously seriously injured. Nearby were two other people. One seemed familiar, the other was not. She felt male energy from both of them.

From Gwendolyn's perspective, both women looked

haloed—surrounded by light emanating from their various energy centers. The hue of Connor's aura was a blue-tinged white
with dark holes here and there. It was also somewhat dim. The
other young woman's energy patterns were unique among anything Gwendolyn had ever seen. Striated waves of light revolved
around her, unfolding themselves into each other, creating new
colors with each revolution. More interesting, this riot of color
periodically swooped around Connor's aura, embracing it, melding with it. The sight was remarkable. It made Gwendolyn's
heart ache with some indescribable emotion.

Despite her unfamiliarity with the form, however, Gwendolyn's experience told her that the girl's life colors were dim-
ming and fading into the surrounding darkness, the movement
of them growing sluggish. The young woman was, without
doubt, dying. As Gwendolyn carefully focused her spiritual
power on holding herself in place, she also searched through her
store of knowledge, and that of her ancestors, for ways she might
summon outside help to the wounded woman and also to her
granddaughter. After all, one did not just run about the universe
tapping the shoulders of unsuspecting persons in other dimensions of reality and whispering to them about emergencies in the
middle of some vast American wilderness.

She supposed she could return to her own physical body and
do things the third-dimensional way, over the phone. Still, she
reached out fingers of energy to touch Connor's cheek, to
whisper moral support into her mind. Her granddaughter's astral plane self rose instantly to meet her. Their eyes met in mute
understanding. The Connor who knelt in the sand was not
aware of all this at a conscious level, Gwendolyn knew. But she
would certainly experience a sense of renewed hope, of re-
stored energy.

Then Gwendolyn reached out those same fingers of energy to the injured woman and stroked along the length of her body, leaving trails of healing light. Her touch paused here and there to try and stop up the widening fissures in the aura from which her life energies appeared to trickle. But Gwendolyn's skills here were limited. She might, perhaps, delay the inevitable, but she could not stop it. And she must return before her own body grew weak from lack of attention. She rarely traveled so far and for so long at a time.

Just as Gwendolyn prepared to release her hold on this place and allow herself to be drawn back to the quiet library in St. Giles, she heard a soft, yet firm voice say, "Make haste, my child. It is time for you to see your granddaughter." An enormously bright light appeared at the corner of her vision. Sounds, indescribably beautiful sounds, swirled around her. She saw the face of another being…a shimmering female figure clad in soft white leather clothing, fringed clothing with shifting swirls of brilliant color. "Who are you?" she asked.

"You will know soon enough," came the gentle answer. Then she felt a sharp tug at the lifeline which connected Gwendolyn to her own physical body. Her mind turned in that direction and, without effort or will, she flew back along the bright, silvery filament with the speed of light.

Moments later, she raised her chin and gazed at the fire, which had reduced itself to flickering embers. She smiled a broad smile. Despite the aches and pains of old age, and the stiffness that came of sitting so long in place without moving, Gwendolyn Broadhurst felt like a girl again. The decades of life lived as a human being, with all their lessons and heartaches and shifting emotions, fell away from her spirit like shackles dissolving into nothingness. The wisdom of many lifetimes remained, but in place of stern dedication and stoicism was simple, childlike joy. She could not explain it, or determine what had touched her during her long journey across the world, but she knew that her own search for truth and her desire to protect her granddaughter had led her to a place few visited before they abandoned their physical bodies to death. She had been granted a rare gift, and she would use it wisely.

Gwendolyn could feel the circulation returning to her hands and feet. She rose from the wing chair, bracing a hand on each arm of the chair to do so, and stood for a moment to be sure of her equilibrium. The clock told her that hours had passed. There was no time to waste. The elderly woman made her way to her desk, more slowly than usual, but without tottering. Gwendolyn Broadhurst made it a point never to totter.

Two hours later, plane reservations confirmed, one small suitcase packed, and necessary phone calls placed, Gwendolyn sat down to wait for the taxi. She looked about her, at the fine old furniture, the cherished keepsakes. But she felt no overburdening sadness, only a little melancholy, perhaps, and a mild amusement that these things had assumed rather too important a place in her life. They had comforted her, to be sure, but they were, after all, merely objects, with no more true substance than a handful of good earth tossed into the wind.

In due course there was a soft tap at the door. Mr. Pensworthy had arrived. She smiled. As Old-World as she, Mr. Pensworthy flatly refused to summon passengers by sounding his car horn, particularly when collecting "one of my ladies," as he referred to his older women patrons, most of whom he had been driving to and from the station or even to London for decades. She opened the door and gestured to her small suitcase, which he immediately took in hand. Then he stepped outside and waited for her to lock the cottage door so he might offer his arm if need be. But she walked briskly ahead of him to the waiting automobile, with only her walking stick for support. As they drove down the lane, she felt no need to look back.

On the plane, she slept well, but she did not dream, for her spirit also rested, content to await the dawn.

CHAPTER SEVENTEEN

I count life just a stuff
To try the soul's strength on.
—Robert Browning

Thursday
Somewhere over Arizona

After crossing over the border into Arizona and reaching the southeastern edge of the Navajo Reservation, Benjamin flew much lower than FAA guidelines permitted. But he wanted to stay well underneath radar tracking, since he had strayed significantly from the flight plan he had filed. He had startled a few people and a number of sheep; that couldn't be helped. His sense of urgency was overwhelming, and he had set down only briefly on a deserted mesa in order to rig up his laptop computer to receive signals from the tracking satellite his department used. It was just a hunch, and a long shot, but he had spent the last couple of hours trying to think like his traitorous assistant, to imagine what steps Marty might take to carry out a plan to destroy Connor.

Obviously, the first rule of tracking was to figure out a way to keep your target in your sights. If Connor was wandering aimlessly through an area where pursuers would surely be spotted, Marty would have devised a method to pinpoint her whereabouts when he needed to. Since Marty was missing, logic told Benjamin he was somewhere nearby. And that meant he had decided to go after Connor in person. Marty was an electronics genius. It would have been simple for him to plant a device in Connor's luggage or clothing that would lead him to her. How else could he be sure she wouldn't elude him?

The rotors had almost stopped turning by the time Benjamin completed his uplink to the tracking satellite. This small but highly efficient orbiter was used by only a handful of authorized people. Benjamin was fairly sure Marty had learned the complex string of access codes and that he would use every tool at his disposal, particularly top-secret resources that few would be monitoring. Benjamin grimaced as he considered how the habit of secrecy, along with naive assumptions of security, had been Marty's best allies. No one would be checking usage patterns on this particular equipment. And even if they had, Benjamin's access codes would never have been questioned. He blamed himself most of all. He should have been more aware, less trusting. And yet that way of life had become so abhorrent to him—never trusting, never believing, never accepting anything until it was fully proved, and even then, only conditionally. Situations changed, people changed, loyalties and alliances changed. He tried to pinpoint the moment when he had grown so careless.

Benjamin had never extended to any other professional colleague the level of trust and friendship he had given Marty. Bitterness boiled up in his throat when he recalled the courtesy and affection with which he had treated the young man. Marty had joined Benjamin and Amanda for countless dinners at the Potomac house, fishing trips out on the Chesapeake Bay. Marty had the run of Benjamin's city apartment, office, home—everything. "It was my own damn fault," Benjamin thought. "I wanted too much to trust someone. I wanted to have someone to take over the work, and I didn't want to risk Connor. She's what's left of me, the best part of me." He was snatched from self-recrimination by the low but insistent beeping of the laptop.

The program had finished processing the information relayed from the satellite. Benjamin set about establishing and inputting parameters to filter out erroneous signals. He knew, or at least he fervently hoped, that he would find what he was looking for—a burst transmitter, a small device that maintained its own power for very long periods of time by emitting a signal only at predesignated intervals, rather than continuously. The type of device Benjamin had in mind would also have its own electronic signature, one very different from other types of transmissions. He narrowed the search grid sector by sector as he tuned and retuned the satellite's receivers. Still nothing. Benjamin felt a wave of hopelessness sweep over him. He was suddenly so tired. He wondered how he would ever find Connor in all that desert. The thought that Marty might find her first made him shudder.

The soft beep turned into a discordant howl. The satellite was tracking a signal. There it was, northwest of his current position. He couldn't imagine why it hadn't shown up earlier. Surely the bursts weren't set to such long intervals. But then again, why not? In this country, even half-hour bursts wouldn't put the target that far out of range. There was nothing else out here, nowhere to go. Movement from one area to another was slow, particularly if the target were on foot, just as Connor and Laura Nez were. The beacon would last much longer with greater intervals of transmission. "Good old Marty, you son of a bitch, you never miss a beat."

Benjamin altered the grid pattern on his screen once more to localize the flashing dot, which represented a locked signal. In the next instant the dot disappeared completely. But he had the location. The spot was northwest of where Connor's car had been found. He had already charted that location from his memory and Malcolm's description, as provided by the Navajo Tribal Police. It made sense that this could be the tracking device Marty had planted. Benjamin could not be sure it was Connor, but he had nothing else to go on, nothing else to follow. He had to hope and pray that the secret he had protected for decades would turn out to be all those things he was afraid to believe it could be. He needed help and he wasn't afraid to ask for it.

Benjamin flicked the starter and set the rotor turning again, kicking up sand and dirt all around the chopper as it rose into the air, hung there for a moment, then headed, nose slightly downward, toward where the pilot hoped he would find his daughter still alive.

Two miles south of Navajo Mountain

The weight of the litter they carried was beginning to tell on the would-be rescuers. Even Malcolm, for all his strength, kept shifting his grip where his hands were blistering. Albert's expression was grim, but he said little. Connor was in the worst shape of any of them. She limped badly on her swollen ankle. Only the tightly laced boot kept it from ballooning. But she kept monitoring Laura's pulse and respiration, though she wasn't entirely sure how good or bad the results were. She had to admit she didn't know much about things like vital signs. She was considerably more familiar with death and the causes thereof. Both of her careers had taught her more than she needed to know about what injuries could prove fatal to the human body. Neither had prepared her for the task of keeping someone alive.

They were resting frequently, both for the litter bearers' sake and for the patient's well-being. Albert signaled for another halt, and they sat Laura down very gently. The wound had stopped bleeding, but Laura was very pale once more. Each step they took jarred her, and her breathing seemed more shallow. Occasionally, she moaned softly. Still, Connor did not lose hope; she simply would not entertain the idea of defeat. Her grandmother had promised that help would come somehow. However impossible it might be, Connor was convinced that her Gwendolyn Broadhurst had been present in spirit and would find a way to help them.

There was even more to it than that. Connor was a stubborn woman, and she was not going to *let* Laura die. Some would have argued that this particular outcome was not within her power to decide. She would not have heeded them. She had been taught never to give up, and she certainly wasn't going to start now, not with Laura's life hanging in the balance. Her arm and shoulder burned with the strain of carrying the stretcher. Her legs trembled with fatigue. Her ankle throbbed with every step. She could feel the blisters on her feet from too many miles in stiff hiking boots. But the kind of person she was, coupled with emotions she didn't even understand, drove her on even when her body threatened to quit.

Only a few days ago (less than a week, she realized with some surprise), the author in her would have honestly described Connor Hawthorne as a tired, angry, sad woman with her feelings tightly restrained under a veneer of social courtesy and natural stoicism—burned out, dead inside. Somewhere between Albuquerque and wherever the hell they were now something inside her had changed, or her assumptions about herself had changed. She was still tired, dear God, she was dreadfully tired. And there was sadness and anger. Such emotions could not be dispelled instantly. But her grief for Ariana was being transformed. It existed still, but without the bitterness. It no longer held sway over her own life.

Where she had been a woman just going through the motions of living, until living was over, now she was fighting for life and holding on to it with both hands—and she was holding on to Laura's as well. By virtue of being chased and shot at and nearly killed, Connor discovered that she still had the ability to care adamantly about life and death. And the reason she was alive to acknowledge these startling revelations was because this one loyal and courageous woman had been willing to die without a moment's hesitation to save Connor.

Hell of a gift, and Connor knew it. Now she understood that, while she wasn't yet ready to let go of Ariana and wasn't prepared to begin again with someone new, someday she might actually entertain the notion of love again. Connor's mind, as usual, was trying to stay several steps ahead of her more adventuresome heart, but was losing the battle for supremacy. She began to suspect that she must abandon altogether her habit of intellectualizing every situation, every obstacle. And she had the novel idea, novel for her anyway, that perhaps there need be no battle at all.

Perhaps there were no "good" and "bad" parts to a human being. Maybe they all had a reason to exist. And here, in this harsh, but strangely seductive land, her powerful mind held no sway. When the land spoke to her, the witch sense answered back. And, for the first time, Connor paid attention to something other than rational thought and logical deduction.

Benjamin was pushing the helicopter to its limits, despite its age. It frustrated him to think of the swift, fully equipped, fully armed aircraft sitting on the ground at Kirtland, and he wondered more than once if he should have risked the security issue. But now that was a moot point. All he had was this eight-year-old economy model, the only virtue of which was its large cargo area. The Glock was all he had in the way of weaponry. It would have to do as he rapidly approached the coordinates of the beacon's last transmission. The program had been busy extrapolating a probable course from the last three transmissions, but there would be no more data. The signal had vanished, there one minute, gone the next. He would have to fly the same course and hope.

His mind turned over possibilities. He might be closing in on someone other than Connor, or she might be with someone whose presence was a threat. Added to that, he could hardly approach surreptitiously in this noisy eggbeater. He might come across Marty, or worse, Marty with his own armed backup team. One handgun would hardly even the odds. And any sort of high-powered weapon or even a .30-.30 rifle could take down Benjamin's chopper if he got too close. He sighed. Too many what-ifs. He kept one eye on the computer screen for the signal that refused to reappear and one eye out for obstacles. He was only 20 or 30 feet off the ground. Even a short mesa could be fatal at this speed. Benjamin cleared his mind and kept flying, straight and true on the designated course. And he kept praying.

———⊶⊷———

Albert was the first to hear it, partly because the noise was alien to the area, partly because he was an unusually observant man. It was a faint, but steady, pulsating thrum. "Listen," he said.

Connor, whose attention had been utterly focused on Laura, was startled, not by the noise, but by the fact that Albert stopped so abruptly she ran into his back. "What?"

"Just listen," Albert repeated

They put down the stretcher, and Malcolm and Connor looked at Albert interrogatively.

"What?" Connor frowned. She was impatient to keep on. But then she could hear it, too. And so could Malcolm. It was getting noticeably louder. Albert swiveled his head back and forth.

"I think it's coming from behind us."

Malcolm nodded. "I think you're right...that's what it sounds like."

The three of them turned to scan the sky to the south. At first the sky seemed empty of anything but that sound. Then Malcolm pointed.

"Look, right there, at about one o'clock."

They stared at the little dot on the horizon with mixed feelings. Connor felt a stab of fear. It could be more of Marty's people, coming to finish the job. What if they had found his body?

"What do you think, Albert? Could it be the chopper from Farmington?"

"I don't see how. I would have heard something on the radio by now. They'd be close enough to transmit." He pulled his hand-held unit from its belt holster. "Can't hurt to try and raise them. At least we'll know." He keyed the transmit button. "Farmington Search & Rescue helicopter, this is Lieutenant Albert Tsosie, do you copy?" He released the button. Nothing but a soft hiss. He stabbed the key again. "Repeat, this is Albert Tsosie, do you copy?"

He shook his head at Malcolm. "I don't know, they could be monitoring the wrong frequency, or...." He didn't have to elaborate on what might come after "or." Connor looked around. There was no appreciable cover in any direction closer than 75 yards. A scattering of rocks near a shallow ravine was probably the nearest spot that would give them any protection, which was to say, not much at all. But they had the shotgun and two sidearms. "Pick her up," she barked. "We need to get to those rocks."

The three desperately weary people snatched up the makeshift stretcher and started to run. But despite the surge of adrenaline, their progress was impeded by the difference in the length of their strides, and the fact that Connor was almost crippled by her ankle. Running was painfully awkward, and they weren't covering much ground.

The sound was overtaking them now. The blades of the approaching helicopter beat the air savagely. Waves of pulsating sound slapped against every hard surface. She jerked a glance over her shoulder. It was more than a dot now; it was gaining on them faster than she would have thought possible. Cover was only a few more yards, just a few. Everything seemed to be moving in slow motion. It was like a nightmare. Connor could hear the harsh breathing of Albert and Malcolm, the sound of their boots pounding over the dirt. She stumbled, almost fell. The chopper was less than a hundred yards away, bearing down on them. They lurched behind the rock outcropping just as it passed overhead, spraying them with an explosion of dirt, gravel, and tumbleweed. As they dropped the stretcher, Connor threw herself over Laura to protect her from the mini-hurricane the chopper blades were kicking up.

Malcolm drew his service revolver. Albert slid two shells into the double-barreled shotgun and snapped it shut, then peered over the rocks, expecting to see the helicopter taking another aerial run at them. He took aim, ready to pump both loads into its underbelly, for all the good it would do. Connor looked behind them and her heart sank. If an assault came from that direction, there was no cover at all. Albert tugged at Malcolm's sleeve, pointing. The chopper wasn't in the air anymore. It had touched down some hundred yards or more away, the pilot's door facing toward them, the blades spinning down. Someone got out.

"Not exactly an aggressive maneuver," Albert stated. "What do you suppose he wants?"

Malcolm shook his head. It didn't make sense. Connor squinted in the bright sunlight, trying to identify the figure who advanced slowly toward them, hands out to the sides. Something about the outline, the way the man walked was familiar. Connor cupped her hands over her eyes, trying to decide if her reprieve from death had been only temporary. She got to her feet. Her gut told her this was no threat. A moment later, her head knew it too. A clear voice rang out over the high desert. For a moment, Connor and Malcolm looked at each other in mute disbelief. It couldn't be. It wasn't possible. Albert simply looked confused.

———◦◦◦———

From the air Benjamin knew he had to be almost on top of
whoever he was following, and as he zoomed over the next small
rise, he saw them—three small figures standing beside something
on the ground. He whipped out the binoculars and focused.
"Well I'll be a son of a bitch," he said to himself, grinning as
wide as any man ever grinned. The figure of Malcolm Jefferson,
head and shoulders above his companions, was absolutely unmistakable. Then he recognized Connor and a man in a uniform
who could not possibly be Marty.

Benjamin felt as if his heart would explode from sheer joy, and
he turned right toward them. To his surprise, though, the three
snatched up their burden and began running toward the rocks.
In a flash of understanding, Benjamin knew why. He could have
kicked himself for being so oblivious to how they might react to
an unknown helicopter. He quickly flew past them and set down
out of range of their sidearms. Making sure they could see he was
not armed and was alone, he began walking toward them.
"Wouldn't it be ironic if one of them shoots me?" he asked himself. Then he called out.

"Connor, Malcolm. It's me—Benjamin."

He saw that the big cop was standing now, and then out from
behind the rocks a figure began to limp toward him. He broke
into a trot, and, for a few seconds, it seemed like the longest
piece of ground he'd ever covered. He reached out for her and
crushed her in his strong embrace. Over and over he murmured,
"Connor, oh Connor, thank God, thank God, you're safe."

She stood there trembling in his arms, her face pressed against his denim jacket. She had been afraid she might never see her father again; it certainly never occurred to her that he would end up here, now, when she needed him most. After all, lightning was not supposed to strike twice in the same place, and she figured she'd used up a lifetime of luck when Malcolm appeared out of nowhere. It had seemed nothing short of a miracle, until this moment.

Benjamin looked over Connor's shoulder at Malcolm Jefferson with a look of wonder on his face. "How the hell did you get here?" he asked, smiling.

"That's kind of a long story. Maybe later. We've got a woman wounded. She needs help."

Benjamin looked puzzled for a moment, then it came to him. "Oh my God, Laura? Is Laura hurt?"

Connor pulled away from her father and looked into his face. "She's hurt really badly, Dad." Connor steeled herself to deliver the worst news. "It was Marty. He shot her. He was going to shoot me." To her surprise, Benjamin didn't even blink.

"I know. I figured that much out. That's one reason I'm here. Where is the son of a bitch?"

"I killed him." Connor's voice was harsh. Benjamin looked closely at his daughter, read the anger and satisfaction in her face.

"Good. You've saved me the trouble." He pointed toward the figure behind the rocks.

"Who's that?"

"Friend of mine, Navajo cop. He helped me find Connor and Laura."

"Dad, we've got to get her out of here."

Instantly, Benjamin was all action. He came around the outcropping and saw Laura. Kneeling beside her, he checked the

young woman's pulse, pulled back an eyelid, then looked under
the bandage. "She's weak, but stable. We need to get her on the
chopper."

Malcolm realized his Navajo friend was still in the dark about
the new arrival. "Albert, this is Senator Benjamin Hawthorne."
If Albert was surprised, he didn't show it.

"Ah, then I take it he's on *our* side."

Malcolm grinned. "Damn right! There really is a cavalry after
all."

"That's what my ancestors tell me," Albert said, the hint of a
smile playing around his mouth.

Benjamin looked at Albert. "When we have time I want to
thank you properly for saving my daughter and Laura."

"Thank *him*," Albert said, nodding at Malcolm. "I was just
along for the ride."

"Connor saved herself," Malcolm protested. "My contribution was one poorly placed bullet."

"Oh, stop it," Connor said. "I needed you both, and that one
bullet kept me from being the one lying back in that arroyo. But
let's wait until later to worry about who did the saving. We need
to get moving."

"Let's get her into the chopper. There's room in the cargo
area." Benjamin was already reaching for one side of the
stretcher. The other three took hold as well. Almost as an after-
thought, Malcolm scooped up Connor's briefcase. They secured
Laura as best they could on the floor of the cargo bay. Malcolm
and Connor squatted beside her, and Benjamin suggested Albert
take the left-hand seat up front. "I need you to help me find
something," he said, offering no further explanation as they
strapped themselves in.

"I take it we're not headed for a hospital."

"Too far, and I think someplace else would be better."

"That would be her grandmother's place?"

Benjamin looked at Albert curiously. "How do you know that?"

"She told me in Navajo. Said her grandmother could cure her. At least that's what it sounded like."

Benjamin eyed Albert for a long moment. The Navajo cop was an unknown quantity here. If he took Albert along, things could get even more complicated. He sighed. He would have to trust to fate this time. The voice in his head told him to come quickly. There was no more time for internal debate. He hit the ignition switch and set the rotors turning. Within moments they lifted straight up and began moving northwest again. Benjamin motioned for Albert to don the headphones next to his seat so they could communicate.

As Benjamin spoke, Albert listened carefully, nodded, asked a brief question, then listened some more. Whatever they discussed, they appeared to agree on it, and the helicopter skimmed at top speed across the desert toward their ultimate destination.

CHAPTER EIGHTEEN

If a way to the Better there be,
it exacts a full look at the Worst.
—Thomas Hardy

Friday, December 6
Brussels, Belgium

Franklin Ulysses Bordman, accustomed to absolute compli-
ance, if not fawning obedience from his subordinates was furious
to the point of outrage. He had not received a single field report
in 48 hours, either from his advance team in the United States
or from his second-in-command, currently stationed in Paris.

Even his everyday duties as a U.S. Army staff officer were
being hampered by a series of inexplicable, and apparently insol-
uble, technical problems with computers in the Communications Unit. Overseas calls were being limited to high-priority
only. The file server for his staff's local area network had been
down since the previous afternoon, taking with it e-mail, databases, and even the news wire. Whatever afflicted the file server
was apparently contagious. The computer dedicated as an Inter-
net server was also useless, returning constant network-error
messages whenever he tried to link up with other systems on the
Web.

His blustering and roaring had done precisely nothing to improve the situation. The staff sergeant assigned as technical support had yet to discover the cause of the "crash," as he called it. He reported that there was no apparent cause for the series of equipment failures and that there was nothing he could fix. The colonel vented his rage in the form of half a dozen insults, which included not only the sergeant himself but every member of the sergeant's family and ethnic group. When the colonel stalked out again, he was not aware of Staff Sergeant Woznowski's heartfelt salute at his back, consisting of a single finger.

The minutes ticked away, then hours. Still nothing, still no reports of success. Bordman stared at the walls, then at the picture of his son. Irrational fear pricked at his heart. Something was wrong. He just wasn't sure what. But he did know he couldn't stand it here another moment. He picked up his heavy overcoat, his cap, and his briefcase. On his way out, he gave his aide, Captain Wilding, a completely unwarranted dressing down. That made the colonel feel a little better, but not much.

Outside, it was bitterly cold. Dense, gray clouds promised snow within the hour. He belted his coat and set off at a brisk pace, muttering to himself as he went. His plan was to check into a nearby hotel and make some calls. No sense risking the use of the telephone in his quarters.

So wrapped up in his planning was he that he failed to notice the two men who peeled away from a concession and sauntered casually after him. Across the street from the NATO headquarters, a small, unobtrusive sedan pulled away from the curb.

Bernard Brel blew out a thin stream of blue smoke. The car reeked of the Gauloise cigarettes he puffed incessantly. They were fat, unfiltered, and far too strong for the average smoker—at least the average American smoker. Bernard, however, was French and had been chain smoking them for 20 years. He had the morning hack to prove it. He crushed out one and lit another as he watched the front of the building. His eyes rarely strayed for more than a second.

Bernard didn't miss much. He didn't make mistakes, or at least he had made very, very few in his long career. What that career was, precisely, would be difficult to define. He was not strictly a spy, though that was sometimes part of the job. Nor was he a thug, though some would no doubt call him one. In reality, Bernard was an intelligent, thoughtful man who avoided "wet work" (as some of his old compatriots in the States used to call it) whenever he could. He took no pleasure in bloodshed. And yet, sometimes violence was an unavoidable part of his job. He didn't much care for his occupation anymore, but had no will to escape from it. At 54, his secret dreams were frayed at the edges, brittle with age, no longer any comfort to him in the darkest times. He knew there would never be a vineyard in the south of France, nor a wife, nor children, nor grandchildren. There would be no restful retirement for Bernard.

Whom he worked for—exactly—was also a matter for debate. Few men knew the surnames he used, even fewer knew his real name. But that was necessary, too. The nature of his assignments made Bernard acutely aware of the proximity of death, and though he took all necessary precautions to avoid it, he didn't fear it particularly. He had outlived most of his "colleagues" in the business. He accepted that he had probably outlived his luck, too. So, when he took a deep drag from the Gauloise in his hand, the potential health risks of smoking were hardly at the forefront of his mind. In his work, the potential health risks of bullets were of greater, and more immediate, concern.

Just as he contemplated opening the vacuum bottle on the passenger seat to fill up his coffee cup, Bernard saw the tall Army officer exit the building. He turned on only the parking lights. Then he rolled down the window and tossed his cigarette in a high arc of scattering sparks. His two associates responded to the signal immediately and strolled after their quarry. Bernard waited for a few beats, then pulled away from the curb. The plan was to do it quickly and attract no attention to themselves. Bernard's boss had made it clear that this phase of the operation was not sanctioned by the U.S. military in Brussels.

Colonel Bordman, in his agitation, heard nothing but the sounds of traffic, which he ignored. Thus, he was stunned when his arms were pinioned behind him, the briefcase wrested from his grasp. He struggled until he felt cold metal against his neck, just at the base of his skull. He knew instinctively it was the barrel of a gun. "Christ Almighty," he thought. "Goddamn muggers." He stopped struggling.

"All right you Belgie bastards, my wallet's in my breast pocket. Take it and get lost." Of course, the colonel was 100 percent wrong in his assessment of the situation, although, in retrospect, no doubt he would have wished it were just a mugging. But it wasn't. It was time to answer for his sins, such as they were. As the pundit once said, "Paybacks are hell."

Bernard slid the car smoothly up alongside the trio and swung open the back door. The two men shoved the officer into the back seat, slammed the door, and they were out of sight within moments. The entire operation had taken less than a minute.

"What the hell do you bastards think you're doing?" The colonel tried to lean forward to grab at Bernard, but the other two men yanked him back so hard his head slammed against the rear window. The brim of his cap was knocked down over his eyes. He tried to move his arm to raise it, but both arms were gripped firmly. Bernard looked in the mirror and chuckled softly. "Don't worry, monsieur, you don't need to see where you're going."

The colonel experienced that unique form of numbness that accompanies visceral fear. Since he was not entirely bereft of insight, the meaning of what was happening to him was chillingly clear. He had been found out, somehow, or, more likely, he had been betrayed. Anger seethed in him as he considered whom the traitor might be. Probably that goddamn wetback, Martinez...slimy little creep, which might even mean that Hawthorne was onto him. Damn! He tried to calm his heartbeat and think. Who were these men? Where were they taking him?

Surely he would be interrogated. And just as surely he would be able to make some sort of deal. He knew how the game worked. He'd lose his commission, obviously, but they wouldn't put him in prison or execute him. He knew too much; he had information to trade; his trial would be an embarrassment. He'd keep them on a string, wondering just how much he could tell them, until he got a chance to escape. He could join his own people, take control from a new headquarters. The more he thought about it, the more he liked it. The colonel was sure he could talk his way out of this, if he could only get to the right people.

⚬⚬⚬

Captain Wilding was shocked to see Lieutenant General Alejandro Herrera walk into his office. He leaped to his feet, knocking over his chair, and snapped to attention. Behind the general were two MPs, a captain, and a lieutenant. Wilding had never seen the two junior officers before.

"At ease, Captain. I take it your colonel has left the office."

"Yes, sir. I don't know when he will be back, sir. We've had a lot of technical problems today, sir."

"I'm aware of that, Captain. How many staff are assigned to your unit?"

"There's the colonel and myself, sir, Lieutenant Fromer, three non-coms, PFC Gold and three civilian clerks, sir."

"Is all the staff here?"

"Yes, sir. And Staff Sergeant Woznowski is working on our computer problem."

"We're aware of the computer problem. Tell Sergeant Woznowski to return to his own office immediately, Captain. And assemble the other personnel in the conference room. You will close the door and wait there with them until you receive further orders. You will not talk among yourselves, and you will not discuss my presence here. Is that clear?"

Captain Wilding stood at attention once more. "Yes, sir!" The general went directly into the colonel's office with the other two officers. The two MPs stayed in front of the door to the corridor. Captain Wilding could feel himself starting to sweat. Something was wrong, very wrong. But he couldn't imagine what sort of crisis would merit the attention of a lieutenant general. He didn't want to imagine it, and he certainly didn't want to be involved in it. He stepped into the next room and ordered the staff to report to the conference room. Everyone looked baffled, particularly the civilian clerks, but they did as he instructed. When they had filed in, he closed the door, noticing as he did so, that one of the MPs came to stand in front of it. Everyone began talking at once but he held up his hand for silence.

"I have been ordered to wait here with you while some inquiries are being made. We have been ordered to wait quietly and not talk or speculate about the reasons."

His military subordinates nodded glumly, accustomed to obeying even the most obtuse orders. The three civilians, however, two women and one man, were not so easily subdued. They immediately protested, loudly, until Captain Wilding was able to finally interrupt.

"Look, people, I'm sorry for the inconvenience, *but...*" he said, looking at his watch, "you're employees who are still on U.S. Government time. If I want you to sit there and do nothing, that's up to me. You're still getting paid, and I'm sure this will all be resolved shortly."

It wasn't. Almost two hours passed before the door opened and the general stepped inside, to be greeted by a gabble of voices from the civilians. The military personnel, on the other hand, swiftly came to attention. General Herrera dealt with the civilians first, holding up his palms as a plea for their attention.

"I understand that this situation is distressing. However, we believe there may have been a breach of national security related to the operation of this unit."

The room was completely still. Captain Wilding felt his heart drop. He could see his entire career going up in smoke, even though he was sure, absolutely sure, that he had done nothing to jeopardize his country's security. But he'd heard of cases like this. Everyone associated with a traitor was tainted. Suspicion was never quite laid to rest. But who was the traitor? Surely not the colonel. But they had gone directly to his office, even though they knew he was gone. That must be it. His own commanding officer? Sweet Jesus!

Captain Wilding tried to focus on what the general was saying.

"...and it will be necessary for all of you to remain here a while longer. Then you will each be escorted to another area where you will be interviewed individually. This may take some time. I assure you that we will conduct these interviews as expeditiously as possible, particularly for those among you who are Belgian citizens. In the meantime, I have ordered the commissary to send up some food and coffee. If anyone needs to use the facilities, Corporal Johansen here will escort you to and from. That's all."

General Herrera didn't wait for protests or questions. He turned on his heel and left the room. The enormous MP, Corporal Johansen, closed the door behind him and remained in the room, a fact which made them all feel even more like prisoners. The civilians began chattering in French, until the corporal cleared his throat loudly and gestured with one finger to his lips. The message was unmistakable, and the Belgians fell silent, their resentment simmering.

Wilding knew that when a security breach was suspected, this was SOP. It was treated like an infectious disease. The initial treatment was quarantine, isolation, until each potential "carrier" could be examined and given a clean bill of health. Wilding's conscience was clear. He looked around the room at his staff and wondered if each of them could say the same. The door opened and a private came in wheeling a trolley with sandwiches and two coffee urns. He put the trolley in the far corner of the room and retreated without a word. Before the door could completely close, though, the captain that Wilding had seen with the general earlier pushed it open again. He whispered something to Corporal Johansen. The MP stepped across to Wilding.

"Sir, the general requests your presence in Colonel Bordman's office."

When Wilding got up, he felt his knees shake. "Come on, buck up," he said to himself as he followed Johansen to the door.

He went straight to the colonel's inner office and knocked at the door. It was opened by the lieutenant. The general was sitting in Bordman's chair. Every picture in the room had been taken down and propped against the wall. All the file cabinet drawers were open, and they were completely empty. There was nothing left on the surface of the desk itself. Several military issue crates were stacked in the center of the floor, presumably filled with the missing files and other items.

Captain Wilding saluted. The general nodded and said, "Sit down, Captain," gesturing to a visitor's chair. Wilding perched nervously on the edge of the seat. He couldn't even pretend to be relaxed. The general leaned forward, elbows on the desk.

"Captain Wilding, this is Captain Fitch and Lieutenant Fujima. They are charged with overseeing certain areas of internal security within our NATO mission." Wilding understood what that meant. These men probably did as much of their work out of uniform as in it. "Now I don't want you to feel that you are being accused of anything, because you aren't. But we do have reason to believe that your commanding officer, Colonel Bordman, has been engaged in subversive activities harmful to the interests of the United States."

Wilding's mouth dropped open. He could not conceal his shock. The colonel was a son of a bitch, sure. But a traitor? It didn't make sense. He was as military as they came. He was a 30-year man for God's sake.

"I find that very difficult to believe, sir."

General Herrera got up and came around the desk to lean against it. "Captain, I admire your loyalty, but our suspicions have been confirmed by certain materials we have found here.

Now what I need you to do is open that wall safe for us. We need to examine the contents."

Wilding looked confused. "But I can't, sir."

"And why can't you, soldier? I gave you a direct order."

"I know, sir. I'm not disobeying the order, sir. I mean that I can't open it because I don't know the combination, sir."

"You're asking me to believe that you, as the colonel's aide, do not know the combination to this security safe?"

The poor captain was squirming in his chair, his face getting redder and redder. "I know, sir. It's standard procedure for the senior aide to have access to the security safe in case the officer in charge is incapacitated. And I have the necessary security clearances for any work we do here. But the colonel...he wouldn't give me the combination. The one time I asked him about it, he just about tore my head off. Told me to mind my own business, sir."

Wilding swallowed hard. The whole story made him sound totally incompetent and he knew it. He sat, head down, waiting for the brunt of the general's wrath. Instead he heard the metal on metal sound of the slide being drawn back on an automatic weapon as a shell was pumped into the breech. The next thing he knew, Captain Fitch was standing beside him. The barrel of the .45 sidearm was pointed at his left temple.

"Let me ask you again, Captain. Will you open the security safe? Because, if you do not, I assure you that Captain Fitch will fire on my order. We don't have time to waste with you."

Captain Wilding felt the bottom drop out of his world. He loved the Army, always had. His one dream was to wear the oak leaf clusters of a major. Now that would never happen. His career was in ruins, for reasons he didn't understand. He couldn't open the safe, and a fellow officer was going to shoot him. He was going to die. He wanted to get on his knees and beg, but Wilding wouldn't disgrace his uniform. He knew he was innocent. That was all that mattered. He took a deep breath and in a quiet voice said, "Sir, I can't open the safe because I don't know the combination. I wish I knew how. I wish you believed me. I would never betray my country. But I have no choice, because I have no way to comply with your order. If Captain Fitch is going to kill me, then get it over with." He closed his eyes.

Moments passed, but nothing happened. He opened his eyes. The general's face was not angry. Wilding could swear there was even a hint of a smile there. The .45 was no longer pressed against his temple. Wilding heard the soft rasp of leather as Captain Fitch replaced the gun in the shoulder holster under his uniform tunic. The general put his hand on Wilding's shoulder.

"That's all right, Captain. We just wanted to be sure."

"Sir?"

"Sure that you couldn't open the safe."

"But, why? I don't understand."

"If you did have access to what was in that safe, young man, you'd never see the light of day again. I can assure you of that." General Herrera walked back around the desk and swung the door of the safe open. "We've already examined the contents, Captain, and, believe me, I'm deeply shocked by what we've found."

Wilding looked bewildered but relieved. Apparently, he wasn't going to die after all. He did, however, feel an urgent need to visit the men's room. The general stood staring at the wall safe for a long tick of the clock, and Wilding stood up. He assumed his presence was no longer called for. "Will there be anything else, sir?"

"Yes, Captain. We are going to conduct interviews. We will

start with you, although yours will be brief. You will then assist with the rest of the personnel interviews and add whatever knowledge you may have about the individuals who work in this office. Please try to keep them calm and cooperative. That's all." Wilding could hardly suppress a grin when he snapped off the most enthusiastic salute of his career.

Captain Fitch accompanied him from the room and stopped to speak to the MP at the corridor door. The guard looked at Wilding once and nodded. Fitch motioned to Wilding. "You're free to come and go, Captain, but we're going to start the interviews in about 10 minutes."

"In that case, Captain, I'd really like to go."

Fitch smiled and nodded. "Understood."

The MP opened the door for Captain Wilding, and he double-timed it down to the men's lavatory. Standing in front of the urinal, letting nature take its course, he could not remember ever being so grateful to be alive, or taking a whiz ever feeling so good.

Back in Colonel Bordman's office, General Herrera flipped through the pages of a black leather binder that had been found in the wall safe. Its contents shocked, frightened, and infuriated him all at once. The magnitude of this treason and the impunity with which Bordman had used his position to further his crime were almost incomprehensible.

"*Madre de Dios,*" he murmured softly under his breath. "Did he actually think he could get away with this?"

Captain Fitch was still leafing through files, but he tossed the handful he had back into the case. "Sir, I think we had better move to search the colonel's living quarters immediately. If he dared keep that book here, there's no telling what we may find there."

"True, Captain. That's true. But not yet." He looked at the chrome banded watch on his right wrist, a model designed for left-handed individuals so the stem and alarm buttons were on the left side for accessibility. "Right now you will get through the interviews. We will reassemble here at 2200 hours and proceed to the colonel's quarters."

"But, sir, with all due respect, Colonel Bordman may get wind of this and try to run. We need to get him into custody as quickly as possible."

"No, Captain, we don't. The colonel's fate is in someone else's hands, and that's all I'm going to say on the matter. I'll see you at 2200 hours." He took the binder under his arm and left the room.

The two officers stared at each other for a moment, then the lieutenant shrugged. "I guess he knows what he's doing. Did you get a look in that binder?"

The captain looked less convinced about the general's orders, but he nodded. "Yeah, some of it. The guy must have been a certifiable Section 8. Let's get on with it before we catch hell from the State Department about those Belgian citizens."

General Herrera took a staff car to the guest residence where he was temporarily billeted. With him went Colonel Bordman's "bible." He sat in the study for a long time, flipping through the pages. One by one, he tore out those pages outlining the colonel's so-called plan for world domination and tossed them into the fireplace.

The last section contained specific information about the

colonel's little army. Most of the people were identified only by code names, but he knew that problem would be overcome. He removed those pages from the binder and slid them into an envelope. The information would travel by diplomatic pouch to his old friend, Senator Benjamin Hawthorne.

General Herrera poured himself a brandy and sat down again. He was tired, and he was sick with anger and sorrow. A fellow officer had betrayed his country, his uniform, his oath. And those around him had remained blind to his treachery. All of this was hard to bear, especially for a man who had fought his way up the promotion lists, whose career was a shining example of what dedication could yield. He wore his hard-earned stars with pride, but not with arrogance. He knew all men were fallible, all had weaknesses. But even that understanding did not help him right now. This particular weakness had cost lives, had jeopardized others. Worse, the U.S. Army had overlooked the presence of a madman in its ranks. How many more were there, he wondered? Were there more Bordmans using their rank and their privileges to undermine the very government they served? The general shuddered at the implications of that possibility.

He poured himself another brandy and looked at the clock over the mantel. He knew what they would find when they went to the colonel's living quarters. Benjamin's message, passed on from an operative he both knew and trusted, had been quite clear on that point. Herrera didn't like it, but he saw the necessity for it. He was neither a cruel nor violent man, and he didn't relish the thought of any human being suffering. But he understood that some cruelties were necessary, some violence unavoidable. And in this case, the colonel had brought it entirely upon himself.

If Franklin Bordman was surprised to find himself in his own study, he didn't show it. He had regained most of his strutting self-confidence and, even though his assailants rudely shoved him through the door, he quickly caught his balance and began taking off his coat. He even went so far as to go directly to the small bar and pour himself a whiskey. The fact that none of the three men did anything to stop him further inflated his cockiness. Obviously, they were waiting for a superior to come and interrogate him. Fine. He could handle some damn spook from NSA or the CIA or whatever rock they crawled out from under. He sat down at his desk, a thin smile playing over his lips. He was ready to take charge of the situation.

"So, gentlemen, perhaps you'd care to have a drink while we wait for whoever we're waiting for."

Bernard stepped forward, hands in the pockets of his dark blue raincoat. He was a short, thick-set man with heavy, dark eyebrows threatening to meet in the middle of his brow and a thick mane of black hair, streaked with white, that rarely succumbed to grooming. His face was lined and scarred, almost as if he'd spent his life losing prize fights. Bernard didn't generally impress people positively, not, at any rate, until they got to know him. Their final impressions depended on whether they were friends or enemies. He looked more the part of the henchman than the mastermind, but then first impressions are often misleading. He spoke in thickly accented English. "Colonel." He pronounced the rank as the French would, in three syllables. "I'm afraid you're laboring under some misapprehension. We aren't waiting for anyone."

The colonel's smile faded. "But then...why...?"

"Why have we brought you here?"

"Yes, why? If you think I'm going to be intimidated by a bunch of thugs, you're very mistaken."

Bernard sighed. Always the stereotypes. "But, it is not our intention to intimidate you, Colonel. Intimidation implies an intention to use strategy to obtain some particular end. I have no need of games such as that. We are going to wait until sufficient time has passed so that evidence of your misdeeds has been secured. Even now every document, every file, every bit of information is being removed from your office. And in a little while, I am going to kill you."

The other two men who had stood silent near the door, moved swiftly across the room to take up a position on either side of the colonel. All the color drained from the army officer's face. But he wasn't ready to just give up.

"Now you listen to me, you froggie moron, I insist on speaking with your superior. I have information I am sure they would find valuable. And I am just as sure that you are not authorized to kill me until they have interrogated me. So get on the phone."

Bernard smiled a slow, menacing smile.

"But that is where you are very wrong, my dear Colonel." Bernard could be very charming when he wanted to. He especially appreciated the irony of being charming to a snake such as this one. "We have all the means necessary to extract any useful information you may have about your very illegal and traitorous activities."

He pulled a small, black zippered case from his pocket and moved closer to the desk so he could open it and display its contents. Two hypodermic syringes nestled in one compartment.

Six small vials, marked only with letter and number combinations, occupied individual slots. The colonel started to rise, but strong arms took hold of him. Hands unbuttoned his uniform tunic. He was slammed face-forward onto the desk as the tunic was removed, then jerked backward again until he was facing Bernard. The man on his left rolled up the colonel's shirt sleeve.

Bordman struggled, but the two assistants were remarkably strong. Before he knew it, both of his arms were strapped to the arms of the chair. Another cord secured his torso to the back of the chair. Still, the captive struggled and bellowed.

"You goddamn motherfucking piece of shit. You can't get away with this."

That enigmatic smile once more spread across Bernard's lips as he plucked a vial from the case and, with the other hand, retrieved a syringe. He stuck the needle into the vial and slowly filled the syringe to the halfway mark.

"But of course I can get away with it, Colonel. I already have." He came around the desk and took the place of the man on the colonel's left.

"You know," he said thoughtfully. "I have many tools here. All of these chemicals produce very much the same effects, although they all have quite different side effects. Now this one," he tapped the syringe and slightly depressed the plunger so that a drop of the liquid seeped out, "has very, shall we say, unpleasant side effects. Those who have experienced it describe the sensation as...hmm...I think the most picturesque phrase was 'acid in your veins.'"

The colonel's eyes were riveted on the syringe in Bernard's hand. He kept trying to convince himself that this was all a put-on, a ruse to make him talk. Something in the colonel's ego wouldn't let him admit that perhaps, just this once, he was on the losing side after all. He tried to steady his voice, rediscover his tone of command. "I told you I want to speak with someone in charge immediately to discuss a deal. I have vital information to trade. I demand that you call your superior."

"Ah, but you see, Colonel, you are in no position to demand anything. Besides, all of your so-called 'vital information' will be mine very shortly." He reached over and took another vial from the case. "The effects of this particular drug can only be neutralized by the drug in this bottle. I am quite certain that, before too long, you will wish for just one shot of the antidote. But for now, we wait, and *you* will not say another word."

The four men sat silently as the minutes ticked away. More than two hours had passed since his abduction. The colonel could feel his arms and legs going numb from sitting so long in one position. He could not take his eyes from the vials of liquid on the desk and the sharp points of the syringes. The stillness was broken by the sound of the cellular phone in Bernard's coat pocket. He casually pulled it out, pressed the send key, and said, "Yes?" He listened for several moments, nodding, his expression growing grimmer with each movement of his head. "You have all that you need then? Good." He hit the "end" key and replaced the phone in his pocket.

"It seems you have been a very bad boy, Colonel. You are a traitor, a murderer, a terrorist, a killer of innocents, and a very sick man." He strolled across to stand in front of his prisoner. "So you are the brains behind the White Aryan Resistance. WAR, I believe is your very clever acronym."

The colonel's heart felt as if it were being squeezed in a vise. His head buzzed. They knew, they already knew. But how? And now it was all slipping away—his power, his plans.

Bernard read the defeat in the man's face. "How easily you

give in, Colonel, you, the brave murderer of school children and innocent bystanders. It would appear that we have you to thank for the 47 dead eight-year-olds in Lyons, and the busload of Jewish tourists in Palestine, and the 132 people who burned to death in that incendiary attack on the movie theater in Bonn. You have been very busy dealing out death. But then you were not there to hear their screams." Bernard looked at him in disgust. "But let us proceed to the subject of your death. Perhaps this way is best under the circumstances. It is the one thing that will spare you the humiliation of trial, though I daresay the parents of all those children might prefer to see you publicly hanged, or worse."

Bernard quickly wrapped a rubber tourniquet around the officer's upper arm and tapped his exposed forearm until he saw a likely vein. He didn't bother with antiseptic, just plunged the needle in, emptied the syringe, and withdrew it. Blood trickled out of the hole he left behind, but he ignored it and quickly unfastened the tourniquet. Within seconds, the colonel felt like his arm was on fire.

Bernard tossed the vial and the syringe onto the desk. Bordman could feel the pain spreading now. God, it really *was* like acid coursing through his circulatory system, spreading, spreading everywhere—his chest was burning from the inside out, then his stomach, his penis, his legs...and his head. He began to whimper, then he began to scream, and his whole body writhed. Bernard motioned for Derek to stuff a gag in his mouth and tape it there.

Bernard looked into eyes that had lost every ounce of arrogance, though the madness was now there for all to see. Those eyes watched in disbelief as the Frenchman put away the syringe and zipped up the case.

"I must admit I was a trifle dishonest with you. There really is no antidote to the drug ravaging your body. But I do have a message for you, Colonel, something for you to think about as you die. Senator Benjamin Hawthorne says he hopes you enjoy hell."

———◦◦◦———

At 2230 hours, General Herrera, Captain Fitch, and Lieutenant Fujima entered the quarters of Colonel Franklin Bordman. Ostensibly, they had come to arrest the colonel on suspicion of treason, subversion, and other charges and specifications yet to be determined. They discovered, however, that the colonel had chosen to avoid the disgrace of a general court martial. The once proud and arrogant would-be dictator lay across his desk, his head in a pool of blood. Near his right hand lay the Colt .45 automatic that had blown away a large portion of his skull and brain. Splashes of blood and gray matter clung to his hand and to the desk lamp.

All three officers stood without speaking for what seemed an eternity. They had all seen death, and the General, for his part, had some idea of what to expect. But the gory remains of a human being still disturbed him. The air was heavy with the smell of blood and human waste. Lieutenant Fujima turned on his heel and left the room. Fitch and Herrera heard the front door being flung open and the distant sounds of retching. Neither man held that against the younger officer. Somehow the setting of this bloodshed made it all the more difficult to look upon. This wasn't a battlefield. This was a quiet home on a quiet, lovely street in the midst of beautiful city. This gore was almost an insult. But then, the General thought, so was scum like Franklin

Bordman. He gave the desk a wide berth as he circled around to take a look at the dead man's face. It was almost enough to bring up the brandy he had drunk earlier. Herrera swallowed hard as he looked into the haunted eyes and the face twisted into a rictus of mortal agony. Colonel Bordman had been a long time dying. The bullet in his head had been an act of final mercy.

Herrera turned to Captain Fitch. "Call Prentiss and tell him to send four of his best men with a wagon to collect the body and clean up this mess. No lights, no fuss. I want this kept absolutely quiet. I don't want the civilian authorities to get any hint of this. All official reports will indicate that Colonel Bordman took his own life while at the desk in his office, not here at home. Is that understood?"

"Yes, sir." The captain knew that something other than suicide had occurred in this room, something frightening and vengeful. But he knew better than to question his orders. He could hardly use the phone on the desk, which was covered with blood and brain tissue. Instead, he went out into the hallway where he found another one. He dialed a number and, while he waited for Prentiss, he spoke to the lieutenant who had come back inside, his face deathly pale. "Just wait out here. We're sending for someone to take care of that."

———◦◦◦———

There were no grieving relatives to ask awkward questions and demand awkward answers about the passing of Colonel Franklin Ulysses Bordman. His service record concluded with a terse paragraph.

"The officer took his own life by means of a self-inflicted gunshot wound to the head, using his own registered firearm.

Reasons for this action appear to be impending charges of misconduct."

There was no mention made of what these charges were, but all official reports bore the stamped signature of Lt. Gen. Alejandro Herrera.

The vault hidden beneath a carpet in the quarters of the late Colonel Bordman, and removed before the Army officers arrived to discover Bordman's body, yielded sufficient additional information (combined with pages removed from the so-called WAR bible) to track down most of the budding dictator's strike force. Bernard and company eliminated them one by one over the course of three months, until only the very smallest fish remained, a handful of foot soldiers too terrified to do anything but hide in the deepest holes they could find for the rest of their lives. Bernard, himself, took some degree of satisfaction in running to earth the actual perpetrator of the Lyons school incident. The daughter of his cousin had been among the pile of tiny bodies.

Selected information regarding the colonel's terrorist activities was shared with Interpol and with antiterrorist task forces in allied countries, so that certain cases under investigation could be closed. (The final estimate of casualties that could be laid at the door of the colonel's private terrorist army was approximately 1,403 people over the course of more than ten years.) But the fact that an officer of the United States Army was behind the acts of terrorism was never shared and never would be. Later, every document, except for those retained by Benjamin Hawthorne, was shredded.

Colonel Bordman was buried next to Robert in their family plot in a small town in Georgia. There were no pallbearers, no ceremonies, no salutes. Father and son were once more reunited—in death and in dishonor.

General Herrera, Captain Fitch, and Lieutenant Fujima returned to their respective commands. Captain Wilding was promoted to major and transferred to Okinawa after signing a supplementary oath of nondisclosure. The world of duty and order went back to normal.

———◦◦◦———

From the *Santa Fe New Mexican*
Saturday, December 7

Accident Victim's True Identity Revealed

The woman killed in a hit-and-run accident on Wednesday, and identified from papers she was carrying as French author Celestine Trouville, is, according to FBI sources, not the individual she claimed to be. When the U.S. State Department contacted French authorities for assistance in notifying next-of-kin, they discovered that the real Celestine Trouville is in a Paris hospital recovering from a serious skiing accident. FBI sources say they have, however, matched the fingerprints of the victim with those of an individual being sought for questioning in connection with the brutal slaying of a Washington, D.C. woman.

CHAPTER NINETEEN

Imagination, which, in truth
Is but another name for absolute power
And clear insight, amplitude of mind,
And Reason in her most exalted mood.
—William Wordsworth

Friday, December 6
The Navajo Reservation

The simple act of waking up was unexpectedly arduous. Connor's mind flailed about, trying to disengage itself from a dark, heavy blanket of unconsciousness. In reality, however, her mind, as it sluggishly affected the shift from sleeping to waking, was simply misinterpreting her body's efforts to untangle itself from the confinement of a sleeping bag. Having finally identified the problem, she stopped struggling and let her head fall back onto the pillow beneath. Pillow? Why was there a soft, white pillow here? Funny, she did not remember getting into a sleeping bag either. Then a more significant question surfaced. Where was she?

Far above her, 40 or 50 feet, she could just make out the roof of a cavern hidden in shadow. Connor sat up and tried to get her bearings. She had been asleep on a cot or pallet set against a stone wall and roughly fashioned from pine logs and strips of leather.

Over that were laid animal skins, bear and sheep as far as she
could tell, not being much of an expert on wildlife. The cave
was circular in shape, perhaps 75 feet across. In the center, a
good-sized fire burned in a ring of stones. Beside her pallet, her
hiking boots stood side by side. Next to them, her parka was
neatly folded.

Completely disoriented, Connor felt as if she had been
dropped into the middle of a stage set without benefit of script.
She unzipped the sleeping bag and flipped it aside. But she
quickly discovered it was quite chilly. So she wrapped it around
her and tried to figure out, logically, how she had gotten here.
Before events fell into place, however, one word floated to the
surface of her mind—Laura! Laura was wounded, dying. Where
was she now? Connor fought down a wave of panic. The silence
around her was so absolute it was spooky.

She called out, "Hello? Is anyone there?" Her voice, rusty
with sleep, had rather less than authority than she would have
liked. Unnaturally weak and hollow, it probably hadn't carried
very far. But just as she was about to try again, she heard a noise
coming from one of the passages on her right. Footsteps. The
sound was preceded by a beam of light, which swayed and wavered as it approached. She could just make out a figure as it
came through an opening in the cavern wall, someone with a
flashlight. As the figure approached the circle of light cast by the
fire, Connor could have wept with relief. It was her father.

"You're awake, honey." He came directly to the couch of
furs and sat down, taking her in his arms. She clung to him, her
body trembling.

"Hey, it's okay now. You're safe."

Connor drew a ragged breath. "But what about Laura? Is
she…?"

"Dead? No, of course not. I told you it would be okay."

"But how? And what is this place? Where's Malcolm?"

Benjamin smiled. "Hold on there, Ms. Impatient. I'll answer all of your questions, one at a time. Maybe we'd better start with where you are." He paused, as if gathering his thoughts. "This cavern is an outer chamber. It's part of a network of caves under the mountain. I thought it would be better if you all woke up here. Malcolm and Albert were your roommates last night." He gestured at two other fur-covered couches across the cave.

"What do you mean by 'better' if I woke up here?"

Benjamin hesitated. Connor sensed that his lifetime habit of secrecy was difficult to shed, even where his daughter was concerned. "The inner chambers are different, each one more so than the next as you go toward the center. This is the place I've been protecting for over 30 years."

Connor stared at him. "This *cave* is what you've been protecting? This stupid cave is what got Ariana killed, and what sent Marty chasing after me, and what almost cost Laura her life?"

Benjamin laid a hand on her arm. "Please, honey, don't prejudge me, or this place. You'll have to see for yourself. Then maybe I can explain more."

Connor had never known her father to be so deliberately cryptic about anything that directly affected her. She was caught between curiosity, puzzlement, and resentment, but she leaned over and put on her boots, lacing them badly, but swiftly. Benjamin stood up and held out his hand to help Connor up. "Let's go find the others, and you can see Laura."

He flicked on his flashlight again as they started down the passageway from which Benjamin had emerged. It was too dark for Connor's taste; she nursed a severe phobia about enclosed spaces. But she followed at her father's elbow, staying within reach. Before long, they came to an arched opening leading into a cavern even larger than the previous one, but it was divided into smaller areas by arms of living rock protruding from the walls. Each "room" was made up of three walls. The fourth side was open to the main area.

Connor noticed immediately that it was much brighter here, and she looked up to see if there were some sort of opening that admitted sunlight. But the roof of the cavern was as solid as the first one. It finally dawned on her that the light appeared to come from everywhere. The walls themselves glowed with a sparkling incandescence, as if tiny lamps were embedded in every surface.

"Where is the light coming from?" she asked.

"There's something about the mineral composition of the walls that seems to reflect ambient light, but you'd have to ask a scientist who understood geology." He grinned. "That wouldn't be me."

Connor suddenly heard a loud voice. Before she knew it, she was being swept up in a particularly enthusiastic Malcolm Jefferson bear hug. When he finally released her, she looked up at his beaming face. She noticed instantly that all the fear and worry were gone. His smile was broad, the lines that usually creased his forehead were nowhere in evidence. He looked, well, he looked like a different man. He grabbed her arm and led her over to an alcove. There was a wooden table surrounded by several chairs. Malcolm steered her into one of them. "Now sit and have something to eat. You must be starved."

Connor realized he was absolutely right. She felt hollow inside. There was a noise from a neighboring alcove, and Albert came around the corner smiling and stirring something in a wooden bowl. He looked as well and rested as Malcolm. For that matter, she suddenly noticed, so did Benjamin. Even their clothing bore little evidence of their arduous trek across the desert. But before she could ask about it, Albert put the bowl down in front of her, along with a large spoon.

"Ms. Hawthorne," he said, "it's good to see you again. And here is your breakfast."

She looked doubtfully at the golden-brown substance in the bowl, which appeared to have the consistency of oatmeal, or cream of wheat, both of which she hated. "So what is this?"

"My special recipe. I guarantee you'll not only like it, you'll want seconds." Benjamin and Malcolm took a seat at the table and watched amusedly as she dipped the spoon gingerly into the mystery food. Connor had been brought up to be polite. Courtesy required that she at least try Albert's dish. After one mouthful, however, courtesy was no longer required. It was delicious! Sweet and yet not too sweet, with a hint of saltiness. Her spoon picked up rhythm. Albert chuckled. "See, told you."

"What is it?" she asked between bites

"Tsosie's World Famous Corn Meal Mush with Bacon and Honey," he proclaimed proudly.

Connor eyed him suspiciously. "You mean I'm eating something which actually is called 'mush?'" He nodded. "Well then," she said, grinning, "I want more."

While they waited for the chef to come back, Malcolm poured water into an aluminum cup from the canteen beside him and handed it to her. She drank it down gratefully, and he refilled it. She sipped a little then sat back to enjoy the presence of the two dearest men in her life. Their apparent contentment still baffled her. All the events of the past few days seemed like a brutal nightmare, and yet they had happened. They had almost died, hadn't they? All her questions, temporarily derailed by hunger, came flooding back.

She looked at Benjamin. "Dad? What about those answers you promised me? And where's Laura?"

Benjamin had been lost in thought, it took a second or two for him to focus on Connor. "Laura is just fine, I promise. You'll see her soon, but she's still resting. It was pretty close there. She almost didn't make it."

Connor saw the image of Laura in her mind's eye, pale, silent, so near to death she seemed. Malcolm, seated next to her, patted her hand. "He's telling you the truth. She's going to be fine. I've seen her." He looked at Benjamin expectantly and smiled again. Connor got the distinct impression that everyone was in on some secret that she had not yet learned. It was vaguely annoying. She didn't like being kept in the dark.

"So, Dad? You want to tell me what is going on here, and maybe where 'here' is?"

Benjamin leaned forward, his arms resting on the tabletop. Albert returned with the second helping and set it down in front of Connor quietly. She toyed with the spoon, waiting for her father to speak.

"It's a long story," he began, "although actually my part in it is fairly brief when you think about it, but that's the part I know, so we'll start there." He took a sip of water. Connor sensed that telling this was somehow very difficult, and yet clearly he wanted to finally share this secret.

"About 30 years ago, back in the 60s, John Keneely and I were working on a temporary project at Los Alamos."

"I just visited Uncle John a few days ago."

"I know, he told me." Benjamin hesitated for a moment, then decided not to share the news of his friend's death just yet.

"So one weekend we decided to get away from the lab and take a hiking trip. John wanted to visit Navajo country." He paused. "Sort of like you did, ironically enough." He sipped the water again. "We wanted to get really off the beaten path, so we came across the northern part of the reservation until we saw a mountain. John was immediately taken with it and was all for doing some climbing, and I went along with him even though it was midafternoon and I thought it was too late to start. I wanted to camp and begin in the morning. But John was always stubborn, so we locked up most of our stuff in the car and started hiking. The distance turned out to be a lot farther than we thought and it was late in the afternoon by the time we got to the foot of the mountain.

"But he wanted to start up anyway and maybe find a ravine or someplace where we could put our sleeping bags and build a fire. I admit I was really getting pissed off at him. Here we were without our tent and our food and cooking equipment, and he wanted to find some dirt and rock to bed down on. But we didn't have much choice by then. The sun was setting; the moon wasn't out and I didn't feel like hiking back to the car in the dark. So we started uphill. "We couldn't have gone more than a quarter mile when it happened."

Connor, watching him intently, interjected the appropriate cue. "What happened?"

"John fell. He tried to climb a ridge and lost his handholds. He started sliding right toward me. I tried to catch him, but I couldn't. He went about 30 yards past me and slammed into a rock feet-first. I picked myself up and scrambled down to him, but he was already unconscious. There was almost no light left and I couldn't find my flashlight. I must have dropped it when John rolled into me. I had a small flare in my pack and I lit it and, God, I couldn't believe how hurt he was." Benjamin closed his eyes for a moment, remembering the awful picture revealed in the reddish glow of the flare.

"I could tell that both of his legs were broken from the way they were jutting out at weird angles. His head was bleeding and one arm was caught underneath him. I thought maybe it was broken, too. I'd seen a lot of wounded men in battle and I knew this was bad. And there was no one, no one around for miles in any direction as far as I knew. If I tried to go for help, it would be hours, and John would surely die of exposure and shock. If I stayed, well there wasn't anything I could for him except wait with him until…." He didn't finish the sentence, but they all understood what he meant.

"So I couldn't leave him there alone. The flare was fading and I still hadn't found my flashlight. I looked around me for some wood to make a fire, but there wasn't much. It wouldn't last long. I kept talking to John, I didn't know if he heard me or not. Later he said he did, but that just might have been kindness. John was always a kind man."

Connor looked puzzled that her father had referred to him in the past tense, yet before she could ask, Benjamin hurried on with this story.

"So there I was, with this tiny little fire. It got colder and colder. I covered John with the sleeping bags, but he still shivered, probably from shock. I remember how angry I was because I was helpless to do anything to save him. I was cursing occasionally, pounding my fist on the ground." The Senator said nothing for a minute or so, until Connor prompted him to continue. "But you must have figured out something, Dad. John lived."

"Yes, he did. And that brings us to this." His gesture took in the entire cavern. "Sometime in the night, I heard a sound. Now I'd never been much of a hunter, never liked the sport. John and

I hadn't brought any weapons with us anyway. But I was afraid it was some wolf or coyote or something that had smelled blood. I didn't know how I would keep it away if the fire died down completely. I was digging in my pack hoping there was another flare I had overlooked when I realized there was someone standing just a few feet away.

"I looked up, trying to think what I could use to defend John and myself if this person was hostile, and there she was, the oldest woman I'd ever seen. She was dressed like a Navajo and her face was ancient beyond belief. And yet, when she came closer, she didn't move like an old woman. I was startled, but I wasn't afraid, even though she didn't speak at first. Instead she just stared past me at John for the longest time. I sat there like an idiot. I couldn't even talk.

"Finally she pointed at John and said, in this odd voice, 'Your companion is injured. His body grows weaker with each breath. He will die.' I had sort of gotten over the way she appeared out of nowhere and I was inclined to assume she was friendly. But the way she just pronounced that John was going to die made me really angry. I jumped to my feet and looked her right in the face, spouting off something about John not dying, and I wouldn't let him die, and so on, but even while I was ranting away, I knew there wasn't anything I could do to prevent it.

"Then she just smiled at me, which was strange under the circumstances. But her smile didn't seem callous or cruel at all, but more like...." Benjamin searched for the word. "More like an embrace I suppose, even though that doesn't explain it either. But that was only the first of many events that night that I could never have explained in rational terms." Benjamin paused to take a sip of water from his cup.

"She held up her hand and two figures came out of the dark-

ness. They were also Navajo...tall and strong. They went right
to John and started to pick him up. I remember trying to stop
them, saying they couldn't move him because his back might be
broken. But the old woman waved me aside with a gesture, and
I swear it was as if someone had physically pushed me away. I
actually tripped over a stone behind me."

Albert nodded. Apparently this story did not seem strange to
him, but then his perspective was likely different than those of
the others who sat at the table and he was perhaps the most
open-minded of the listeners.

"These people picked him up and the old woman turned and
walked away. They followed. 'You may come, too,' was all she
said. So I did. I followed them through these winding, narrow,
declivities in the side of the mountain until I was completely lost.
I only hoped they knew what they were doing. Finally we came
to a small cave entrance and I followed them and went inside. I
was not going to let John out of my sight, even though I didn't
know if he was even still alive. "After the small cave came another passageway, and then another, and then another. I remember how afraid I was, afraid that I would never get out of
there. Then we came into that big cavern where you slept, Connor." He nodded at his daughter. "I felt a little better then, when
I saw the furs and the fire burning. But we didn't stop there. We
went on down the passage and came in here." Benjamin stopped
the story once more to let them catch up. Connor leaned forward.

"But I still don't see what they could have done for Uncle
John in a place like this." She looked around the primitively furnished cavern with its rough-hewn tables, cots, and animal skins.
"The walls are pretty amazing, I admit, but still, this is no emergency room."

Benjamin smiled gently. "No, and I'm not sure a whole team of doctors could have saved him." He paused, trying to find the right words. "I don't claim to be really religious, you know, beyond the usual weddings and baptisms and the occasional visit to church for a Sunday service. My life hasn't really followed what I've always thought was a Christian path." He looked so troubled that Connor reached for his hand.

"It's okay, Dad. You're a good man."

"I'm not sure everyone would agree with that, honey. I'm not even convinced of it myself. But," he raised his hand to stave off her protest, "that isn't the point. I'm trying to explain why what happened that night was so difficult for me to accept." He looked at Albert. "I think you know more about this than I do."

Albert shook his head. "Senator, there are many levels of knowledge and very few Navajo understand the mysteries of our people anymore. Even I know very little. My understanding is that of a child. The teachings, the most ancient of all wisdom, it is lost to us. Or at least I thought it was, until now." He smiled and Connor recognized that same contentment—a glow in his eyes that mirrored the one in Malcolm's.

Benjamin looked at his daughter. "What I'm trying to say is that I didn't have much faith—in God, or in magic, or miracles, or even in the special abilities some human beings claim to have. Of course, our government has worked on that sort of idea for years, always trying to find a way to get an edge on the competition. They've researched and tested for every kind of extra sensory perception, and they've found some apparently gifted people—psychics, telekinetics, and such. But I always scoffed at my colleagues who worked on those projects. I believed in myself and my own people." He abruptly broke off and they all knew he was thinking of Marty, but no one spoke of it. After a few moments, he went on.

"That night long ago, we came in here. The two men placed John on that little platform." He pointed to a low dais, perhaps 14 inches above the floor of the cavern. It, too, was covered with skins. Around the raised area was a circle some 12 feet across, bounded by small stones. Within the circle, the floor was covered with sand. "The old woman told me to sit down on a couch by the wall and to be quiet. There was something about the way she spoke that prevented me from even thinking about doing otherwise." He shook his head, smiling a little. "She's an imperious sort of person. So I sat, but I'm embarrassed to admit that I don't really know what went on that night. She began to speak in Navajo, later to chant. I didn't understand the words. At least I thought I didn't. But somehow images came to me—images of spirits, demigods. I don't know. They weren't threatening, but I knew they were powerful. The singing, or chanting, grew louder and louder. It echoed off the walls. I thought I heard the sound of drums but I couldn't see any. After what seemed like hours, I must have fallen asleep." He took a sip of water.

"When I awoke, I didn't know what time it was, or even what day it was. But I saw John lying very still on that platform and at first I was afraid he was dead. The old woman was standing outside the circle, and I remember jumping up and running toward him. I was angry. I thought I'd given in to some bizarre superstitious ritual and slept while my friend died." Benjamin's voice trembled. "But just as I reached the edge of the circle, she waved me back. Again, it was like an invisible hand restraining me. 'Don't disturb the patterns,' she said with that same commanding voice, and I looked down at my feet. All the surface of the circle was covered with symbols, images, pictures."

"Sand paintings?" Albert volunteered.

"Yes. But not like those things you see in the tourist shops."

"No, of course not. It would be sacrilege to reproduce and sell a holy image. Those are just for souvenir hunters." Albert went on. "The sand paintings used in ceremonials are produced just for that ceremony and they must be perfect. Then they are erased, and the sand scattered according to ritual." He looked at the circle in the middle of the room, where only pale white sand now lay.

"Go on, Dad, please." Connor could feel herself growing impatient with these conversational asides. She was still just as worried about Laura, and nothing had really been said about what had happened.

"So, she made me wait. I asked her if John was okay, and she was her usual cryptic self. 'That's up to him,' she said. 'If he wishes to return, he will.' So we waited. She sat down in a chair at the edge of the circle and motioned for me to sit at this table. The two men brought me food and water, and we waited."

"How long?"

"By the date on my watch, it was four days."

"Four days? You sat and just waited for four days?"

"Yes, I did. I could see John's chest rise and fall ever so slightly so I knew he was alive. And it just didn't seem that long until I checked. More like hours than days. And during that time, she erased the paintings, just as Albert said, and when I awoke from a nap, I saw that she was just completing yet another set. John's color was good and he was sleeping peacefully. Finally, she erased the paintings again, went to him, and told him...she just *told* him it was time to get up." He grinned. "You'd have thought she was rousting a lazy kid out of bed. He sat up, blinking and stretching. He didn't remember a thing since he fell."

"So you're telling me that some magic ritual mended broken

bones and fixed a concussion?" No one could possibly mistake the skepticism in Connor's voice.

"Yes, honey. That's exactly what I'm telling you. I don't know how, I don't know why. But that's what happened. And John and I have never told a single soul about it."

"And that's your big secret? Some pagan ritual, some miracle healing? People are dead because of it? What sense does that make?"

"Believe me, honey, I would gladly have changed places with Ariana, anything to save you from this pain. But let me finish, please. Then you can judge my choices however you want to. Yes, John was healed, but we also discovered something else in this place that could prove so dangerous to the delicate balance of our world we did not dare let it be known."

"And just what would that be?" Connor's anger was not to be assuaged by double-talk.

"I'm not sure how to explain it."

"And that's supposed to be an answer?"

"You'll have to see for yourself and then perhaps you will understand. But for now, why don't you pay Laura a visit?" He pointed toward another of the partitioned rooms, this one screened off by blankets hanging from a pole across two of the short walls.

The need to find out if her friend was really all right overcame both her curiosity and annoyance. She got up from the table and went to the chamber behind the blankets. Within was a cot, much like the one on which she, herself, had slept. Connor stared at the utterly still form. Laura did not even seem to breathe, yet her cheeks were a warm pink. Connor heard Benjamin behind her.

"But how, Dad? I don't understand. Is she really going to live?"

"I don't know the answer to that, honey. It's beyond me to understand it. But John Keneely survived, so I tend to believe in the power of this place and what goes on here."

"It is good of you to believe at least that which you can see with your eyes, Benjamin Hawthorne."

Connor was startled by the strange voice. She had been quite sure they were alone in the room with Laura. She whirled around and saw the dim figure standing in the corner of the room. Benjamin, however, did not appear at all startled. He turned around and smiled. "You know I believe more than that, Grandmother Klah." Her father held out both of his hands toward the old woman, and she placed one of her hands in his. "Please," he said, drawing her gently forward, "I want you to meet my daughter."

The old lady smiled, her ancient face creased with a hundred lines and wrinkles. She was dressed in long, dark skirt and colorful blouse of aquamarine and pale rose. Over this she wore a white shawl. Her long, gray-white hair hung loosely down her back. "But I know your daughter rather well, Benjamin. We met recently, although I don't believe she remembers."

Connor remembered her certainty that someone had been nearby when Laura was first wounded. She stammered a bit. "But I thought that...wasn't it my own grandmother? Grandmother Broadhurst?"

"Ah, you do remember. Yes, my child, she was there also. And she will be here, in this place soon."

"You mean here, as in physically here?"

"Yes, she left her native country to travel here on the day when this young woman," she gestured toward Laura's still figure, "was first injured. I invited her to come here."

"You did?" Connor was overwhelmed. Ordinary rationality

seemed to be out of place here.

"Yes, although she saw me in a somewhat different form. And yet, she knew me well. Thus, she answered my summons." She glanced at Benjamin. "You must see about assisting her to find us, my son. She is very near now, and very weary."

"Yes, of course," he nodded with uncharacteristic meekness.

Connor shook her head slightly. "I don't understand any of this." She felt the old woman's wizened hand touch her cheek.

"You understand more than you wish to admit to yourself, my child. Remember, 'there are more things in heaven and earth, Horatio, than are dreamt of in your philosophy'."

"But isn't that...?"

"Shakespeare? Yes. Even very old Indian ladies can quote from literature, child. Much of humankind's redemption lies in its artists and poets." Her clear, blue eyes twinkled.

"I'm sorry, I didn't mean to imply...."

"I know, you didn't intend any disrespect. None taken. But tell me why it is so difficult for you to admit that you *know* many things to which most others are still blind?"

Connor wasn't sure how to answer. "I suppose I haven't *wanted* to know. Things I can't explain—they sort of scare me."

"Ah, well, in that you are like most others human beings. But you have the power within you to overcome that troublesome habit of being afraid."

"I thought fear was a natural human emotion."

"Only if that is what you believe." The old woman smiled at Benjamin. "There can be no doubt she is your daughter, Benjamin. She has the intellect of a scholar and the heart of an angel, yet she cannot reconcile the two." Her gaze wandered to the still form which hovered nearby. Connor's eyes followed.

"Is she really going to be all right?

"The answer to your first question is yes. It would take more than a single bullet to end her existence, although time was running short when you finally got her here." She said this with a frown, as if they had been somehow derelict in their duty, but Benjamin said nothing. He seemed unoffended by her somewhat irascible demeanor. Connor, on the other hand, didn't appreciate being criticized. They had all done their best under the circumstances. She opened her mouth to protest, but the old woman waved her off with a dismissive gesture.

"We will go elsewhere and let her rest. She is being disturbed by our energies." Connor could see no outward change in Laura, but she followed the elderly woman and her father back beyond the curtain and over to the table where Malcolm and Albert sat, talking quietly. Both men rose as the group approached, and the old woman smiled at them.

"Courtesy in ones so young is surprising, gentlemen, but please let us dispense with formalities such as this." She lowered herself slowly onto one of the seats.

The thought suddenly occurred to Connor that this could not possibly be the same woman her father had spoken of meeting more than 30 years ago. He had described her as very old then. Granted, she looked about 100 years old now, but still.

This train of thought was interrupted, however, when Grandmother Klah nodded at Benjamin. "As you see, one of our number is not yet with us." She motioned to the one empty seat at the table. "You must see to Mrs. Broadhurst at once, Benjamin. Take your helicopter to the airport in Albuquerque and bring her here. I have sent her a very clear message to wait for you."

Benjamin stood up. He looked at all of them and the expression on his face was more calm and content than Connor had ever seen, but the reasons for the transformation still nagged at her. That, and her father's acquiescence to everything the old woman told him to do. It wasn't like him to be so docile. The questions in her mind were multiplying by the minute, yet she hesitated to act the part of inquisitor, particularly since the three men treated the elderly woman with such deference.

Instantly, those piercing blue eyes turned on her, fixing Connor in an invisible grasp. She was unable to look away. "You are troubled, child." Connor blushed. "No, don't be embarrassed. Part of your charm is your tendency to question things. That is as it should be. Your difficulty, and yours…" she said, looking at Malcolm, "is that you have not learned the value of the heart in discerning truth. There are times, my children, when truth can only be felt. Experienced, but not explained."

"Why do you refer to us as children?" Malcolm asked quietly. Connor wondered the same thing, but she realized that she would have asked the question with a touch more defensiveness.

"Because I am guardian of the mysteries and, in a sense, you are my children. Not biologically, of course. I am not your ancestor, though there are ties between Albert's clan and my own." Albert gazed at her. His face was an inscrutable mask, expressing neither skepticism nor agreement. After a few moments he nodded almost imperceptibly and the old woman turned back to Malcolm once again.

"What mysteries?" Naturally, the question came from Connor.

"The mysteries of life, of spirit, of death which is not death."

"What does that mean?" Connor asked, a little more sharply than she intended. "Everyone dies eventually."

"Do they?" the old woman asked, a small smile playing over her lips.

"Of course," Connor responded, though not as convincingly as she would have liked.

"Since you're so sure of yourself, young woman, perhaps we need not have this talk."

Connor was shamefaced. "I'm sorry. Please, forgive me. I'm just very tired and the last few days have been...."

"Yes, the last few days have been very difficult, not least of all for Laura. But we will get to that. Now, let me continue." She pointed to the canteen. "May I have some of that water, young man?" Albert poured her out a cup.

"I am aware that this is difficult for you to grasp, but you need not understand everything at once. Even Benjamin, who has long known of this place and has experienced some of its wonders, does not fully understand. But he is a good man, and a strong one. At the very least, he grasped the importance of concealing its existence at all costs."

They were all silent for several moments. Connor's voice sounded small when she finally spoke. "The costs were high for some of us."

The old woman's voice was gentle. "I know that, child. I know that you lost the one who was your mate and lover, the one called Ariana. Others died, also, in pursuit of this mystery. Benjamin lost someone he once trusted, and he also lost his best friend."

Connor looked up sharply. "Marty wasn't his best friend."

"I didn't say he was. I was referring to two different people."

"Then, if Marty is the one he trusted, who is the second?" Connor was suddenly afraid to hear the answer.

"The other man who came here...the man who was healed of his injuries, the one you call John Keneely."

"But why do you say my father lost him?"

"Because he is dead, child. John took his own life to protect the knowledge he carried with him for so long."

Connor's face crumbled, and she cradled her face in her hands. Her Uncle John was dead. It didn't take her long to make the connection between her visit and his suicide. "It was my fault, wasn't it? It's because I went there and someone followed me?"

"His actions are no one's fault, child. Why are you so quick to take blame for events over which you have no control? To feel guilt where none is called for? John made a decision based on many factors, and yet it was not just out of pure logic that he chose that path. His heart and spirit guided him."

"But why did he have to *die*?" Connor's voice was angry through her tears.

"Why shouldn't he, child? Was he not growing old? Why are you so caught up in this issue of death?"

"Because he's gone, damn it, and...."

"And what? You didn't say goodbye? You still think it is your fault?"

"Yes, that."

"First of all, please try to abandon this arrogance that most human beings have, thinking they are in charge of other humans' lives. Everyone is in charge of one life, the one he is living. And, secondly," she held up her hand to stem the question about to erupt from Connor, "stop taking this whole notion of losing a physical body so seriously. Do you think your Uncle John, the person you knew and loved, simply ceased to exist because his *body* is gone? Really, child, I thought you had progressed farther than that." The old woman shook her head, a mildly exasperated look on her face.

"You're talking about heaven? Something like that? Souls going to heaven? But they're still dead, they're not here. They're not here with us." Connor was as miserable as she looked, her voice thick with grief and anger. Malcolm put his arm around her. The old woman looked at them for a while before she answered.

"No, Connor, I'm not talking about heaven as you call it. That's a myth for the childhood of your species. Just as some of the stories of my ancestors were myths in a way, myths to explain why magic works, why spirit is pure and all powerful. But those stories, however pleasant and comforting, don't begin to describe the joy of what is possible beyond physical existence. Life really *is* eternal. Each of us is just one expression of the consciousness you call God. We have all of eternity and an infinite universe as our playground. All of creation is ours and theirs— Ariana, John, even Marty and the other man who wished to kill you and died in the process."

"I hope Marty burns in hell!" Connor spat out the words, but the old woman shook her head emphatically.

"Hell is another one of those stories, child. Do you actually suppose that the One who created us, the One who *is* love, would punish any of us with fire and brimstone?"

"But he should be punished for what he did."

"And will *you* sit in judgment, child? Will *you* decide that any soul shall be forever banned from light and love? For all eternity? Will you do what even Mother/Father God would not do?"

There was complete silence in the cavern. Connor wrestled with the question in her mind and in her heart. Her first reaction was, "yes, of course." She believed she could kill Marty again with her bare hands and send him off to eternal punishment with great satisfaction. But some greater understanding stirred softly deep within her, and she held her tongue. Anger, revenge, grief. Were any of these enough to give her the right to condemn a soul for all eternity? She supposed the truest answer was no. But she couldn't bring herself to say it aloud. She was stubborn. It was as if even the tiniest admission of tolerance or forgiveness for Marty would betray Ariana.

The old woman seemed to know her thoughts, however, because she smiled and said, "I thought not. You are learning, child, you are learning. And now let me try to finish this little talk before your father returns, for then there will be other matters to which we must attend. And, yes, I know you have questions upon questions, but there is no time to teach the history of creation, not even that small part I am privileged to have been taught.

"All you must consider at this moment is that every single atom in the universe is part of God, and that means that each of you is an expression of God. You came here for different reasons, but each of you in some way seeks knowledge of yourself. Some, like John, were destined to come here for the healing it is within my power to give. You can call it a miracle. I simply call it a gift and a responsibility. And it is not my most important task."

This was making Connor's head hurt. It was too much to grasp, and philosophy had never been her strongest subject. But the old woman pressed on.

"The universe is filled with wonders of light and dark, each seeing itself in the reflection of the other. My own ancestors passed down, among our myths and legends, that there are countless other beings throughout creation and that there are other places than this simple reality—places like the dreamtime where you, yourself, have been. There is a gateway here to other places. I am the guardian. Others have done that work before me. Others who come after me will fulfill that task."

"How long have you been here?"

"Since I was a girl. My mother brought me here to learn the mysteries. That was many, many decades ago."

Connor's eyes widened, as did Malcolm's. Finally, Albert, who had not uttered a single word, cleared his throat. They looked at him expectantly.

"Why do you seem so familiar to me, my Grandmother?" He used the traditionally respectful Navajo form of address to an elderly woman.

The old woman smiled at him. "There were many among our people who once understood how to travel to other dimensions, other planes, leaving their physical bodies behind. Even you have dreamed your way there from time to time. Your spirit is of the People, my grandson, and, although the People fade away now, they were chosen to hold the places of Light." She looked at them in turn.

"Of course all of you have dreamed your way to other places. Your souls are adventurous ones, and you, Connor, are so much like your father, particularly when he was younger. Once I had healed John, I had a chance to talk to Benjamin. I was immensely impressed with him. His is a very remarkable spirit. He, too, started asking questions. He had a thousand of them. I tried to answer some. Gradually he came to understand, at least as far as he was able. What was most important, though, is that he immediately realized that he could never reveal his knowledge of this location."

"But why? Surely people should know about you, that you can heal people and that there is some—what did you call it— gateway to different parts of the universe."

"Not necessarily the physical universe, Connor. It isn't some sort of time traveling corridor, or a convenient way to visit other planets. It is a place where the barriers between realities are very thin, where one might pass to places you dream of—even heaven." The old lady smiled. "Besides, even I do not fully understand why it exists, or what it means. Would you have your scientists, or, worse, your soldiers come here and violate this holy place? Would you have them try to exploit the wisdom of the ancients? Do you believe that would be best for our world?"

Connor stared at her, thinking of the way government worked, of the secrecy, the greed, the ambition, the aggression. "No, I guess not."

"But that is what would have to happen. Benjamin saw that even before I said anything to him about it."

"Why would it have to?"

"Think, child. Outside, in that world you live in, people feed on a steady diet of anxiety. Your governments live in a constant state of fear that there really is magic, that God is very real, that Spirit is more powerful than flesh. What makes you think they would allow all this to be known? Your father understood, and he is a wise man."

"I think he is, too. But...."

Grandmother Klah shook her head. "All in good time, child...all in good time." She raised her arm and pointed toward the chamber where Laura was resting. "Right now, you have duties elsewhere. She is awake and has returned to this time and place. See to her."

Connor was too relieved and overjoyed to resent the imperative tone. She jumped up and barely resisted the urge to break into a run, going headlong through the blanket curtain. She was caught up short, however, when she saw that the young Indian woman was sitting up and yawning in a most mundane fashion. She was stunned.

"Laura!" Connor was across the small room in two strides and, without thinking, threw her arms around the would-be patient, who returned the hug with equal enthusiasm, despite a soft gasp of discomfort.

"Hey, take it easy, girl. I do need to breathe just a little."

"Sorry. It's just that I wasn't sure I'd ever see you again, alive anyway."

"Thanks for the vote of confidence. I seem to remember telling you I'd be all right."

"If you did, you probably said it in Navajo. Only trouble is, I don't speak Navajo. If Albert hadn't been there, we wouldn't have known what to do. But he told us you wanted to come to your grandmother's." Connor looked in the direction of the outer room. "Is that your grandmother?"

Laura smiled. "Well, if you mean the really, really old lady with the long, gray hair, then yes, sort of."

"Sort of? Why is it so hard to get a straight answer around here?"

Laura laughed. "You, of all people, should know better than to look for 'straight' answers." It took Connor a couple of beats to pick up on the joke, and when she did, she laughed out loud. Not that it was all that funny. It was an old joke among lesbians, but it felt so good to laugh.

"Seriously, though. Strictly speaking, she isn't my grandmother, but she has been like one to me, and, among my people, women like her are revered as grandmothers. She is a relative, kind of, and very grandmother-like, don't you think? Besides, this is the second time she's saved my life."

"The second time?"

"The first time was when I wandered in here one day half starved and dying of thirst, or so I thought. I felt driven to come here but I didn't know why. She explained it to me."

A few pieces fell into place for Connor. "So that's why you and my father know each other." Connor digested this for a moment and shook her head again. "But I'm still confused."

Laura reached up and touched a lock of Connor's hair which had fallen over her forehead. "Always thinking, my friend, but some things have to be felt...here." She put a hand on Connor's heart. "Don't worry, you'll grow into it."

Laura's touch and the soft timbre of her voice made Connor feel lightheaded and indescribably happy. The sensation startled her so much that she involuntarily took a step back. Laura sensed her unease and stood up. "Shall we go and see the others, and you can fill me in on what has been going on?"

"Sure, but Dad's not here. He went to pick up my Grandmother Broadhurst."

"The sort of silvery lady who came to see us?"

"Us? Silvery?"

"Back there in the desert, in that ravine after I got shot. Her aura was silvery."

"You knew she was there?"

"I figured she was related to you somehow, and, although I couldn't see her face, I had a sense of her presence. Of course, I knew Grandmother Klah was there."

"Why doesn't any of this seem to surprise you at all?"

"Why should it? Never has," Laura answered in a matter-of-fact tone.

"Geez, what is it with you people?"

"Is that 'you Navajos' or 'you free thinkers'?"

"Damned if I know."

"Then while you figure it out, let's go get something to eat, I'm starved."

Malcolm greeted Laura effusively, Albert slightly less so, but not because he cared any less. Navajo men avoided public displays of affection. But his beaming countenance said it all. He really had not believed she would make it.

The old woman was gone, though neither man knew exactly where. Laura didn't seem to mind. "Don't worry, she's always doing that disappearing act. Now what's for breakfast? Or lunch?"

Albert said there was food in the other cavern, but Laura told him not to worry about it and sat down at the table, anxious for a recap of the previous day's events. During the next couple of hours, Connor and Malcolm took turns telling the story of the trek, how scared they were when they thought the approaching helicopter belonged to the bad guys, and how utterly relieved when it turned out to be Benjamin.

Malcolm filled in the next part of the story, for apparently Connor had completely succumbed to hunger and exhaustion during the helicopter ride; she passed out. She had, after all, been racing across the desert on foot for four days. She had had very little food, but a double helping of sheer trauma. When Benjamin finally set the chopper down in a shallow ravine, Malcolm had carried first Laura, and then Connor, into the caves. Albert had helped Benjamin spread some tree limbs over the chopper.

"The old woman healed your ankle, too," Malcolm added. "But we couldn't stay awake for the entire ceremony for Laura." Connor was startled. She had forgotten all about the painfully sprained joint. It should still be hurting a lot, but it wasn't.

Laura spoke up. "I guess I needed more than the laying on of hands."

"I'll say," Malcolm interjected. "I couldn't even feel a pulse when I put you down over there. But Grandmother Klah wasn't worried." As he spoke her name, she emerged from another small room on the other side of the cave. As she approached, she looked at Laura with a critical eye toward evaluating her condition.

"You need some more rest, child. I suggest you and your friend," her chin pointed at Connor, "go back to the first cave and take naps. You can also be there to greet Benjamin and Gwendolyn when they arrive."

The two young women repaired to the cavern where Connor had first awakened. Despite the admonition to rest, however, neither Laura nor Connor was in any mood to sleep. They sat together on a pile of furs and skins near the fire, talking quietly about all that had happened. After a particularly long lull in the conversation, Connor said what she had on her mind for some for hours.

"You saved my life, Laura. How can I thank you for that? For a while there I was afraid you were going to die because of me. I don't know if I could have lived with that."

Laura smiled broadly. "Well I couldn't have lived very well with it, either."

"Come on, I'm being serious."

"Okay, I'm sorry. I was just teasing. But why are you being so serious? We survived. And I, for one, am very happy to still be here. What about you? Are you glad to be alive?"

"A week ago there's every chance I would have said no to that. These past few months I've felt as if I were just going through the motions anyway, so what did it matter. Ariana was dead and buried, and I didn't *care* about anything."

"So what happened to change that?"

Connor thought for a while. "A lot of things. Mostly because since I've been here, I've allowed myself to feel...not just the emotions, but all those other sort of spooky things I've always preferred to ignore. I let the dreams become important. I listened to a voice here and there. And then I looked down the barrel of Marty's gun and realized how much I wanted to live. Just like Jimmy Stewart in *It's A Wonderful Life*, my mind was screaming 'I want to live! I want my life back.' I know, sounds kind of silly."

"Not at all."

"I can't say I'm filled with joy right at this moment. Ariana is gone, John Keneely's dead. And both of those deaths were pointless."

"You can't know that."

"Maybe not. But either way, at least I know I'm glad to be alive. And maybe someday I will be overjoyed about it."

Laura looked at her. "I hope so, my friend. I want that for you, more than anything else."

Perhaps it was the compassion in Laura's eyes, or the gentleness in her voice, or the way she had called Connor her friend. But whatever it was, she felt her chest tighten with emotions— ones she couldn't begin to sort out. Laura moved closer and put one arm around Connor's shoulders. They were still sitting side by side two hours later when Benjamin appeared with Gwendolyn Broadhurst on his arm.

Malcolm, Albert, Laura, Connor, Benjamin, Gwendolyn, and Grandmother Klah sat around the little table and talked quietly, sharing accounts of the events of the past few days. As they talked, each of them, at some level, sensed the symmetry created by the seven who were assembled there, seven whose lives, through a completely unexpected set of circumstances, had intersected at this particular moment in time. Grandmother Klah, naturally, saw more than symmetry. She saw a coiling of destiny into a tight circle. She saw, with eyes that looked beyond this tiny reality, the coalescing of past, present, and future. But she kept her own counsel as the others filled Gwendolyn in on all that had happened.

Most fascinating, however, was Gwendolyn's account of her astral travel to New Mexico and the fact that she behaved as if Grandmother Klah were an old friend. When pressed for further explanation on this point, though, she deferred to their hostess, who rose to her feet. The old woman looked at each one of them in turn, slowly, carefully, perhaps even a bit critically. It was as if she were evaluating them in preparation for making some very important decision. When her gaze finally reached Gwendolyn, however, she did not pause. She went to stand beside Connor's grandmother and said, "It is time. You will all follow us."

The two elderly women led the way, arm in arm, through a small passage opposite the one through which they had entered the cave. Suddenly, they were immersed in absolute darkness. Instinctively, they each reached out to clutch on to someone else in the group. But even though they had been only a foot apart from each other, not one of them could find another arm or hand to grasp. Connor began to panic. The air was dense and hot, the blackness profound. The human brain is unused to dealing with any environment containing not even one tiny glimmer of light. She felt as if she had drowned, forever lost in the dark. Her fear was overwhelming, she could not move, and just as she was determined to make some sound come out of her mouth, she could see again.

They were all standing in a small chamber, much smaller than the others. It was not bright, yet she could see everyone clearly. Connor could not understand how they had gotten here. She had no recollection of walking once they had been plunged into that impenetrable darkness. Yet, here they all were.

Connor's attention was drawn to the source of the illumination in the little cavern. She was speechless, which, as far as she was concerned, was getting to be a bad habit. The light came from an archway, but within the arch there was no door, semi-transparent or otherwise. Where a door should be, colors of every imaginable hue swirled over the surface of the opening. At the same time, though, it did not seem flat, two-dimensional. It more closely resembled a deep pool whose bottom was unfathomable. Connor stared at it. Her mind became blank, and she felt herself drawn irresistibly to the doorway. She wanted to know, had to know, what was in there. But she felt a restraining hand on her arm. It was Laura's.

Connor snapped out of her trance when she heard Laura's voice. "No, Connor. You can't go there." She realized that Benjamin had likewise gently restrained Malcolm and Albert from approaching. Gwendolyn and Grandmother Klah were apart from the others, talking quietly between themselves.

"What is this place?" Connor whispered.

"It's the gateway I spoke of. This is the chamber where it exists."

"But where does it lead?" Her eyes traveled up toward the ceiling. "And what are *those*?" she gasped, pointing at 13 crystal objects sitting in niches where the chamber's walls intersected the domed ceiling. Except they weren't just objects; they were shaped like skulls, down to the smallest detail of jawbone and tooth. And they glowed! Each of them emitted intense light from within.

Grandmother Klah interrupted her conversation with Gwendolyn and turned to Connor with a wry smile. "No one could accuse you of a lack of inquisitiveness, child. To answer your last question first, those are the gifts received by my ancestors. We do not know how precisely they work, but they are a part of this place. At the very least, they protect this chamber and the mountain from prying eyes and minds. And I perceive that they amplify my abilities, such as they are."

Connor looked dazed, as if someone had landed a roundhouse punch to her head, and she was trying to figure out who or what hit her. Grandmother Klah looked at her with kindly concern. "None of this can hurt you, Connor. You have to reach out with your heart and with your spirit, and discover that for yourself. As to where this leads...I only know that it is a place where those who are ready to leave this life may go if they choose. But so much knowledge has been lost." Her face was sad. "Now there is only a little left with me." Her gaze fell on Benjamin, whose eyes were afire with some inner joy as he spoke.

"I went in there, just once, for an instant. In that brief moment, I knew that I could have left this place forever. I could have flown free with only the power of thought to propel me. There were spirals and paths and roads leading to the past, the present, the future...." His voice trailed off, and Connor could see he was actually quivering with the effort to keep from rushing to the gateway.

Grandmother Klah saw his dilemma, and her tone of voice was soft and compassionate. "That was a great gift, Benjamin, and you are a courageous man. Few have ever seen what you saw that day so long ago. Almost all of us must allow our physical bodies to cease before we journey onward. You wanted to stay in that place where you felt yourself closer to your Creator, and yet you returned. Why, Benjamin? Why?"

Benjamin twitched as though startled. A wave of sadness washed over his countenance, but then he looked at Connor and smiled. "I had a little girl," he said. "A beautiful little girl. And I knew she would need me."

"She did need you, Benjamin. As did many others. That is why you were allowed a taste of infinity—or heaven." She smiled softly. "So you might protect that which the world is not yet ready to understand. The magic of spirit as yet has no place out there." She turned to Mrs. Broadhurst. "But you, Gwendolyn, you do not need to resist your yearning. Your time to enter is at hand."

Connor was aghast. "What do you mean, 'her time'? Where are you going, Gran?"

The dignified old gentlewoman smiled at her granddaughter. There was so much love and joy on her face, Connor's heart ached with some unnameable emotion. Clearly Gwendolyn wanted to go. But how could she lose her Gran now? It just wasn't fair.

Grandmother Klah, who had proved herself perfectly capable of reading everyone's thoughts, wagged an admonishing finger at Connor. "Child, you cannot keep other people around simply because you need them. Everyone has a life to live and a destiny to pursue, a destiny of her choosing. When I saw Gwendolyn on another plane, she had come to try and help you. She did help you, but I also saw, as I experienced her presence, that she was not long for this particular world, and she understood my thoughts. This is why she came here, so that she might forego a painful death and say goodbye to you while she is yet strong. Surely you would not deny her this choice."

Gwendolyn came to stand in front of Connor and gently

wiped the tears from her granddaughter's cheeks. "Connor, my dear child, you know I love you dearly, and you know I shall always be within call if you need me. But there is indeed a time to every purpose, and my purpose has been fulfilled. Besides, what Grandmother Klah says is true. I've been quite unwell for some time now. I wouldn't be with you long in any event."

She hugged Connor close. "Take care, my dear, and promise me you will look for joy wherever you can find it. Now, now, dry those tears. Is that any way for a Broadhurst woman to behave?"

She reached for Benjamin's hand. His eyes, too, glistened. "And you, son-in-law. You're a dear man. I'm sorry to leave you with the difficult task of explaining my mysterious departure, but I know you'll take care of it somehow." She looked at him for a long moment. "I hope my daughter will someday see reason, but I have my doubts. Just don't let that keep you from finding happiness. Sometimes you must learn to let go." He nodded, unable to speak through the lump in his throat, and held her close for a moment.

Gwendolyn moved on to Malcolm. "We don't know each other well, young man, but I've heard very laudable reports on your character. Thank you for helping my granddaughter." She laid her hand on his cheek briefly, then turned her attention to the Navajo policeman, who stood aside from the rest, trying not to intrude on this family moment.

"Lieutenant Tsosie..." she stumbled over the pronunciation slightly, but he smiled gently, "you, too, had a part in rescuing Connor. Thank you for your faith. Not every man would chase across this wilderness without understanding the reasons why." She took his hand and squeezed it gently.

"And, of course, Laura." Gwendolyn took both of Laura's

hands in her own. "You, young woman, are quite amazing. Even my granddaughter might learn a thing or two from you. Thank you for your courage." Tiny trickles of dampness glistened on Laura's bronze cheeks. Gwendolyn leaned closer and whispered something. Laura smiled and hugged the elderly woman, who, having finished her goodbyes, strode briskly toward the shimmering opening.

Just before she stepped through, Gwendolyn looked back at her loved ones and friends. "May God be with you all," she said, and then she was gone.

The somewhat forlorn group stood silent for a long time. Benjamin put his arm around Connor, who kept her eyes fixed on the opening, half-hoping Gran would change her mind and come back. But she knew in her heart that wouldn't happen. And, as Connor Hawthorne, former skeptic and former cynic, stood there wondering and hoping and grieving, she also knew that someday, when it was time, she would return to this place and find out for herself what lay beyond.

That evening, both rescuers and rescued left the mountain. Grandmother Klah told them it was time to go, and no one was inclined to argue with her. Benjamin set the helicopter down briefly near the sight of the crash because Laura was determined to retrieve the satellite communications device she had buried. The wrecked vehicles were gone. No one made any reference to the scorch marks on the pavement, or to what had happened there.

The next stop was in Tuba City to drop Albert off. Malcolm shook his hand until Albert thought his arm would come off at the shoulder, and the two young women hugged him hard (despite his natural reticence), which was less painful, and more pleasant by comparison. Malcolm said he would be in touch soon, but Albert's mind was already engaged in devising some creative tales to explain his absence, his return by private helicopter, and why his carryall had been abandoned so far away. He wasn't a dishonest man by nature, but no human would ever hear from his lips what had really happened. What he had seen cast an entirely new and wonderful light on the history and spirituality of his people. And yet his heart told him that it was not yet time for the Navajo to reclaim their true role in the affairs of humankind. Someday, perhaps even in his lifetime, Father Sun and Mother Earth would once again live in the hearts of men.

Laura left the group when they reached Albuquerque. Once they all stepped out of the helicopter, she hugged the two men.

"I can't find the words," Benjamin said, "to thank you for protecting my daughter."

"I had quite a lot of help," Laura smiled. "So don't worry about thanking me. And, besides, your daughter saved my life, too. I think we're even."

She turned to Connor, whose eyes looked suspiciously misty. "That was one hell of an adventure, my friend. We'll do it again sometime, *without* the bad guys."

"It's a deal," Connor replied as Laura hugged her long and hard.

"I'd better be going. I've got some explaining to do about that Mercedes." Laura felt the need to get away quickly, before Connor suspected how difficult this parting really was. "Bye, all."

They watched Laura walk away, the long braid swinging back and forth across the shoulders of the soft doe-skin shirt she wore.

"Hell of a woman," Benjamin said softly.

"Yes, she is," was his daughter's reply.

After a moment, the Senator looked at his two companions. "What say we have some dinner? And get ourselves a flight home."

Connor suddenly wanted, more than anything else, a good strong dose of everyday reality—real food, a real bed, and to go through a day in which she didn't have to question or understand the laws of the universe.

EPILOGUE

———————◦◦◦———————

So, break off this last lamenting kiss,
Which sucks two souls, and vapours both away,
Turn thou ghost that way, and let me turn this,
And let our selves benight our happiest day.
—John Donne

———————◦◦◦———————

June of the following year

Connor unfolded her legs from their lotus position and took one last look at the sun as it slowly spread its last glimmers across the horizon. The early evening wind off the Mediterranean was still brisk at this time of year, and the Lido was fairly deserted. It was the last stop on her six-month long pilgrimage, if one could call it that, visiting every place she and Ariana had shared during their years together. Connor had been searching for acknowledgment that so many years of living had not been simply wiped away with Ariana's passing. In each place she found a good memory, and, one by one, they filled up the empty spaces and healed her anger.

She used part of the time during her travels to finish the book she had been working on when Ariana died. The mood of her newest work was markedly different from those which came before. Her publisher questioned the changes. There was more depth to the characters, perhaps too much. The ending was not as tidy as usual. There were questions left unanswered. Some loyal readers might be startled, some might even abandon her. But Connor was not concerned. Her priorities had changed, and with them, her writing.

She had been thinking about Laura more and more during these past couple of weeks. It was impossible not to. Connor admired her, even envied her, perhaps, because she recognized that Laura's true strength came from within. Connor wondered if she could find that resource within herself. And Laura was intelligent, her instincts were sharp, and she was a beautiful, proud woman who rejected the temptation to arrogance. Lately, every now and then, Laura was in her dreams, her long, dark hair shining, eyes aglow, her soft voice murmuring something that Connor wanted desperately to hear, but could not decipher. If only she were not so reluctant to go back into the dreamtime.

She tried not to think too much about what had happened inside the mountain. From this distance, it seemed unreal. She knew it wasn't, and yet everyday reality, with its mundane concerns and events, faded the memories of Grandmother Klah and the rituals of healing as the weeks passed. Connor knew that someday she would have to tackle the issues that had been raised in her mind—about God, about her own soul, about what really was out there—but they would have to wait. Still, she could not deny the fact that her Grandmother Broadhurst was gone. Aunt Jessica and Katy had found notes left behind explaining about the cancer and that she preferred to be alone when the end came. Connor dearly wished she could explain everything to them, but that was impossible. She had to formulate a benign lie, insisting that although she had known where Gwendolyn was, and had visited her at the last moment, she had promised to respect the old lady's wishes to be left alone. Though both women had been deeply distressed, they took it in stride.

Benjamin had smoothed over a number of legal formalities. In late December, an empty, weighted casket had been shipped back to England for burial in the churchyard at St. Giles on Wyndle. Connor attended the funeral, where she briefly spoke with a bereaved and embittered Amanda, who was furious at being denied a visit to her own mother's deathbed. Their meeting, like their relationship, did nothing to comfort either of them.

As she watched her grandmother's friends and family gathered beside the grave, Connor regretted the subterfuge, for she knew Gwendolyn was off on an adventure far from this cold, rainy churchyard. She had to swallow the protest she wanted to shout aloud, "She's not in there. She's alive. I watched her go." But the dozens of mourners who gathered, huddled under their umbrellas, were left with only a casket, and they, too, needed to say farewell to a woman they had loved and respected.

After the funeral, Connor resumed her travels, communicating little with anyone back home other than her father and Val, who was always ready with a bit of wise advice and a Yiddish wisecrack or two. "So, isn't it about time you stopped schlepping around the world and came home?" Val had asked, never one to mince words.

"Soon, Val, pretty soon. But not quite yet. And don't worry, I'm not chasing ghosts. I'm setting them free."

"Glad to hear it, because my rates have gone up and I don't have an opening for a new patient."

Connor had laughed out loud then and assured Val that everything was just fine. She needed total solitude, unfettered by social obligations and safe from the well-meaning encouragements and sympathies of her acquaintants. Thus, she walked among strangers, quietly, thoughtfully, wrapped in her cloak of invisibility, and was not at all lonely.

When Connor got back to the hotel, she found another letter from her father. His gentle words of encouragement and comfort had followed her all over the continent. It saddened her that her parents had not been able to reconcile, though she was not blind to the reasons why. She suspected they never would. Amanda remained a veritable recluse at the Potomac house, and Benjamin took up permanent residence at his club. His Christmas letter had brought unexpected news—he had resigned his government position. After he returned from New Mexico, he had only stayed long enough to clean up some details, details she assumed had to do with Julius Martinez. Careful investigation revealed that Marty had been a traitor from day one. He had murdered the real Julius Martinez more than 15 years earlier and assumed the man's full identity. Marty was a carefully planted agent, working on behalf of many interests aside from those of Colonel Bordman. Connor did not ask for any details, because they no longer mattered to her.

She read her father's most recent letter while sitting on the veranda outside her room. As always, he asked after her and provided a brief update on their mutual friends. Malcolm and his family were doing fine. They were living at the townhouse now, as Benjamin and Connor had arranged. Her father added that all the necessary legal formalities had been taken care of, which included putting it on the open market first (at a price intended to discourage buyers) so that anyone still interested in Benjamin's vault would assume it had been removed (which it had) and would not threaten the Jefferson family's safety. The handwritten journals and maps pinpointing the location of Grandmother Klah's mountain were destroyed. After two months, the "For

Sale" sign was removed and Malcolm moved in. He thought he was on an extended house-sitting assignment and leaped at the chance to put his kids in the excellent neighborhood schools. Of course he was sure to raise a fuss when he discovered the house was being deeded to him, but Connor wanted him to have it. She would never live there again.

At the foot of the page, just under the "Love you, Dad," was a cautiously worded postscript. "Laura called to see how you were doing. She didn't ask for your address, so I didn't offer it. But she gave me the enclosed directions to where she's living now, just in case either of us happened to be out there sometime."

Connor read the postscript three times, then folded the letter carefully and replaced it in the airmail envelope. She hardly noticed the sharp chill in the air. Her mind was somewhere else. Images swirled and merged in her thoughts. Ariana, lovely and sweet and wonderful, was now, she hoped, off adventuring and working her magic somewhere else, perhaps even with Gwendolyn. But, at any rate, she was not here anymore, in this world of mortal human beings. And yet, somehow she *was* here. For the first time since Ariana had died, her presence was suddenly so near that Connor thought she could almost reach out and touch her.

She pondered, not for the first time, all the things Grandmother Klah had said about death, eternity, and immortality. Intellectually, and taking into account what she had seen, Connor accepted that they were very likely true. But, in this particular moment in which Ariana's presence was unmistakable, Connor *felt* the truth of it. With the sudden inspiration that stems from the soul, she understood why she hadn't wanted to fully accept what Grandmother Klah had tried to tell her.

In Connor's mind, those explanations somehow diminished the significance of her own loss. If she accepted eternal life for each soul, Ariana might well be happy and content and even better off somewhere else, somewhere Connor could not reach. And if she did let go of bitter grief, she was letting go of Ariana. Wasn't that betrayal, infidelity? Surely if she truly cared, she would mourn forever.

The truth came full-blown into her mind and her heart. Connor's life was here and now; it was a gift to be cherished rather than endured. Surely that was what Ariana would expect of her, not this empty-hearted wandering. Ariana had loved life, had lived every moment, be it sad or joyful, with intensity and abandon. Then she had moved on.

A silvery shadow passed between Connor and the rising moon. She felt a softness brush against her cheek, inhaled the scent of perfume, and, perhaps, only imagined a soft whisper that rode the evening breeze. "Farewell, *cara mia. Ti adoro.*" Slow tears welled up in Connor's eyes and trickled down her cheek. But she did not raise a hand to wipe them away, for she no longer resented them. After a very long while, she went back inside and began to pack. It was time to go home.

Laura stepped out of the hogan when she heard the whine of a laboring engine in the distance. She could not see the car since the road approaching her homestead dipped below a ridge. She wasn't expecting visitors, but one would be welcome. A distant neighbor might even be dropping off the mail. Perhaps, finally, there would be a letter from Europe—a pale blue airmail envelope like the first (and only) she had received four months ago.

Dropping the hammer she had been using to nail the last roof support into place, Laura wiped her hands on the legs of her jeans. The car, if indeed headed her way, was probably still two or three minutes away, so she went inside to put on coffee. Returning to the yard, however, she no longer heard the engine noise. Perhaps she'd been mistaken, imagined she'd heard it. "Loneliness can play strange tricks," she thought. "I'll have to get hold of myself." She listened a moment longer, shook her head, and reclaimed the hammer.

Inside the hogan, she resumed wailing away at the 16 penny nails that were all they had at the trading post. The racket was almost unbearable in the small space, but she didn't really mind. It kept her from thinking too much about things that couldn't be changed, and she experienced a deep satisfaction from building her own hogan. It was important to create something with your own hands, something that fed the spirit as well.

When the last nail was finally driven home and there was absolutely nothing else to hammer, she sighed and hopped down from the wooden crate she had been using as a stepladder. An instant later, she heard a soft, scraping noise, followed by the one voice she wanted to hear more than anyone else's on earth.

"You wouldn't happen to have a Slim Jim and a Dr. Pepper, would you?"